DIGITAL BOOK

The Xerox DocuTech Book Factory

PRINTS BINDS AND TRIMS PERFECT BOUND BOOKS ON ONE MACHINE

The Book Factory is an automated, in-line solution for producing perfect bound books, made up of components supplied by Xerox and its finishing partners. The base configuration consists of the Xerox DocuTech 61xx printer and the Bourg BB2005 binder

For more information on the Xerox DocuTech Book Factory or the rest of the DocuTech 2000 Series,

Call 1-800-ASK XEROX
or visit the web site at:
www.xerox.com/docutech2000

XEROX
DIGITAL BOOK PUBLISHING TECHNOLOGY

The Xerox Book Factory options include:

- **BOURG BPRF** www.cpbourg.com
Perforates, Rotates, and Folds printed sheets as they come off the printer, creating 4-page signatures. This module reduces printing costs by enabling the most efficient image imposition layouts.

- **ROLL SYSTEMS DOCUSHEETER.** 781-229-2266
This option reduces the labor overhead and cost of cut paper supply by replacing a paper tray with a roll paper feeding system. Produces up to 50,000 sheets from a roll to continuously feed a DocuTech printer.

- **CHALLENGE CMT 330 TRIMMER**
www.ChallengeMachinery.com
The CMT 330 is a three-side trimmer with full digital control of the trimming process: servomotors control all adjustments normally done by hand with a traditional trimmer.

- **XEROX DIGIFINISH BOOK INTEGRITY** 716.427.6325

Xerox DigiFinish is a server-based system that provides a digital connection to Xerox partners' feeding and finishing equipment, both in-line and off-line. It is used for machine set-up and closed-loop process control.

Xerox DigiFinish Book Integrity is one of several solutions built on the DigiFinish platform. It is available with the Bourg BB2005-DF perfect binder.

XEROX
DIGITAL BOOK PUBLISHING TECHNOLOGY

Color Cover Production

Proofing

Xerox DocuColor 12

- Up to 12.5 color impressions/min at 64-105 gsm
- 600 x 600 x 8-bit resolution for vibrant colors
- Straight through paper path using Intermediate Belt Transfer Technology to increase reliability and image consistency
- 6-micron toner particles for sharper images with higher toner yields
- Choice of controllers to get the combination of color management, job management, and workflow control for optimum output

Production

Xerox DocuColor 2000 Series

- Production class sheet-fed digital color presses
  - DocuColor 2045 produces up to 45 color impressions/min at paper weights of 81-105 gsm
  - DocuColor 2060 produces up to 60 color impressions/min at paper weights of 81-135 gsm
- 600 x 600 x 8 bit resolution generates offset quality output
- Excellent reliability
- Wide range of weights and types of substrates handled
- Patented I-TRACS technology system automatically inspects images as they appear on the actual printed page after fusing, providing immediate feedback on any required readjustments

For more information about Xerox Color Printers:
www.xerox.com

Lamination

GBC ORBIT 2000 LAMINATOR

For more information on Cover Lamination:
1-800-GBC-ROLL   or Visit   www.commercialfilm@gbc.com

XEROX
DIGITAL BOOK PUBLISHING TECHNOLOGY

XEROX PAPER

The book block was printed on Xerox Digital Laser Opaque 24 lb. or 28-lb. stock.

For more information about Xerox Paper:

1-800-822-2200 in the USA
1-800-668-0199 in Canada

The cover was produced on a DocuColor Printer using Xerox Digital Color Xpressions 98- 80 LB Cover Stock.

Scan and Make-Ready

XEROX DIGIPATH
SCANNER & PRODUCTION SOFTWARE

- DigiPath's Document Scan and Make-Ready offers a true end-to-end solution for customers who require hard copy scanning or make-ready capability.

For more information:
1-800-ASK-XEROX ext. 281
www.xerox.com

ScenicSoft preps software

Preps electronically imposes PostScript, PDF, EPS, DCS, TIFF, and DeltaList source files into signatures. These imposed signatures can be output on any PostScript compatible device such as a digital press, imagesetter, platesetter, on-demand, or laser printer.

For more information:
www.scenicsoft.com

From
Honor
Bound

FROM HONOR
BOUND

Paula La Sala

FirstPublish, Inc.
Orlando, Florida

ISBN
1-929925-14-X

Library of Congress Cataloging in Publication Data
00-107444

Paula La Sala
From Honor Bound

FIRSTPUBLISH, INC.
170 Sunport Ln. Suite 900
Orlando, FL 32809
407-240-1414
www.firstpublish.com

Dedication

To Joe, Joan and Adrian

PART 1
Marisel's Honor

Chapter 1

On the big flat ground before the new cave two men fought. They were both huge men and they fought for their futures, though the men lying around the edge in various attitudes of relaxation didn't care who won. They roared approval of a good hit and roared equally loudly to disapprove a foul, but they found the fight amusing, since they were not involved in the outcome.

For the two fighters, the moment was grim. They had been fighting since mid-morning without a break. It was late afternoon now, and they were both tired. They used battle staves, but the weapons were feeling heavy, and all their skills in wielding them were gone the way of their strength. They fought as if their feet were held in mud, and the air was too heavy to breathe. One man had a longer reach and a careless grin always about his lips, as if the outcome were less serious for him. The other, with the sturdier legs, peered out of cunning eyes, searching always for a weakness he might use to end this endless battle.

"Have an end," called a voice. "You're both past winning. Try again another day."

"Let them alone," called another. "If one of them wins, they'll have beaten all of us, and we'll go to a Challenge. You know there is an Honor nearby that hasn't been challenged in years. Let them be."

With a grunt, the grinning man gave a mighty swing of his battle staff. It was as unscientific a move as any yet in this messy battle. For once his opponent's sturdy legs were not placed sturdily. He fell on his back. He fell where the platform of rock ended and rolled over the edge, unable to get any kind of purchase on its surface. He rolled on down the hill. It was an ignominious end, but end it was.

The entire pack of Wilder men got to their feet, laughing. Hurden, the winner, leaned panting on his battle staff, grinning still.

"So, when will you make the Challenge, Hurden?" came the question they all wanted answered.

"Tomorrow," he gasped. "Give me time to eat and sleep, first. I'll go tomorrow. Anybody coming with me?"

The men laughed again. A few women came forward and started lighting fires on the rock platform. The men went and gathered up food to prepare a makeshift meal. Those without women built their own fires.

Chag, the loser, climbed back up the hill. "Somebody feed me at their fire tonight," he demanded. "I'm too worn down to build my own." For all the cheerful words, he looked mean enough to kill for a place. Hurden turned his back and went to his own fire.

"Over here," called Zolg, the healer. "You can eat with us. I'll look you over in a minute, but I'll see Hurden first. He may as well be ready to win the Challenge, eh?"

Chag sat down with ill grace. "I will not go tomorrow," he announced. "I should bring the Challenger ill luck."

There would be no need. Among Wilders, each man did as he pleased. There would be enough of them to offer support to Hurden the next day.

Hulia, the scout, dropped to her belly and pressed her lips together to quieten the sound of her harsh breathing. She had been running heedlessly through the trees, careless because she was so close to the Honor. Stupid, stupid! She had burst from the woods, not a hundred paces behind a medium large pack of Wilders. The only thing that had saved her from detection was their own concentration. They moved quietly towards the Honor in a loose group, their eyes turned to someone she could not discern among them all. It was an average pack, with a few elders, a few youngers, but in the main made up of males in their prime. She saw no women among them. She glanced at the sun. At this hour of the day there could be only one reason for a pack of Wilders to be approaching an Honor. At daybreak there would be a Challenge.

She made up her mind. Backing into the trees, she got to her feet and ran to tell Carasim, who was the leader of the hunting party, not bothering to be particularly silent. These Wilders were not out to garner women. They would camp the night in sight of the Honor, letting themselves be seen and their intentions be assumed. The Challenge would be sounded at dawn. Her party could enter the Honor easily before dark, even giving the Wilder pack a wide berth. They would be expected. The gates would not be closed before they were inside the walls.

Teq was bringing his goats in for the night when he saw the first signs of the Wilders gathering. He couldn't remember the last time he'd seen Wilders anywhere near the Honor. He'd heard about Challenges, of course. This gathering pack almost certainly meant there would be a Challenge against the Sieur. It would be pretty exciting to see one. In another year, he reckoned, he'd be gone from the Honor for good, and he would have hated it if he had never witnessed a Challenge.

Teq checked to make sure the little boys were all inside the walls and safe. Not that Wilders had any interest in small boys, but the little ones might get frightened if they were caught outside in the fields.

The hunting party jogged in through the gates, ahead of the sunset hailing. The wall guards shut the gates behind the last of them. They were back early. They were supposed to have gone east, through the hills to the edge of the desert, if necessary. It might have been days before they were back, though the wall guards called their names every sunset anyway, so long as they were out.

Teq had resented their going without him. He'd only been out that far once, and his maps - which everyone laughed at anyway - lacked detail. He knew he was too old to go out hunting with the women, but he argued his case, as far up the ladder as the Council.

Marisel herself had heard him in Council and denied him sharply. "Isn't it time this boy had his Drumming?" she demanded, turning to Tarabeth, Teq's true mother. "Maps indeed! The extent of my Honor is known. Say it, boy."

"The rift to the west and south, the desert to the east, the hill forest to the north," Teq mumbled. He glanced at his true mother and saw she was nodding and smiling at him. At least she didn't seem to think his maps were stupid.

"There, you see? What need is there of a map? Carasim has chosen her hunting party. You are not included."

Teq bowed his head and went to stand with the other boys. They grinned and nudged him and made faces behind their hands. Teq ignored them. They were all too small for him to bother with, and they obviously did not understand. He wished for the thousandth time there was another boy in the Honor of his own age.

The idea for making maps came to him the very first time he was taken on a hunt. His hunting skills were fine, but he was much more fascinated by the lands far from the Honor which he knew so well. His eyes naturally seemed to see things in the form of a plan - a map.

The youngers of the Honor were usually taken on the great Autumn hunt for their first time out, because game was plentiful and the needs of the Honor could wait a little in preparing for winter. The great Spring hunt - this one - used the most skilled hunters. The Honor was hungry after winter rations, and the hunters had no patience for mistakes.

The hunters were women, of course. They were the permanent population of the Honor. They held rank within the Council. They became the matrons of the Sieur and the mothers of the Honor's children. There was no reason at all for a boy child to work at a trade. At the first signs of manhood, he was drummed out of the Honor and joined a Wilder pack. While he was little, he was schooled to read and write and calculate along with the girls, as well as how to hunt, naturally. The boys were also taught the art of battle by the Sieur. After schooling was finished, a boy could go on herding the animals and maintaining the Honor walls until his voice broke and he needed to scrape the hair from his face. That was the sign for his Drumming. Teq would be drummed out alone, lacking age brothers. Teq wondered if his older brothers would have understood his wanting to do something else, like make his maps. He actually doubted it. He couldn't remember any of them doing anything special. All he could recall was them fighting each other until their drummings set them free.

After the Council was dismissed, Teq wandered over to the goat pen, where he normally went when he wanted to get away from his little brothers. He sighed heavily, longing for his own freedom. Belleth, his true sister, found him there.

"I can't decide whether you're as brave as the Sieur or too stupid to know what you were doing, calling on Marisel in Council." She glanced at him sideways, grinning.

The two were much alike to look at. Both of them looked more like the Sieur than any of his other children. This made for a good looking boy, but Belleth was already too tall and broad and strong to be a beauty like their mother. She would be a formidable leader of the hunt one day. Carisim, who was the leader now, always chose her, which many of the other girls envied. But Belleth wept to have her mother's gentle grace. She knew what it was like to yearn for the unattainable.

"When I'm a Wilder I shall go everywhere and map everything," Teq grumbled.

"Well it would be better to wait until then instead of making an ass of yourself in Council."

"I can't wait, Belleth. I can't wait to get out of here and be something. When I'm out with the herd I keep circling round the edges of the Honor. I just want to go on and on." Teq sighed.

"Being a Wilder isn't so much." Belleth gave him a shove. "Seems to me there wouldn't be time for anything but finding food, fighting other Wilder packs and fighting hunting parties for their women. Doesn't sound like much to me, and I can't see that you'll have much time for making maps then, either. Truth is, little brother, nobody much gets to be what they want."

"You want to be a hunter, and you're the best there is of your age. You'll be a hunt leader as soon as Carisim gives up."

"Truth? she asked.

Teq nodded.

"That's just what I let people think. The truth is I would much rather be just like Tarabeth. I want to play the lute and dance and be wise..." She turned away so that he would not see her eyes filled with tears.

"... and get chosen first of the matrons by the next Sieur. Do you really want that more than hunt leader?"

"Yes," she sighed, "but you'd better not dare tell anyone. Swear it."

"I'll swear if you'll look out for details and marks when you're on the hunt, that I can fill in on my maps. You are going tomorrow, true?"

"True, and I would do that anyway. You're my only true brother and you'll be gone within the year. Come on over to the well and help me fill the water bags for the hunt. That's what I'm supposed to be doing out here. Not talking to the herd boy."

Now the hunters were back. Teq watched them safely inside the walls before the gates were shut. The party had obviously come upon a herd of gumbuck nearby somewhere. They carried seven of the tasty beasts slung from poles by their hoofs. And their belts were hung with birds. It had been an excellent hunt: rich as well as short. Belleth came in nearly last, stained and sweaty as the rest. She waved to him on her way to the bath house.

The matrons came out to meet the hunters, pulling out the long tables for cutting up and skinning the meat. Challenge or no challenge, the meat had to be dealt with and the skins boiled clean. Fires were lit in the smoke and boiler houses. Torches were lit all round the walls. Joints of meat were carried off to the kitchens for cooking. Tonight they would eat sparingly. There would be very little time for a meal. Tomorrow there would be a feast for more than one reason. They would either be celebrating the victory of their Sieur, or welcoming a new one.

The matrons worked at the butchering well into the night. By the time the birds and the gumbucks were disposed of, the young girls were scrubbing tables with their eyes half shut. Because the Honor must be ready for the dawn Challenge, even the hunters helped out, which was a thing Teq had never seen before. They carried water from the well for the boiler house and the scrubbing; and sand to clean the tables and soak up the blood beneath them. They even carried the readied meats into the smoke house.

Teq was put to work trimming the torches and lighting new ones as the old burned down. Clay lamps did not throw enough light. How often did they need more than moonlight to deal with an emergency in the dark hours? Only the very youngest children slept through the whole of that night.

And the Sieur. For the sake of the Sieur, the huge effort in the central yard was carried out silently. It was a thing to behold, the great work carried out by torchlight in utter quiet. There had never before been a night like this one. Only Marisel, Holder of the Honor, and Tarabeth, first among the matrons, did not join in the labor. Marisel directed, pointing at this or that to be done and the person to do it, saying not a word. Tarabeth stayed with the Sieur. At first the workers could hear the gentle sound of her lute from the Sieur's quarters, but later, even that was silent. The matrons nodded to one another, smiling. The Sieur slept. It was vital that he rest in order to be ready for the Challenge at dawn.

By moonset the labor was over. The women dragged their way to their beds, leaning on one another, or supporting the younger girls, as they walked. They were exhausted, but pleased with themselves. A short sleep of restoration and then they would dress in their best and be ready for the dawn.

Only Teq was too excited to sleep. So long as he was wakeful, he thought he might as well be useful. He drew up washing water from the well, filling all the basins by the women's quarters. Then he set some water on the fire in the kitchen, ready for the morning brewing. There would need to be hot beanbrew to drink if everyone was to be wide awake for the Challenge.

He had finished by the time the false dawn briefly greyed the sky. He threw in the beans to simmer, then scooped himself out a cupful because he was tired at last, and now it was too late to sleep.

"Get me a cup too, Teq isn't it?" The deep voice of the Sieur startled him so much he nearly spilled his own.

"Lord," he said, and bowed, blushing like a girl child, to be noticed and named. "What is your command?"

"Well, it's not a command, son, but I really would like a cup of beanbrew. It's been a long night and it's an early morning."

Teq raised his eyes. It really was the massive form of the Sieur standing above him, but he was smiling and his eyes were twinkling.

"Lord," he said again, trying to mind his manners, and scooped out the largest clay cup he could find.

"Thank you, boy. Have you been up all night too?"

"Yes, Lord. I couldn't sleep. But the women said you were sleeping... as soon as my true mother stopped playing the lute."

"Yes, you are Tarabeth's son, of course. You don't look much like her, do you? No, I stopped her playing so that the women would not worry about me. The worry of so many women can be a burdensome thing, Teq. You'll discover that when you become the Sieur of an Honor."

"Are you rested enough for the Challenge, Lord?" Teq blurted out.

"As much as I can be. It's possible I may lose, you know. If not this one, then another. This is my fourth, though it's been a few years since the last. So. I am prepared. Are you?"

"I, Lord?"

"Yes, you. You should see a Challenge as part of your battle training. All that training I gave you is as much for this as for life as a Wilder. Are you prepared to see me lose? Are you prepared for your drumming? Can you see yourself as a Wilder offering Challenge? That's all my other sons seemed to think about."

"I can see myself free."

The Sieur laughed. "Yes, I see. Free of the Honor, eh? That's a good and a bad thing - at least I found it so. There's no structure in being a Wilder. No peace. And yet here... perhaps too much? Well, it's a good Honor and today I must fight for it. I must dress. You too, son. Will you be there to support me? Another man?"

"Of course, Lord, of course. Of course I will. If they tried to send me herding today... But I am not yet man."

"Near enough, I see. I will be glad to know you are there." The Sieur smiled again and handed his empty cup to Teq. "We'd better hurry now. It has been good to talk to you."

"Lord." Holding the two cups, Teq bowed, bent nearly double as he watched the retreating back of the Sieur. He was awed and elated. Never before had he held casual speech with the Sieur. Nobody had - well Marisel and the matrons, of course.

He might have stood there longer, but there was a rising noise as the women and girls stirred from their beds. He really did have to hurry. Not only did he have to dress himself but he had to check that the little boys had washed.

He rinsed out the cups and dashed off to the boys' room. But the little boys were up. They were even dressed, knowing the excitement of the day. They tumbled all around him as they hustled out through the door on their way to the kitchen.

As Teq pulled his best tunic from the room's only chest, the deep sound of the Challenge horn split the morning.

CHAPTER 2

Marisel allowed herself a minute alone. There had been no time to meet with the matrons before this Challenge. She needed a moment to think. It was time enough for a new Sieur, certainly, but she must be getting too old. She was used to this one. She liked him. She dreaded the thought of going through the slaughter and the training which a new Sieur would mean. Yet, here it was. A Challenge. They could be neither predicted nor ignored. Perhaps it was time she was replaced as the Holder of the Honor. Nonsense! She was tired. That was all. This was no time to be doubting her own place and authority. She shook herself and walked firmly down to the courtyard. There were youngs who needed to become matrons. She should be glad of this. With a firm back and a head held haughty, she walked ahead of her matrons to the gate.

The horn sounded a second time, blasting a noise which must have been heard as far as the desert. The silence which came after seemed to be louder than the horn. Nothing moved or made a noise for full minutes. At last, at Marisel's nod, slowly from the courtyard came the sound of the Honor drums. They were responding to the Challenge.

There was a solemnity and steadiness about the drumbeat as of a hunter walking to claim the prey she had slaughtered. There was none of the wildness of a young man's Drumming. Teq ran for the courtyard, fastening his tunic and using wet hands to plaster down his hair. The women were gathering in columns. Marisel stood by the gates, and in descending seniority the women formed behind her. They all wore their best finery. In the early morning light, the courtyard glowed with color. Teq looked round hurriedly for his brothers and was astonished to see each standing with his true mother, as were the smallest girls. His eye hunted for Tarabeth and saw that she was beckoning him.

"I have a message for you from the Sieur," she murmured, twitching his tunic into better shape. "You look terrible," she added, "as if you'd been up all night."

Teq cleared his throat. "I was, Lady. What did the Sieur say?"

"If he should lose this Challenge today, you are to run away and hide until he finds you."

"Finds me? Why? Where would the Sieur be going?"

"Hush. That's enough. We're moving." Tarabeth had already said far too much. She had done as the Sieur bade her - she always did - but if Marisel of any of the other matrons were to hear of it...

It really hadn't occurred to Teq to wonder what happened to the beaten Sieur when someone else won the Challenge. Of course he knew that the new man moved in and became the Sieur, but where did the old one go? Old? His Sieur was not old! Just the same, although he would naturally not lose this Challenge, he would lose some time, and then what?

The gatekeepers peeled back the gates and Marisel led them out of the Honor. Teq realized that as no man except the Sieur COULD come into the Honor, the battle had to take place outside the walls. The women moved, with their children beside them, in time to the solemn cadence of the drums. As they got outside, they formed themselves into two columns, making an aisle from the gates to where Marisel stood.

The drums stopped.

"Who are you who sounds the Challenge horn?" Marisel called in a clear voice.

"I am a man in my prime who has beaten the best of these in fair battle," came the answer, as a very large Wilder strutted forth from the pack.

The man was tall, as tall as the Sieur, and as well muscled. He was notably younger. His hair was black, tied high on his head in Wilder fashion. There was black hair on his chest and on his arms and legs. He wore no tunic, just his breeches. He seemed to have large feet. His eyes were very bright, and he was smiling. His teeth looked good, like those of a man who has fed well. In his hand he held his battle staff. It was taller than he and thick as a thigh bone. Formidable.

Once again the drums sounded. A single note, quite fast. Down the aisle of women strode the Sieur. As soon as he reached Marisel the drums stopped.

"Your Challenge is accepted," he said. His voice sounded strong, though not loud, yet it was clear to the whole assembly.

There was a sigh from the women and from the massed Wilders. The sun was creeping into the sky, inching upward. The morning was cool and dry. No ground mist. By noon it would be warm enough. The day smelled clean and fresh. It was spring in the land and the earth looked too innocent to be roiled by a battle.

But Marisel moved again. She led the women to the left, where they formed a half circle, the older women formed the points of the crescent. The young women were safely in the middle, far from contact with the Wilders. They also moved, stirring as a pack, until they muddled themselves into the other half of the circle. Only the Sieur and the Challenger stood inside the arena they formed.

The opening moves of the battle were the classic ones, such as the Sieur taught the young boys of the Honor in their battle classes. Teq took a step forward to get a better view, but Tarabeth jerked him back beside her and draped the edge of her fine cloak around him as if she wanted to hide his very presence. He was getting rather tall for this kind of treatment, and it irritated him to be treated like a small boy, but this was not the time or place to show it. He could actually see perfectly well anyway, so he held still and watched avidly.

The tempo of the battle increased. The crack of staff on staff grew louder and more frequent, as if the combatants had found their pace. Both men were breathing deeply, but neither seemed to want for breath. The Sieur looked serious but unworried. The Challenger, Hurden of course, grinned cheerfully, as if he had waited all his life for this - as indeed he had. A quick thrust from the Sieur caught the Wilder on the cheekbone, and he staggered for a moment, losing both balance and grin. The Sieur waited courteously for him to regain his balance. The Wilder came in at him whirling his staff like a leaf caught in the wind. The combatants were getting serious.

The two men concentrated in a way which caught the watchers up in the battle as if they were themselves participants. Teq was unaware of the difference the outcome could make in the lives of the women of the Honor. How much the character of the reigning Sieur meant to the quality of living. Marisel was master of the Honor, true, but the temper of the male, his concern for the women, effected their every day; their every night.

Meanwhile, the Sieurs were confined within the Honor, while the Wilders lived out of doors, fighting other Wilder Packs and hunting for their food. And they were young. The Challenger was always younger than the Sieur he challenged. It was only the practiced skill of the Sieur which was holding this young fighter at bay. Each thrust was parried. Each swing was knocked aside. The Sieur twirled his staff, blinding the Wilder to the direction of the next attack. The younger man was kept running, jumping aside, leaping to avoid a hit. He had not the sense of strategy to recognize that all he needed to do was maintain pressure and the older man would tire. After all, he had not had sense enough to wait a day or two after his battle with Chag before making this challenge. The Sieur allowed him no time to think, but kept the pressure on him hard and heavy.

The pace grew faster, hotter. Both men were breathing heavily. A crack from the staff of each broke through the guard of the other. The Sieur was caught on the ribs, the Wilder on the upper arm. The sun continued to slide upwards in the sky and dazzled first one and then the other, as each circled to take advantage of this ally.

It was clear the two men were well matched. The battle could go on and on. The day wore towards noon. The pace slowed. The breathing of the combatants could be heard now, rasping. Women and Wilders eased their positions, but steadily maintained the circle. The children twitched restlessly and were soothed into stillness. The battle seemed endless, as if it had been going on for days instead of hours. Teq was no longer following each move with wide-eyed interest.

And suddenly it was over. With a low, sweeping cut, the Wilder caught the Sieur across the front of his left knee. He stumbled and fell down heavily upon the right one. Without pause, he drove his staff upward with a sharp jabbing motion. He caught Hurden in the eye. Before the man could so much as raise his free hand to the hurt, the Sieur struck again, catching him this time on the jaw. The Wilder fell flat, as if swept from the arena by a giant broom. His legs twitched once, and then fell still. The sound of his breathing slowed. He made no move.

In the utter stillness which followed, only the sound of the Sieur's gasping breath broke the silence. The collected crowd was holding its own breath waiting to see who would rise. With both combatants down, there was no winner. Using his staff, the Sieur climbed heavily to his feet. The challenger still made no move.

With slow steps, leaning his weight upon his staff, the Sieur limped past the women to the gates of the Honor. The women curled round behind him and reentered the Honor two by two. Just as the gates of the Honor swung shut, the Wilders broke rank and went to their fallen comrade.

Teq noticed. "Perhaps they do care for one another," he thought. "Everyone always said that Wilders were a useless lot, each out for himself with no concern for anyone or anything else. "But how do they know?" he asked himself. Only the Sieur would know for sure, and he could hardly ask him. Teq snorted at the idea, and Tarabeth rapped his head in displeasure.

As everyone inside the Honor began to scatter, Teq realized that Tarabeth had released him, and the fatigue which had grumbled at the back of his eyes all day, finally swept over him. He just made it to the coolness of the boys' room before he fell flat on his face on his bed, still wearing his best tunic, and was asleep in seconds.

Tarabeth went to the Sieur at once, terrified, now that she allowed herself to be, that he might have been beaten. That he might have been lost to her. She loved him as deeply and as eternally as if she was a young dreaming about her first Sieur. But Tarabeth was not a young, and her love was a deep and abiding thing which filled her heart and satisfied all her senses. She could show this to no one. Certainly not to Marisel, who would have disdained such feelings. They were matrons, were they not? They had too many responsibilites to the Honor to allow time for such nonsense. Love indeed!

Nor could she speak of it to the Sieur himself. He had made her first matron, which spoke of his preference. He liked her beside him in the night. He seldom sent for one of the youngs now. She felt he did so only when his duty demanded he father another child. Yet she felt such jealousy at those times that her heart turned sour in her breast, and her songs dried on her lips.

But now he needed her. He lay on his bed, his face twisted in pain. Sweat pouring from every part of his body. "You have come," he managed to smile at her. "I am glad it is you."

"Of course I have come," she answered, composed now. "Show me the hurts. I have ordered a bath for you. Being clean will help you to feel better. I have brought you a draught to ease the pain a little and ointments to help the bruises. Is anything broken?"

"My leg. Cracked a little, I expect. Below the knee there. Aah," he gasped as she probed it.

"Yes. Not a bad break. You will walk on it well enough, though it will be weak there for many months, I think. Now," she accepted the jugs of hot water from the youngs who brought them from the kitchen, "the bath. Have you drunk what I brought you? Good. Now, off with the clothes and into the bath."

"Have you no other words for me, my Tarabeth?" he asked, relaxing a little as the pain killer and warm water eased him.

"Am I glad you won, you mean?" She knelt beside him and stroked his hair. "I am glad my lord is still my lord. There could never be another for me." She kissed him and he kissed her back with an ardor which moved her almost to tears.

"I'm glad too," he grinned. "Play to me, my lady, while I soak here, and when I rise from this bath, you will anoint my wounds and bandage my leg and I will be as new."

She laughed and picked up her lute. "There will be time for everything before my lord must appear at the feasting. Even sleep." She plucked a gentle tune from her instrument and he closed his eyes in contentment.

It was the smell rather than the sound which woke Teq. Feast day! He rolled on to his back. He remembered the battle and he remembered the hunt and he knew there would be a huge feast tonight. He realized he had eaten nothing at all, all day. The noise from the courtyard clattered loudly into the room, from the women setting up for the meal. Incredible odors were wafting in with the noise. The food must be nearly ready. A glance at the sky through the window slot, and he could see that it was almost dark. Excellent. No waiting. He jumped off his bed and plunged his head into the stale washing water he had used in the morning. The last of his sleepiness vanished. He slipped off to the eating room, trying vainly to straighten his crumpled tunic so that he didn't actually look as if he'd slept in it.

Last night's butchers' tables were now set up in the eating room, with benches alongside to accommodate the feasters. He slipped into a dark corner near the bottom table where the boys ate, hoping nobody would see him and find him a job before the food arrived.

At full dark, the people of the Honor began to gather, wearing the morning's finery. They took their proper places at the tables, chattering and laughing with one another. As soon as some of his brothers appeared, Teq slipped out of his corner and sat down with them. The younger women seemed less ebullient than their older sisters. They smiled quietly, seeming less glad than polite.

Women swathed in covers to keep their best dresses clean, carried in the food. The first dish was a gumbuck, roasted whole on a spit. Marvelous mixtures of the winter's dried fruits and nuts were blended with the roasted fowl. Vegetables were piled high, some raw, some boiled in precious salt water.

The cooks disappeared and came back with their fine clothes showing, and slipped into their places, high in the hierarchy of the Honor. Only the high table was above them. And at the last Marisel entered with the Sieur and Tarabeth, first matron. The Sieur's left leg was bound rigidly between rods of wood, so that he was unable to bend his knee. He sat on the bench, his face knotted in concentration, and swung the injured leg up beside him. The two women sat on stools at either end of the high table, allowing him the room.

"This is a feast of double meaning to the Honor." Marisel spoke in a ringing voice. We give praise to the hunters for this bounty before us which they have bestowed upon us all. We give praise to the Sieur for his valor and his victory once more over an insolent challenger. Eat, drink, and sing praise in your hearts as you do so. What is your pleasure, my Sieur?"

The carvers rose, the girls picked up the pitchers of wine and water and stood to their posts.

"I will eat from the haunch of the spitted gumbuck, and the breast of fowl, and I will taste of each other dish." The carvers bowed their heads in quick acknowledgment. The Sieur's voice was strong, untroubled. He smiled warmly at the assembled company. "I am glad to be present at this feast."

The women roared approval. The older women showed their real enthusiasm, banging their utensils on the tables. The younger women shouted politely and that was all. Teq noticed it and wondered why.

Tarabeth picked up her lute and played a cheerful chorus from a song they all knew from childhood. Voices picked up the singing of it as the carvers and servers distributed the food. By the time any food got to the boys' table, Teq was almost desperate with hunger. Tarabeth plucked a final chord and at last they could eat. At last.

Teq over ate. He had some of everything, and then went back and heaped his plate again. His little brothers eyed him with awe.

"You want to be a big boy, I bet," said Mem, the very smallest child in the Honor. He had just left the women's quarters for the boys' quarters and had yet to stop talking. "You want to be as big as that man that fighted the Sieur today. I know." He nodded his head solemnly and watched Teq eat each bite. "It's OK," he added kindly. "You are a big boy already."

Teq didn't bother to answer. For one thing he was too busy eating, and for another, Mem was too small a person for him to notice. He actually thought Mem was very bright, but it was beneath his dignity to show it. Mem's true mother was Salsi, the youngest of the matrons.

By the time the feast ended, not only Mem, but a couple of his brothers were fully asleep with their heads on the table. Teq woke them up and led them away. Mem was tottering about, half asleep and terribly muddled, so as soon as they were out of sight of the women, Teq picked him up and carried him to bed, before he lay down on his own.

But he couldn't sleep. There was a massive weight of food, churning and grumbling audibly in his stomach. Besides that, his brain was working as if he were Marisel with the problems of an Honor to solve. In the end, he got up, wrapped his cloak around him over his sleep shirt, and slipped barefoot into the courtyard.

There was a moon of sorts, hidden most of the time by rags and tatters of clouds. It was brighter than last night, though, when they'd needed so many torches. He could see a figure sitting on the well wall, feet swinging. There had been no lights on the way to the courtyard to impair his night vision so he was pretty sure it was Belleth.

"I thought you'd be out. I saw how much you were eating," she said before he could get close enough to verify it was she.

"Got things on my mind," he answered.

"What mind? Sure you don't mean your stomach?" she rejoined.

"So why are you here, Lady Clever? Sure you didn't wear yourself out watching me eat?"

"Couldn't sleep either," she changed her tone from the bantering. "Too much excitement this last couple of days. And too much gossiping going on in the youngers' room."

"Isn't there always?" It always seemed to Teq that the young women talked as much as Mem.

"I suppose. Couldn't shut my ears tonight, though. They're all worked up and upset" Belleth jumped to the ground and peered into the well at the moon's reflection.

"I noticed that. They didn't seem to like it when the Sieur spoke at the feast. That seemed odd. To me, anyway. What could be the problem?"

"Oh, there's a problem, all right. They were hoping the Sieur would lose the Challenge."

"What?" Teq was outraged. "Our own Sieur?"

"Well it's got to happen some time," Belleth said reasonably, and until he does lose, none of us can be a matron. Everyone younger than Salsi is the Sieur's daughter, so we're stuck, you see? They liked the look of that Wilder, too. His smile was really wonderful."

"It seems to me that there are far too many things I've never thought about," Teq mused. "I suppose it could it be that I spend too much time on my maps, and not enough thinking. I feel really stupid. I mean, I don't even know where a beaten Sieur goes when a new man wins the Honor!"

"I don't either. There hasn't been a Challenge for ages, so that's probably why we haven't thought about it. Life was just going along comfortably in the same old rounds until yesterday. And anyway, I don't think any of your brothers ever thought about this at all before they left to be Wilders. I remember them, even if you were too small."

"Well, you're my true sister, so I can talk to you."

"The others had true sisters too."

"I suppose... Do you know I was up all night last night and I actually spoke to the Sieur? And he spoke to me - one to one!"

Somehow Teq didn't feel he should tell her about the message he'd had from the Sieur later, through Tarabeth.

"When we have a new Sieur, I'll get to talk to HIM one to one. Perhaps he won't notice I don't look as pretty as the other youngs, and then I'll have a child of my own. Oh," she sighed, "I do know what they mean. I can't wait either."

"I can't imagine anyone being better than our Sieur," Teq replied with all the hauteur he could muster. He really wasn't used to the idea of his true sister being somebody's mother. Another new thing! "I'm going to bed now," he added. "It's going to take me a few days out with the herd to think through all this stuff about Challenges. I wish there was someone I could ask. Goo'night."

He walked away, head down, wanting peace to think.

He had nearly disappeared when Belleth called to him as loud as she dared, without waking the whole Honor. "Wait. Teq. There's more. There's another important thing. You should know..."

But he didn't hear her, the moment passed, and Belleth never again got the chance to warn him of the danger he was in whenever there was a challenge. And in a moment the shadows were empty.

CHAPTER 3

It was winter. Very little snow fell in the plains around Marisel's Honor, in fact, some winters there was none. But now a little snow had fallen and it took the edge off the iciness.

There was still plenty of food, but among a few of the young women there was a winter restlessness, that archery practice and gathering firewood did not allay.

Carasim pulled Belleth to one side after the evening meal. "Feel like a day's run to check traps and set new ones?" she asked.

Belleth's face lit up. "Yes, I would. What a good idea, Lady! Hulia would like it too, and so would Salsi. How many will you take?"

"About six of us will be enough. You know the two youngs who made it out of the girls' room after the autumn hunt? We could take them along. Get them blooded."

"Twitter and Tweet? Good idea."

Carasim laughed. "Is that what you call them? Maybe the names will suit them less after a hunt run. Setting traps in the cold has a way of freezing the silly out of greenlings."

"When, Lady?"

"Tomorrow unless it's snowing hard. Any reason why not?"

"None. The days are so short now, you'll want us to leave at first light?"

"First light, yes. I wouldn't go without Hulia to scout, and Salsi can come if she wants. She's always useful. You tell them and I'll round up the other two. Twitter and Tweet!" She walked off smiling and shaking her head.

The party slipped out of the gates as soon as they were opened, to the sound of the dawn drum. They wore their boots skin side out for traction, trotting easily, and making first marks in the light snow which had fallen during the night. The crisp air bit at their breath. The stars lingered in the gray dawn light, vying with the sparkle off the snow to light their way, more than with the sullen sun.

Carasim directed them around to the rift edge of the forest where the trees were sparse. Hulia led, with Carasim shepherding Twitter and Tweet, Belleth and

Salsi bringing up the rear. The two youngsters wanted to dash ahead, wild with energy. Carasim had to snap at them to slow them down to the tireless trot which would keep them going for the whole of the day.

Once within the forest walls, they kept silence. It was not a discipline which was hard to maintain. The awesome presence of the giant trees themselves required it. There was little secondary growth, once they were past the outer edges: only here and there where some mighty tree had fallen, creating a clearing for the light to enter.

Hulia knew where the traps were set and led them unerringly from each to each. It was their pattern not to set traps in the same place again, so they gathered and carried the game they had snared as well as the traps which had snared it. They stopped to eat their noon meal at the side of a swift, bitter little stream, which raced angrily through the forest from the high hills in the north to the rift in the west.

"There's no time to work the rest of the forest. We'll save that for another day," Carasim decided. "We'll go back the way we came, setting the traps as we go. Ready?"

"Wait." Hulia held up her hand. "Look there."

A line of goats trotted out of the bushes on the other side of the stream, disturbed, no doubt, by their voices. They crashed through to the rising ground, while a large billy goat stood facing the hunting party, daring them to move. There were young in the herd, and some of the females showed swollen with pregnancy.

"A few of those would bring fresh blood to our herd," Salsi said, admiring them.

"They're a healthy looking lot, and that's a fact," Carasim agreed. "Want to catch a few?"

"It would be a marvelous run," Belleth grinned. And more soberly, "and useful to the Honor."

Carasim grinned back and nodded. "All right. Belleth, Hulia, Salsi, go after them. See what you can do, but be back by sunset, mind. We won't keep the gates open for you. You have binders enough? Take some from the traps, if not. We can make more. I'll take these two with me, trap-setting. Off you go."

The three young women were the swiftest runners in the Honor, which was just as well because by the time they had leapt to their feet the goats had disappeared. Salsi reached for her share of the game and traps where she'd dropped them when they stopped to eat.

"Leave those. You'll hardly be able to catch up, unburdened. We'll take them," Carasim said.

Twitter and Tweet groaned, but the others dropped single file to the stream's edge till Hulia found a way across, then they were gone. Belleth turned once and waved, as they plunged after the goats, and then they were out of sight.

"Come on, you two. We've twice as much to do and no more time to do it in," Carasim urged as she loaded herself and the two youngsters. "Show me how you would choose good places for the traps. You should have been picking them out as we came along."

They did well, they were so anxious to prove they could do anything any hunter could do. Carasim felt Twitter never would make a hunter, but she was neat fingered with the traps. It was Tweet who could pick out where to set them, as instinctive a hunter as any predator. They concentrated hard and wove their snares with few mistakes. They were noisy on the way back, but they were cheerful and proud of what they were doing, so Carasim did not reprimand them. One lesson a day, well learned, was good enough. With each trap set and left behind, their burden lessened.

"Hulia won't know where we've set these, will she Carasim? Perhaps we can lead next time we come this way."

"Perhaps," Carasim smiled at their eagerness, "though I think we'll have to clear the snares before you're old enough to be scouts. What do you say?"

But it was a good day, satisfying. Even burdened with all the game, they got back to the Honor with an hour to spare before sunset. The drummers were just beating the tattoo to call in the herd and the wood gatherers as they got to the gates.

"Take the game to the kitchens and get a warm drink while you're there," Carasim told her charges. "You did well. You've earned it."

She herself went to the gate captain. "Belleth, Salsi and Hulia have gone after a wild goat herd" she told her. "They want to see if they can catch a few. Salsi's idea. Bring fresh blood to the herd."

"Bringing in diseases, I'll be bound. Best to leave the wild to the wild, I always say," snorted the captain. It was years since she had ventured beyond the gates herself. She was cautious about what came in from the fields. What came from beyond the Honor was not to be considered. It was to be despised.

Carasim chuckled. "They're a healthy looking bunch. You'll see. Be on the lookout, though, and sound the alarm if you see that billy goat chasing them. He looked big enough to take on the Honor."

"Hmph," said the captain. "Our hunters are equal to any wild thing. But maybe you shouldn't have left them alone with mad male creatures about." She was only half joking.

Teq drove his tame goats through the gates a few minutes later and penned them for the night. He pulled down some straw for them and went off to the kitchen to find himself some beanbrew. While he was drinking it he heard about the new goats. He made his way up to the walls to wait for Belleth and his new charges.

The last of the wood gatherers straggled in bearing her load, as the weak paleness of the winter sun began to edge below the horizon. The edges of the rift rose a little above the plain and cast ground-eating shadows towards the Honor walls. There was no sign of the three hunters.

Slowly the drummer beat the sunset drum and the captain called the three names in each direction. There was no response. Reluctantly the gates were closed for the night.

The wild goats had chosen the steepest route on the other side of the water, because goats always do. They seemed to know they were being followed but didn't seem to care - at least the billy goat was leading them and not taking up a defensive position in the rear of the line.

"Where *are* they going?" Salsi asked, exasperated after an hour's run.

"I don't suppose they know themselves," Belleth panted. Even for the hunters the leisurely seeming pace of the goats was surprisingly fast. They had covered a lot of ground. "This is getting into real hills now."

"Be quiet," Hulia chided. "Save your breath and keep your stealth."

"Nothing lives over here in the forest," Belleth objected.

"We know very little of this side of the stream," Hulia cautioned, "but there's probably bear."

"It's winter. They'll be sleeping," said Salsi.

"Let's leave them that way," Hulia answered.

They scrambled on, always upward, always steeply. They were at the northern edge of the forest when a huge, rock crag suddenly hove into their sight as if it had just jumped into position there. The goats tripped easily up its almost perpendicular face. They did have a destination after all.

"Climb THAT?" whispered Salsi. Being all but out of the trees seemed to call for extra caution, so she whispered.

"Look over there." Belleth pointed, whispering too. "Those two are heavy with kid. They haven't gone as high as the others. I bet we could catch them."

"I'd hate to go back with nothing after all this. Is there time?" Salsi asked Hulia.

"It's downhill all the way back," Belleth put in, grinning.

"Separate," Hulia whispered. "Climb there and there and come down at them from each side. Drive them to me here. I'll rig a tunnel trap while you're getting in place. One chance, then we go home."

The two slipped silently away and disappeared from sight. Hulia bent the saplings at the forest's edge and tied them to form a rough tunnel, where the goats had created their path to the crag. She worked as quietly as she could in spite of her haste, but the goats seemed placid enough, secure on their rocky castle. One of them even eyed her working for a while, chewing its cud peacefully.

Then suddenly the goats' heads went up and they were leaping in all directions over the crag. There was no sign of Belleth or Salsi.

"Stupid, stupid," muttered Hulia, and threw up her hands in disgust.

And her hands were caught from behind in two strong ones, while yet another hand clamped over her mouth. She went rigid from shock. Before she was back to herself enough to struggle, she was pinned tight against a large chest while her hands were tied tightly on either side of her body. A leather was thrust into her mouth, the second the hand released it, and that bound in place too.

The voice which came from the body that was tying her up was male. "That's all three," he called out gleefully.

"All right then," called another. "All bound tight and their mouths stopped? Good then. Carb, Hort, Wex, get them moving. You others take their weapons, then kill us some goat and follow along. Better be quick. Not much time till sundown."

Hulia was dragged over to the edge of the outcrop and then round to the other side. The crag was less steep there, easing down on to a boulder strewn valley, before climbing again to the hills. Belleth and Salsi were propped against the rock, already bound. With all three of them helpless there was no way to send word back to the Honor. They would never be sure whether the three were dead or Wilders had them. They could do no more than look their despair at one another.

The Wilders were a mixed bunch of males, none as large and fine as their Sieur, but they looked fairly clean and decently fed. There seemed to be discipline among them. They could hear the voice of the leader but had not seen him. Nor did they know how many there were in the band. The three with them each took charge of one of the women and pushed them ahead, across the valley floor.

How could they have been so careless? How could they have heard nothing? Rumor said Wilders crashed about in the forest like marauding bear, not like true hunters, yet they'd heard no sound. Suspected nothing. They were caught like greenlings. Like Twitter and Tweet. The Wilders must have heard them coming, even traveled with them through the forest, flanking them. When Belleth and Salsi rounded the rock they ran into the Wilders' waiting arms. The pair who captured Hulia were probably there with her in the forest. When she made so much noise building the tunnel, they'd been able to walk right up to her. And she'd been worried about frightening the goats! The goats didn't even react until the Wilders all jumped out of hiding at the same time.

Misery dragged at the feet of the three women. They realized how far they had already come today and there was still nearly two hours of daylight they were apparently to walk through. The Wilder pack must have their camp up in the actual hills. The three Wilders who had been named, presumably, each took charge of one of the women, keeping them in motion.

Again they traveled upward. Well, it was true: they knew the Wilder packs owned the hills. It was madness to have crossed the stream and traveled north. They didn't need new goats in the Honor as badly as all that! Salsi blamed herself for mentioning it. Because of her, they would never see the Honor again. Salsi thought of her children and mourned deep in her heart. She knew they would be cared for, and even adopted by another matron, but never to watch them grow, or hold them again...

Hulia blamed herself for carelessness. They had been so heedless in their wild race after the goat herd. How could she have forgotten Wilders, forgotten to listen to the forest, forgotten to take even normal precautions? She could not help feeling some respect for the Wilders who had trailed them, though. Nothing had betrayed them to her, and she the Honor's scout...

And Belleth decided she was on an adventure. Better to make the best of what had occurred. There was no way to change this. Of all the stories told of women captured by Wilders not one spoke of the women's return. But they did know that they had been caught to be matrons within the pack. They would not have the dignity attached to being a matron within the Honor, and they would never rule the pack. But they would be held in some esteem, she estimated, and that might never have happened to her in the Honor. She regretted the worry they would cause to the people they cared about by not appearing before the gates shut. Teq in particular, she regretted. She had wanted to tell him... Well, the chances were good that he would have his drumming any day now and become a Wilder himself. He might even join this pack. For herself, she knew that no Wilder pack had enough women to go around, so nobody would care if she was too big and too ugly. She would have her own babies now, for sure. She settled down to endure the trek...

At the same time as Carasim's party reached the Honor, their small group reached the Wilder camp. It was well set up, at the side of a stream - perhaps the same one they had crossed over so many hours before. Rough huts were built in a circle before a cliff face which held small caves. A stand of trees sheltered the approach, both from prying eyes and from the east wind. Sentries were posted. Fires were lit on the flat ground in front of the caves. It was apparent that the men gathered around the fires were cooking food. Imagine that!

Once past the sentries, the group was greeted by roars of approval, as they were led to the largest of the caves. Inside, their bindings and gags were removed and they were pushed into a sort of pen.

"Later," their captors grinned at them. "Don't make a noise, now."

It was two more days before their loss was accepted at the Honor.

"No," Marisel decided, "I will risk no more of my women. Wilders have them now and it is too late. They would not be acceptable to a new Sieur now, anyway."

"But think, Marisel," Tarabeth urged, trying hard to keep the tears from her voice. "Salsi is a matron with children here, and Belleth is my true daughter."

"There is no other scout in the whole Honor like Hulia," Carasim pleaded. It was not just that their loss made her angry for the Honor's sake, it was that she felt such guilt that they had been in her care. She should never have left them.

Marisel's voice was kind, but she was adamant. "I do understand your pain. It is my pain also. And Carasim, if you had been there, no doubt we would have lost you and the young ones as well. There is no point in considering what might have been. The loss of each of them is an agony to me and a sad loss for my Honor. But we cannot fight an entire Wilder pack, even if we knew where they were. You both know that as well as I do. We will care for Salsi's children. I will announce a mourning."

And Teq beat his battle staff on the ground in angry frustration. His mind was so full of rage that he wanted to run out on to the plain and just keep going. Of course nothing could be done to make yesterday out of today, but he was bursting with fury. He was not sure if he was angrier that his true sister was lost to him, or that very soon he would be a Wilder himself. Very soon he would be joining a pack. Very soon he would be hunting for women.

Was this a right way to live?

Chapter 4

The three young women looked about them at the place where they were penned. "Penned" was clearly an exaggeration, since the door opened outward with a push from within. Only a looped binder held it closed. On the other hand, the outer cave as well as the cave's forecourt was overflowing with Wilders, so there was no place to go. In fact, they were probably better off in the pen where they were out of sight.

The pen itself covered quite a large area and was well padded with bracken. There were even blankets piled in a corner. There seemed no particular need for caution, and they were tired and cold now that they had stopped moving. They banked the bracken, wrapped themselves in the blankets, and stretched out to rest.

Hulia was the first to speak. "This is my fault. I do not deserve the title of scout. I was in charge, and I took no care. I never once thought of Wilders. Stupid, stupid. I know you must despise me, and I deserve that."

"Don't talk foolishly," Salsi said severely. "There is no point in talking about what we might have done or not done. What we should be doing is planning escape. My children..." She turned away to hide her tears.

"You're one as silly as the other." It was Belleth's turn and she was angry. "What is there to plan? What is there to do? We're caught. That's that. We're here and here is where we will have to stay. If by some wild magic, we were to get away, where would we go? We know where we are, more or less. If we went back, they would follow. Even if we could outdistance them, we would lead them straight to the Honor. If they don't know where it is, do we want to let them know, so that they could capture more of us? Weeping and bemoaning demean us. We must put our minds to dealing well with whatever happens to us from now on. This is our lot. What's done is done! We serve ourselves better by getting some rest so that we can face whatever happens next."

The other two were much too astonished at Belleth's diatribe to have anything to say. She made a sort of sense. Much as they resented the idea, acceptance really was the only response to their capture. But from Belleth, the youngest of them! Had they known her excitement and eagerness to know what would happen next, they would have felt less properly chastised. As it was, they each rolled over to face away from each other in silence. And although Hulia gritted her mind in agony over her sense of guilt, and Salsi wept quietly for her children, in the end, they slept.

They were surprised that they were awakened by a woman. "I am Frata," she greeted them, " captured more than a year ago. There are seven women here - well, ten now, so you are not alone." She smiled reassuringly. "I have brought you water for washing and a comb to tidy your hair. Is anyone hurt?"

Belleth answered her. "No. Our only hurt is to our pride and to our hearts." She smiled back. "Are we to fear what will happen to us here?"

"Why no. Not at all. Boredom will be your worst affliction, as we never go hunting, or leave the main camp at all. Otherwise, life is like that of any matron in the Honor, except that there is more than one Sieur, if you will. Were you all matrons?"

"I am," Salsi answered. "I am Salsi. Belleth and Hulia are not." She indicated them as she named them.

"I was too young to be a matron," Belleth put in. "The Sieur of our Honor was my sire."

"Here we are all matrons. We are assigned exclusively to certain of the men. This is accepted, and there is no fighting over us or abuse of us because of that. The other difference from an Honor is that only the men have a voice in Council."

Hulia growled.

Frata went on. "That is hardest to bear. We can influence our men if we are able. Some listen, some don't. Otherwise we tend our fields and the smoke house. Make clothes, tend to our children: much the same as in the Honor. A lot of the time we spend together."

"How does this 'assigning' happen?" Belleth wanted to know.

"That will be tonight after the meal, which is ready now. Tidy yourselves, so that you will look your best." Hulia growled again, so Frata added, " it is a matter of pride."

"Can we not refuse?" Hulia asked.

"You can refuse one of the men, but it is usually better not. They are assigned as a reward for something that has benefited the pack. The three men you are assigned to - it is usually three - are friends with one another. An outsider could cause friction and that would be hard on everybody."

"But can we not refuse altogether?' Hulia asked. "I could aid the pack in other ways. I am a scout."

"Not any more," Belleth said dryly.

"No you cannot refuse altogether." Frata lowered her eyes. "You were captured because you are a woman. Scouts come in aplenty. Think. Could you have refused your Sieur?"

"Didn't have to," Hulia muttered. "I just told Tarabeth I didn't want to be chosen."

Belleth was surprised by the revelation, but decided to change the subject, particularly as Salsi looked ready to weep again at the mention of the familiar names. "What is this place used for?" she asked, indicating the pen.

"Oh, women can come here during their monthly, if they want to. And it's used for birthings. That's all I ever use it for now. Yours is the second capture since I came," she added.

"What about our weapons?" Hulia wanted to know.

"You'll get your knives back, or some knife. No spears or bows. We don't hunt. I told you."

"So they're afraid of us," Hulia sniffed.

"Not really. What is there to fear?" Frata handed Hulia a cloth to dry herself while Salsi combed her hair. "There are so many men here, and they really are stronger than we are."

"Yes," Salsi murmured. "Even my little Mem was growing strong at battle practice." Her eyes were filled with tears.

Belleth held her peace. She washed and tidied herself as well as possible, brushing bracken off her tunic and braiding her hair. She was still too tall and too big and too plain of face, but she did her best. She couldn't help reflecting that, no matter what happened, Mem would never reach manhood. It would be easier for Salsi to forget that away from the Honor.

The rest of the women arrived to accompany them to the evening meal. They varied in age, but only two were nearing their middle years. The others, like Frata, were roughly of the ages of the new captives. They all carried children or had little ones holding on to their hands or their tunics. It occurred to Belleth that these youngsters would never know the life of an Honor. It had never crossed her mind before that most Wilders never did get to be the Sieur of an Honor. Most just remained with the packs for ever. The children might never know the discipline and schooling of an Honor, but then again, the little boys would not meet Mem's fate. Belleth was overcome for a moment with thoughts of Teq, but she resolutely put them aside. Surely he would have time to grow and reach his drumming. She shook herself. It would be necessary to be alert for the evening.

The arrangements for eating the evening meal were so loose that the three women were astonished. The men were already eating. Noone spoke. The women picked up bowls and scooped out food for themselves and their children, looking in each pot before deciding what to take. The men were sitting round the fires in groups. They eyed the newcomers speculatively but made no moves towards them of any kind. The three newcomers found it impossible to distinguish one from another in the dim light. There were no visible leaders, no high table, no visible servants. The oldest and the youngest among the men tended to cluster together, leaving the men in their prime to gather with one another. But it all seemed to be a matter of preference, not planning. The women and children joined one group or another - presumably their 'assigned' mates - as they picked up some flat bread from the piles near the fires and squatted down to eat. Frata led the newcomers aside.

"Why don't you eat over here. I will be at that fire there, if you need me. My mates were the three who brought you in. They asked me to see that you were fed. When you finish wash your bowls over there, and stack them. When everyone has finished eating, you will hear your assignments." She smiled again and left them.

"Well!" Hulia said.

"Oh stop being insulted, Hulia," Belleth said. She was tired of Hulia's posing and Salsi's weeping. "Look about you for which fires have no women. That is where we'll be going, I expect. See what you can of the men there."

There was no signal. No apparent plan. Still not a sign of a leader. As the shadows deepened to full dark, and only the firelight kept the shadows at bay, a man rose.

"I was chosen leader of today's hunt. I claim the right to choose a mate," he said.

There was a general murmuring, but no voice of dissent. The man walked over to where they sat. Two more men from the same fire rose and joined him. The three women shifted uncomfortably under their scrutiny. The men talked together, obviously deciding who to choose. The speaker stepped forward and took Hulia's hand. He pulled insistently until she rose. She resisted all the way to their fireside. The more she resisted, the more they grinned. Belleth and Salsi drew closer together, shivering.

"This cave site is keeping us warm through this long winter. I found the site." While they had been watching Hulia, another speaker had risen. "I claim a mate to warm the fireside of myself and my brothers." This speaker was very close to them and they could see him well. Again there was no dissent. There were four, this time, who came to discuss the two women. They seemed smaller and younger that the last group. They argued together for a long time before the speaker stepped forward and took Salsi's hand.

Salsi went with them quietly. She did not glance at Belleth who was appalled to find she was mortified. Shamed. Even here where women were so few, she was too plain to be chosen, even by young men who were closer to her age than to Salsi's. She had dared to hope it would not be so. She closed her face down to show no hint of her feelings.

Two men rose at the same moment. The murmuring from around the fires stopped. Perhaps this was unusual.

"I am your carver." The voice was loud and self-assured, even arrogant. "I have been a Sieur. I need a woman again to my bed. So does my brother here. We are big men with big appetites." He paused waiting for a response. There was silence. "We have not been with you long, but we claim a mate now. This one will do very well."

Another voice spoke. It was quiet, but firm, unintimidated. "I am your healer. My brothers and I tend you all. We eat of the meat you bring, but we have a right to claim a mate for ourselves as much as any hunter. We claim that right now."

"Both claims are good," shouted one voice.

"No need to have been with the pack since birth. All have the same rights," shouted another. "Let the carver have her."

"No the healer has grown up among us. The carver has had mates when he was a Sieur. Just because he was thrown out of an Honor doesn't give him a right of preference."

"Yes," from another voice. "The healer serves us well. He has the right."

A general clamor broke the darkness. Unchosen? Belleth thought wryly that she had never expected to have a pair of suitors. She was well aware that it had nothing to do with her. She was simply a woman. Any woman. Still, it was a nice idea. She grinned to herself, heartened. She had a random thought: so this was what happened to a Sieur after he was beaten. She wished Teq were here so that she could tell him.

"Call a Council," someone suggested.

"Let the woman choose," said another voice. Everyone laughed. "Why not?"

And the whole pack roared with mirth.

A hand pulled Belleth into the firelight and the two speakers stepped up to her.

One was large and red of face, made more so by the firelight. A jagged scar ran from the corner of his mouth to just below his eye, distorting his face. But even without the distortion his face carried an expression which made Belleth shudder. It was an expression which was foreign to her - to any woman from an Honor. It was a leer. "Choose," he demanded. His voice was very deep and rough. "I was a Sieur. I know how women want to be treated. You would do better with me than with this cripple. Look at me. Look at my brother. We are men."

Another man had come up behind the carver. His size owed as much to his girth as to his strength. He stood with his fists on his hips and an identical expression on his face.

"Aye choose." A quiet voice spoke from Belleth's other side. Perhaps not quiet except in contrast. He was tall and unnaturally thin. He limped into the firelight on a foot twisted beneath him so that he must walk on its side. His face was long and brown, and seemed closed to sorrow and gladness alike. He looked at Belleth with such a certainty of defeat in his expression that her heart was touched. And in those same eyes, away in the depth, so that she was not sure in the uncertainty of the firelight, she thought she saw a look of self-deprecating humor, as if he were amused at his own temerity. She knew what he was feeling. Both the courage of his challenge and the sureness of his rejection were known to her. She stepped over to him and offered her hand.

The carver and his brother roared in unison and lunged forward, but every man at every fire rose in his place. The chance had been given, the choice had been made, the peace would be kept. It was the purpose of assignments.

The healer spoke again, smiling at Belleth. "I am Zolg," he said. "You honor me as you honor my brothers."

"Honor! Yes, I suppose that is the meaning of 'honor'." She laughed. "I am Belleth. Together we will be Belleth's honor. We will deal well together."

"Not so," Zolg replied, gently. "Here we allow no talk of Honors. If we are lucky to have a wife at our fire, we do not spoil things by talking of the past. We create a present. A good present, we hope. Come and meet your other husbands."

"I am frightened." Belleth was astounded to discover she could confess her vulnerability to this man she had met only minutes earlier. She was so startled at herself that she could think of nothing to add.

"We are not a very frightening group," Zolg smiled at her. "This is Dern and this is Hezer. They are my brothers."

"True brothers?" Belleth asked as she smiled shyly at them.

"If you mean, did we have the same mother, no we didn't." Hezer's voice was very deep. He was a short, pale man with a broad chest and long arms.

"We choose one another as fire companions when we leave our mothers," Dern explained. He, on the other hand, was as tall as Zolg, but dark-skinned, with very long hair. In the dusky firelight, it was all Belleth could see of them.

"We are not men who are like to grow into Challengers, you see," Zolg explained. "We are not handsome men, with good physique..."

"We have learned to be healers. Zolg is our elder brother. He knows a lot about healing. We are helpers. It is my task to fetch the sick to him, and carry them to the isolate cave when they may infect others," Dern told her. "I have never infected my brothers, though men avoid me because of that. Please do not fear me, lady."

"And I seek out the herbs which Zolg uses in his cures. He has trained me to seek for them. I am slow of wit. My pack brothers have told me so. Often. Only Zolg and Dern would accept me at their fire. We hope you will like us when you see us, lady."

"I am Belleth. I can hunt. I am good at it, but it is all I know how to do. I would like to learn about healing. As a woman I am not pretty. Tall. Much too tall. Well, you can see that. I feared a Sieur would not ask for me, and I would never have a child. You asked for me. I think we will support one another, if you can accept me as I am. I will do my best for you."

"We do not expect you to love us, lady," Zolg added. "But I think we will love you."

"I think I shall love you, if you are kind to me. We will be a support for one another. I mean to do well."

"We do too," Zolg told her. He lifted her hand shyly and kissed it. She moved closer to him at the fire.

"I know we will do well together," she whispered.

And they did. Belleth learned to accept and give love, which was a concept Hulia never mastered. In time, with the birth of a son, even Salsi ceased to weep for her lost life. Because Belleth, like her brother, was of an inquiring mind, she learned the healing arts from her mates, and enjoyed them. Her first pregnancy brought her fulfillment, which turned her so far inward, that in midsummer she did not even notice that the camp was nearly empty. Most of the men were gone. It was Salsi, pregnant also, who brought her the news.

"The men are back," she said to Belleth, her voice heavy with sadness.

Belleth who was happily pounding roots into powder looked up, smiling. "I hardly noticed they were gone," she said. "But then my Zolg and his brothers do not go on the hunt. You're crying! What's happened?"

"Oh I don't know for certain, and they won't tell me, but they went with Chag to make a Challenge. They weren't on a hunt."

"Oh yes, Chag. He always kept apart, and he is certainly big. As big as the Sieur. Why should that make you cry?"

"He hasn't come back with them. It means he won his Challenge. I'm sure. And oh, Belleth, I just know they went to Marisel's Honor."

"You can't know that!"

"I know in my heart. My Mem is dead. And I am here. Oh Belleth," she wailed.

"Belleth was quiet for a long time. Salsi was right. Of course she was right. Marisel's was the nearest Honor and the Sieur was sure to be Challenged again since he had been wounded at the last Challenge. "Teq," she said once, and grabbed on to Salsi. They could only hug one another to give comfort.

"It would have been worse if we were there," Belleth said at last. "We would have had to see everything."

"Perhaps I could have saved Mem. Hidden him."

"How? He was already in the boys' quarters before we left. It is a bitter world. But Salsi, our children here will be safe. Perhaps it's better here."

"Nothing will ever matter to me again. Never again. " Salsi stopped her tears and walked bleakly away.

Belleth sent her heart seeking. Was Teq safe? She had never warned him, and she had meant to. Perhaps his drumming... She returned to pounding the roots. She would never know. She decided to believe he was safe.

Chapter 5

Teq lay on his stomach at the far southern edge of the Honor. It was spring, and for once the day was dry and bright. It was a day to prod weary hearts into hopefulness with the sheer force of its scents and colors. Certainly the goat herd was attesting to that. They were frisking and leaping with unwonted energy - even for goats. As he watched, two of the winter's kids ran at each other, butted heads and leapt straight up into the air. But for Teq the pensive, even gloomy, mood which had overcome him with the disappearance of Belleth, weighted him down still. He felt as if he were due to learn dreadful things and be called upon to do dreadful deeds. As if his childhood was over.

His map of the south lay on the grass before him. It showed what the eye could see and as far beyond that as he had traveled with the hunters. The southern reaches of the rift were wide, forming a flat, rock strewn valley below the steep escarpment on whose top he lay. On the farther side of the valley, the terrain rolled upward in barren rocky curves, stretching higher and higher. Sharp chasms split the rock hills, which ended in a flat topped mesa, dotted with scattered shrubs. All of this he showed on his map, but it ended abruptly with the mesa. He knew nothing of what lay beyond. That was the trouble with all of his maps: lack of knowledge. At this season of the year, the bottom of the rift was alive with the rushing torrent of snow melt, depositing rocks, bits of trees, and even dead animals in the broad vale, as it slowed here to a mere frenzy. The high hills where the snow fell, rose far to the north of the Honor. Where the rift ran to its west, it was narrow, and the wild water was fierce and strong enough to carry the detritus with it.

Disgusted at the paucity of his information, Teq lifted the stones from the corners of his map and allowed the skin to roll shut. He sat up and clasped his knees, thinking about the oddity of the morning's encounter with his true mother. Tarabeth had passed him as he was releasing the herd from their pen, ready to take them out. She paused as if admiring the kids, and spoke to him so softly that he was forced to strain to hear her over the bleatings and jostlings of the goats.

"I will speak to you near the well when the Honor is asleep," she said, not waiting to hear his startled "Lady" in response.

What could it mean? Quite frankly, boys were beneath the notice of the matrons, except for ordering chores. Certainly Tarabeth was his true mother, but she was also first matron. Any chore could be ordered in full hearing of the Honor: mend this, carry that. Yet the demand from his true mother delivered so secretly, argued that she did not want their exchange to be overheard. Perhaps this was the way that a drumming was announced, but that didn't seem likely. Even his singing voice - which he tested constantly - still rang pure on the highest notes, and he despaired of finding even one errant hair on his face. Could it be that he was to train some of his little brothers in tending the herd? No, that was silly. There would be no need for secrecy about that, and anyway, they were all still in battle training with the Sieur, and there were plenty of girls who could do it.

He sang the song he usually used to try his voice, having enough high and low notes to test his range. He hit all the high notes with such ease that it sent him even farther into gloom. He felt as if he would be trapped in the Honor for ever, even though his limbs had grown so long that he never got to take a meal without hearing some teasing from the women.

Teq sighed, and then a thought struck him. Perhaps the Sieur had another message to pass to him. It was a fact that the Sieur never addressed one of the youngs directly, except in battle training, and then they were *very* young. He hugged to himself the memory of the morning before the Challenge when the Sieur had asked him for beanbrew, in undiminished warmth. What could it be? The Sieur ordering him to stop herding and assist in battle training? He cheered up. He knew it was a fantasy, but it kept him dreaming happily until he heard the warning drum, faint on the evening air, to bring in the goats for the night.

In fact, Teq's speculations were not so far awry. Tarabeth *was* carrying a message from the Sieur. And it was certainly not to be overheard. They had discussed it as they lay in the Sieur's quarters the night before.

"My lord is in pain," Tarabeth said, as she laid her lute aside, watching him massage his aching knee.

"I do wish you'd stop calling me 'my lord'. I have a real yearning to hear someone use my name again. I am Galt. You are my beloved first matron. Would it be so hard to say?"

Tarabeth laughed. "Not hard, but wrong. Suppose I were to use my lord's name in front of someone else. The shock would tear the fabric of the Honor. Marisel loves tradition. But you are not answering me."

"You know the pain will always be there in some degree. I barely won the Challenge, and he did wound me sorely. I had to damage his eye so that the same one would not return. I will definitely lose the next Challenge. I am strong, but no longer strong enough to win against a Wilder in his prime. Spring is here. It won't be long now. Among Wilders, even from pack to pack, it is known where there is a weak Sieur. The packs will be drifting towards us. It is only a matter of a little time. Will you miss me?" He smiled at her.

"I will not be matron to your successor. It will not be forced on me. Marisel would not allow it. I shall refuse, if I am asked."

"You will be asked. You are beautiful." He kissed her.

She responded to his kiss, loving him. "You are my only lord. You do not have to ask if I will miss you."

"In all other ways, I will be glad to lay down this burden. To be Sieur is no burden in the beginning. It is all joy and triumph. But now, the responsibility seems heavy, and anyway, it is time for the youngs to have a new Sieur."

"You miss Salsi, my lord." Tarabeth lowered her eyes. It was Salsi's youth which had caused her pangs of jealousy: pangs which had frankly astonished her by their unexpectedness and inappropriateness. It was the duty of the Sieur to produce more young.

Galt reached out and stroked her hair. "Never as I shall miss you. I mean only that it is time. Our own Belleth was in need of becoming a matron, and there are others, older than she."

Tarabeth was contrite. "I know it is true. I would just delay it a little longer. Certainly until Teq has his drumming. I will lose both my children, but I would rather watch him leave to be a Wilder than watch him die."

Galt frowned. "I have been thinking about that. You remember the message I gave you for him at the last Challenge? It was spur of the moment, but do you not think he could save himself if he were warned? There is the chimney. It might help him. He is so close to his drumming, I know he could survive. And he is your son. I could not bear to be responsible for his death. For the little ones, even Mem who is so bright that my heart breaks to watch him, there is no hope. But Teq... Could we not conspire to save him, my Tarabeth?"

Tarabeth rose from the bed and began to pace the room. "I am first matron. I have a responsibility to uphold the laws of the Honor.

"You do," Galt agreed.

"But he is my true son, and he is yours, my lord, and made in your image."

"He is," Galt nodded.

"I have already lost Belleth, who should have been here as my comfort, when I lose you."

"You have."

"I worry about her so much. I still look for her. How is it with her? How is her life in a Wilder pack?"

"She is probably well and even happy. We may even be on the way to becoming grandparents by now."

"Grandparents?" Tarabeth did not know the term. Honor matrons were all just matrons. The Sieur was just the Sieur, even if his identity changed. A true daughter's child might well be the near sister of a matron's second child.

"I mean that she may be carrying a Wilder child. She may, probably does, have mates of her own. She may well be happy with them. It is usual," Galt explained. "At least it was when I was a Wilder. In the Pack I lived in."

"But she is lost to me."

"She is," Galt agreed.

"To lose Teq in such a way... And he is no ordinary boy. He is so accomplished."

"Accomplished? He is excellent with the battle staff, I know. Is he an accomplished herder? Hunter?"

"He makes maps. Wonderful maps. He thinks I do not know, but I have seen them. Belleth showed me. And yes, he did well enough with the hunt, and he is good with the herd. They follow him, you know, he does not drive them."

"Then with all this, can you not see your way to warning him, my Tarabeth? It would be such a waste... It is likely that there will be a Challenge before his drumming."

"A warning is not specifically forbidden."

Galt smiled. He had won his point. He did not wish to show her the fallacy in her argument with herself.

"I will warn him. I will show him the chimney. He is so nearly of Wilder age," she resolved.

"How true, my wise Tarabeth. Come. Lie beside me. We will take comfort in being still together."

As soon as the little boys retired, Teq sought his own bed. He lay tense, aware of every tiny sound in the Honor. Wakefulness was far from uncommon for him, but he feared that he would fall asleep this night. He kept tiptoeing from his bed to the basin to splash water on to his face. It seemed that the Honor would never fall still.

Silence at last. He counted every number he knew. Twice. And then he dared to venture from his quarters. There was very little moon, but his night vision was good, and he could make out a shadow by the well. Tarabeth was before him.

"Lady," he whispered, compelled to make little noise by the stillness of his true mother.

She had watched his approach, going over and over the arguments she had used the night before, and convincing herself again and again that what she was about to do was right.

"Come with me," she greeted him, and grasped his hand. "Do not make a sound."

He was as tall as she now, suddenly it seemed, perhaps even taller. Being led by the hand seemed silly, now that he was so large, but he kept the silence she imposed as much from bewilderment as obedience. They entered the kitchen area, dominated by the tables and the immense, jutting chimney which housed not one, but three, cooking hearths. The room was dimly lit by little dish lamps, left burning to aid early rising cooks to unbank the fires and start the day.

Tarabeth laid an unnecessary finger to her lips. They were already soundless. She led Teq to the left of the chimney. There she chose some of the stones of the chimney, and where they met the outer wall, and pulled on them. The whole side of the chimney opened just like the gates of the Honor, only narrower. The space was just wide enough for a broad person to enter. On the right side of the chimney there was a deep alcove with shelves. The cooks kept their clay cooking vessels there, and it was full to overflowing. Teq was disgusted with himself that he had never questioned why there was not a like alcove on the left. The older he got the more, he realized, he simply took for granted. There were so many questions he should be asking, every day.

Tarabeth took down a dish lamp and stepped into the gap, motioning Teq to follow her. An alcove did exist to their right, and space to move straight ahead. The air was smokeless and surprisingly cool, so close to the fire. They walked forward two paces, then turned abruptly left. A short passage zigzagged sharply, first right then left. They walked through it, a matter of only a few paces, then stopped short. Had it not been for the lamp, they would have walked into a bush. They were outside the Honor.

Once she was certain Teq knew where he was, she led the way back inside. She shut the chimney, then pushed him forward to find the right stones, so that he could open it and close it for himself. Then she replaced the lamp and led him back to the well. They spoke no word until they got there.

"You have seen that which few have seen, Teq," the solemnity in her voice clear even in the hushed tone.

"Lady," he answered, completely at a loss to know why he had been so distinguished. He thought he might sound foolish if he said anything else, so he held his peace.

"It was the wish of the Sieur that I would show you, and I agreed."

"My lord is gracious," Teq mumbled, almost incoherent in his elation at being so noticed by the Sieur. But still, he was puzzled. Why?

"There is a reason for this. There is that which I must tell you." Tarabeth turned her face away from him in the night, as if she could not bear to say any more. There was a pause of such length that Teq feared she would not continue. He did not dare to make a sound in case she would not.

At last she spoke, in so low a voice that he had to lean close to hear. "You recall the message I gave you from the Sieur at the last Challenge?"

"I do, Lady. I still do not understand it."

"It is because..." Her voice took on a bleak quality through the whisper. Teq shivered, though the night was not actually cold. "It is because a new Sieur has the duty and the right to kill all male children remaining in the Honor at his accession. They are the offspring of the Sieur he has conquered and so he eliminates all trace of that person. If you have not reached your drumming by the time of the next Challenge you will be killed and I will be unable to stop it. Therefore I - we - decided to give you the means to save yourself." Tarabeth finally turned back to face him. Her face loomed pale in the dim light.

Teq could find no words. At first he could not make himself understand what he had been told. It was too monstrous. And then he blurted out the first words which came to him, "but why?"

"The children of the Honor must be strong. A Sieur who is conquered is not as strong as his conqueror. Thus his children will not be as strong. The girl children will become his matrons and carry his get. The boy children have no function, and serve to remind him that he had a predecessor. Worse, they remind the matrons of their sire. The matrons must be willing to get children by the new Sieur - oh, all this is beyond your understanding. You are not even of Wilder age yet. You do not, cannot, know what I am saying. All you need to know is that you will be killed by a new Sieur and I have shown you the means of escape. It will be better, so much better, if your drumming comes first. You show no sign, no sign at all, of readiness?" her voice pleaded.

"None, Lady," he said impatiently. "But Lady, my brothers! I am to show them? I am to lead them?"

"No!" Her voice took on a note of desperation. "No. You must say nothing. Nothing to anyone at all of what I have told you and shown you. That is an order."

"I could not leave my brothers," Teq said flatly. "I will say nothing until the time, and then I will simply take them with me."

"You will, you must leave them. Oh please, do try to understand. These little ones could not survive outside the Honor. No Wilder pack would accept them. They would just be extra mouths to feed. Worse, you would never get beyond the bounds of the Honor with them. They could not move fast enough to outstrip a Sieur. They are all too small. Can you not see that?"

"Yes, I can see that. But, Lady, what am I to do? This is too much for me. You tell me I must knowingly leave my brothers to die. I cannot. I do not know what to do."

"Save yourself. It is my order. It is what the Sieur wants you to do. He knows you. Sees you. He wants you to do this. He cannot save all his sons. He wishes to save one. I was persuaded. I also do not wish to watch you die. I was easy to persuade. I have lost your sister. I want you to be safe." She began to weep, deep wracking tears, no less punishing for their near silence.

"Lady, do not cry. I understand the orders of my Sieur and of my lady. I will do as you say. But, Lady," he almost wailed, "how am I to bear this knowledge? My heart will burst. You should not have told me this."

Tarabeth straightened her shoulders and quieted her weeping. She drew herself up to stand straight, by the well, as if donning authority like an extra garment. "You will prepare yourself. You will make ready as if you prepared for your drumming. Ready your weapons. Prepare journey food. Put them in the chimney, secretly. If, as we all hope, your drumming time comes, then retrieve them. If not, then you must escape. It is your duty, laid upon you by your Sieur and your first matron. You will succeed. I charge you in my name and the name of the Sieur. Pledge yourself."

"I do so pledge, Lady. I understand my duty. I will disclose the secrets you have passed to me, to nobody. I will prepare, and I too will hope my drumming is soon." He spoke without inflection, the words wrung from his belly.

"Then take my blessing now." Tarabeth clasped his face between her hands and laid a solemn kiss on his forehead. "Be my true son. Leave me now."

Teq rose in obedience and stumbled to his bed among his brothers, walking as if he had aged a dozen years in that night encounter. There began, with that sleepless night, a time of torment. Whatever else might happen to him in his life, nothing he might be called upon to bear could be a greater burden. Each time he looked at his brothers, he knew himself to be their betrayer, and his misery deepened.

It was a short, wet spring. Still Teq's voice did not break. And then it was summer.

Chapter 6

As spring eased into summer, Marisel put the whole Honor to work scrubbing and whitewashing and patching. Everyone was exhausted. For safety, hunting parties only went out now in large numbers. Large hunting parties meant larger quantities of meat to deal with. Large hunting parties and scouring the Honor meant less people to work in the fields. Everyone fell into bed weary beyond measure every night, and was nervous and irritable during the day. Life in the Honor was not pleasant.

Teq was put to work, on at least half of the days, patching and mending walls. He had less days out with the herd where he had always been in the habit of doing his thinking and planning. He let his brothers help him with the patching and mending so that he could spend more time with them. And yet he found it impossible to be close to them and not remember that there was no point in teaching them. They had no future. He was as irritable as everybody else. It seemed to Teq that the Sieur was being cruel in seeking to improve their work with their battle staves. They would never in their lives have the chance to use these skills, learned at such a cost in bruises and tears. Sometimes, when he could sneak the chance, he would stop and watch, renewing his own old skills, and then he would get even angrier with the Sieur. And then one day he realized that the Sieur could not allow himself the certainty of losing the next Challenge, in spite of his slight limp and weakened left arm. If he did, then failure was certain. Even the chance of success meant life for Teq and maybe some of his brothers. The thought cheered him up and made him look kindly on the Sieur.

When Teq did go out with the herd, he worked on making himself a new bow. His old one was too short for his growing arms, and so was his battle staff. One thing at a time.

His preparations for escape - if he ever had to do so - went along easily. The journey food, which was made of berries, nuts and meal pounded together, was piled in the pantry alongside the smoked meats. Whenever a hunting party was going out they would help themselves. Teq just went along behind them and stole

36

some. His stash in the chimney alcove was shaping up nicely. He was aware that escape meant running and climbing, so the collection had to be sorted carefully for what was really necessary. It could not be everything he would take if he were leaving on a proper drumming. If that did happen, it would be easy enough to add to the store. If not, he had to have refined what he could easily carry. He spent the night time making his bundles. He found he enjoyed doing it well, in spite of the fact that he was only carrying out an order he did not wish to.

One problem was that his winter cloak was far too small, and summer was hardly the season to ask for a new one. At least he could use the old one to wrap his bundle into a final pack. Beside the food, he had a spare tunic and shoes... and his maps. He could not bring himself to leave his careful maps behind, even though he knew their contents by heart and had no need to consult them as far as they went. He made the pack secure with as many binders as he could filch. There were spare binders for his waist where he would carry his knife, his sling, his water bag and his pack of arrows. The pack could be tied to his back, with his battle staff and bow shoved down behind it. His hands would be free for climbing. He wished he could practice carrying it, because it was a bit awkward and quite heavy, in spite of his refinements. But there was no place to do so. Even at night someone was sure to be wakeful if he was pounding up and down the courtyard. He had to content himself with practicing putting it on quickly.

At the beginning of the summer he had to beg hides to make new shoes. Two pairs, because running all day and every day would be hard on them. "Two pairs?" the matron asked. "My feet are growing so quickly, I thought I'd make one for now and one for later," he explained. It made very little sense, but with all the animals the hunters were bringing in, there were plenty of hides, and in any case she wasn't really listening. She said no more than "Hmph" when she gave them to him. He made two pairs and had enough left for a new water bag. His old one was wearing thin, and he wanted to make one which flopped about less. He had to unmake his pack to change the shoes, but he was pleased.

The daytime activities, obviously so hectic because Marisel was readying the Honor for a new Sieur, and Teq's furtive activity in the dark hours, wore him out. He had little time to think, nor did he lie sleepless any more. The minute he got to bed, he was asleep.

He did sing his test song every day. There was no sign of change in his voice. And he still explored his face for hair. One day, nearly at midsummer, he thought he found one. It was just one, but his heart leaped high with excitement, and he wanted desperately to tell someone. But who? Who would care? It was one of the days when he had taken the herd out. Perhaps she was waiting for him, or perhaps it was just luck that Tarabeth was by the pen when he brought the herd in.

"I believe my drumming may be soon, Lady," he blurted out, as soon as he saw her.

He forgot for a moment the resentment with which he had been regarding her, ever since she had ordered his fate. For some reason he blamed her for the terrible things she had told him. The messenger was held responsible for the message. With his words, her face lit with a whole heart smile. Some of his resentment melted in its warmth. She was a beautiful lady, his true mother, and he could not help loving her.

"Wait here," she told him.

While he waited he examined his feelings. He realized he had told her his news because she was the only person other than the Sieur (and he could hardly speak to him!), who knew the significance of the hair. He had no intention of bringing her happiness. That was for himself. And yet, when he saw her smile, her happiness still made him happy. In the weeks which had passed since she told him, he had put as much of her message from his mind as he could. Not thinking about it, he had come to realize a little, what had motivated her to place this terrible burden on him. She must feel the loss of Belleth still, as acutely as he did himself. She would lose the Sieur, for whom he did not doubt she had high esteem, if he lost the Challenge. And she would lose her true son also. That was the only thing she might be able to change. At least, although he would still be gone from her, it would be no worse than if he had his drumming. Her true son would be alive. His true mother cared for him!

When Tarabeth returned, she carried her lute and a bundle. She was both surprised and delighted when he smiled at her. He had never done so before. Naturally, sons would not display emotion before their true mothers once they had gone to the boys' quarters. It was a childish way of asserting manhood. Since she had given him her dreadful message, he had frowned, not even remained impassive, when she was near. The smile was as close as she would be likely to come to forgiveness, and she was warmed by it. She smiled back.

"There will be nobody in the eating room," she said. "Let's go there."

People were hurrying to prepare themselves for the evening meal. The tables in the eating room were piled ready with bowls and spoons and beakers. At this hour the room was deserted. Teq and Tarabeth walked there in a companionable silence, more comfortable together than they had ever been. He is growing up. Already he is a man in his heart, she thought.

Tarabeth settled herself on one of the tables. "Sing with me," she said. "What is that song you are always singing? Ah yes, 'The Moon Hunt'. Begin."

Teq sang. No false note marred the beauty of the song. His treble was as perfect as ever.

"Alas, not yet, my true son. Soon." In spite of herself, tears came into Tarabeth's eyes. "No matter," she added. "I have made you this. It is your drumming gift. Take it now." She handed him the bundle she had been carrying.

Teq shook it out. It was a new cloak: large, and heavy; of the softest leather, lined with felted goat hair.

"It will serve to keep you warm and dry, though I am afraid I made it rather heavy. I hope you will be able to carry it, when you have to take so much else. Do you like it?"

Teq too began to weep silent tears. He knelt before his true mother. "It is a gift fit for a Sieur, Lady. I had been at my wit's end, how to ask for a new cloak at this season. It will never weigh heavy to me."

Tarabeth wept with him. She rose, graceful always, and reached out her arms to him. For the only time since he had left her for the boys' quarters, she hugged him to her.

"You have prepared, Teq?" she whispered.

"I have prepared, Lady. Just as you ordered."

She nodded her head, and again kissed his forehead. "We are both blessed, then," she said. "Go now. We must not be seen talking together for so long." She walked away, hugging her lute to her, her head bowed.

Teq rerolled his new cloak, and hurried with it to the boys' room. It would have to be bound to the top of his pack tonight. Until then he shoved it noncommittally beneath his pillow, and none of the little boys even noticed.

The next day, Teq was again out with the herd. In fact all the mending was about finished, and the Honor looking renewed. He managed to finish his bow early in the day. He had taken the herd to the west, right up to the rim of the rift. He had decided that, if he had to escape indeed, the best way would be to cross the rift here and travel west. For one thing, the crossing was made difficult by the very steepness of the cliff, on both edges. For another, hunting parties, put off by that very difficulty of handling game up and down the cliff, never went that way. And thirdly, now that the river had all but dried up, the slit of a gorge was narrow at the bottom, and hard to walk along, but it offered a lot of cover, with its wrinkled cliffs, and huge boulders. Teq explored the edge to find a way down which he could negotiate with all his equipment. He found a short chimney which ended in a fairly substantial ledge. He could lower his pack to that, while he chimneyed down. From the ledge there appeared to be a defile which went all the way to the bottom. Not impossible.

When the evening drum sounded, he started back with the herd. He was not sufficiently alert to note the extra warning beat in the summons, so that he was nearly at the walls before he saw the gathering Wilders. The Challenge would be tomorrow!

He stopped short, momentarily taken in such a panic that his heart seemed to stop and his knees began to tremble. He had no idea what he was supposed to do. He began to sweat. Then, as suddenly as he had panicked, his mind cleared, his muscles steadied, and he knew exactly what to do. How lucky that this was a day with the herd! His whole plan for concealing where he had gone rested with them. He planned to scatter them to cover his tracks, and for this, it would be necessary to leave them outside the Honor. It was not unprecedented. If there were a reason, such as when they were whitewashing the pen, they were left outside. The leaders were hobbled, and the rest stayed close. Teq led them to where the bush concealed the chimney exit, and hobbled them there. He planned to explain that, in such summer heat, leaving them penned during a possible day-long Challenge, would be bad for them, if anyone asked. Here they could forage. He slipped inside and brought them water, then back inside before the gates closed for the night. The gatekeepers were busy keeping an eye on the Wilders and had none to spare for Teq.

The evening meal was eaten in near silence. The room was so full of tensions and undercurrents that any conversation seemed unnaturally loud. Each group was preoccupied with its own thoughts, either gladdened or burdened with thoughts of the morrow. The Sieur made little pretense at heartiness as he had done on the previous Challenge eve. He looked about him gravely, as if memorizing the scene, and ate sparingly. To Teq's new awareness, the true mothers of sons seemed to be pretending to eat. Any that were servers, lingered at the boys' table, adding to their food and patting them in passing. Those who were not servers made excuses, carrying drink jugs perhaps, to make some physical contact with their sons. Only Tarabeth did not. She and Teq did not look at one another. The little boys were too tired and excited to notice the extra attention. Teq was so unsettled by it all, that he left the room as soon as the high table had retired. He found it unbearable to be near his little brothers. He flung himself on his bed; but as soon as they came to bed, he flung himself off again, and went to hide his thoughts from the sight of others in the empty herd pen.

The sound of Tarabeth's lute, coming softly from the Sieur's quarters made him think of them. He wondered if they discussed their parting. He thought about her feelings, playing for a new Sieur in all probability, on the morrow. Would she be able to do it? Perhaps she would play out of duty. Perhaps she did so now. He knew nothing of the world of the women, in spite of his talks with Belleth and living all his days among them. He felt that there was so much in the world to know, and he would never learn it all. He was totally inadequate! How did he suppose he could escape, go off on his own, and even survive until he was of Wilder age, let alone make a better life?

Nonetheless, when all was quiet, he checked his supplies one last time and filled his new water bag. At least he could do this much right. Then he went to lay on his bed, certain he would be sleepless. But he was not.

Tarabeth was. She had helped Galt prepare for the morrow. So sure were they that he would not succeed that she had made a bundle of supplies for him, rolled them in his cloak, and hidden them in the bush outside the chimney. The presence of the goats there startled her, but she deduced Teq's plan from their presence and approved. She checked his preparations on the way back in and was satisfied. What could be done for her men, was done. For herself, nothing could be done. She did not care.

Galt slept eventually, her soothing fingers massaging his shoulders and back. Only Tarabeth lay wakeful that night. Before dawn she did what Teq had done on the morning of the last Challenge, and started the beanbrew early. She carried some to Teq, waking him with a hand on his brow, so that he hardly knew she was there until he smelled the brew. Then she woke Galt.

"It is time, my Lord Galt," she told him, smiling.

"So my lady has spoken my name at last. She honors me." He smiled back. "I slept," he added in some surprise. I may be readier than I expected."

But he knew in his heart that this day would end outside the Honor walls and he checked around his quarters for the last time. There was a sash of Tarabeth's tossed on to his pillow, and he took it up to wind around his waist. She saw him, and was pleased, then told him where she had hidden his cloak and journey food. "It is the last service I can perform for my lord," she said, her eyes full of tears. He kissed her then. "How I shall miss my Tarabeth," he told her. "But you will be with me this day, at least. Come. There are the drums. Be strong. Teq is ready?"

"He is ready," she assured him, letting him go.

Galt went to arm himself, and Tarabeth picked up her lute and her cloak. She arrived last among the women gathered behind Marisel and hurried to her place. She carried her lute on her shoulder, under her cloak, bulging her outline as if Teq might be with her. The gates swung wide immediately and the women processed out of the walls, forming their passage for the Sieur. Once again the Challenge was made, the response given by Marisel, and the Sieur marched to the drums down the aisle of his matrons and young women, to accept it. The arena was formed. The fight begun.

It was Chag, indeed, who was the challenger, though the fact that he was known to Belleth, Salsi and Hulia, and they to him, would never be known to anyone at Marisel's Honor on that day. He was a young man of great strength, powerfully endowed with a sense of his destiny, very sure that he was to be Sieur. But he had very little security in his dealings with people. Among the Wilders, only his prowess of strength and valor had any value. There was no need there, to charm. He had no knowledge of dealing with women, but was somehow sure that he would know when the time came. They were obviously weak creatures who could be dominated, of that, at least, he was certain. In all ways he seemed a proper Challenger for the role of Sieur, to those who saw him now.

Chag was of a height with Galt, though his reach was longer. He was shorter of leg and longer of body. His sturdy legs were short and muscled as rock. There was no moment when he did not command the battle with his strength, though Galt fought with a skill which gave Chag more trouble than he looked for. As the day grew towards noon, the heat took a toll on the fighters. Sweat poured into their eyes and over their bodies, so that even the battle staves became slick and hard to hold. Galt knew that if he was to survive this day, he must call up all his skill. He was not as strong as this ox of a man, that was obvious.

Galt fought slyly. He did not seek to disable his Challenger with mighty blows, but rather to wear away at him with tiny hurts. And to make him angry, so that he would cease to control his fight. The strategy began to work. Galt's blows hurt. He hit vulnerable places: the hand, the arm muscle, the ankle, the ear. The Wilder began to roar and to flail with his staff, so wildly that Galt could evade him easily. Though as the day progressed, that became harder. It grew hotter and hotter, with a damp heat which sapped both contestants of their strength. It was harder on Galt. He eased back, letting the staff work for him. Surrounding his opponent with whirling confusion. It was the most he could do. Galt knew that now, this very moment was the time. He must best this Challenger now. Or it would be never. He wanted him static. Unmoving. He knew exactly what he would do. He was astonished to realize that he was going to conquer this day, after all.

And then, Chag, who was standing block still just as Galt intended, whirled suddenly and hit Galt a blow on the side of the head. It felled him. At that same moment, Galt was thrusting forward and low with his staff. The momentum of his thrust carried forward, even when he was himself falling. It tripped Chag in his moment of triumph. He stayed on the ground, flat on his back, for a breathless moment, more from shock than hurt. He was furious. He felt that falling before these women spoiled his certain victory. His rage took him to his feet in a single leap, where he stood over Galt, daring him to waken and rise. But Galt, though coming muzzily back to his senses, lay where he was. This was a fight he must now acknowledge he was not going to win. He was near enough spent to be glad that it was over. It was already too close to noon. The fight had lasted far too long.

Triumphantly Chag waved his staff over his head, to an approving roar from the Wilders. It was enough to assuage his embarrassed fury. He was able to reassert his dignity. Without a backward glance he strode through the gates of the Honor, leading the women in.

Marisel led him to his quarters, making sure all signs of the previous occupant were gone. She ordered the eager young women in with fresh bedding and clothing and water for washing. Food was ordered to keep him attended and occupied while the evening meal was prepared. Chag found all the attention somewhat unnerving. He had no idea how to deal with servitude. He was gruff and ungracious with the women, and was sufficiently aware of how he sounded to be displeased with himself.

It was not until Marisel was at last at leisure, that she realized that Teq was not present. He would not have gone out with the herd so late in the day as noon. She sought out Tarabeth, mildly irritated.

"Where is your true son?" she demanded.

"I do not know," Tarabeth answered truthfully.

"Was he with you at the Challenge?" She was becoming suspicious now.

"He was not."

"He was warned. You warned him! Did you not?"

Tarabeth did not deny it. She said nothing.

"The Sieur will be told." Marisel was really angry. That Tarabeth, the first matron, should have so betrayed the laws of the Honor! She felt that she had been deeply betrayed by someone she had always trusted.

"Of course," Tarabeth murmured.

At the evening meal, only Marisel sat at the top table with the new Sieur. There was as yet no new first matron. The whole room waited in silence to hear Chag's voice for the first time, as he selected his portions of all the dishes. It was his right as Sieur to have first choice. He did not understand the silence. His chagrin at being reminded by Marisel of his right was annihilating. Worse, he had been the focus of all those eyes for several minutes. He cleared his throat, and the young women tittered nervously. He had fought for this. He kept telling himself that all these women were now his. He spoke gruffly and smiled not at all, doing his best to hide his embarrassment. He focused his anger on the table where the little boys sat. They were dying to ask each other where Teq had gone, and they were wriggling around, waiting for the chance to speak to one another. Chag roared them into stillness, venting his spleen and at last able to eat with some equanimity. It was a long time before normal conversation got started.

Quietly the matrons who were true mothers to the boys brought them the special trays with the heavily drugged food. If they were not to survive the night, they would at least feel neither fear nor pain.

Chag reached his quarters after the meal, nervous about the night to come, and restless because of his performance in the Honor so far. That the women expected a new Sieur to be strange to their customs did not occur to him. He felt that he was putting up a poor showing before them. He wanted action. He remembered a task that was still to be carried out.

"I will deal with the boy children now," he announced to Marisel. "They will by now all be gathered in one place, I assume."

"My lord, one is missing," Marisel told him, embarrassed in her turn that there was something amiss in the custom of her Honor. "I have instructed his true mother to await you in his place."

Chag did not quite understand what Marisel was telling him. "His true mother has killed him for me?" he asked, astonished.

"No, my lord. His true mother has warned him of his fate and has helped him to run away. She is to stand before you to tell you this herself. She is in the boys' room."

"Ah," said Chag, still slow to understand and disapproving now, "she had your permission."

"She had not. I am angered by her actions."

"Then I am angered too. Why did she do it? The boy will not survive alone in the wild. He will die anyway."

Marisel was too angry to explain that Teq was nearly of drumming age. That was not the point. The point was that she had been defied. And by the first matron, whom she had trusted. "There is no explanation for my lord," she answered.

Chag really was angry now. He had been embarrassed too often in front of this woman, so obviously more experienced than he in the matter of command. There had been his tripping right at the moment of his victory; there had been the matter of amusing the young women with his forgetting to choose his food; and now he had been defied by one of the matrons. He was thoroughly aroused. "Lead on," he said grimly.

Although the boys' room was brightly lit with burning torches, the deep breathing from their beds made it clear that each of them was heavily asleep. One woman stood by the empty bed. It seemed to add to his chagrin that she was so beautiful. More beautiful than any other woman he had seen in the Honor. She stood completely still, looking down, and yet she appeared graceful, even in her stillness. Chag wanted to make her beauty notice him, but she refused to raise her eyes, even when he stood beside her. Ignore him, would she?

"Speak to me, woman. Where is your true son?"

Tarabeth said nothing. Her eyes remained on the ground.

Chag reached out a hand and grabbed her hair, pulling back her head so that her face was raised to his. Still her eyes were cast down. "I asked you a question," he said.

Tarabeth said nothing.

"Her son has been searched for? You are sure he is gone from the Honor?" Chag asked, keeping hold of Tarabeth's hair.

"He has been searched for. He is gone," Marisel confirmed. "She warned him, my lord. It is against all custom and the laws of the Honor."

"Then she shall be punished," he said, pulling his knife from his belt. He placed it at her neck, where a tiny bead of blood formed and ran down in a thin trickle. "Will you speak now, woman?" he asked.

For the first time Tarabeth raised her eyes. She looked into his, and he saw in hers a look of utter contempt. That a Sieur would treat one of the women of the Honor like this was an indictment of his fitness that was unacceptable. That Marisel was condoning it, was partly due to her anger at Tarabeth, and partly due to her not knowing this Sieur. Tarabeth spat. The spittle landed accurately in Chag's right eye.

There was no time for thought, just for reaction. At almost the same second, it seemed, he moved so quickly, he drew his knife across her throat. She made no sound. The gasp was Marisel's.

As soon as he released Tarabeth's hair she fell dead at his feet. In a frenzy of rage, with no pause, still blind in his right eye from the spittle, Chag killed the little boys.

As she had known she would, Tarabeth lay dead in her true son's place.

Chag was breathing heavily. His rage was unabated. The sight of the carnage all around him served only to make him angrier. He felt especially infuriated that he had been somehow manipulated by Tarabeth. He should have possessed her. Made her one of the matrons of this place. She had diminished his victory. No, not her! The missing boy. He was the real culprit. Chag turned to Marisel.

"What is the name of this boy who has run off, and where will he have gone?" he asked.

"His name is Teq, Lord," Marisel answered grimly, appalled at the sight of Tarabeth lying dead. Such a killing was unprecedented. She had the feeling that Tarabeth had been deliberately provoking. Courting her own death.

"Tomorrow I will hunt him and bring him back," Chag snarled.

"Tomorrow, I will send hunters to discover if he is still on Honor lands. If he is, then they will return him to you, Lord. My Lord will not be leaving the Honor himself, of course." Marisel spoke steadily. Her voice was charged with years of authority. It was clear to her that this one needed controlling. There would be no point in permitting the one day to roam the Honor lands, before he settled within the walls. It was tradition to permit it, but in this case...

Suddenly Chag understood. He would never step outside the walls until the day he lost at Challenge. It would be years and years before he would again have converse with men, and only then if his Challenger did not kill him.

He turned to Marisel and roared, "send girls to me. Not matrons. I want unused girls. Send them at once. And clean up this mess."

"It shall be done, Lord. Does my Lord wish an escort to find his rooms?"

"Girls!" he shouted, not listening. "Not just one."

Marisel escorted him out of the boys' room and beckoned to two of the matrons. "Escort my lord to his room, and bring him drinks that he may rest. Later he will begin his duties to my Honor."

They understood her. He needed to be drugged to sleep until he calmed down. Otherwise he might harm her youngs.

She watched him go and sighed. He would serve. Some Sieurs were more tolerable than others, but he would serve. She didn't like his small eyes. She found his body odor offensive. He was not used to bathing. Were they ever? She went to find people to clean up the boys' room. A waste, but a necessity, she supposed. It was custom, and that was what counted. Still, it always took the true mothers of the boy children time, before they were ready to serve a new Sieur.

Marisel sighed again. Was she getting too old? There was something about this change which sickened her. Was it the loss of Tarabeth? How could she have betrayed them by warning that boy? She deserved to die. No, she didn't. But traditions could not be flouted. The matter could not go unpunished. Who knew which other matron might not follow her lead next time? And the boys. Tarabeth's true son was nearly at his Drumming. He should survive. But what if little ones were loosed? No. It was the right way. It was the proper way. There was always a good reason behind tradition. It was merely fatigue which was troubling her. She was not too old. True, to run the Honor was a never-ending burden, but so long as it was her Honor, it would be done well.

Part 2
The Journey

Chapter 7

While everybody was responding to the Challenge horn by milling about getting ready to march serenely out of the Honor, Teq got himself to the kitchen. He scooped out a mug of beanbrew, and while it was cooling, busied himself emptying pots and rinsing mugs. When the last of the matrons noticed he was still there, he splashed some beanbrew on to his best tunic.

"Hurry up, boy," she grumbled at him.

"I must wash this out, Lady, or my true mother will be furious." He tried to sound contrite and not nervous.

"The tunic is too small for you, anyway. Your workaday one will have to do. Run along and change."

"Yes, Lady, but I think I can wash this stain out."

"Well whatever you do, hurry up. I have to get myself ready and in place. Make sure you are not late," she threw at him as she hurried off.

Whew! He had wrapped his working tunic round him under the already straining best tunic. The best one was much too brightly colored - not to mention too small - to wear on the open fields. He would stand out like a banner.

As soon as the matron was out of earshot, he slipped his fingers into the slit and opened the chimney. He was inside with the door shut before the matron could change her mind. It was cramped inside the chimney for changing his clothes and tying on his pack, besides which he was trembling with excitement. At least he had practiced tying on the pack, so with that part he was reasonably swift. Just as he slid into the open air, he heard the drums beginning. Once outside, he had room to push his staff and bow between the pack and his back. He took care to hang his new water bag with a double binding. Now it sat across his stomach, instead of bobbing about against his leg. Ready or not, it was time to go.

He pulled out his knife and cut the goats' hobbles. The whole herd crowded round, glad to see him. As soon as he heard the new drumbeat announcing the arrival of the Sieur, he set off towards the western boundary of the Honor. He had considered whether just being outside the boundaries would mean the pursuit was over, and decided he could not risk it. He would assume there was pursuit until he was far enough away to make it implausible. During this first, most dangerous, part, he would be at most risk of being sighted when the Honor and the Wilder pack were forming their circle. Eyes wandered then. After that they would all be too concentrated on the battle to be aware of his progress.

At the first clash of battle staves he was off. He angled a little south to keep the high walls between him and the fight scene for as long as possible. Running was awkward with all that equipment, but he found a jogging rhythm which seemed to cover the ground and not throw things out of balance. In the middle of the summer, the ground never really cooled off, but there were no rain clouds about. As yet the air was dry and merely warm. Teq began to enjoy himself. He was free at last. The herd was certainly enjoying itself, used to his more sober walks in the past. They followed Teq as faithfully as ever, obscuring every mark of his footprints. When they showed signs of flagging, Teq grabbed the horn of the leader and dragged him along. They could all rest for a bit when they reached the rift.

The sun was well up when they got there and the heat increasing. Teq allowed himself a sip of water. The goats knew where to find their own. He cast up and down the edge of the rift until he found the chimney he had noted yesterday; then he untied his pack, cloak, bow, and staff, and put them on long binders, so that he could carry out his plan. It was only by using his staff as the holding end that the line was long enough to reach the ledge, but he got everything down there. So far the plan was working. As soon as he had wedged himself into the chimney, he threw a sod at the lead goat. It shied away, offended, and set off without a backward glance toward the rivulet which trickled over the edge further south. The herd scampered after. Teq hoped that it would appear that he had gone over the edge there himself. The path down was much easier, but a long way south. The new Sieur should be well behind him, then. That is, if there was a new Sieur, he amended. Maybe his own Sieur would win the Challenge. He hovered for a minute, half in and half out of the chimney. Too late for doubts. He was committed now. Perhaps the new Sieur would not learn about him... Or bother to pursue him... Assume the worst, hope for the best, he told himself, and get going.

The wedge part, down the chimney, was pretty simple. He got as far as the ledge without even scraping his hands. He gathered up and strapped on his belongings, full of new confidence, and then examined the defile. Suddenly it didn't seem so easy. Teq lowered himself gingerly over the edge, and immediately the weight of his pack threatened to pull him off the cliff face, backwards. This was serious. He considered climbing back up and knew he could not get back up on the ledge. Not being pulled outwards as he was. He jammed his fingers into the cracks he found, carrying his weight on their tips, as he groped for footholds. All the way down. He banged his feet into the stone so hard that he bruised his knees; leaned into the cliff so far that he scraped his face; breathed stone dust from the flaking surface so far down into his lungs, that he threatened to choke on it and throw himself into the valley with a cough. But make it he did, as far as the next ledge: half as wide as the upper one, but enough.

Teq lay there on his face, catching his breath and looking all the way to the bottom for the first time. He could see absolutely no way to get there from here. It was not so far now - no more than twice his own height - but the bottom surface was a jumble of rocks. If he jumped and fell awkwardly, he could break his leg, which would probably be the end of his life right here. If the new Sieur didn't get him he would starve to death, at least. Even the tiny stream would be out of reach. He could die of thirst...

Well, he couldn't go back up, so he had better work out a plan! He could lower his pack again. Without it on his back, he would have a chance if he jumped. Untying it, lying on his stomach, and with bloody fingers was almost too hard. Besides that, he was afraid that if he wriggled about too much, he would burst his water bag. It was already driving him to despair that he couldn't reach it. As soon as he had thought of dying of thirst, his thirst had become intolerable. Once he nearly went over with the pack, but in the end it was down. The bow landed well, following the pack down, but his staff bounced off one rock, then over to another, and cracked. Teq was ready to cry at this point. No battle staff! No way to defend himself... He gritted his teeth. Nothing to be gained by worrying over what was already done. He had to get himself down there. He could either hang from his bloody fingers and drop, or launch himself from a sitting position, which the ledge would allow now that the pack was off his back. He decided on the latter. There was one level place he should be able to reach if he could look at it. He reached it, but only just. One leg buckled under him as he landed with one foot half on a boulder. He cracked his shin, and cried out. There was an echo. He could not allow himself to do that again. Well, he was down! The worst was surely over.

Noon in the bottom of the gorge was as hot as the kitchen on a feast day with all three fires blasting heat. There was still a little water in the stream, edging its way down the center, appearing to bear no relationship to the springtime spate which had washed the cliff walls. Teq didn't even bother to stand up. He slid down to it and splashed water on to every exposed bit of his body: all of which appeared to be stinging. The water stung worse but felt better. It was clear enough, so he slaked his thirst at last with sips from his cupped hand. It was a while before he felt ready to stand up and gather his belongings. He looked around.

His sense of urgency returned, lost in the perils of descending the cliff. He scanned the cliff face anxiously, but it betrayed no sign of where he had come down. The dust at the bottom marked the place, though. He used his new cloak to scatter the dust, while he stood on a rock like some goat shaking its beard. Stronger now, he hefted his pack in his arms, and jumped from rock to rock, leaving no trace. He carried his bow in one hand. The battle staff was a complete loss. He left it where it lay.

The gorge was so deep that no sound penetrated. Teq looked straight up. The sun was staring straight back at him out of a searing sky. His eyes began to tear, but before he closed them, he caught sight of some kind of hawk riding the thermals. Nothing else stirred. It seemed there was nobody looking for him yet. There was no way to determine the course of the battle. Come to that, he had no idea how long it took a new Sieur to set about his bloody business of hunting the male children. For the first time it occurred to Teq that his own Sieur had probably killed boy children when he first came to Marisel's Honor. The thought revolted him. You hunt animals - for food - not people! The battle staff was not a killing tool, merely a disabler. His whole training emphasized that. He felt a mixture of loyalty and disgust when he thought of the Sieur.

The Sieur must still be battling for his place. Then what? Still, perhaps not. Perhaps he was already felled and a new Sieur in search of Teq. Maybe the new Sieur would make use of his whole pack of Wilders to help in the hunt before they left him to his triumph. Teq began seriously to plan his next step. Here, he was far too visible to pursuers. He could hide temporarily behind a boulder, but not for long. He decided he had better walk along the stream bed, since leaping rocks was slow and precarious. He would get as far north as possible so long as there was no cause to believe he had been seen. He would have to find a place to climb out before he got to the forest. He knew that the gorge became narrower at the forest's edge, and the cliff much steeper. An impossible climb. Just ahead he could see a place where the western cliff jutted forward. If he could find a climbable route behind that, he might be fairly well hidden from the eastern edge. He put his head down and trudged resolutely forward up the stream.

Once round the corner, which took far longer to traverse than he had supposed, he stopped and strapped all his belongings back on. The sun was past the visible part of the sky now, so that he could better scan for movement. Just as he found a place he thought he could climb, there was a clatter of birds rising on the far side of the gorge, but he heard nothing more. They wheeled a while in apparent agitation, then settled again. It was sign enough. There was someone up there.

What Teq had found was a traversing crack which went about half way up the cliff. There, at that point, there seemed to be a vine growing into or rooting out of the crack which went all the way to the top. With enough footholds he should be able to make it. It was a bit of a scramble - how he wished he were full grown! - to reach the first handhold, but from there, easing up the traverse was fairly easy. His feet fitted well into it, and his hands found places to cling.

When he got to the place where the traverse stopped, he had to reach out at full stretch to catch the vine in a place where it was not attached to the cliff. He then had to kick his legs free so that he could grab at the vine with the other hand. For a second he was swinging free from one hand. With the weight of the pack adding to his own , it needed three tries to make the catch, and then he was still swinging, albeit from two hands now. It was at this precarious moment that he heard the threatening rattle of a gourd snake. One foot found purchase. The other still swung. Teq peered down between his legs, paralyzed in terror. The venom of the gourd snake was without a cure. Instant death. But there was absolutely nothing he could do to avoid it. The snake swayed out of its coils, just at the spot the free leg had stepped from the instant before. Sweat poured out from all over his body. His fingers began to slip on the vine. He did not dare to seek out a foothold with his hanging leg to ease the strain on his arms, lest it attract the snake's attack. He had never felt so helpless. It felt like a full day while the snake eyed Teq and he eyed the snake. Whether he hung too far for its reach, or whether it decided he was no threat, it was the snake who backed down. Teq could not have done so, willing as he was. There was nowhere for him to go.

By the time he dared to move his leg, his arms felt as though they were dislodged from their sockets. It took all his resolution to pull himself grimly upward. There was no way to determine if more snakes had chosen this cliff for a home, but common sense told him he had probably been more at risk in the traverse, which went deep, than here on the cliff face.

He began to tire long before he reached the top. He had supposed that climbing up would be easier than climbing down. So much for that! The heat of the afternoon was as brutal as pain on his exposed head and neck. Teq could run for days with the goats or a hunting party. He could stay awake all night if there was something he wanted to think about. He could outlast anyone in the Honor except the Sieur, in training battles. But he had never before tried to spend a whole day climbing. It used muscles he didn't know were there. The pack became such a burden to him that he would have cut it loose, if he could have spared a hand to do so. Shins, calves, shoulders, fingers shouted individual agonies into the furnace of the rock face. Had it not been for the vine, always there, he would not have made it.

The sun was reddening in pleasure as it lowered itself into the pool of night when Teq finally hauled his trembling legs over the rim. He lay gasping, his limbs convulsing in exhaustion. He was ready to lay there forever, so long as it was level. But gradually, the nerves of the hunted clanged in his brain. Surely the new Sieur would not climb at night. He might... Teq pulled the knife from his boot and wearily sawed through the vine. There. It would not help the hunter. There might be an easier way up, though, that the new Sieur would know. He had been a Wilder. Perhaps around here, and he might know the cliff like Teq knew the lands of the Honor. The moon was on the wane, but there would be some moonlight. He could not stay here. Forcing himself into motion at last, he limped away from the rim at a tottering trot, to a place where some rocks hung together in an odd formation. A scrubby bush grew to one side. He reached the place in the last of the light and became one of the shadows.

He had no staff to thrust among the rocks to explore for snakes. He chose the bush as the safer shelter. At last the pack could be loosed. At once he knew how hungry he was. And how thirsty. He had not eaten all day, and not drunk since he started the climb. He ate a little, drank a little, wrapped himself in his cloak, and fell totally asleep.

And just at the point when his body was fast asleep and his mind ready to follow, he heard from far, far away, a voice calling his name.

Chapter 8

As soon as the world fell silent, Galt rolled over and flopped on to his back. He wanted his mind to start working before he made any further moves at all. First, he mentally checked all his body parts. Bruises certainly, but nothing worse. The Challenger had not been such a good fighter. Merely strong. There was no doubt about his strength. He could have outlasted Galt's stamina three times over. The only place which hurt really badly was his head, and that made up for all the rest. Very cautiously he opened his eyes. The midday sun was almost directly overhead. He scrunched them quickly shut. And then a shadow fell across his face. With caution he reopened his eyes. A Wilder stood there.

"You fought well," said the Wilder. "Better than Chag."

"Thank you," Galt answered. "Didn't do me much good, though, did it?" He smiled a little. "Chag's his name, eh? Who are you?"

"I'm a healer. Are you badly hurt anywhere?"

"Not really. My head and my dignity suffered the most. I am thirsty, though."

"I thought you would be. Here's some water." The Wilder proffered his water bag. "Can you sit up? I don't want to choke you."

Gingerly Galt sat up. He glanced towards the Honor. The gates were shut. It was a sight he had last seen when he came here as a Challenger. He breathed deeply, then smiled up at the young man, and reached for the water bag. "This is good of you. If you can spare the water, I would like to pour some over my head too."

"Do that," said the healer. "Colder water would do you more good. If you're coming with us, the water in the river is cold."

Galt looked around, more easily turning his head now. The Wilders were drifting off in small groups, northward towards the forest. "How far away is your camp?" he asked.

"Near enough a full day. We won't reach it tonight. No real hurry at this time of year, is there?"

"In the high hills, then. North?"

"Northeast."

"No," Galt said thoughtfully, handing back the water bag, "I don't think so. I may come later, on my own, if that's what I decide to do. It's good to know where to find a pack if I need a place. It's as you say: no hurry at this time of year."

"Well, I'll be on my way, then. It takes me a while to catch up, and I prefer to travel in company. You'll be welcome if you come. A good fighter is always welcome. We have another once-Sieur with us."

"Thank you for the water, and the invitation." Galt struggled to his feet. The young healer handed him his battle staff, and he leaned on it, as he raised his other hand in thanks and farewell. He watched as the young Wilder limped away, one of his feet badly twisted. A surprise that! Not all Wilder packs would tolerate a cripple. Still, healers were valued. He must be good at the work.

Apart from the ache in his head, Galt began to feel recovered enough to move on. The last of the Wilders was already out of sight. Nothing was moving on the plain in the full heat of the day. It would be wise to take his own aching head into the shade. There was an odd insecurity about being alone in this emptiness. It had been years and years since he had been on his own. He knew he must be watched by the wall guards, but he could not see them, and certainly he could expect no hail from them. As soon as the battle ended he had ceased to exist for all the women of the Honor. Probably the guards' eyes were more turned inward today, hardly watching the surrounding plain. What would be out there with a large pack of Wilders wandering all over it? Galt shouldered his staff and set out to walk the circumference of the wall.

Smoke was rising from the chimney when he got to that side. He headed to the bush where Tarabeth had said she had hidden his possessions, grateful for her thoughtfulness. He was doubly grateful when he found a full waterbag and a sack full of journey food. He had not realized how hungry he was. The day had begun with nothing more than a mug of beanbrew. Propped against the wall under the bush, he would not be visible from above, even if anyone cared to look. He sat there and ate comfortably while he considered his next move.

He could see the goat herd fairly far south on the rim of the rift. From the droppings around him, it was obvious that they had spent the night right here. Idly he examined the ground. There was a footprint - just one - near his hand. He brushed it away. Teq's? It must be Teq's. So the boy had the sense to use the herd to cover his tracks, had he? Galt felt a sense of pride. This was his son, and Tarabeth's. There was cleverness there. Galt thought about him. The boy was alone. Perhaps he ought to follow and see that he was all right. After all it was his idea that he had escaped. He had the responsibility. No point in leading straight to him, though. This Chag person might be a vindictive type. If someone told him about Teq he might be angry at the escape and follow him. Galt decided he would just go and see if the boy got away all right.

Knowing now that there was a Wilder pack to the northeast, it might have been the best way to go. But Teq didn't know that, any more than he had himself until this morning. The most sensible thing to have done was to get out of the Honor quickly by crossing the rift. The boy would have been in a hurry. He would have gone directly west. Indeed that's where the goat tracks led. Better, then, if Galt were to go south, where crossing the rift was easier, then follow Teq up the rift from the other side. If Teq had crossed safely, and he could discover it, and that would be enough.

It was time he was on his way. The afternoon was already well advanced. He hefted his belongings and set out, walking. It had been a long time since he had done even that. His head throbbed, but nothing could be done about it other than simply endure. Time would take care of it. He really wanted to be out of the Honor before nightfall, and that meant descending the rift wall while it was light. He had time enough if he found an easy route down, by a stream for instance.

And that's exactly where the goats were, munching placidly at the rich grass near a stream. It was not much more than a tiny trickle of a stream, coming from a spring which welled up near the rim. It poured cheerfully over the side, as it had done for long enough to carve out a near staircase, through the alternating hard and soft stone of the wall. Galt was delighted with it. He began to glory in his freedom.

The glory was well over by the time he reached the rift bottom. The morning's bruises were stiffening. The ache in his head had become a fiery throb, and he was tired. All those years in the Honor had turned him soft! He was hungry again and nobody was going to cook a meal and then offer him first choice of everything. Nobody was ever going to do that again. Nor was anybody going to ask him how he felt. With each step downward he force out a grunt against the exertion. He began to feel a little sorry for himself. Only the thought that the Chag person might be following Teq and find him in this state, drove him on. His pride would not allow him to give up - and anyway he was halfway down a cliff!

When he did reach level ground, the shadows of evening were purpling the bottom of the rift. Galt was much too weary to do more than choose the boulder he would sleep beside. He found a soft place in the dust to the lee of a giant, which looked as if it had stood there as long as the rift walls. He ate a bit more of Tarabeth's journey food. Old habits made him scrape out a soft place for his hip, before he rolled into his massive Sieur's cloak and settled himself to sleep. Ha! The Chag person would have to wait until somebody made him a cloak like this. He grinned to himself and drifted towards sleep, thinking of Tarabeth. And just as he slipped into slumber, he thought he heard her voice calling, though he couldn't make out the single word on the wind. He smiled again and slept.

Galt wakened stiff and groaning. He had lost the art of sleeping quietly and had long ago rolled out of his prepared place. Each bruise made a separate protest as he sat up. A crow perched on the boulder made a derisive caw at his awkward movements, as it rose easily to join its circling fellows in their hunt for breakfast. At that moment, Galt would have given all the freedom in the world for a mug of really fresh beanbrew, hot from the fire, to start the day. He wondered if Tarabeth had packed some of the dried beans, but then he really didn't want to stay here long enough to start a fire. And anyway, he had nothing to boil water in. He settled for more journey food and a sip of water before he got himself down to the stream to splash water on his face and the worst of his bruises. There! He would do for now. What next?

He stood at the point where the rift began its long, slow curve from north/south to west/east. In anticipation of the curve, the walls had widened, and the farther slope leaned back. He decided he might as well climb out here where the climb itself would be comparatively easy. It was obvious to the eye that the walls of the rift got steeper and steeper to the north. His guess was that Teq would head north once he was across the rift. The edge of the forest and the hills, if his memory served, would provide better game than the plains. He was interested in that himself. His supply of journey food would not last forever.

Far away on the wind, he heard the morning drum as the gates of the Honor were opened. He guessed that someone would soon be out after the goats, if nothing else. Best to get moving. Settling his goods on his back, Galt chose a route and started to clamber up the rift wall. It was not an easy climb. Before he was half way, he was forced to use hands as well as feet. Even tacking back and forth, he had to cling hard to the miserable bits of shrub which grew bitterly from the pitted surface of the rock. It took all morning to reach the top, and he was winded when he got there, much to his chagrin. But his bruises were giving him less trouble, even though the throb in his head was back, and the old wounds in knee and shoulder were protesting. He reflected that he might have shown more stamina in the battle, if he could have made a climb like this every day. Life in the Honor did not offer that kind of flexibility. The confinement came with the position of Sieur. No point in regretting it now. He flung himself down on to the grass, after a sip from his water bag, and slept again.

When he woke he felt much better. He looked out across the rift and saw some of the little girls among the goat herd. They would not be looking this way. Neither girls nor women looked beyond the Honor. It was their world. He scanned the plain for signs of Chag. There seemed to be no other movement. But then Chag could be anywhere, on this one day. After this, he would not be leaving the Honor, so the danger to Teq would not be long lived.

Galt started north, munching on some journey food as he went. He followed the edge of the rift, looking into it for signs that Teq might have been there. About mid-afternoon he saw the broken staff. He let his eye travel up the cliff from that point. A difficult place to come down! He was pleased to see no sign of trampling at the bottom. The boy must have erased his footprints. A bit pointless with the staff lying there, but it showed he was stopping to think, at least. Now how had the boy gone on from there? Perhaps his progress would have been easy to track at the bottom of the rift, but from up here there was no way to tell. Galt was impressed. This Teq of his was showing a lot of sense. He was obviously not just running in panic. He was putting thought into what he did. A grown man might not have done as well, given the sureness of pursuit that must have been in his mind.

Galt looked across the rift. The walls of the Honor loomed large from here. Teq must have moved on north. He was altogether too visible. Galt did the same, looking all the time for signs of the boy's movements. The ground sloped gently downward towards the west, giving some invisibility from the walls of the Honor to a traveler, if he was far enough from the rim. Galt stuck to the edge, however as he pressed on to the north. By late afternoon he found the severed vine. The thing was well rooted in every crack and crevice to half way down the cliff face. Severing the top made no difference to its stability, but he followed Teq's reasoning, and he was pleased again. Where the vine ended, he saw the defile to the bottom. A perfect place for a den of gourd snakes. Hm! Would Teq have known that? In any case, he had apparently made it to the top as the severed vine witnessed.

Face down on the grass, Galt stayed still, looking down and following the progress of his son, for a very long time. When he did roll over, he nearly fell on top of a nosy ground dog, which froze in panic. One quick blow of his battle staff and he had his supper. Now he really felt better. He got up and looked around him. The pile of leaning boulders seemed like a good place to spend the night. He carried his kill over there.

It was clear from the beaten down grasses, that this was where Teq had spent the night before. It must have provided him with small comfort, but he was sure now that the boy was doing fine on his own. He had planned his escape well, and executed it with care. He would be safe enough now. The Chag person would not follow him this far outside the confines of the Honor. If he should be vindictive enough to try, Galt would be perfectly happy to fight him again. He chuckled to himself, as he rooted round in the sack Tarabeth had provided, to find his fire makers. Moss from the rocks and dead branches from the bush would give him enough kindling to cook his ground dog. A cooked supper, another long sleep, and the morning would be time enough to decide what he would do next.

Galt began to feel good again.

Chapter 9

The chill of the morning was enough to waken Teq. He clutched his cloak around him and groaned his way to his feet. The rift was outlined in the gradually increasing light of morning by a dappled mist rising from its depths. The sunlight dazzled from beyond the Honor walls and seeped on to his side through the mist. He walked round the pile of boulders to snatch some warmth from the early rays. He had fire makers in his kit, but didn't want to stay here long enough to build one. He would be warm enough when he moved. Too warm before long, no doubt.

He tried roping on his pack, but his shoulders were so chafed from yesterday that he couldn't stand it. He devised a way of hanging it from his forehead and strapped around his waist. It would do. He had taken out some journey food to munch on while he ran. His main need was to put himself beyond the sightline of the Honor wall guards. If he could see the Honor walls - and he could, clearly - they could see him. Since the ground sloped down from the rift edge, he moved off west, angling gradually more and more to the north. He felt fairly secure that he would not be pursued beyond the territory of the Honor itself until he remembered the voice calling his name. In the light of morning, he wasn't sure he had not just dreamed that. He decided to act as if it were real: assume that he was still hunted.

On the open plain, there was very little Teq could do to render himself less visible. Movement itself could be seen for miles. Far to the west he could tell that a very large herd of something or other was moving at much the same speed as himself, and in much the same direction.

The pace of his jogging was comfortable, easily eating up the miles. He would have liked to do something to vary his diet of journey food, but reasoned that it was better to outdistance his hunter than take time to become a hunter himself. There was no doubt in Teq's mind that he could find enough food to sustain him, with or without finding a Wilder pack to join. He had been out with the Honor hunters since he was old enough to keep up - though not recently, it was true. If he reached a forest, he could find enough nuts and berries to keep himself alive, even if he didn't manage to kill some prey.

What did bother him was where he was going. He was heading north to the hills, of course, which were forested, and where he should be able to live hidden until he identified a Wilder pack to join - and until one would accept him. No, it was not only the place, but the rest of his life towards which he was jogging, and he was very disturbed by what he had always taken for granted. Like his older Honor brothers, he had always known he would have a drumming to mark his reaching manhood, and then go out and join a Wilder pack. Then what? The idea, he had always supposed, was to gain strength and battle cunning as a Wilder. As Belleth and he had discussed, life as a Wilder was one long battle: for food, with other Wilder packs, with parties of Honor hunters to steal women. When you reached your prime, having done all that for years, you sought out an Honor and made Challenge to the Sieur. Then you were Lord of the Honor. Granted the women ruled in everything that mattered, but you were still the revered Lord. And the first thing you did was to kill all the boy children!

Teq snorted in disgust. What kind of a goal was that? He had never questioned it before, never really thought about it. It was simply what was. He didn't really know about the killing part of it until a month ago, it was true, but still... Was it really a goal worth fighting to achieve? Did he, Teq, really want to do that? No, he didn't. Honestly, he didn't. But what else was there?

Teq's mind was so far from where he was going, that a lamewing ran, tottering, right out from under his feet, squawking most pitifully. His sling should have been in his hand, instead of wrapped inaccessibly around his waist under his pack. What sort of a lone hunter was he turning out to be? The lamewing had run far enough away to launch herself into the sky. The chance of making her into dinner was lost. Well there was still the nest. That's what her whole broken-wing charade had been about: leading his eye away from the nest. He searched about and found it. Three fine eggs. He sat heavily down and eased off his pack so that he could swallow the eggs down. As the first one slipped into his throat he had a sudden picture of himself acting the part of a new Sieur. He was killing the children! He gagged on the egg he had just swallowed and left the other two.

A person had to hunt to live. But babies? Shuddering, he tried his pack on his sore shoulders and decided he could now tolerate it. His forehead was just as sore as his shoulders now anyway, and rubbed raw where he had sweated under the binder. Let that egg count as his nooning and keep going.

As he jogged, Teq thought about the Honor he had left for ever in such a hurry, only yesterday. He had been able to say goodbye to Tarabeth, which was more than had been possible for his brothers and sisters. Or Belleth. Especially Belleth. He wondered if she thought about him, wherever she was. She had made no goodbyes either. The thought made him feel better. It was as if they had both turned their backs on the Honor and gone adventuring into new lives. The thing they had always talked about. He had not known how heavy the misery was which he carried with him. He felt lighter now, the running easier. He was on his way to the freedom he had been longing for. His jogging steps ate up the afternoon.

Looking away to the east he could no longer see the walls of the Honor. He had come fairly far. He was close to where the forest began on the other side of the rift, far north of its closest point to the Honor. On this side there was no forest, but just before the ground began to rise into the hills where the Wilders roamed, there was a copse of trees. Quite a substantial one. There must be water in there, to sustain the trees. With luck, animals would come there at evening to drink. With even more luck, he could get there in time to bag something for his supper. At worst, he should be able to fashion a trap or two to catch something when they came again at dawn. He increased his pace. It was already past mid-afternoon.

His pack had become unbearable by the time he reached the trees. Dusk had fallen, but Teq reckoned it would still be worth trying to get something to eat. His mouth was already watering in anticipation. He dropped the pack thankfully, and unwound his sling from around his waist. He thought he could try for something small tonight. There was no time to get all set up with his bow. In any case his arms were too sore. He wasn't sure he could control a bow properly.

Step by step he moved quietly but quickly through the trees. His arrival at the copse had already caused all the birds to rise and circle. The animals, if there were any, would all be wary. He made sure there was no sound to advertise his exact position. He tested the wind and moved around so that he could approach the center of the copse facing into it. He wanted to make sure even his scent didn't alert his dinner. There was very little undergrowth and he could walk softly on the detritus which lay quietly underneath the trees. It was getting very dark now, under their shade. He could see a lightness ahead, which must denote the water. Two trees stood very close together on the edge of the clearing. They would provide a place where he could stand still and blend into the copse. He would be almost invisible to any creature within the clearing, however wary. He eased up to the trees, his eyes on the light ahead. Whomp! With a yell and a whoosh he was carried aloft, upside down. He had placed his foot as neatly into a snare as if he had been planning for it. A vine had him gripped around one ankle. He swung violently to and fro, bumping his head once against one of the trees, before he steadied. Now, neither tree was within reach of his hands unless he started himself swinging again, and already his leg felt as if it had been jerked out of his hip.

Rage brought tears to his eyes. He had been through enough these last two days. He did not need this. Just when he thought he was clear of pursuit, he was neatly caught. Not that he was analyzing, but he could not have told whether his tears were in anger at his pursuer for setting a man-snare, or at himself for his carelessness. What kind of a world had people setting snares for other people?

Regardless of the moral of the situation, he was in immense discomfort. The blood had rushed from all over his body into his head. He had a quick thought that he was grateful not to be wearing his pack. It would have throttled him by now. Even upside down, his hands were free. He should be able to do something.

If he could reach his knife, if he could somehow climb up his own body, he should be able to cut himself free. This was ridiculous! He would have cursed, or even laughed, if he wasn't choking on his own spit. He tried to jackknife his body to reach the weapon at his waist. The knot around his ankle tightened painfully. He cried out. The pull on his leg was much worse.

"Be still," said a deep, male voice.

Teq was still swinging back and forth as a result of his effort. He was now in danger of blacking out. He could just dimly see a figure, apparently holding a bow with an arrow nocked and ready to fly at him. He gurgled. He was trying to say, "get me down."

"Wait," the voice said. "I am going to tie you, then I'll cut you down"

Wait!

Teq felt a vine being tied to one hand and the hand yanked up along his side. He smelled sweat, but the other was taking care to stay out of his line of vision. "Hurry," he forced through his teeth. It was hard to see anything at all now in the fading light. He felt himself being lowered at last. His head touched the ground, none too gently, and the rest of his body followed. Quickly the vine was wrapped around his free foot. He was trussed like a bird ready for cooking.

"Now," said the other, from behind him, "what are you doing here, so far from your Honor?"

Chapter 10

"Who are you?" Teq tried.

"That's my question."

Considering that Teq was the one tied up, there was no advantage in antagonizing the other, though he would have been happier to be able to yell and scream. He wished he could see him better. "My name is Teq", he responded.

"Was this trap set to catch man or animal?"

"Man?" said the voice incredulously. "Why ask a question like that? I could tell I had caught something big, but not a man. Are you from a Wilder pack?"

"No. Not me. I just left my Honor yesterday. Are you?"

"No. What do you want here?"

"I wanted dinner. I thought there must be water in these trees, and I'd get something which came here for the evening watering. I saw no smoke or sign of a camp"

"Where is your Honor?"

"Well, it's not my Honor any more. I told you. I left. It's across the rift."

"Nobody could cross that!"

"Not here. Farther south. I really didn't come here to attack you. Do you think you could untie me?"

"You don't sound as if you reached your drumming. Is there a hunting party with you?"

"No. Truly. I told you. I left. I ran off." Teq was finding it hard to keep talking, trussed as he was, but he didn't dare stop. He gulped hard, trying to clear his mouth.

"Ran off? That's stupid. I never heard of anyone running off before their drumming."

"Well, I did. I really am alone. Are you alone, or is there a Wilder pack near here? Perhaps they would let me join?"

"I'm here alone. No Wilders. Look, I'll untie you, but I'll keep any weapons. I'll undo your hands and you can untie the other binders. Be careful. I can't afford to cut up good binders."

"Fine, " Teq choked out. He had decided by this time that this was not a man in his prime. He sounded young, even though his voice was deep. He sounded nervous too. It might be that here was someone to join up with. It would be a good thing to be friendly. "What is your name?" he asked, as the other unbound his hands.

"My name is Vork."

Vork was close enough now for Teq to see that he had guessed right. In the last glimmer of the daylight, he could make out that Vork was a youth, not much older than himself.

Vork took the knife from Teq's belt, then backed out of reach. Silly, thought Teq, I could throw the binder and trip you, and I have another knife in my boot. But he went on carefully unwinding the binders and making no sudden moves. His night vision was fairly good by now, so Vork's must be also.

"I find only a sling and a knife. Is that how you were armed in leaving your Honor?" Vork questioned him.

"No, no. I left my pack and bow at the outer edge of the trees, so that I could move more quickly and quietly. It was so close to dark, and my only thought was to catch something to eat. I have eaten nothing but journey food for two days."

"Why?"

"I was in a hurry to get away. I told you I ran off. There." The last of the binders was freed. Teq wound them carefully.

"Stand up."

Teq found the leg which had been caught in the trap was unwilling to bear his weight. He limped about in a circle, stamping to bring the foot back to life. "It's not broken," he said.

Vork was silent. He seemed to be considering. "I will go with you to collect your pack," he said at last. "Then I will bring you to my fire. I have food cooking."

"Food? Really? But I saw no smoke."

"You will see. Which way is the pack?"

"South. I came from the south." Teq looked up at the stars. "This way, I think."

Their progress was slow because Teq was limping. Vork insisted on staying behind him. Worse, it was hard to find the pack in the dark. In the end, Teq fell over it. No complaints. He was so glad to find it. He groped about until he found his bow, and then handed it to Vork.

"Where is your battle staff?" Vork wanted to know.

"Broken."

"Broken? Were you fighting?" Vork sounded shocked.

"No. I dropped it down the rift and it fell the wrong way."

"Hm!"

"Look, if I had one, I would be glad enough to lean on it. My foot hurts and I'm tired. I've been running all day. I really don't want to attack you, and I'm starving."

For the first time Vork seemed to relax. "Come on, then," he said. "My fire is not far from here. I'll lead the way."

Teq concentrated on walking. His foot was swollen and suddenly he was more weary than he could bear. Vork didn't set a very fast pace. Frankly, if he had, Teq would have had to let him go. He was trying to work out why Vork was on his own. His guess was that he had been drummed out of his Honor very recently, and hadn't yet found a Wilder pack to join. He was as much alone and as vulnerable as Teq himself. Apart from his carelessness in stepping into the trap, Teq decided that his luck was holding. He had found a likely friend. Best of all, a thing which he not dared to think of too much, Vork was not from the Challenger's Wilder pack and out hunting for him.

The night was full of cloud and very dark. As far as Teq could tell, the place where they finally stopped was just on the pond-side edge of the trees. He could see the dim glow of water a little downslope from where they stood.

"Sit there," Vork said. "I'll get us some food."

He squatted down and started lifting sods with a pair of sticks left close by. As each sod was lifted, a glow of banked firelight and the smell of cooked meat became clearer and clearer.

"I killed these birds this morning," Vork volunteered. "I cooked them all to preserve the meat, so there is plenty. They should be ready by now."

"I've never seen this method of cooking." Teq was impressed.

"Really? The women of my Honor use it for feasts. It takes all day, but the herbs cook with the meat and the flavor is usually good. I've only been able to find mint, but it should taste all right. Can you get some water? We can make tea when it boils. I have leaves, ready dried. Here." He handed Teq a pot. "Use this."

"Metal? This is metal!"

"Oh. Yes. It was given to me." Vork chuckled. "I'd never seen a metal pot either. The water heats fast, and nothing drips on the fire. It's the best thing to heat water in that I've ever seen."

"Who gave it to you?"

"Look, it's a long story. If you get the water while I get the food up, we can talk when we eat. I think we have to talk, about each other as much as the pot, but I'm hungry."

"I'm starving," Teq agreed. "You're right. I'll get the water."

Teq winced his way down to the pond on his sore foot and scooped water into the metal pot. Metal! There had been talk in the Honor of metal knives. A long time ago, a hunting party from the Honor had been attacked by a Wilder pack who carried them. It was far out in the desert. Marisel had led the hunting parties in those days. There had only been a few Wilders, and the hunting party was large enough to chase them off. One of the Wilders had dropped a knife. It was said that Marisel kept it in her own quarters, afraid to let anyone else even see it, because it could best any weapon they could make, in the Honor. Certainly Teq had never seen it. He'd heard the tale once when he was much younger and out with a hunting party.

The smell of cooked meat drew him back to the fire quickly. Vork handed him a whole fowl, wrapped in charred leaves. The meat was not charred, but was falling from the bone. Nothing had been said about trust, but Vork had stuck his knife in the fowl. So Vork had decided that he was not an enemy, eh? Good. The metal pot was set on a stone in the midst of the fire while they ate. They did not talk. They were far too hungry. The meat was delicious, and true enough, tasted of mint. Teq discovered the long leaves stuffed down inside the bird.

"I have never tasted anything so good in my whole life," he said, licking the fat from his fingers. "Thank you. I have never been so hungry, either. Tomorrow, it will be my turn to get some food for the fire."

"Or you could accept my offering, if you would." The voice came from the trees behind where they sat. Both boys leapt to their feet, eating knives in their hands. They could see nothing.

"It is a wise man who guards his own fire," the voice added. "I bring an offering of food, and ask the right to join you at your fire."

The boys looked at each other in the uncertain firelight. By the voice, this was a man grown. What could they do? They had sat, heedless, and it was too late now for caution. They shrugged at one another. Something about the voice nagged at Teq's memory.

Vork cleared his throat. "Step forward, then, and be seen," he said, keeping his voice as steady as he could.

A figure stepped heavily from among the trees, laden with a pack and a small doe gumbuck, draped across his shoulders. Even thus disguised, Teq gasped in recognition.

"It is my Sieur!" he said.

Galt laid the doe near the fire. "Galt," he said. "Sieur no longer. A fugitive from Honor life, like yourself. Teq, my son. Young sir. May I know whose fire is offering me hospitality?"

"My name is Vork, sir... Galt, sir... Sit and be welcome, Galt, sir. Would you care for one of these birds? We have just eaten but..."

Galt grinned. "Do stop calling me 'sir'. I am Galt. A man among men, as you are. I am grateful to come to your fire, and the smell of those birds was enough to draw me to your fire from far away. Thank you, I will certainly accept one." He turned to Teq. "I am glad to have found you too, my son. I followed you yesterday, but not today. In case of pursuers, you know. I thought you beyond their reach today."

Galt took the offered bird from Vork. He pulled his knife from his belt, squatted down, and set to. So! Someone had cooked for him, after all. He grinned to himself inside, while he ate. Time enough to find out who this boy with the great cooking skills was, after he had eaten.

Vork turned to the fire, where the water in the metal pot was beginning to steam. He picked up some leaves he had set to one side and bruised them a little, with a stone, before he threw them into the pot to make tea.

And Teq said nothing. His feelings about the arrival of Galt, were running about all over the place. His first reaction was horror, that he could so easily be found, when he had taken care to cover his tracks. His second was delight, that it was Galt, his Sieur, or in fact, sire, who had found him. He was disappointed that Galt had not intended to find him. Yet he was honored that Galt seemed pleased to have done so. He was relieved that he and Vork were not spending the night alone, after all. Last night he had been too exhausted to worry much about predators, human or otherwise. Tonight he was nearly as tired, and he feared sleeping too deeply. He was sleepy already. Although his inclination was to trust Vork, he worried that he was wrong to do so. Finally, the nagging feeling that had troubled him for the past couple of days, troubled him still, behind and beneath all these other feelings, modifying them: that this was Galt, who had killed the boy children when he conquered Marisel's Honor. Should such a man be honored? Trusted? Counted as a matter of pride in ancestry? And so Teq said nothing at all. He sat aloof by the fire and sipped from the pot when it was passed to him.

Galt wiped his fingers and sighed in satisfaction. "And so, Vork," he said, "you are on your way to become a Wilder? Newly drummed from your Honor, I would guess."

"No. None of that is so. I have had no drumming. I reached manhood here. Alone. No drumming," he said again, rather wistfully.

"Like me," Teq murmured, and then swallowed his words back into silence.

"Have you young men exchanged your histories with one another?" Galt asked.

"We intended to, after we had eaten, but then you arrived, Galt -er, sir."

"Do stop calling me 'sir'. The chances are that we may be adventuring together. Or not, if it is not what either of you would wish. Either way, there are stories to be told."

"Mine is rather a long one. I would like to tell you both. Perhaps, though, it would be better in the morning. I'm tired, myself."

"Me too," Teq yawned, in spite of himself.

"I have built a place to sleep in that tree over there," Vork offered. "But if you would like to sleep by the fire you would be most welcome."

"We are probably all too weary to concentrate," Galt agreed. "The morning, then." He turned to Teq. "Let's unroll these great cloaks your true mother gave us and get some sleep, then."

Teq nodded, weary but wary. It was not until Galt's heavy breathing told Teq that he slept, that he felt able to slip into sleep himself.

Chapter 11

"This is why I have not left this place." Vork unlaced his shoes and showed them the soles of his feet. They were wrinkled and puckered and shiny pink, with hard patches and soft patches and an overall look of soreness.

"That's terrible!" Teq cringed back involuntarily as Vork put his shoes back on. "Do they hurt?"

"Not any more," Vork assured him.

"Do you know how your feet were burned as badly as that?" Galt asked, serious concern in his face.

"I think someone held them in the fire. I remember the pain and I remember screaming and my sisters screaming, but my head was so sore, I'm not sure any of it really happened."

"Head?" Galt asked.

"Sisters?" from Teq.

"You had better start this story from the beginning," Galt suggested. "Do you come from an Honor somewhere near here? Do you come from an Honor at all?" He smiled encouragingly.

"Oh yes. Of course! Vibella's Honor," Vork answered. "I don't know if it is far from here or in which direction. There was no rift that I ever heard of, and no hills. There were sheer mountains capped with snow all year round to our south, and a huge lake, but I don't know where it is. If I knew that, I'd have gone home when they left me here."

"But you couldn't have stayed there. Your voice has broken. You are too old." Teq tried to keep the envy from his voice.

"That's true, but I would have gone nearer. Into country that was familiar, at least."

"When did you leave Vibella's Honor?" Galt prompted.

"It was the autumn hunt."

"That's nearly a year ago!"

65

"I suppose so. A small party of us were sent away from the main group to track a herd of pala. It seemed like a large herd moving slowly. We were supposed to get one and bring it back to the others. Instead we were ambushed by a party of men. We fought. They didn't look like Wilders - at least their hair wasn't dressed high on their heads, and their clothes were too neat looking. But they were still out to capture women. I was shot with an arrow in my arm, which hurt badly. I was still fighting, though, when somebody clubbed me.

"After that I only remember snatches. I was being carried, by my Honor sisters, I think. I would wake sometimes, bouncing on somebody's shoulder, and sometimes lying on the ground. All the time my arm was on fire, and my head was sore and dizzy. I couldn't focus. I thought I was dying, and I didn't care.

"It seems as though we stopped moving, or at least I wasn't jouncing around any more, before the part where my feet were in the fire. Perhaps it was a dream, but you've seen my feet. They look burned, don't they?"

"Definitely." Galt was grave.

"One day, I just woke up. One of my Honor sisters was binding my feet in bags of fat. There was a smell of meat cooking, and I was thirsty. We were here. I could see all my sisters and the men who had attacked us. Lanja, who had led our small hunting party, came to talk to me. I don't think it was the first time I woke. Maybe a couple of days later. I seemed to wake and sleep a lot.

"Lanja told me what was happening. These men had captured us, and the women were going on with them. They had been forced to agree to go peacefully - not try to escape - by some means."

"Probably burning your feet," Galt suggested.

"Oh! Yes. Perhaps. That could be it. I don't know. Lanja didn't say. Anyway, she told me they'd waited until I was well enough to leave, before they went. They'd built me a shelter, and they were leaving me food and stuff, but they had to go with the men now before the snows came.

"A little later one of the men came to talk to me. He brought the metal pot with him. He said one of the women had told him I could build true. This was because, the year before, we had been enlarging the Honor, to make better shelters for the goat herd. They were building the wall all wrong. As soon as we got a heavy rain, one side would sink and it would fall down. I don't know if you know what I mean. I could see it, and I convinced the matron in charge, Vibina, to let me show her. I worked it out in my head, and my plan was better than Vibina's. The walls of the new goat pens stood firmer than the walls of the Honor, when the autumn rains came. The Honor walls weren't really very safe.

"The man who brought me the metal pot wanted me to tell him what I did - especially the bit I worked out in my head. He asked me a lot of questions, and then he went away and talked to their chief. The chief's name is Kambar, and he came over to talk to me next.

"Were these men Wilders?" Teq wanted to know.

"No. As I told you, they even looked different: neater, better dressed, more disciplined, more serious. I don't remember ever seeing one of them smile, let alone laugh. I haven't seen all that many Wilders, but they always seem raggedy. Do you know what I mean?"

Galt and Teq both nodded.

"Anyway, this chief, this Kambar, said they had a long way to go and they must leave me, because I wasn't yet fit to travel. Then he said I would be welcome in their town, if I could get there this year."

"Town?" Teq asked. "What's that?"

"It sounds wonderful to me. Kambar said he and his men were all confraters, who lived together in a huge walled town. He said you could fit dozens of Honors inside it, and a few Wilder packs beside. He said the place was run by men, with a Dignus in charge, and any man who could contribute - that's what he said, contribute - would be welcome to join them. They had come out to harvest women. He said harvest..." Vork paused and giggled.

"Galt and Teq looked at each other in surprise. "Go on," Galt said.

"He said I would be welcome because I could build true. His confrater had been testing me, asking me all those questions. His confrater was a bit of a builder too. Kambar said he was giving me the pot to use, but also to show when I got to the town. I could ask for him when I got there and show them the pot. He told me there were metal workers in the town! If I show the pot when I arrive, the guards would know he'd invited me. Then he told me how to get to the town, and very soon after that, they all left."

"So you do know how to get there," Galt considered. "Why have you not gone? The snows have been over for a long time. Perhaps you do not trust these men who tortured you."

"I'm not sure they did. That was your idea." Vork was confused. "I liked them. I might have dreamed that part about holding my feet in the fire. I might have rolled over when I was ill and stuck them in the fire by accident."

"I see. But you are certain that they ambushed you and took away your Honor sisters."

"Yes... I told you I had stayed because of my feet. The truth is I was afraid to go alone. I mean, it's so safe here. But I really do like the sound of being in that town. I do want to go. It's that I'm afraid of being caught by Wilders, or anything else, on the way there. My arm isn't very strong any more. I'm not sure how my feet would stand up to the journey... so I've just stayed here, not knowing what to do. And then you both came," Vork finished, looking anxiously at Galt and Teq. "I've been thinking, perhaps we could go together."

He was greeted by silence. It lasted a long time, so long, in fact, that Vork got up and started to pace nervously up and down. There was a crash from the far side of the pond as one of his traps worked and caught some creature.

"I'll get that," Galt said, finally, getting to his feet.

"I'll come with you." Teq leapt up, glad of the excuse to do something without answering Vork. He wanted time to consider.

Vork looked hurt and puzzled. He had told them everything, and he could not see what he could have said that was so wrong.

"Give us time to think a little," Galt told him kindly. "You have told us so much and it needs pondering. We will go and get whatever is in the trap. In fact, Teq, you go around that side of the pond, and I'll go this way. We can make sure we get something for the fire. Vork fed us both last night. The least we can do is provide something tonight."

Teq walked over and got his bow and his sling. He felt chastened by Galt. He should have thought of it. He was determined he would not return to the fire empty handed. In the end, he was lucky to catch a couple of coneys with his sling, on the edge of the trees nearest the plain. That took him all day to accomplish. His foot still hurt a little, and he moved more clumsily than was usual for him, alerting all the game in the wood of his coming.

When he got back, Galt and Vork were talking and seemed content with one another. Galt had brought back the carcass of the cadger which had been caught in the trap. He had skinned and jointed it on site, and then rigged the trap again away from the smell of blood. He now worked, spitting the joints over the fire. While he worked, he told Vork his story. It was certainly common enough: a challenged Sieur, beaten and departing an Honor.

"Tell Vork your story," Galt said, when Teq limped in with his trophies.

"I'll just do my part in getting the meal first," he answered, wanting to put off speaking in front of Galt, unsure how the tale would be told. Unsure if he would cast Galt as hero or villain when he actually began talking.

"No, I'll do that," Galt smiled. "I can see you are tired. Vork told me what happened to your ankle. Better to sit down and rest it a bit. Talking will keep you occupied without hurting the foot."

Teq did as he was bid, and began his tale. As well now as later, he supposed. He told it well, giving full details of Belleth and Tarabeth. He explained how each of them had talked to him. He spoke of his own thoughts and doubts as he jogged across the plain. In telling it, he cleared his own mind, clarified his thinking. It seemed to him now that the tale showed that there were good things and bad things in all actions; in all people. To expect people to be all one or all the other was the expectation of a child. People simply were not. All you could do was choose for yourself which way you wanted to go. There were new choices to be made all the time. This question of Vork's was only the most recent. One thing he was sure of, he didn't ever want to be the Sieur of an Honor even if he did become skilled enough to win a challenge.

"So you don't want to be a Wilder, then?" Vork asked, all eagerness. "You would be willing to come with me to find the town."

"I haven't said that. I'm not sure about being a Wilder yet. It sounds to me as though the confraters aren't much different, except for living in a town."

"Oh no! Anybody can be a Wilder, but not all Wilders are acceptable in the town.

They'll only take men with skills. Like me," Vork added. "Besides, they are very disciplined. When they left here, they were marching along with the women herded into the middle. They had scouts placed ahead and behind and on both flanks. Just like a large party from an Honor on a journey, would. They weren't roaming about all over the place the way Wilders do. They're better than Wilders."

"You already know they'd accept you for your skills, but we don't know that we'd be acceptable. What skills do we have?" Teq asked.

"What about your mapmaking that Tarabeth told me about?" Galt asked. "That sounds like a skill to me. However you're right about me. I don't have anything acceptable to offer."

"You have been the Sieur of an Honor. You've given battle training to every boy. Surely that would count as a skill," Teq argued.

"I'm sure it would," Vork agreed. "Kambar seemed to be just such a leader. You could lead us. You know so much more than we do." Vork sounded wistful.

"What happened to the shelter they built for you?" Teq was suddenly suspicious. "How do we know this story of confraters and towns is true?"

"There's the pot," Galt said. "I've never heard of any Honor with metal working."

"I destroyed the shelter as soon as winter was over. I thought that if I did that, and burned it, I would have no excuse not to leave. But I have been too scared, as I told you, to go alone. I kept putting it off. I know I want to go. It seems as if it would be possible if we all went together. Don't you think so?" He looked at Galt.

"Why not?" Galt decided. "I've already been a Wilder once. I was happy enough, but I don't know that I want to go back to it. I do know how to reach a pack, if you want to join one, Teq. We can't leave until your foot is strong, in any case. You don't have to decide now. I can tell you how to find the Wilders, or we can go and find the town together. Whatever you decide. I'm going with Vork. It will be something new. Is it far to go, Vork?"

"Yes, very. Kambar said they only harvest women far from the town, so that the Honors don't hear about them. It's west and north, perhaps a full moon or more away. You have to find a certain pass through the western mountains, and it's beyond that."

"I'm coming too," Teq said suddenly. "I can map the way as we go. It's what I told Belleth I had always wanted to do, and it is. Even if the town doesn't exist, we'll be seeing new places."

"Good!" Galt smiled and pressed his shoulder. "We can make you a new battle staff - I saw your broken one - and prepare some new skins before we leave. Another half of a moon and your foot should be as good as new. Then we can be off. What do you say, Vork?"

"You're the leader." Vork sounded elated. "I'll do whatever you say."

"Me too," Teq agreed. "It's much better to have a leader."

"We already sound more disciplined than Wilders. This bodes well." Galt responded. "Let's eat and drink to that. The food is ready at last. We'll have a celebration by Wind and Sky! I didn't think to see one of those again so soon. Ha!"

Chapter 12

It rained for days when they started out. Either the grayness of the weather reflected their mood or they reflected the dismal skies. Considering they were beginning an adventure en route to a new life, their gloom seemed incongruous; yet each carried a private burden which fitted well with the silver substance of the world.

All the years of confinement within the walls of the Honor were taking their toll on Galt. His first days out, following Teq, had seemed like a release into freedom. That had filled him with a bounty of energy which was tempered only by leaving behind the comfort of the matrons, the delight of loving Tarabeth, and the loss of his little sons. The knowledge of his having saved Teq had counterbalanced even that, at the time. But with each gray day of this journey, the pain of his griefs penetrated deeper. The calm which had been with him during their days of preparation at the copse, deserted him now, and he fell into silence while he led the two young men climbing into the foothills away from the familiar plains. They climbed, gently at first, moving steadily north by northwest, leaving everything they had ever known behind them. Placing a final patina on the total grim of his mood, his body was betraying him. The power of his muscles had weakened immeasurably during the years of virtual inertia. The battle training had prevented them from total atrophy. He wondered how he had kept up the amazing pace when he crossed the plain - and then killed a doe - in Teq's wake. Admittedly the doe had been just standing there when he entered the copse, but still... He had covered the whole plain in no more time than it had taken young Teq. He found it necessary to rest frequently and to force himself to action at the start of each day. Only the necessity of showing leadership to the two young men kept his pride alive and prevented him from complaining. Instead, he gave them silence.

Vork was afraid. Even with the security of two companions on the march, he feared constantly that they would be attacked by overwhelming numbers of Wilders. He walked always in the huge shadow of Galt, flinching at every sign of life. He felt the safer for the rain and the consequent impairment of visibility. Besides that, his feet were genuinely fragile. Before they left the copse, he and Galt had fashioned padding for his shoes from the skins of coneys. They were thickly constructed from alternating layers of fur and leather, fastened snugly to his feet before he tied on his shoes. They provided a sympathetic cushioning, but still the constant walking was proving very hard on his feet. He stepped cautiously, and slowed their forward progress. He developed a ginger, limping walk, almost hopping from one foot to another, which would stay with him for the rest of his life.

Since Teq was the most able-bodied of the three, the task of ranging wide to hunt for the pot, fell to him. He was glad of it. He could hardly bear to be near the other two, depressed as he was by Vork's whining and Galt's silent misery. He considered abandoning them. He speculated on the progress he would have made by now, had he been alone. He thought of going off by himself in search of a pack of Wilders to join. From these he did not fear attack. What did they have that was worth fighting them for - weak as their party obviously was? Their only possession of value was the metal pot, and that was carried hidden in Vork's pack. Their clothes and weapons were more easily made than stolen. What Wilder men in their prime would bother with them?

On top of his disgust with his companions, Teq was questioning the choice he had made. It was true that they were covering new terrain, and the nightly camps were called so early by Galt, that he had plenty of time to mark his map from the rapid notes he had made with charcoal as they marched, hard as that was in the rain. Vork had elected himself cook. After he had helped Galt to clean the day's kill, Teq's time was his own until they ate. He went off by himself and brooded as he drew, under cover of his thick cloak. His reservations about the confraters were growing. People who would torture a sick youngster in order to force their will on the women, were no better than conquering Wilders who killed boy children. The women had always been the leaders in his world and he was used to them; but looking back, they seemed kind and sensible by comparison, even bound as they were by traditions. They had arranged the comfort and care and sanity in his life. It seemed wonderful now in retrospect, and infinitely desirable. The piercing anxieties of his new life made him forget how smothered all that care had made him feel at the time. And yet the women knew about, and conspired in, the killing of the boys! Was this any better than actually doing the killing?

The evenings at the copse had been punctuated with stories. After they ate, one or other of them would begin the tale of some memory evoked by the food or the weather. They had been peaceful and cheerful times. Evenings now were just quiet. None of them spoke from anything other than necessity.

The rains were not heavy, just dampening. But the damp caused friction where wet clothes rubbed the body, and misery where water dribbled into beds. Days began and ended with the smell of mold as cloaks were rolled and unrolled for sleep. The grasses of the plains lay flat and the high hills were hidden in mist. The world smelled of mud.

Then, on the fifth morning they woke to sparkle. Sunlight danced on the dew and the sky glowed peach and violet in the sunrise. The rising mists of morning burned off while they drank their morning tea and they smiled at one another.

Teq fell flat on his back, waving his breakfast meat in the air with one hand and grinning. "It's going to be a beautiful day," he said unnecessarily.

"Look how far up we are," Vork said, awed. The sun spread its rays fanwise over the vista. It still had the force of summer, although it was waning. "Look!"

They looked. The plains were far below them. They had been walking along a ridge, where the plains penetrated deep into the hills. Now they had climbed past and above it and they could see how far they had come. The rift was barely visible on the horizon, showing as a thin black slash in the endless plains. The forest was a smudge, disappearing rapidly from their view. The hills rose ahead of them and to their right. Peaks of mountains showed pink and white in the dawnlight in the far, far north. Below and ahead of them a river ran, swift and narrow, that they must cross on a narrow ridge of stone. Water poured across the ridge and dropped a few feet to a deep pool below.

"Come on." Galt leapt to his feet. "We'll cross that and then we'll make camp. We may as well cross while everything is wet. Once we're on the other side we can spread our stuff to dry in the sun, while we catch some fish for supper. I may have lost my skill, but we'll have all day for trying. Don't sit around gaping. It's a glorious day."

They caught his mood and jumped into action. They smothered the fire, and gathering everything together anyhow, they ran down the hill to the river crossing. They got soaked in the crossing, but they didn't care. The sun was heating the morning, and their spirits rose with every inch it climbed into the sky. They pulled off all their clothes and spread them on the hillside to dry. Then they all jumped into the pool below the little falls, and plunged under the water where they stood, rising to blow and splash water at one another like children. Naked as they were, they crept up along the river bank to the shadowed pools where Galt assured them that fish were lurking. He showed them how to trail their fingers in the water until they touched a fish, and then make a grab for it. It did take all day, since the fish were not willing, but in the end Galt got two and each of the boys got one. There was cress and mint growing along the river banks in plenty. They gathered it up, and Teq collected wood for their fire, while Galt built one and Vork prepared the fish. They turned their clothes and watched the steam rise, and then fell asleep near the fire. It was the first cool tendrils of evening which woke them, to dress, gather everything up, blissfully dry, then eat the dinner they had caught together.

After that progress improved. Vork discovered that the soles of his feet had hardened, and he could walk with confidence, though with no improvement in his gait. Galt's muscles had imperceptibly firmed during the gray days, so that he was leaner and fitter than he had been in years. The limp from the injured knee was all but imperceptible, except when he was exhausted, and his arm seemed itself again completely. They were now totally enclosed within the foothills, in a world of climbing and descending. Each day's climb carried them a little higher.

They had all learned, by now, to walk with the easy hillman's stride, and the miles were passing faster. The heat was being leached from the sun by the approach of autumn. The crispness of the air lent a briskness to their movement which carried them mile after mile with little effort. They came, at last, to a place beneath a cliff which lay just below what must be the pass. The true mountains still lay to their north, but they were now very high within the hills, so that trees were growing stunted and gnarled from the strength of the winter winds and snows. There would be a stiffish climb up the cliff's side, although the way was easily defined. Galt decided that it was too late in the day to risk the climb. Better to start fresh in the morning, when the rising sun would light their way.

It was there that Teq came at last to manhood. There had been many restless nights to foreshadow the event, but he had been too healthily tired at the end of each day's march to take any notice. It was when he decided to try shouting at the cliff to see if there was an echo, that his yell started high and ended an octave lower. Both Galt and Vork looked up from settling their things, startled.

"Well, then," said Galt. "It's come."

"We would both have our drummings now, if we had still been at our Honors," Vork put in, somewhat wistfully. He was plucking and gutting the ptarmigan Teq had brought down with his sling as they had walked.

"Drumming," Galt said, putting down the wood he had started to gather. "Good thought. Let me see what I can do while you two get the supper ready. Yes, we should all arrive at that town as men, good enough to be accepted by these confraters, I'd say. Hm! A drumming. Good."

He walked off without another word. Teq set up their camp and gathered plenty of wood, while Vork prepared the meal. There was time enough to take care with it, adding herbs that he had gathered along the way. The meal would be much better that most of their meals on the journey. Quite a feast, in fact.

When Galt reappeared, he carried with him a part of a tree trunk, hollowed out long ago by rot. He said nothing until they had eaten the feast and lay back to stretch their filled stomachs. Then he pulled a skin from his pack, and bound it across the top of the log. Across that, he bound their three staffs. Picking up two strong sticks from the pile Teq had gathered, he beat out three separate notes from his drum, skillful as a matron.

"This is your drumming, boys," he shouted, laughing. "Dance and be men. What are you waiting for?"

Vork stood up, uncertain, but Teq leaped into the firelight, holding a shadow staff in one hand. He lunged at a shadow enemy, flickering the shadow staff through his hands with such a show of dexterity that Galt laughed again.

Vork caught the spirit of the dance. He crouched low and feinted at Teq's legs with an imaginary staff of his own. Teq leaped high and twisted in the air, to bring his crashing down on Vork's head. But Vork rolled out of range. Galt laughed louder and drummed harder. The boys threw themselves into a battle which was a dance, or a dance which was a battle. Vork hopped and rolled to counter Teq's leaps and lunges. The drum beat ever faster, and the two boys lost all consciousness that they were performing an imaginary dance of war. They were warriors. They were hunters, challenged by the greatest of all prey, and by the wildest of Wilders. They fought each other, and they fought together, and the drum beat faster and faster. At last, each boy called out an involuntary yell of triumph, forced from his throat by the pace and the excitement.

At once the drum changed to a slow, solemn beat. First Vork and then Teq stepped up to Galt and bowed low. He was now the Sieur of the Honor and the Holder of the Honor, as well as the matron drummer. The two boys stepped back. Shaking their shadow staves high in the air, they marched from the fire, from the Honor, men now, to the steady beat of the drum.

Galt stopped. "That was a wonderful drumming," he told them. "I am enlarged by the company of two such men. Come back now. Tonight we must rest and drink some tea in celebration. Tomorrow we have to go back to being adventurers." He unbound their staffs and the skin from the log, and dismantled his drum. He threw the log on the fire. "There," he said, as they returned to collapse by its warmth. "You are both my sons and I am proud of you."

The water boiled in the metal pot, and they had barely enough energy to make some tea and sip it where they lay. They slept, exhausted by the emotions they had spent in the drumming, as much as by the energy. One danger was past. Teq could no longer be counted a child. The hazards to be met on the other side of the pass, were hazards they did not consider that night. The moon, rising in a wind-dark sky, shone on three sleeping men.

Chapter 13

Beyond the pass the hills were steeper, so that their descent was accomplished more swiftly than their long, slow climb. The progress of autumn exactly matched their descent, so that the climate never appeared to change for the travelers. Each night they slept cool, but comfortable, though in the hills away to their right they could see storms passing in the heights, and the snow continued to creep down the mountains in the distance. They spent their second night through the pass near some trees and a quiet stream.

"We are being watched," Galt said. "It is something I have not felt since my Wilder days, but it is a sensation you do not forget."

"The game has been behaving oddly," Teq offered. "Ever since the pass, when I am hunting, I only go a short distance and it runs right at me. I have been thinking that perhaps there was another hunting party out there, and the game was escaping them, but hardly for days in a row. I've been wondering what to make of it."

"Who would watch us?" Vork asked, nervous as he crouched over the fire, cooking as usual.

"What about these confraters of yours?" Galt suggested.

"That's true. They might be on the watch to see what we are doing. What anyone would be doing who comes through the pass," Teq agreed. "What do you think, Vork? You know them."

"I don't really know them, but they were very disciplined like I told you. They probably would do that. But they did invite me. It's all right if it's them, isn't it?"

"It's all right for you," Teq said.

"If they didn't want to be found, they might well stop you wandering about by driving game to you." Galt was thoughtful. "They must be wondering who you and I are, though. There will be a testing of some sort before we are allowed into the town, I would guess. I'd as soon it wasn't in battle. That's a bad way to begin..."

"There's not much we can do about it, is there?" Vork sounded worried.

"You don't have to worry either way," Teq said. "You've been tested already. I suppose I could make a great display of marking my map every evening."

"Good idea," Galt agreed. "Not much I can do, though."

"You could give us battle training. You could do it after we eat, or while the meal is cooking or something. We could use the training, and it would show your skill." Teq was excited.

"I suppose I could."

"Vork would do it, wouldn't you? You and I could fight one another while Galt instructs us. What do you say?"

"Well..." Vork was less than eager. It wasn't a thing he had enjoyed doing when he was smaller, and Teq was much bigger and stronger than he was.

"Good, I knew you wouldn't say no," Teq grinned. "We can start tonight."

"In fact, it's a good idea," Galt agreed. "It would show what I can offer, yes, but it would also be good to demonstrate to them that Vork has his strength back. It may be that they refuse to accept the weak. It had occurred to me that this was the reason they left him behind. If he could get here, all this way, he would be acceptable."

"Do you think so?" Vork asked nervously. "I wouldn't want to be turned away now that we've come so far."

They began that evening while the meal was cooking. It was true that Vork needed a great deal of instruction; and Teq, no longer a little boy, found out how much he had forgotten. They fell ravenously on the food when the practice was over. They hardly noticed that, without Vork's usual care, the meal was half burned. Used as they were to vigorous days in the open, the concentrated work-out came hard. They slept heavily. In some way, the knowledge that they were watched made them less, rather than more, wary, and they slept without disturbing dreams.

For two more days, they threaded their way through the hills, climbing up and climbing down, but overall getting lower and lower. Trees grew more numerous. They noticed a considerable forest to their north on the slopes of the foothills there. The forest was so thick, that they could no longer see the mountain peaks beyond. Where the mountains curved round to the west, however, the rising sun sparked each morning from their snowclad tops.

On the fifth day beyond the pass, the ascending slope was so steep, that they decided not to stop for their nooning until they reached the top. The hill stood solidly in their path and there was no way around without turning away far to the north. They had been walking almost all the way on grass, but this was a boulder strewn slope, and required all their concentration to reach the top.

Teq made it first. They heard his gasp. "Come quick," he called to them, "we have arrived."

Galt made it next. "So that is a town," he muttered. "Well, well!"

"But it's huge!" Vork gasped.

They looked down at the town they had come so far to find. The trip had been easy. Recently even the weather had been sympathetic. Kambar's directions to

Vork had been clear. There had been no hazards along the way. They had grown complacent. Nothing had prepared them for what lay below them.

They were looking at an immense bowl set among the hills, though the southern side was not much of a rising. The town was spread over a large portion of it. On the farther side of the valley, the hills were steep enough to form a kind of cliff, down which a river of water cascaded mightily, throwing drops high into the air. The mist over the plunging water sparkled like a rainbow in the noonday sun. At the foot of the falls, the waters ran through the town, forming a lake in its center, and ran out as a gentle stream under the walls to the south.

The entire immensity of the town was surrounded completely by two walls, twice the height of a man. Gates were cut into the walls on the northern, eastern and southern sides, but the gates on the inner walls did not correspond to those on the outer. Thus anyone entering or leaving would have to pass through the passage between inner and outer walls before gaining entry or exit. Guards were visible walking along the tops of both walls.

From the inner gates, broad avenues crossed the town. The largest buildings were both at their center point and surrounding the central lake. From there, all the other buildings were set in tidy patterns, stretching away in all directions. Unlike the wall-hugging structures in the Honors they knew, these structures were free standing or leaned together in pairs. None abutted the walls.

Smoke rose from the chimneys, high into the air, but the upper winds caught it and dispersed it, before sight of it could go beyond the surrounding hills. There was abundant sign of life. People hurried about the street of the town in a patternless way, intent on matters that could not be guessed at from so high above.

As they stood on the ridge gazing down, a party of men arrived at the northern gate, leading beasts laden with wood, apparently culled from the hill forest.

"It would take a lot of that wood to keep all those fires burning," Galt observed. "They must have people out there cutting at that forest every day."

"What about food," Teq wondered. "There can't be any game left in these hills. Think where you'd have to go to find meat for so many."

"Look there," Galt pointed to the south. The gentle hillside was covered with a huge herd which seemed to be of mixed types of animal. It was too far away to make out what they all were, though there seemed to be antlered deer of some sort, as well as goats and something woolly. There appeared to be a number of people guarding them.

"Well, Vork," Galt asked, "what do you think of the place now we're here?"

"It looks safe," Vork answered. "A man could live there without worry or distraction. You know what I mean. And there seems to be a need of building. Did you see? They're working on the wall to the south, and there are buildings going up all over the place."

"That's true. Your talents would be useful. And indeed they have taken exceptional pains to keep the place secure," Galt mused.

"Who do they fear?" Teq wondered. "You don't need walls like that against predators."

"There must be some warlike people to fear. If Wilders don't attempt to breach the walls of an Honor, they certainly wouldn't attempt those," Galt agreed.

"We fear no one!" said a deep voice behind them.

The three whipped around to see a tall, saturnine, bearded man standing there. He flicked a finger and six more bearded men rose from the grasses, dressed in green so that it provided near invisibility. In each hand was held a spear pointing steadily at the party of adventurers.

"Kambar!" Vork exclaimed.

"So you have chosen to show yourselves at last." Galt spoke calmly.

Kambar flicked a glance in his direction, narrow-eyed and considering. "Vork, who are these men?" he demanded. His refusal to answer, made Galt irritated and wary.

Teq was furious with himself for failing to hear their approach. In spite of being so fascinated by their first sight of the town - BECAUSE they were so fascinated by their first sight of the town - they ought to have been more alert. He held his silence.

"They have come with me. To join you," he stuttered, suddenly unsure. "I met them at the copse where you left me. "See." He fumbled his pack from his back. "I have brought back the pot you left with me."

"I asked who they were, not where you met them." Kambar's voice was harsh. Uncompromising. "And why you felt at liberty to bring with you whomever you chose."

"They didn't want to be Wilders." Even to Vork's ears that sounded weak. "They are my friends," he added more resolutely, "and I decided to ask for their company on this journey."

Galt nodded approvingly.

Kambar did not. "You may have brought them to their deaths. It is the right of confraters to decide who may enter their town, and who may know of it. You do not have that right. And yet you have elected to bring them to where they have seen the town, and know now how to reach us. This knowledge may not be carried from here. We cannot allow these men to join some Wilder Pack and spread the word of our presence. We accept only the skilled, who earn the right to our protection and our resources. Others are put to death. You." He turned to Galt. "What is your name?"

Galt raised his eyebrows, and Vork put in hastily, "he is Galt. The one time Sieur of an Honor."

"And you are Kambar, who abandons young persons to fend for themselves during the long cold. My name is Galt indeed, who was bested at Challenge and left the Honor. This is Teq, my son, who fled the killing just prior to being drummed into manhood. That drumming was accomplished for both these young men on this journey."

"The sound of it woke the hills," Kambar replied dryly. "We watched at the pass to discover if the noise makers were coming this way. Imagine our surprise to see Vork as one of these."

"Ah! Well then, you acknowledge us all as men like yourselves. Let us begin again from that point. We formally request acceptance into the brotherhood of confraters who have built this noble town." Galt smiled calmly.

Kambar nodded, acknowledging Galt's status. "We have watched you giving these young men battle training. It is a skill which is of value to us," he conceded. He touched the metal collar at his neck. I am a chief. Guards and hunters are led by men of my hierarchy. We wear the green." He nodded toward his unmoving men.

"You lead the men and women in the hunt, then," Galt concluded.

"Women? Women do not hunt here!"

"How are my Honor sisters?" Vork blurted out.

"I hardly know." Kambar turned to him. "They were assimilated into their proper places. I have not taken further note of them. It is possible one or another may be a wife by now. It has been long enough since we left you."

"Alone and ill," Galt pointed out.

"He mended."

"He did. And befriended us when we came to the copse. He elected to invite us to join him on this journey, as was his right as man alone. You do not dispute this, of course."

Kambar looked at him for a silent moment then turned to Teq. "Vork has been tested, and we have agreed to accept your battle skills, but what of this young man, this Teq?"

"He is my son. He has..."

"Let him speak for himself. You. Teq. What can you show as a reason for acceptance into the confraternity? We have hunters enough. All men past apprentice, help with the hunt. Not just the guards. We will need more than that for a reason to spare you." Kambar seemed nasty.

Teq had been silent throughout the entire exchange. He had been impressed with the way Galt had wrested the initiative from Kambar. With Kambar he was not impressed. He disliked his tone, his treatment of Vork whom he had damaged so badly, and his offhand dismissal of the matter of Vork's Honor sisters irritated him. Had he not been sobered by the light in Galt's eyes, he might have given a very rude answer to Kambar's demand. Instead, after a pause, he stepped forward and shrugged off his pack.

"I am a maker of maps," he said. "I will show you the map I have been making of our journey to this point from the copse."

Kambar snatched it from his hand. "Did it not occur to your foolish mind that some Wilder pack might have stolen this from you, and learned the route to the town?"

"How would such a thing be possible, when the town is not marked and the route still incomplete?" Teq asked with calm. "I map only the known. I do not make maps of dreams or other people's words. I also ask, what pack of Wilders would attack a small group of men without valuables? You have yourselves been watching us since the pass. Did you have to fight off marauding Wilders on our behalf?"

"How do you know that?" Kambar demanded.

"How could we fail to?"

"You are insolent." Kambar looked at the map in his hand, giving it his full attention. "This is a good map," he said at last, with seeming reluctance. It is a skill we value. Very well. You will be acceptable to us, but you had better learn to mind your manners. You are to remember to show respect when you are addressing a chief." He turned to Vork. "Your arrogance in bringing the uninvited with you was at best, foolhardy. We considered killing you all as soon as you had come through the pass."

Vork shuddered, and picked up his pack. Teq held out his hand for his map, but Kambar ignored him. Galt shrugged and gathered his belongings, nodding to Teq to do the same.

"We will take you in now." Kambar again flicked his fingers and the six men deployed without further orders. Two men each flanked the three, separating them from one another. Argument against the readied spears would have been merely foolish.

As Kambar led the way towards the eastern gate, Teq reflected that there was little to indicate that they were being escorted to the town as accepted confraters. To any observing eye they were prisoners. Well, they had arrived. And they were all alive. How long they would be glad to be among this group of brothers would remain to be seen. Teq, at least, reserved his judgment.

Part 3
The Town

Chapter 14

The way through the gates was distinguished by the number of times Kambar was challenged. Instead of being irritated, as Teq thought reasonable, he seemed pleased. It was clear that Kambar was well known to all the wall guards who stopped him and asked him to identify himself and his party, so Teq could not see the point. He amused himself with the idea of reentering the Honor at the end of the day and reeling off the names of his goats to the wall guards; or of watching a returning hunting party, worn out and glad to be home with food for everyone, being asked if they would state their names and that of the dead animal being allowed in. Since Vork marched between the first pair of Kambar's men, Galt between the second, and himself between the last, he was unable to see how either of the others was accepting this. What or who were these confraters afraid of? Since Kambar gave all their names every time they were challenged, by the time they had negotiated the passage between the walls and entered the town itself, Teq felt quite well known.

Once inside the walls, the party split. Galt and Teq each made a protest, but they were ignored, and their arms seized by their escorts. Not wishing to seem as if he were entering the town as a prisoner - though he was not totally sure about this - Teq shook off their hands and walked between them without further comment. He did take note that Galt's group followed Kambar, while Vork's group struck off in another direction. His own guards led him straight ahead for some distance before turning off down a side street.

The street they walked down was broad, with buildings close to one another on either side. Each building was as different from its neighbor as was possible for such simple structures. Some of them had one floor piled up on top of another, which was a thing he had never imagined possible. No wonder they valued a person like Vork who could build true! In the center of the line of buildings on his right, they stopped at one which was double high. It took up more space than any other they had passed. And it seemed more than twice as long. Smoke came out of a chimney which led up out of the center of the roof, unlike any of the other chimneys, which all leaned against the side of their structures. A sign swung creaking over the door. It was painted with the signs of all four directions, painted as arrows in bright colors.

His escort didn't bother to knock on the door, but pushed it open and walked in, with Teq between them. Teq was astounded to see that the room before them had no back wall: just a series of posts holding up the ceiling. Beyond the sullen fire in the middle of the great room, sat a huge table, part inside and part outside the house. There was shade over it, but the open, walled courtyard beyond provided exceptional light for the table. A man worked alone at either end of it. Along the sides worked a scattering of young men and boys, all apparently unaware of their visitors, since none of them looked up. Not a word was being spoken.

A man rose from one end and came towards them. He was tall and thin and quite old. His tunic fell almost all the way to his ankles, and he wore a sleeveless coat over it. Around his neck was a metal collar like Kambar's, which appeared to be immensely heavy for so frail a person to bear; but he kept touching it with long, gray, proud fingers, in apparent rhythm with the tiny swaying steps he took as he walked. It seemed to take a long time for him to reach them.

"Yes?" he asked.

"Chief Kambar has sent you a new apprentice," said one of the escort, and then, with a pause which was long enough to indicate lack of respect, he added, "Master".

"He's been tested by the Chief."

"I shall see to that myself."

"This here's Master Mapmaker Kinnysinny." The man shoved Teq forward. "All right, then. We'll be off." They suited action to word, not waiting for the Master's rather irritated dismissal.

"Kinnasen. My name is Kinnasen." He turned on Teq.

"Er... yes," said Teq.

"You will address me as 'Master', and only when requested to speak. What is your name?" The Master found some relief from his irritation in being able to chastise Teq. He almost smiled.

Teq thought Kinnasen sounded like a woman's name, but bowed politely and responded, "Teq of Marisel's Honor, er, Master." He bowed again.

"Don't mention Honors in this Town, boy. They count for nothing here. Less than nothing. How did Chief Kambar test you? As if he would know how to do so..."

"I showed Kambar the map I had been making of our journey here. He kept it."

"Chief Kambar. And address me as Master. You have now been told twice."

"Yes, Master."

"Well, what can you show me?"

"I have another map, of the land around the Honor, Master." Teq was becoming irritated himself, but he had an honest respect for his elders and only resented being despised for coming from an Honor. He could think of no reason to be ashamed of that. However, he was in no position to quibble. He dug in his pack and found a copy of the map he had mentioned. He handed it to Kinnasen.

"Ah. It is rudimentary but adequate. The detail is clear." Kinnasen walked closer to the fire as if the room chilled him. Teq followed. "Yes. Good. Very good. I will accept you as an apprentice. Yes. You may stay. Is this the only map you have?" Kinnasen rolled up the map in his hand and placed it under his arm.

Teq realized he would not see this map again either, so he decided to lie, or nearly. "I was unable to bring all my possessions when I ran away from the... when I ran away. I had made more maps, though, Master."

"Too bad. Too bad. Well, there it is. Bardon," he called.

At the table, a boy put down what he was doing and hurried over. He had an unctuous air. Teq did not like his looks. He was plump, narrow-eyed and pale, and a little older than Teq. He bowed in silence.

"I want you to meet -um Teq, isn't it? You may finish for the day now. Take your work to the Competent and introduce Teq to him. Then take him to find a bed, colors and food. Tomorrow he will begin work as an apprentice here. That is all."

Still Bardon spoke no word, but bowed to the Master in silence. He jerked his head at Teq in a "follow" way, and walked back to the table.

Teq looked with interest at the work in progress on the table. There were pictures of the land, made on leather, like his own maps. But on these charts, the mountains looked like mountains, the trees like trees, rivers like rivers. All the people were working with brushes and colors. The maps were marvels.

Bardon picked up the skin on which he had, presumably, been working, and checked whether it was dry. He rolled it and carried it to the older man, working at the opposite end of the table from where Kinnasen had been. This man wore a collar of leather. The Competent? In front of him was a pile of maps on which he was lettering with a brush so fine that his nose nearly touched the table in concentration. He acknowledged Bardon with a nod, and stared at Teq after the whispered introduction. He offered no word, and neither did Teq. He just bowed yet again. The Competent returned to his work as Bardon led Teq away. Nobody else at the table acknowledged their presence by so much as lifting their eyes.

They walked to a ladder attached to a wall in one corner of the room. Teq knew what it was, because there had been one like it for the guards to mount to the walls of the Honor. Bardon started up and Teq followed, determined not to speak until Bardon spoke to him. They entered a room at the top, similar to the one below, but with all four walls in place. It seemed slightly broader. Probably the floor of this room extended over the table to shade it from sun and rain, Teq thought. He was rather pleased with himself for working that out. A dozen bedrolls were opened on to the floor, a peg in the wall over each. Spare clothes hung from some of these.

"We can talk up here," Bardon spoke at last. "There's a free bed near the chimney, and one beside the ladder. Take which one you want."

Teq chose the one near the ladder. It seemed important to be able to reach the way out, quickly, though he could tell that was silly, even as he thought it.

"Why can't we talk downstairs?" he asked as he piled his pack on to the bed.
"The Master says it disturbs the work. We get instruction at the beginning of
the day about what we are to work on, from the Competent. Then we just go on
doing it until we finish for meal times. You see?"

"Do you like it here?" Teq asked.

Bardon looked startled. "Why not? Mapmakers are honored among the confraters - except by the green shirts: guards and hunters - but they don't count. It's
better than being some Wilder thing, if that's what you mean, or some Honor
grubby." He snorted. "I never had to put up with any of that. I came here on my
mother's back. Too young to walk. When I'm a Competent I shall go outside the
Town and look at where I came from, probably. That is, when I go out with a
hunting party."

"I am a hunter myself. Kambar said everyone is."

"Oh, well, yes. We are in theory. Mostly it's just the brainless gorms, the green
shirts, like those two who brought you in. They're the hunters and guards. Can't
learn any other trade. You see? We don't waste our time on that stuff."

"You mean you never leave the Town?" Teq was dismayed to have confirmed
what he had begun to suspect.

"I told you. Mapmakers - well Competents - get to go out with hunting parties
and map new places. I'll be getting my Competent's collar soon. I'm working on
my project now."

"Er-congratulations." Teq thought this seemed to be the answer called for.

Bardon smiled. It must have been. "Hungry?" he asked.

"Yes, if you are."

"Let's go, then, before the horn sounds. We'll worry about your colors later.
We can get in ahead of the crowd if we eat first."

"Horn?"

"To end the day's work."

"Oh, I see." Teq thought of the drum which called the Honor home at day's
end. Must be the same sort of thing.

All of a sudden it struck Teq that he was alone. He had no idea where, in this
vast Town, Galt and Vork had been taken. Presumably they were now apprentice
builder and guard or hunter, or whatever Kambar had decided they were. And
where was that? The Town seemed huge and the walls impassable. He felt
trapped. Trapped and alone! Swallowing his sudden panic, he followed Bardon
back down the ladder, taking his pack with him. He threw just his cloak and blanket on to the bed to claim it. The pack was his and he wanted it to stay his.

When they reached the bottom of the ladder he tried a question. "Do all trades
eat together?" He had suddenly had the idea that he might see the others there.

"Hush," said Bardon.

Once in the street, conversation was allowed again. "We can eat anywhere we
like, but who would want to eat with any other trade? I mean who would a mapmaker want to eat with? You see? We eat at the Matted Vine. It has the best food,
of course. They mark down what we eat, and present the bill to the Competent.

" Seeing Teq's puzzled expression, he added: "what is owed... The Competent pays for all the apprentices. Simple. You see?"

"Pays?"

"You don't know about credits, do you? I've met Honor grubbies before." Bardon sniffed with a sort of pleased contempt. He was enjoying being the authority. This particular Honor grubby looked as if he could fight just about anybody and win, but he was still helpless in the Town. He knew nothing.

Bardon sniffed again. "Think of a credit as... as a stone," he explained with enormous patience. "Every hour of work you do is worth so many stones. You see?"

"Why?" Teq asked. "I mean, you're doing it because you want to, aren't you?"

"Farting grubbies! It just is. Accept that, or you won't understand anything that goes on here. Now. You need a new shirt, say. You can go to a market that has shirts to offer, all right? Each shirt is worth so many cred... stones. You give them the stones. You have some because you earned them for your work. You give them because you owe them for the shirt. Paying what you owe. Then they give you the shirt. You see?"

"It seems like a good idea," Teq answered slowly. He was quite pleased with the notion. "Not everyone could use a map in exchange. I see. Like where we eat, for instance. They wouldn't need a new map daily. Yes. That's a good system. When do we get our stones?"

"Credits, grubby, credits. You don't. Not as an apprentice. Not until you're a Competent. While you're an apprentice, the Hall pays for what you need. You are working to learn the trade. They can sell the work they have you do. They teach you, and feed you, and clothe you and house you. You see? Mapmakers wear brown. You'll need proper brown shirts. We'll go and get them after we eat. The Hall will pay. Here. This is the Matted Vine. This is where we eat."

The square building they were entering was full of smoke. There must have been a blow-back from the fire. An older man and a pregnant woman were trying to deal with it by fanning it through the door. There were mats forming one wall, which one girl was trying to roll up, to let the smoke out. She was having a hard time as she was very young and small. The cooking pots hung in the fireplace, and the pregnant woman was obviously trying to get back to them. The rest of the room was full of long tables and benches, set in rows. They did not look too clean, to Teq's eyes. The eating tables in the great room at Marisel's Honor had been scoured with sand daily, until they gleamed. But if the food was good, he didn't care much. He was hungry.

Two girls were racing about bearing heavy trays, setting up the tables with wooden bowls, beakers and spoons, piled at the end of each. The smallest girl finished rolling up the mats, though not very high, and came to help. The smoke was clearing at last.

Bardon chose a table, picking up utensils as he sat down. Teq did the same, and sat down opposite him. The oldest girl came over. She seemed about his own age: already a woman. Her hair was long, and would have been very fair, if it were not grimed with ash. She looked hot, gray-skinned, and tired. All the women were wearing night shifts, Teq noticed, though belted at the waist, and shoes made of cloth. He wondered why.

"You're early," she told them.

"Is the food ready?" Bardon did not look directly at her when he spoke.

"Two?" she asked.

"Thank you, Lady." Teq smiled at her. She looked up quickly, startled. She smiled back and the smile was wonderful. She suddenly didn't seem so dirty. Her smile made him think of the wide outdoors on a misty morning. Bardon looked at her sharply. She lowered her head and scurried off.

"Lady! "You are too raw for your own good, grubby. What do the women do to the men in these Honors? Fraternity preserve me from it!"

Teq was saved from a snarl by the blast of a horn, so loud that conversation was impossible. Just as well. He was getting heartily tired of being called a grubby.

"Work's over for the day. We were just in time." Bardon rubbed his hands in anticipation. "That girl should get herself back here with our food before the others start arriving. Hurry up, girl," he shouted.

"She's a woman, not a girl," Teq said evenly.

"Here, she's a girl till she works in a Pleasure House. But you're right," he added graciously, " she looks old enough. They'll be sending her off any day now. Probably waiting for the next Distribution of Women so they can get her replacement first."

"All right," Teq sighed. "Tell me about Pleasure Houses."

"You can't use one until you're a Competent or a Merchant or a Captain. Certainly not if you're an apprentice. I don't have to tell you what they're used for, surely?" He gave a hissing laugh, which made Teq want to hit him. But he needed to know how to go on in the Town. He wouldn't get anywhere if he didn't. And Bardon seemed more than willing to tell him. He held his expression neutral with an effort.

"When they bring in a bunch of females they've captured, they divide them up. The Chief of the party that brings them in, Chief Kambar mostly, decides who goes in which bunch. The old ones are bought as servies in the private houses or Halls, if they're needed, all the way up to the Palace of the Dignus. The young ones are used in the inns and wine shops. People who need them bid for them at the Distribution of Women. It's how the Chief's people earn their credits, as well as by bringing in food. The credits go to all the green shirts, hunters or guards. The women in their prime go to the Pleasure Houses. Of course the ones who get to use them pay the Pleasure House Keepers for their use. Once one of these women gets pregnant, anybody who has enough credits and has a house can bid for her. Then they're called wives. Like that one over there. I mean to save for a house quickly, once I make Competent. I want a woman of my own. If they don't become pregnant, they just stay on in the Pleasure House. They get rather well-used and wear out, then. They end up as servies, of course, but they don't increase the value of anyone's house."

It was a while before Teq could bring himself to speak. He was appalled by these Town ways. He could not understand why the women allowed it. Perhaps they had no weapons to fight with. He asked Bardon, non-commitally, "the women never hunt, then?"

"Of course not. If they were allowed outside the walls, they'd form a pack and run off. We can't have a Town without women. You know... am I boring you?"

Teq's expression must have been showing too bland. "No, no, of course not," he ground out. "I'm becoming educated."

"Oh, well then, I was just going to say, there used to be a time when this Town was all just like a huge Wilder pack. Just men, always fighting each other, with no organization at all. I've heard a lot about it. They say the men killed each other when the first women were brought in, just to get at them. And the women fought back. There had been a Dignus chosen, but the women killed him and almost got away. The Dignus we now have was a young man then. He chased them, and brought them back. He's the one who restored order and got the Town organized. He built up the walls, and set up the Council. Set up the order of things as they are now. He's a great man, though he's very old now. You might get to see him on Founder's Day, or one of the other feasts. We have three feasts a year, you know," Bardon said proudly. "Nobody works at all on feast days. You've missed Summer Long Day, so Founder's Day is next. It celebrates the day the Dignus made the Town a confraternity, with all the men equal, under the Chiefs and Masters and all that. It's a wonderful thing to be a confrater. Winter Long Night is the other feast day. You don't have any feasts - out there - do you?"

"Yes, of course we do," Teq answered shortly. "We celebrate Summer Long Day and Winter Long Night too. And then there are the Drummings, of course."

"Drummings? Oh yes, I've heard of those. When you grow up, right? And then you're thrown out of the Honors and have to join a Wilder pack. Is that what happened to you?" Bardon gave his hissing laugh.

In spite of himself, Teq sounded wistful. "Join a Wilder pack? That's right. Only I never did. I had my Drumming when I was already on my way here."

"Well here it doesn't count." Bardon was pompous. "Here you have to prove yourself to become a Competent. Ah food. Finally!"

The blonde girl carried a jug and a platter of bread in one hand. In the other was a huge bowl, smelling of a rich stew. There was a ladle in it. She set down the jug and platter, and silently ladled stew into their bowls.

"Thank you, Lady. I am Teq of Marisel's Honor. Will you tell me your name?"

"I am Athirra of Alagith's Honor. Hunter of fish." She gave him her smile again, but wiped it from her face when Bardon looked up with a frown. She snatched up the stew and slipped away. Groups of young men were spilling into the Matted Vine and filling all the tables, as pervasive as a leaf fall in autumn. They didn't speak until they were seated, as if the habit of silence had followed them down the street.

"You watch yourself around women," Bardon warned with a full mouth. "Apprentices don't get them, and that's that. You could end up with your apprenticeship extended for ever, if you are a trouble maker. Never would make Competent. You see?"

"She's just another Honor grubby like me. Like seeks like." Teq grinned inside himself as he started on his food.

And that was the truth. She was trapped here too, and his heart went out to her. Indeed, it was beginning to ache for himself. Like him, she was a hunter, used to open spaces and moving free - at least fairly free. He had jibbed at the confines of the Honor lands. This was worse! At least, he supposed hunters of fish were used to moving around in open spaces. Anyway, the principle was the same. But at least, he had come here of his own free will. That would teach him to make decisions when he knew too little about what he was going to face. He had learned this much, approach the unknown with caution. Teq tore savagely at his bread. It was worse for this Athirra. She had been captured and brought here by force. Like Belleth, his true sister. Perhaps he could find a way to help this woman. He had been able to do nothing at all for Belleth. At least, perhaps, they could talk. He resolved to find a way.

Chapter 15

Teq had two immediate ambitions: to find Galt (and possibly Vork), and to rescue Athirra. The latter really came from a need to talk to women again. Talking with her about a chance for her to escape, would certainly fulfill that need. And, of course, such conversation was forbidden to apprentices, which, he suspected, actually drove his desire to help prevent her being sold to a Pleasure House. And anyway, women were what he was used to. He'd spent his whole life among them until his escape. He could not accept that these confraters had the right to forbid them to him. The whole thing of buying and owning women was something which made him, at least, uncomfortable. Actually, it appalled him Though he was honestly trying to fit in, it made him squirm to watch the innkeeper's newly-purchased wife (he noted the pregnancy), constantly trying to please her owner. The innkeeper's name was Famal. He was not a bad fellow, though fattish and less than clean. He was obviously bursting with pride at having a wife, and he was grimly determined that none of the apprentices would so much as look at her. In fact, she always stayed near the fire, filling the bowls of the servies, and begging Famal to taste and approve every dish. Famal would smile and pat her in praise, while he glared round to make sure the apprentices were busy with their food.

Teq's ambition to seek out his erstwhile companions ought to have been easier than trying to talk to Athirra. Wearing his brown shirt, he was a readily identifiable apprentice mapmaker, and therefore excited no comment wherever he went. He was free to roam the Town at will whenever he was at liberty. On two days each week the horn sounded at noon, and apprentices were free to fill their time and vent their spirits as they would. They could eat at other houses and wander to the markets. Except, of course, that they could not leave the Town, visit Pleasure Houses or wine shops. For the most part they went to the game courts, of which there were four: one in each quadrant. There they vied with apprentices from other disciplines either with battle staves (called simply staves, in the Town), or a game played with a bladder. It involved keeping the bladder in the

89

air with game sticks - a sort of flat staff - and then hitting it above the heads of the opposing team to hit a marked target. Teq had gone with a group of his fellow apprentices to each of these activities, in the interest of fitting in, but only once to each. He had been so inept with the bladder as to never again be invited. On the other hand, he was so adept with the battle staff, that he was hissed from the court as being a ruffian and guard material.

He had rather enjoyed the exercise with the staff. Not only was it a break from the confinement of every day in the Mapmakers' Hall, but it was nice to show he was good at something. However, it furthered neither of his ambitions, so he accepted with good grace the fact that he was welcome with neither group. Added to his "Honor grubby" status, which Bardon had made sure everyone knew, he was fairly unpopular with his fellow brown shirts. Bardon's plumpness made it clear that he did not spend his free time in any form of exercise, so Teq followed him one day to see what he got up to. Bardon was quartering the entire Town, noting the location of every Pleasure House. Either this was for his Competent's test, or it was his intent to sample them all as soon as he reached that exalted rank, without having to waste time seeking them out. Well, Teq supposed, tolerantly, being prepared was always a good thing.

The first step in his own research came gratuitously. Gaveril, the mapmaker Competent, who oversaw his training, decided he had enough practice with free drawing. He needed the discipline of detailed copying. He was set to work making maps of the Town, showing every house on every street. Errors or carelessness of detail required a scraping clean of all his work and beginning again. Everything had to be produced to precise scale. At first, Teq found the work tedious, but as the beauty of the design and the reality of the streets began to grow on his map, he learned to take pride as well as pleasure in his work.

There were other maps in greater or lesser detail on which apprentices worked. The Competent himself was working on a huge map of the known world, in itemized detail. Some of the senior apprentices worked with him. The Town sat in the center of the skin like a heart's jewel, lovingly displayed, with its walls. streets and waters. The immediately surrounding territory was designated "Town's Lands", and no boundary was shown. To Teq's astonishment a large part of the eastern and southeastern sectors were designated "Honor Lands", but what surprised him, was that the names of many of the Honors were known, including Marisel's, much to his chagrin. Boundaries of Honors were marked, and even the type of livestock they owned. Not all were named. He searched in vain for Alagith's Honor to discover where Athirra, the hunter of fish, originated. Hills to the north and east were designated "Wilder Lands", with many permanent camps painted in. The far north showed simply as the "Desert of Snow", while a vague area to the east and south, stretching past the Honors in the south, and then higher to the east of them, was marked "Desert of Sand". To the west, stretching from the Northern snowy mountains, all the way south past the edge of the Town itself, very high mountains were marked, and named simply "Unknown Lands". At the edge of the map in the south, and vaguely indicated in the far west, was the title "Great Sea". The map was purported to be for the Dignus himself. Teq noted that nobody who worked on it ever had to scrape down their work at the day's end. Each mark was perfect. He sighed for the day when his own work would be as good.

It was fascinating to Teq that the Great Sea was designated. Seas were known to him only as the stuff of legend: the beginning place, "from which all life began". The beginning myths were full of tales of the Great Seas. "And the sun burned upon the waters until those crushed by the depths rose to greet the light. And they crawled out upon the land, so that their limbs split apart from their bodies, and they could stand and grasp at living things which were plants. These they tasted and learned that they could live upon the land and that it was the proper thing. So they spurned the waters...", that sort of thing, chanted by rote by all the youngs of the Honor. He had never actually believed that such things as seas existed. They were said to be deeper than the rift, splashing water higher than the trees when they were angry, and wider "than the eye could behold". It had all seemed most improbable. Now that he was trapped inside the Town, he desperately longed to seek out the Great Sea and see it for himself. He asked the Competent if anyone had actually seen it, and was told his business was to copy, not query. He wanted to ask how any map could be made without a seeking, but he held his tongue. He was still working on fitting in with the group, though not succeeding very well. At least the rule of silence in the workroom was immutable.

And, of course, there was his agenda to be considered. As he drew each part of the Town, starting at the center and working outwards, he committed each quadrant to memory in exact detail. Where mistakes were made and he had to repeat his work, part of the value lay in committing the streets and buildings to memory. To reinforce both his work and his memory, he would go each free afternoon, to walk the streets he had been copying. He intended to know this Town as well as he had known every inch of the Honor.

When he came upon the Builders' Hall he began to search for Vork in the area. It was the Barracks of the green shirts he had hoped to reach first, to look for Galt, but he had not been looking where he was going, so he came among the gray shirts first. Builders wore gray. The dinner hour was approaching and he was hungry from his long afternoon spent walking around the Town. He watched as the gray shirts began to converge upon their eating house and followed them. He had a vague plan that he could intercept Vork and they could eat together. The Builder apprentices converged upon the Grain Barrel, at the sign of a huge vat with grain spilling from it. Teq placed himself in what, he hoped, was an inconspicuous corner, and waited. With any luck, Vork would arrive alone or on the fringe of a group, so that Teq could attract his attention without making himself too obvious.

The smell of baking bread overlaid by roasting meat was reaching out and stirring his stomach. He was really hungry. He told himself sternly that he had been hungrier on the journey, when it was necessary to catch, kill, gut and pluck or skin the meat before it could be cooked. His stomach gave a mighty rumble.

"Rude as well as ugly, isn't he?" said a voice from behind him. He had planned, with his back against a wall, that there would be no way that anybody could creep up behind him. He spun round. He was wrong. A slit between the Grain Barrel and the next building was actually an opening into an alley, which was, incidentally, missing from the map. Two large gray shirts were easing their way out of the alley.

"Lost your way? Didn't think mappies would have a problem reading a map, did you?" asked the second.

"No. I came here on purpose. Got a problem with that?" Teq flared before he had the sense to guard his tongue. "Er... I came looking for a friend," he amended lamely.

"Friend?" roared the first. "I don't think he'd be likely to find a friend here. What do you think?"

He was addressing a group of gray shirts which had by this time gathered round.

Teq decided not to be intimidated. "We came to the Town together," he shouted, just as loudly as the gray shirt. He knew that if he showed any sign of weakness or fear, he would be lost. "His name is..." As he spoke Vork's name, the blast from the dinner horn sounded, and the name was lost.

"Don't know anybody here named honk. Do you?" jeered a voice from the crowd.

"Oh, let me through." Teq decided things were getting unpleasant, and retreat would be the better part of valor. He still hoped he might catch a glimpse of Vork in the crowd. He scanned them as he pushed forward.

"Mind who you're pushing," yelled a voice.

"Pushed you, did he?" called another. A hand shoved at him, hard. He fell against someone's shoulder.

"Shove me, would you?"

No more words. They set upon him, pushing him from hand to hand as he got angrier and angrier. He shoved back.

Which was, of course, the signal they had been waiting for. With a joyous roar they laid into him. Teq fought hard. He was big and he was angry. He was, in fact, much angrier than he knew. His fury at allowing himself to be led to and trapped inside this Town was every bit as enraging as allowing himself to get into this predicament here. The anger lent strength to his fists, and he laid about him with as much joy as the gray shirts. Of course there were far too many of them. He was ready to concede as soon as he had fought his way to the edge of the crowd. He could bolt with a blackened eye and a bloody nose, but his honor intact. But at that moment reinforcements arrived from the game courts. They carried staves.

He grabbed one of their staves in the first of the new fight, and bloodied a few of them before they beat him unconscious. As is the way of fights, the whole incident had taken very little time. It had reached the point where some of the apprentices were becoming disturbed at the unresponsiveness of Teq's downed body, when the innkeeper came to see what all the todo was about, and sent one of his servies to get the Watch. Alarm silenced the crowd, and they allowed the innkeeper to order them inside the Grain Barrel, leaving Teq lying inert in the street.

Consciousness returned unwelcome. There was no part of Teq's body which did not scream in response to merely thinking about it. A tiny part of his clenched mind allowed him to register sound. With an enormous effort he translated it: the tramping feet of the approaching Watch. There was something menacing in the sound. Something he should fear. The fear was atavistic. His body cringed with the certainty that the arriving Watch would beat him again. Logic had no part in it. His body was sure. It took every scrap of his will, but he got his body to move. He could neither stand nor crawl at that point. He rolled. The dusk had almost reached the point of calling itself night. Both eyes were swollen shut, which didn't help him to see, either. The aberration of the unmapped alley came back to him, and he rolled into it. Pain flared in any part of his body which touched a solid object, but he found his way into the alley, mostly by the absence of an impeding wall. It struck him as funny that he was being saved by an alley which wasn't there, according to the Mapmakers' Hall. He opened his mouth to giggle and vomited instead. Silently and wretchedly. Whatever remained of the day's food, left his stomach in painful sourness. He did not feel any better.

The regimented footsteps of the Watch stopped at a sharp, but incoherent, command. The door of the inn creaked open, and they tramped inside. Teq felt as if his hearing was enhanced, so that his ears were seeing what was happening in there. How long would it be before the Watch heard whatever story was being told about him, and came out to find him? He was desperate not to be found. It seemed to him, that if he were simply gone, the incident would be forgotten. If he were captured by the Watch, there would be endless repercussions. He had no idea what. He was still operating on the instinctive level. Using his bruised and swollen hands, he climbed upright against the wall of the inn, one unsure grip at a time.

There were no bones broken. He could walk if he leaned hard enough against the wall. And all the streets had walls to lean on. It took the entire night to negotiate the streets back to his own. Crossing them became a major challenge, and often involved crawling. He could now do that as well as he could walk. There were times when he was certain he could go no farther, and he leaned helpless and weeping - yes, weeping - against some house. It was a fortunate thing that he could find a route which passed no Pleasure Houses, wine shops or inns. These were the only places of activity in the evenings. Later on, the whole Town was so quiet that he could hear the challenges the Guard made to one another on the distant walls. The only thing of which he remained certain, was that he must not be found and questioned by the Watch. All the way back, he worried at this problem. Sooner or later, somebody was going to want to know how he got into this state. No answer occurred to him, other than the truth, and that would not do.

In the first glimmering of dawn, he reached the Mapmakers' Hall. He was finally defeated by the ladder. There was no strength left in him to climb to his bed. He curled himself up and lay down at its foot, finished.

The first apprentices to tumble out of bed, found him there. Two of them shot down the ladder at first light, to relieve themselves, and then be first at breakfast.

"By the Sky, look at Teq," cried the first. "Is he alive?"

The second one poked at him and repeated the question. "Are you alive?" he asked.

He was answered with a groan. Slowly, with infinite caution, Teq unrolled. The full glory of his swollen and multi-hued face was revealed.

"I'll get the Competent," gasped one, and dashed off. He was answered by another groan. Teq was really trying to tell him not to, and to ask them to help him up the ladder instead. But words would not come out. He would have to practice making understandable sounds through his thickened lips.

Competent Gaveril was furious, almost to the point of incoherence, when he arrived. "What's this? Where have you been? What have you been doing? You have been fighting..." He gasped. "The Master will have to be informed of this. Have you nothing to say for yourself?"

Teq had been practicing trying to speak. With immense pride, the answer to the question he had been pondering all night, came to him. It was perfect!

"Battle staves," he forced out between swollen lips. And then he attempted to grin, because it was not a lie.

Chapter 16

Galt accepted his leather collar as if by right. Well, it was by right. He had fought and won every challenge, and there had been some good ones. He was the conqueror. He was the first captain to have achieved the rank without first having fulfilled the role of sergeant. And in less than two years from his arrival in the Town! The men were impressed, enthusiastically, and so were the Chiefs, with perhaps less enthusiasm.

From the very beginning it had been Galt's intention to rise rapidly in rank. Camaraderie in the barracks was all well and good, but he had been the Sieur of an Honor and he was in the habit of command. It took more of an effort of will to mingle with the men and not run foul of the sergeants, than it did to make challenges for his promotion. In fact, he had been too busy with the consequent battles and preparing for them, to bother to bring himself to notice in order to make sergeant.

On the other hand, he had taken care to win the friendship of the men, both guards and hunters, before he made his first challenge. He bought drinks and told stories, which he did well. He had a large number of anecdotes from his Wilder days, which he told with humor and dramatic flair. Soon, the men were buying him drinks to get him to tell his tales. They especially wanted to hear tales of the women from his time in the Honor, but this he refused to do. He remembered Marisel's dignity and Tarabeth's grace and intelligence, and he would not betray them to titillate these men. But he was still popular, so that when he won his first fight, there was enough of a group to bet on him and cheer him on. As he fought his way up the hierarchy of challenges, the group grew larger. By the time the Chiefs awarded him his collar, the Barracks of the green shirts was filled with cheering men.

"Come and sit with us, Captain," Kambar said. "You need to know about your squad. We will assign you men enough. Do you understand your new duties? Come. Fill a cup and tell us what is on your mind."

"The Chiefs do me honor," Galt responded with a bow, and poured a cup of the fiery drink not available in the common inns and wine shops. "Do you have a task in mind for me?" He sat down on the bench at their table and took a swallow of his drink.

It was night and cold. Great fires burned in the hearths at either end of the hall. Chiefs, captains and sergeants had tables at one end. The great mass of the green shirts gathered at the other. Some games of dice were starting up and the noise level at the men's end of the hall was enough to shout down the smoke from the rafters.

"Captains and their squads rotate duties hunting the outside and warding the walls, as you know. You and your squad will be added to the roster. Surely you have served at both," Chief Fergin said.

The three Chiefs were of equal rank and reported only to the Dignus. They ranked with the Masters and Master Merchants. They together comprised the Great Council. Among the Chiefs, Kambar controlled the hunters, and Fergin commanded the security of the walls and their guard. Sedemp was much older than the other two - a contemporary with the Dignus - and in reality his voice counted for more. They deferred to him because of his age, and because he had the ear of the Dignus. Officially his command was the peace within the Town. In fact, when such peace-keeping was needed, Sedemp called upon either Fergin or Kambar to provide him with a squad to handle it. Wall Guards watched within as well as without the walls for signs of disturbance. There had been few times of crisis within the walls since the great uprising which brought the Dignus to power. Nothing had ever caused a threat from without.

Galt spoke, looking from Kambar to Fergin, with a worried frown flickering at the corners of his eyes. "I have been thinking, Chiefs, and I wonder if you would care to hear what is on my mind."

"This is your night, Captain." Fergin smiled. "Speak, then."

"Yes, speak," Kambar agreed.

"I know I have been in the Town a very short time. Less than two years. Yet in that time I have noticed a growing disorder in the streets. My squad has been called upon to respond to disorder with increasing frequency. Too many men are congregating outside the Pleasure Houses at night, without enough credits to enter. Gangs of apprentices roam farther abroad from their own quadrants after the games, as if seeking trouble. Disorder is not yet beyond handling. Yet it has seemed to me that such a thing is waiting to happen. To get out of hand."

"And what are your thoughts on solving such a problem, did it truly exist?" Sedemp asked quietly. "Do not just state a problem. Offer a solution which we may consider."

"I thought of a specially trained guard - a Watch - dedicated to peace-keeping within the Town. There could be four or five sergeants with their corps, reporting to a captain. The corps would take turns patrolling the Town, day and night, ready to get to a trouble spot very quickly. A simple summoning system could be contrived with torch or pennant or horn. This squad would be specially trained to keep the peace among equals. They would be specialists, not overtired hunters or guards. I know I am a newcomer here, and it is probably a foolish idea..."

"You would wish to be that captain yourself, Captain Galt, I assume," Sedemp offered.

"That would be something only the Chiefs could judge, Chief Sedemp. It would be presumptuous in me to suggest, especially as I have held the rank of captain for less than an hour." He grinned at them, disarmingly. "And yet, sirs, I do have ideas as to how that training might be carried out. But, I am as fond of hunting as I am of battle training, so whatever your decision I will be content. All the work a captain may do is of interest to me."

"I find such diplomatic answers wearying," Kambar said brusquely. "Do you want such a job or not?"

"I could do it. The idea is mine. Nonetheless, it is as the Chiefs decide."

"Just so," said Fergin. "Now, we were discussing your squad. I have newly made two sergeants among the Guard. I will spare you one of these, and a veteran. They will each bring a corps of six men. Can you do the like, Kambar?"

"I had intended two sergeants, yes. Two of mine are constantly bickering with one another. I shall be glad to cede you one of these, as well as a new made. Six men each, of course. So, Captain Galt, your squad is complete. Do you have any questions?"

"If the Chiefs permit, when will the allocations be announced? When may I meet my allotted sergeants?"

"I would prefer you make your own choices among mine: one sergeant among the veterans, and one of the new made. Come here at the noon break tomorrow. You may choose then," Fergin told him.

"Mine are already assigned and informed," Kambar said. "You have been allotted the lower floor at the western end of the Barracks for your squad. They are already moving in. You will wish to move your own quarters over there immediately, no doubt. Comments?"

"Only to Chief Fergin. With your permission I will select between the two new made, but would prefer the veteran to volunteer."

"Very well."

"I will also attend at the noon hour," Sedemp murmured, so quietly that Galt had to strain to listen to him. "At that time I will tell you your assigned task."

Galt was fairly certain he would get the peace-keeping job he wanted. He liked the idea of reporting to Sedemp, who was undoubtedly the most intelligent among the Chiefs. Chiefs were appointed by the Dignus from among the Captains, and they were not all chosen for the same qualities. Kambar was a ruthless hunter of both game and women. His men obeyed him through a mixture of fear and respect. Fergin was a man of fixed regimen: a loyalist and traditionalist. He insisted on a rigid discipline among his men and exact attention to detail. He was not an innovative man. Sedemp was a thinker, on the other hand. Galt had been planning for a long time to come up with a scheme to place himself within Sedemp's sphere of control. He thought he had achieved that. Now he needed to leave before he lost the advantage.

"Your health, Chiefs." Galt raised his cup and drank to them. Then he bowed low to them all. "With your permission I will leave before that game breaks up, and settle myself in my new quarters."

"You are excused," Kambar responded.

At the next day's meeting, Galt's hopes were confirmed. Sedemp had presented his idea to the Dignus, and arranged for Galt to set up the Watch, reporting directly to himself. Sedemp had also managed to put together a fifth corps, using a disgruntled sergeant and six trouble makers culled from among both hunters and guards. Galt took them and scattered them among the other corps, giving the new sergeant sturdy veterans to command. And then he trained them all.

Normally, the game courts were not in use during the working days. They were now. Galt marched his squad from one court to another in double time, through every street in the Town, until they knew every building in every street as well as a mapmaker. At first the men of the Town were amused, and laughed at the obvious strain this put on the despised green shirts. Gradually, as they began to run the streets with ease, carrying their arms easily as they did so, they gained the respect of other men. They became known. Recognized. More important, they became known as the Watch.

When they had run the streets and arrived at the game court, they trained. They worked with battle staves in one, at archery in another, using the hurling targets. There was obstacle running in a third, and tactical response in the fourth. Any of these, or all of these, on any day. And at night they were tested on dealing tactfully with a rioting mob: learning to calm and not to incite. To quell trouble, rather to join in with it and make it worse.

Gradually Galt built their skills. On free days, they challenged guards or hunters to try their skills against them. As they began to win consistently, their pride grew. They became both envied and respected by their peers. And respected by the Town. They were now the Watch.

By the spring they were taking regular patrols, and their training had become maintenance. Veterans among the guards were applying for vacancies, leaving the tedium of the walls for new arrivals. Fergin took note and began to urge his captains to increase morale among the Guard. Kambar took note and pressed his hunters even harder. The Watch was now the setter of standards.

This, then, was the Watch called by the innkeeper to settle the battle of the gray shirt apprentices versus Teq, the mapmaker's apprentice.

The sergeant reported back to Galt, laughing a bit. "That innkeeper was furious with those apprentices, and furious we couldn't find the supposed cause of it all. He took a while sending for us, because he didn't want to upset the gray shirts who was already inside his place by getting their pals into trouble. If it hadn't been that he was afraid the Guard would alert us before he did, he wouldn't have called us at all. You can bet on that, sir."

"So what was happening? What did you find?" Galt asked.

"Nothing at all. Bunch of builders' apprentices bashed about, but half of that could've happened in the game court. Everyone was as sober as you please, sitting at tables making believe they was eating. Somebody must've warned them the Watch was sent for, so they gave up and went inside. Probably the innkeeper hisself told 'em. There was teeth missing, and noses bleeding, and blackened eyes aplenty. Just no reason for it. Must've been fighting among theirselves." The sergeant chuckled. "You should've heard the story they told us, sir."

"Tell me, then, and I will." Galt was all patience. This was one of his two older sergeants, and Galt knew he had to tell his tale in his own way. He was a good sergeant, and tended to be indulgent with apprentice set tos.

"They was telling me as how this one, huge apprentice from the mapmakers, said he was there looking for a friend. Likely, isn't it, sir? One lone apprentice going to another guild inn on a free afternoon after the games! What they think we'll believe... I reckon there was some wager among theirselves that got them started, then they thought up this story after they knew we was on the way, Captain."

"Did you search?" By now Galt had pretty much guessed who had been there. And why.

"Oh, yes, sir. We had to make it look like we was ready to believe them. Didn't find no mapmakers, though. Commended the innkeeper for calling us, and gave the usual lecture to the lads, then came on back to report. End of tale." The sergeant chuckled again.

"Yes. Well done, sergeant. Tell the men. Good report. Now, who will be attending the Deployment of Women, tomorrow? I called for an extra corps to be there. Did you draw the assignment, sergeant?"

"Yes, Captain. E corps has been guarding them ever since they was brought in, and A corps takes over for the night. It's been a long time since we got new women, eh Captain? Not since you've been here. Could mean trouble, all right. And then, with a captain and not a chief doing the allocating... I believe you're right to expect a problem, sir. I'll be there, and my men will know what to do. Don't you worry, Captain."

"Well, Chief Kambar would do it if he were here. Chief Fergin did order them brought in after gate-closing time, though, and that was wise. There would have been trouble then if the confraters were still out on the streets. As it was we had the women under cover before anyone knew they were here. Report to me here in the morning. I'll go with you to attend the Deployment."

The sergeant took his men off to eat, and Galt went in search of food himself. His mind was churning. So Teq had gone in search of Vork, had he? Silly boy. Surely he'd been here long enough to know that he'd get nothing but trouble for his pains. What did he expect? Galt had been so involved in settling his own life in the Town, that he'd given little thought to his two journey companions, once he'd found out from Kambar they'd been accepted as apprentices. He'd thought they'd both be as involved with their new lives, as he was. Surely Teq had made friends among his fellow apprentices by now. What did he want with Vork?

Galt decided he'd better go and find out. It was far enough to the Matted Vine, but he knew that was where the mapmakers ate, and of course, he knew where the inn was. As Captain of the Watch, he was familiar with every inn in the Town, and its reputation for the quality of its food.

Inns and Pleasure Houses were places where most of the trouble his Watch attended to, started. Pleasure Houses were especially vulnerable at this time. It was so long since new women had been brought into the Town that the Houses were nearly emptied. Most of the Pleasure House women had become pregnant, one after another, and had been bought as wives. The remaining women were too well used. Too well known. Worse: there was now a large number of young women still serving at the inns who should have been made available to fill the Pleasure Houses, but there were no servies to replace them. The innkeepers kept them drab, so that they would pass unnoticed, most of the time. A few, however, had been the cause of trouble. The Watch was called, but when they saw the reason for the trouble, even his own men had become restless. Only the sergeants had the use of the Houses, though veterans among the men could earn enough credits to buy a home of their own, and hence a wife. The remainder had access to none, and were getting hard to control. This new infusion of women was large, thank the Sky and the Earth (and Kambar). They would ease a lot of the tensions.

Galt was really hungry by the time he reached the area of the Matted Vine. A captain could eat anywhere, but he rarely came this far to satisfy his hunger. He hoped he'd find Teq there, still eating, though it was getting late now. The boy must have run off from the melee with the gray shirt apprentices, very sensibly. He'd be a bit battered, no doubt, and would have taken his time getting back here.

Galt reached the Matted Vine and opened the door on an uproar. Everyone was shouting at once, it seemed. Apprentices were bolting their food, trying to both eat and get out of there. Everyone else was yelling, in particular the innkeeper. One apprentice finished eating and tried to slip out of the door. Galt grabbed him.

"What's going on?" he roared above the bedlam.

"One of the servies has disappeared, Captain," the apprentice gulped, as soon as he took in Galt's green shirt and leather collar. "Word arrived about the new women just a little while ago. The innkeeper sent the girl off to clean up, so he could take her over to be kept with the other women, to be ready for tomorrow's Deployment. She was old enough to go to a Pleasure House, sir, you see. His wife went looking for her after a bit, and she'd gone. The servie, I mean. Now the innkeeper is shouting about one of us apprentices who was always talking to her. He hasn't been in for his food tonight, and the innkeeper's saying they've run off together. He wants one of us to get the Competent. Not me!"

"Run off with an apprentice?" Galt was astounded. "Surely no apprentice would dare. And where would they go?"

"This one is fairly new. Well, he's been here less than three years. And to tell the truth, he's not much like the rest to of us."

"What's his name?" Galt asked, suspicious now.

"Teq, Captain," the apprentice replied.

Chapter 17

The arrival of the intake of women had kept Galt busy creating duty rosters and chasing all over the Town to warn the Watch to be especially vigilant, before the news of the fight at the Grain Barrel came his way. And now the missing servie! The depth of his concern about Teq surprised even himself. It was really the first time he had considered the boy since he had entered the Town and set about improving his own condition with such single mindedness. If he considered Teq or Vork at all, it was to consider that the proscribed life of an apprentice left him little cause for worry. That they must obey their Competent and Master in all things, was so little different from obeying the matrons of the Honor as to be routine. There would be the trade to learn, and the ways of the Town. Quite enough, one would have supposed, to hold their interest. There would be friends to make, besides, and loyalties to establish. What else would a boy need? That there might be any difficulty in settling in was a matter which never occurred to him. They had all come to the Town voluntarily, after all. They should be interested in settling in. In fact, he had once seen Vork, immediately recognizable by his peculiar walk. He was in the midst of a large group of gray-clad apprentices, en route to watch and cheer at a game court. Vork had not seen Galt, but he had looked cheerful and involved with his peers. What, then, was the matter with Teq? To do something as major as running off with somebody else's property was serious, even if Galt did understand why somebody would want to.

When Galt got to the Mapmakers' Hall from the Matted Vine, he found Teq curled on the floor at the foot of a ladder leading to the upper floor. He was seemingly insensible to the invective being hurled at him by a competent Gaveril, wasn't it? A few other brown-shirted apprentices were hanging about, listening with apparent amusement. The arrival of the Watch Captain merely spurred Gaveril to greater efforts. That the Watch had had to be called to his Hall! In a nutshell, it seemed that Teq had completely failed to fit in to the proper mold of apprentices, in every area except his ability to make maps. There was no sympathy in the amusement of the other boys. Galt later discovered that Teq's skill as a mapmaker was actually exceptional, which was why Master Kinnasen would hear nothing against him. But he was the despair of the Competent. He had wanted to vent all this anger for a long time, but Teq had not given him enough excuse to explode. Now he had. Fighting with other apprentices was totally improper behavior - though normal enough, as Galt knew.

"It is unacceptable, Captain," Gaveril was telling Galt. "Quite unacceptable. His punishment will have to be considered by the Master. It is beyond me, to determine, but I will advise the Master to make it severe. He will probably leave it to me in the end. This is not the first time I have warned this apprentice about going his own way."

"Well, corporal punishment would be redundant, eh, Competent?" Galt asked. "We had better get this lad into bed, so that he can heal well enough to be punished. What do you say?"

"I don't see how that is to be accomplished. He is cluttering up the work room lying there, and yet, I have no idea how to get him up the ladder. He is so... large."

"I'll carry him myself, if he's not too broken," Galt offered. "Up then, lad."

Galt's fingers explored Teq's body for broken bones before pulling him to his feet. There were none. Just enough bumps, swellings and bruises to stiffen his body into pain all over, and render it totally immobile by the morning. Both eyes were swelled shut, so that even had Teq been fully awake, Galt would have been no more than a blur. He knew Galt was there, but the loud and angry voice of the competent had made his body decide not to move so much as the flicker of an eyelid. He said not a word.

But when Galt threw him over his shoulder, Teq let out a groan. "Serve you right," Galt said into his ear, as he balanced his way up the ladder.

"Which bed?" Galt demanded.

One of the gathered apprentices shinned up the ladder and pointed the bed out, fascinated to see the Captain of the Watch carrying one of their own.

"Bring water, lad, and wash some of the blood off him. At least the bits that you can see." Galt climbed back down the ladder. "One thing, Competent Gaveril, they are accusing the apprentice, down at the Matted Vine, of having run off with a missing servie. Didn't come to dinner, you see. That's what I came here to check into. Well, it's clear enough he had nothing to do with that. His fight took place with the Builders' apprentices, over in their quadrant. It puts the lad in the clear on the matter of the missing servie. He was very well occupied at the time when she ran off. Now you are free to take care of him, and I can look into that matter. I'll be back to see him another day to ask my questions about the fight. No point trying now, or in haranguing him either. He can't hear us. Good evening to you."

And Galt left. He returned to the Matted Vine. He thought he might as well eat at last, so he asked food of Famal, the innkeeper there, while he explained why Teq could not have been involved in the matter of the missing servie, Athirra. Famal was so delighted that his problem was being looked into by the Captain of the Watch himself, that he outdid himself with the food he offered. Galt was very well satisfied, and feeling much more mellow by the time he left.

With all this uproar, the matter of the new intake of women didn't cross Galt's mind again until he was almost back at the Barracks. He could hardly ignore them, though. They were his responsibility. With a great sigh of weariness he walked over to the Central Square, where so much of the heart of the Town was situated. The lake lay tranquil in the near darkness of the night, lit by fitful moonlight and the torches of the Watch. On one side of the square loomed the mass of the Dignus' Palace, totally dark now. On another side lay the enclave where chiefs and masters had their houses. Opposite that was the Main Market. Behind it lay the women's barracks. The fourth side, opposite the Palace, lay open, so that the confraters could gather, with only the lake between them and their Dignus.

Galt arrived at the square, just as a corps of the Guard was marching in. His own Watch sergeant was gathering his men, it seemed, ready to face off with them.

"What is it, sergeant?" Galt asked, as the Watch sergeant halted his men.

"We're the ones has the duty here, sir. We wasn't expecting no Guard corps. Thought I'd better check out what they was doing here."

"Yes, well, thank you, sergeant. Very efficient. I'll see to it now that I'm here." Galt walked over to the Guard corps. "Sergeant?" he asked.

"Chief Fergin sent us down to see there's no trouble, Captain."

"Very well. Will your captain be coming here?"

"No sir. The Chief ordered us here hisself. The captain's at the wall same as always."

"Good. Then we can divide the duty. It will be most valuable. I had been concerned how I might cover the area adequately with just one corps. Convey my gratitude to Chief Fergin when you report. The Watch corps will continue to cover the barracks themselves since they are already in position. You deploy your men around the square in case we get unwanted visits from overeager Townsmen during the night. Order your men to stop them. Don't use force unless you have to. Any questions?"

"No, sir."

Both sergeants saluted and turned to their men, ready enough to snarl at one another if they had to protect their territory, but glad enough to have authority there to avoid the necessity.

Galt waited until all the men were in place. He chatted a while with each sergeant, giving instruction and praise in equal doses, until he was sure that any disturbance would not come, at least, from the green shirts.

When he got back to the Barracks it was well past midnight. He was ready to groan with exhaustion. A message awaited him from Chief Sedemp. He was to meet the Chief at his house at dawn. Galt groaned indeed. He left orders that he was to be awakened in four hours with a hot beanbrew drink and good bread, then crashed on to his bed like a tree falling to a Wilder ax.

Apprentices were not permitted at the Distribution of Women. That was one less hazard of disturbance. Every other confrater was bound to be there. There was plenty of room in the square to accommodate them, but there was certain to be, at very least, jostling for the best views.

Galt got to the square in time to see the two corps which had been on duty all night, relieved. He wanted to reinforce the rules with each of the duty sergeants before he called on Sedemp. This time he placed the Watch corps to guard the entrances to the square, and placed the Guard corps at the women's barracks. It was rapidly growing light, and the people would soon be gathering. He wanted to be sure of keeping the peace. He trusted the training he had given the Watch to be more apt for avoiding confrontations. And anyway, the Guard Captains would be in charge of the Distribution itself. His role was all in peacekeeping.

Early as it was, Sedemp was ready for him. "Ah, Captain. All is calm? Good, good. We are expected at the Palace."

"The Palace, Chief?"

"Yes. It will be your first meeting with the Dignus, will it not? We are much of an age, he and I, but his responsibilities have been heavier. Responsibilities are aging, Captain. Remember that."

"Yes, Chief. Is there a special reason for this meeting?"

"Naturally. The Dignus will explain it, should he choose to. I have left word that the Distribution will not begin until our return. The Captains will do the preliminary sorting, and assure that the bidders who are placed near the platform have sufficient credits. I believe both of my fellow Chiefs will be there for the actual Distribution, after all. Any news of the missing servie?"

"Not yet, Chief. Where can she go? We will do a door to door search for her if necessary; but no wife would take her in to compete for her husband's attention and resources, nor any innkeeper in deference to Famal of the Matted Vine. The Pleasure Houses are presumably the places she is trying to avoid. I think we have only to wait for the first really cold night, and we'll have her. The cold will drive her into the open. You can safely leave the matter with me, Chief."

"It had better be so. We cannot have some slip of a girl outwitting the Watch."

"I have it in hand, Chief."

"Yes. Good, good." They had been walking as they spoke. Galt veered to the side door of the Palace, where activity could be seen as servies came and went, but Sedemp took him by the arm. "We enter the Palace through the front door, Captain. You are with me."

The Palace's only distinctive feature was a central tower, rising three floors above what was otherwise a two floored structure. It was built on slightly higher ground than the rest of the square, so that the view was panoramic, even from the front door. Activity in the square was stepping up, now that it was fully light, and Galt could see the platform that had been built in front of the women's barracks yesterday, where the Main Market's stalls were usually placed.

Through the front door of the Palace, the two men entered a square hallway, with arches leading into dimly lit rooms, on three sides. A stair rose before them. It was a confusing layout, probably intentionally. If some undesirable broke into the Palace in search of the Dignus, he would have no idea which way to go. Each archway had been built narrow, and easy to defend. Even a large company could be held off by a few men. Again Galt wondered, who did these Townsmen fear? Themselves? Each other?

A silent, stately woman, well on in years, appeared dramatically in one of the archways. Without saying a word, she led them through a maze of small rooms, whose purposes were unclear, except, possibly to confuse. They were all furnished alike, with scattered chairs and tables.

The room where they ended up was just such another, overheated by an immense fire. A very wide chair was placed facing it, and with its back to the entrance. Sedemp led the way round the chair, so that he and Galt had their backs to the fire. The woman remained in the doorway, and startled Galt by clapping her hands twice. Two barely clad young women rose from either side of the bent figure in the chair, and went to stand with her.

Sedemp bowed low before the chair, and Galt followed his example. This little wizened creature must be the Dignus. He was wrapped all about in a rich cloak, as if he were suffering from severe cold. Only a nose, long and thin, appeared above the cloak's folds. , and a crown of wispy, gray hair.

Still bowed, Sedemp spoke. "This is the Captain of the Watch, Dignus. Captain Galt."

"Hm. Ha," said the Dignus, and emerged from the cloak far enough to spit into a cloth he raised to his face. "You've been a Sieur, I'm told," he said in a surprisingly strong voice. He chuckled. "Lucky fella, ha, hm." He spat again. "What do you think of those two?"

"Dignus?" Galt was bent over uncomfortably. What was more it was very hot by the fire. His face was getting red and he was sweating hard. Worst of all, he had no idea what the Dignus was talking about.

"Oh stand up," the Dignus said irascibly. "The females. The females! What do you think of them? Take a good look. No touching, mind. Hm,ha."

Both Galt and Sedemp straightened. "Er, very ripe, Dignus," Galt offered.

"Aha! Just what I say. Hm. Ha. Stout fella. What do you think, Sedemp? He'll do, eh? Hm. Ha."

"Admirably, Dignus."

"Too ripe. Quite right. Need younger. You get them for me. Dismiss. Ha,hm. Go along. That's all." The Dignus was sinking back inside his cloak after spitting once more. Then he reemerged. "Send those two back. Oh, and Galt. You may pick the House these two will go to. They've been good. Choose well. Ha. Hm." The last sound they heard of him as they were led away again by the silent woman, was of him spitting.

Galt disciplined his features with difficulty, not to show the disgust he was feeling. Now he understood Sedemp's oblique warning. Aged by responsibilities? Was that what this was? Well, he must antagonize neither the Dignus nor Sedemp, he supposed.

"Perhaps you would explain my commission, Chief," he ventured. "I am not absolutely clear about the Dignus' wishes."

Sedemp's voice was as calm as ever, but Galt detected an undercurrent of mild amusement. "You are to search among the women before the Distribution and select two of the youngest. He prefers the very young. Just at puberty. He's had those two a while. Seek among the released servies as well as the new intake. They are often softer. More docile. Less athletic. He needs a little plumpness, but not too much. You saw those two. He needs you to select for beauty and grace also, naturally. But above all, youth. Probably more than just two would be better. Then they can relieve one another."

"And their duties?"

"They are for his bed, of course. But he does require them all day now. He has servies enough. These keep him comfortable. Yes, at least four, I think, Captain. It will please him."

"Why me, Chief?" Galt asked bleakly.

"Your experience and your rank are suited to the task," Sedemp said quietly. "I have, in the past, performed this task myself. I recommended you. It is a signal honor."

"Ah," said Galt, unable to manage the thanks which seemed required.

Sedemp smiled.

The square was filling rapidly as they walked to the women's barracks. The other two Chiefs were waiting for them, apparently already aware of Galt's assignment.

"Be as quick as you can, Captain," Kambar said. "We don't want any restlessness out there because we are not prompt."

"But take care, and check them well," Fergin encouraged him. "Don't hurry through this. Are you planning to buy a servie for yourself? You are entitled to, you know. You could take one who would serve you until you choose to buy a wife. Go along, now."

Galt walked along inside the barracks, where the hunters who had brought the women in were standing guarding the sorted groups. Perhaps a dozen older women stood in one group, and twice as many girl children in another, some of them crying. Galt recognized that these were older girls: hunters in training. They would not have come from the children's rooms of an Honor. That they should come to this! For the first time he found himself thinking about the practices of the Town with regard to women, in a personal sense. Up to now he had had no cause to regard it. If he had thought about women at all, and considering his personal agenda he had given little time to it, it was to feel that there was good organization here. Now he looked and saw these women as if they were the women of Marisel's Honor. His own matrons and children. He was discomfited. Disgusted. Further than that he could not allow himself to think.

He passed to much the largest group of women: the young ones. It was heartbreakingly obvious which pretty faces and bodies would go to the better Pleasure Houses where they would be treated with care. He knew what the plain ones would inherit. Settling his mind to the task, he sought four who would suit the Dignus. For some reason his mind fled to the missing servie: Teq's friend. She would have been here. It was true that the servies were softer and plumper - and looked more docile. He began to understand why she had fled. She might have been chosen to serve the bed of that disgusting old man. Perhaps Teq had already understood something like that. Firmly he shut his mind. He must hurry.

In the end he selected five who looked as if they would fit the qualifications Sedemp had described. They also looked a little stupid, which was a qualification Galt had added himself. A little passive. Women to whom their new duties might be acceptable. He supposed there was a kind of status in it. In these five there was no spark of intelligence, or anger, or hatred, which he could see quite plainly among the others. He began to dislike this Distribution of Women.

Galt led his selections out for Chief Sedemp's approval. The Chief nodded, and Kambar chose a sergeant to lead them away to the Palace. No doubt he would return with the other two. Galt sighed.

Chief Fergin stepped out on to the newly erected platform, and stood waiting until a hush swept across the waiting crowd. The Distribution of Women was ready to begin.

Chapter 18

The children were brought out first. In many cases they were purchased in pairs, to fill the needs of inns. Galt found himself thinking that was a good thing. They would be less lonely. He had not expected to find himself thinking about these women at all. He found it troubling that he did so. The children would work hard, it was true, but they would be as warm and well fed as they would have been in an Honor. Indeed, young as they were, they would not yet have been hunting for long, and confinement within the Honor's walls would have prepared them better than their elders for this change in status. At least he supposed so. Mostly he was grateful for the loss of the weepers, if the truth be told. Innkeepers and their wives led the children away as soon as they were paid for, and there was a better sense of order to the proceedings. No wonder they handled the children first!

His attention was caught by his sergeant. "Hunter sergeant to speak with you, sir," he said.

Galt walked back into the women's barracks, where the Hunter Sergeant had a girl at each hand. They wore identical cloaks of some warm stuff. It was the way they stood there, unquestioning, impassive, which identified them. They had slipped his mind altogether.

"From the Palace. Sergeant?" he asked.

"Yes, sir. Exchanged them for five others you sent. The Dignus' woman didn't give us no credits for the difference. I got no answer when I spoke to her of it. What should I do?"

"Ah yes, I see. You'd better talk to Chief Sedemp about that. Perhaps you'd rather ask Chief Kambar to talk to him. I'll back you about the difference in numbers, of course. You can leave these two with me."

Not that he had any idea what he was going to do with them. He remembered that he was supposed to be finding them a good Pleasure House. As well as he knew where trouble was likely to start in the Town, he had no idea which Pleasure Houses were better places for the women to serve. Where they were treated the best. He led the two women to one side and warned the sergeant in charge to exclude them from the general showing. He told the women to wait where they were. He was certain they would not move a muscle until his return. He grinned to himself.

Galt looked out at the Pleasure House Keepers, obvious from their style of dress, grouped near the platform. The young women, new intake and servies interspersed, were being paraded on the platform now. Each had a number chalked on the breast of the shift they wore, so that potential bidders could plan where they wanted to place their bids.

To one side, a couple of veteran Guard Captains stood together, chatting. Galt knew them slightly. He'd been under the command of one of them for a while. He decided they were the best people to answer his question. If he told them the true reason for asking, he should get a straight answer.

"My respects," he began.

"Galt!" his old commander responded. "This has been pretty orderly so far. Congratulations, since this is your first Distribution. The last hazard will be getting this lot off to their new homes without incident. Have you planned for that?"

"I've been warned. I have three corps ready to act as escort. Nobody will be allowed to leave until a corps is ready to escort them."

"Good idea. They had escorts in pairs last time. It was barely adequate. The women were harassed every step of the way, and the Keepers unable to protect them. It reduces their value. And that was a small intake. Not like this one."

Galt nodded his appreciation to them. "I need your advice, gentlemen," he said. I have to place two young women, exchanged out of the Palace. The Dignus charged me to place them well, and I don't know one Pleasure House from another."

"What?" laughed the younger captain. "And you've been promoted for months now. There is a Pleasure House of boys, I'm told. Is that your preference?"

Galt forced himself to laugh. "No. Just been too busy. Anyway, it's not the sampling of the wares I'm talking about. It's how the Keepers treat their women."

The older one nodded. "Of course we know you don't want boys. Forgive my friend, here. We know you were a Sieur. Like your women exclusive, no doubt. That one over there, the flamboyantly dressed one, is Ruper. His women will do anything. The Wicked Woman is a very expensive place. Very fancy trappings inside.

"Yes, but the women look terrified whenever he enters the room. Stands to reason," the younger one put in. "They get abused a bit. People have funny tastes, some of them, and Ruper has never been known to refuse."

"That's true. That group on the left. They're the fancier House Keepers. You can tell by their clothes, and by how they separate themselves from the general run. You could use any of them. Lombro of the Silken Veil is the most decent. Where is he? Do you see him anywhere?" The captain turned to his younger colleague.

"That's odd. I don't see him. He's said to be kind to his women. They certainly act content enough when you visit the place."

"It's been a while since I bothered," the older one nodded as he spoke. "But that is his reputation. Funny he's not here. He's lost his women to wiving over the past few years like everyone else. He's bound to need some of these as replacements."

The bidding had begun. Galt watched the faces of the Keepers as they made their bids. The women were brought forward one by one, they were sold, and the credits of their new owners handed over to one of Fergin's sergeants. The names of the new owners were chalked on to the backs of the women's shifts as they were led back to the barracks to wait until they were claimed.

The trouble, from Galt's point of view, was that the bidders were doing what bidders always do. They showed no emotion on their faces while the sale was going on. The auctioneer was a Hunter Sergeant who was clearly experienced at what he was doing. Try as he might, Galt could get no clue as to which Keeper might be the best owner for the Dignus' women. Yet he must decide. He had watched Ruper. He was bidding on any young women who looked both pretty and bovine - not unlike the choices that Galt had made for the Dignus' use. He again felt a shudder at what he was being required to do.

The young women were all sold, and it was now the turn of the older ones. Galt had made up his mind that he would simply have to go and find this Lombro. He was the only Keeper for whom he had any reference at all. The crowds in the square were thinning out. Galt went to put his Watch corps on standby alert for escort duty, then wandered back to watch the final stage of the Distribution.

Among the older women was one who stood apart. She had an air about her, not easy to define. That was it! She had the habit of command. The other older women deferred to her. She was actually one of the oldest. Her hair was gray and her hands were bent, yet her back was straight and her eye clear. She was obviously a woman who had held high Council office. Galt watched her with interest. She reminded him a little of Marisel.

Her turn came up around the middle of the bidding. Her function, like that of the rest of these older ones, would be to clean houses. Possibly to cook and wash clothes. The ease or difficulty of the task would lie with the size of the house and the personality of the owner. The auctioneer had her turn herself fully around on the platform, and then display her hands. There were no bids.

And then Ruper called out from where he was paying the credits he owed. "I'll take the old hag. A couple of my servies are near to death. I could use another."

To his own astonishment Galt called out, "how much are you bidding?"

The interruption startled the auctioneer. It was not a normal thing to do. He was not pleased, but Galt was the Watch Captain who was running the Distribution. He said nothing in complaint. He simply repeated the question as if it had been his own.

"I've already spent most of my credits on the ones who'll earn them back." Ruper laughed unpleasantly. "Ten, then."

Not one of the young women had brought less than forty. Twenty was the average rate on the older women and children.

"Twenty-five," Galt called.

The auctioneer looked over at Ruper. He shook his head. "Done, then. To the Captain," and the woman had his name chalked on her back.

"Hardly a bargain," the younger of the two captains murmured to him. "She certainly won't serve you till you buy a wife. She's too old."

"Oh, she'll keep my stuff in order, without causing any disruption in the Barracks. I still live there," Galt answered carelessly. The truth was that he was stunned at what he had done. He had only saved up about a hundred and forty credits since he'd been in the Town, and the most modest house cost at least two hundred. He had hoped to buy a house and move out of the Barracks fairly soon. True his earning power had increased enormously since his promotion, but still... Idiot! He didn't even know where he was going to put her. She'd just have to share his quarters, he supposed.

While he was paying up, there was a ripple at the rear of the crowd. The pattern of the watchers was disturbed as if someone was pushing their way violently through to the front. The Distribution was so close to ending and the crowd so much thinner, that the jostling was being accepted good naturedly. All the same, Galt hurried through his payment and walked back to the Watch corps on guard around the platform to see what it was all about.

A battered looking man almost fell at his feet. His clothes were good, but muddied and torn. The man looked disheveled and spent, rather than badly hurt or drunk.

Keeping his feet with difficulty he gasped at Galt, "is the Distribution of the young women over?" He was looking over at the last of the older women as she was led forward, in a sort of despair.

"The Distribution of all the women is over," Galt told him. "Why weren't you here earlier if you were concerned? The whole of the Town knew it would be first thing this morning."

The man looked ready to weep, then composed himself. He straightened up and looked Galt in the eye. "You are the Captain of the Watch, sir? Captain Galt, isn't it? I wish to lodge a formal complaint."

"Go ahead. Sergeant." Galt called the Watch Corps Sergeant to his side. "Act as witness to a formal complaint, Sergeant," he ordered.

"Yes, sir."

"State your complaint."

"My name is Lombro. I am the Keeper of the Pleasure House, the Silken Veil. Last night I was abducted. Yes, abducted, from outside my own back door. It has always been my habit to step out there from time to time during the evening, to take the air. Last night ruffians were waiting for me. I am sure they were Keeper Ruper's men."

"Did you see their faces? Can you swear a complaint against these men from sure knowledge?" Galt asked with a certain eagerness. There was that about this Ruper and his reputation, he was beginning to dislike.

"No. I didn't really see them."

"Then how do you accuse Ruper?"

"Ruper is the only person in the Town who would do something like this to me. The only one who resents me. A judgment went against him in the past. Some Competent swore that Ruper had mistreated a woman, causing serious injury. Chief Sedemp reassigned her to me. I paid Ruper compensation for her. I don't know why he resented me for it. It was none of my doing. I had not asked for her. But ever since then, he has caused me trouble from time to time." Lombro's face twisted as if the thought of Ruper gave him a sour taste in his mouth.

"Did the abductors hurt you?" Galt asked.

"No. Not physically. They took me to an empty house near the waterfall. I didn't know that last night, as they put a cloth over my head and tied it tight. They tied me up loosely and left me there. It took me until now to get free. It was a filthy place, as you see."

"How did you free yourself?"

"I got the knots undone in the end, but it took all night. I don't think they intended to leave me there indefinitely. Just until the Distribution of Women was over. They have succeeded, obviously."

"But why would they do this to you?"

"Why? How can you ask why? The first Distribution of Women in more than two years and I get none for my House! What am I to do? Every other Keeper has replenished his women. Will any of them sell me even one? Only the worst, if any at all. It is my ruin, that I see here. My ruin."

"Can you take me to the place where they left you?" Galt asked, feeling sympathy for this man. It really was a vicious thing to have done to him. He liked the look of him. Except for when he was speaking his complaint, which was fully justified if true, his face was pleasant. Kindly. Certainly compared with those of the other Keepers. It suddenly struck Galt that this was the Lombro he had been looking for earlier. Where was his head today? This was the Keeper he had been planning to seek out. Of course. A solution for them both!

"Lombro." Galt interrupted as Lombro was answering his earlier question. "I think I can solve your problem, at least in part. The complaint we can work on tomorrow. The thing is, that I myself have two young women to dispose of. You can have them."

"You have? You have! How? Who? Where? Captain, this is unusual. How does it come about that they were not with the others? They are not pregnant? Ready for wiving?"

"No, no." Galt laughed. "They are those which were used by the Dignus and now exchanged for new. He charged me with finding them a proper House. I am told yours is well run."

"The Dignus! Oh yes, Captain, It is well run. Two, you say. Two! That will do me well. How much do I owe you, Captain? How can I repay you?"

"You can pay the Sergeant over there, at least forty credits each for them. You'd better hurry. He's closing up now. Here, I'll go with you and explain to Chief Fergin."

"And yourself, Captain. I will owe you something for yourself."

"No, nothing. I'll see to your complaint tomorrow. You can take me to this place where you were held, in the morning."

"But I am in your debt, Captain. I will owe you. Come to my House, free of charge, any time."

"No, I thank you. Let us say that you never know when I may need a favor. I'll call on you then. Now come along and pay, and then I can hand these two young women over to you."

"Oh yes, Captain. You have saved my life this day. Well certainly my livelihood. Whenever I can do something for you, just name it..."

They concluded the business, Lombro still gushing his thanks. Galt was glad enough to see him on his way, and certainly to rid himself of the burden of the Dignus' women.

And then he was free to collect his own purchase. Here was a thing he was going to have to think about.

Chapter 19

At the sign of the Carved Oak, the wife of the innkeeper had died. She had been sickly, even when he bought her, though she did give birth to a healthy son. But he was himself aging and going blind even then, and glad to afford any wife. They lived together twenty years, and for all that time she cooked and kept the place neat, but the inn was not aligned with any of the Guilds, so they made a poor living, at best. The old man alerted the Watch to her death, and wept a little as they carried her away for disposal, perhaps as much for his own loneliness and hopelessness as for her passing. His son was already established as a hunter. He was all alone. There was a small fire and he sat beside it, unmoving.

It was the night of the first bitter freeze of the season. Galt was on his way back to the Barracks. He'd been to see Teq, whose face was the color of sunset, but who was otherwise recovered, if chastened. It was nearly a week now since the Distribution of Women. They had talked while they ate at the Matted Vine. The excuse was that Galt was completing his investigation of the incident. Teq was long since cleared of complicity in the matter of the missing servie, by the very fact of the fight. He had been confined to the Hall and the Matted Vine for a week, by the Competent as punishment, and already he was beginning to chafe at the confinement, even though for the first couple of days he had been barely able to move.

He passed a bundle to Galt. "If you should find her..."

"Oh I'll find her," Galt assured him. "Nothing in this Town escapes me."

"Well all right, when you find her, could you give her these?"

"What are they?"

"My old trews and tunic from the Honor. They have no Guild color, you see. I thought she might be able to hide as a boy."

"Or be arrested." Galt grinned at him. "Oh, don't worry, boy. I shan't arrest her, but you'd better hope I'm the one that finds her. The whole Watch is looking for her. You're right about the clothes," he added, stowing them in his pack. It's a good thought. After that, there's still the problem of housing her."

114

"Perhaps she's already in a safe place," Teq suggested. "She could just stay there, only disguised as a boy. It makes no sense," he hissed angrily.

"What doesn't?"

"I had to run away from the Honor because I was a boy, and Athirra had to run away from the Town because she's a girl. A woman. If she could just get to an Honor..."

"Past the Wilder packs? Alone? In winter? You're dreaming. And who's to say any Honor would accept her. They're careful about blood lines, you know. And watch how you use her name around here. I'd better be off. I shan't come again. It would cause talk, and you're talked about enough already. We'll meet again for a meal at some independent inn one day soon. I'll get word to you. Keep your head down, boy."

Galt walked silently through the freezing night, glad to be wearing the cloak Tarabeth had made for him. He was preoccupied and somewhat irritated by his inability to find the servie, when he heard the scrape of a foot, loud in the cold dark. He stopped, still and silent, under the bleak branches of a tree outside an inn: the Carved Oak as he recalled. In the black silence he listened hard. He heard the scraping foot again, and the barely controlled judder of chattering teeth. The sounds came from over by the bins where the uneaten food would be thrown. Galt grinned to himself. This was the inn where the innwife had died that morning. No wonder the name had come to him so readily. There would be no food thrown out this night. He decided this would be the perfect time to check up on the old man.

Galt opened the inn door and pushed inside. A sullen fire burned red and ashy in the hearth. On the nearest bench the old man sat, his back to the table. His hands hanging limply in his lap.

"No food?" Galt called, loud enough for the sound of his voice to carry beyond the door.

After a long pause, the old man answered in a whispering voice. "I cannot see who is there. My wife died this morning. They have taken her away. Without her this inn will die. I will die. Leave us to do it in peace."

"That's no way to talk, old man." Galt walked over to him. "Here is timber. I will mend the fire. We will at least be warm."

He threw wood on the fire and watched it kindle. "Let me find ale for us," he said. "We will drink together to your wife's passing." He walked through into the back room, where stores were kept in every inn. Once there, he eased open the outer door and stepped quietly through. The firelight from within threw little illumination outside. Galt stood still, then heard again the slight sound of someone between the bins. With two silent-spaced steps he was there. He reached in, grabbed a wrist, and hauled the teeth chatterer out.

"You are Athirra," he said. "I've been looking for you for days. A week. Be still now. I am Galt. Teq's father."

She tried to say 'father' as a question, but her teeth were clenched so hard against the cold that she could not speak.

Without letting go of her wrist, Galt reached under his cloak and pulled out his pack. With one hand he found the bundle of Teq's clothes and thrust it at her. "Put those on," he told her.

She was too cold to argue, or attempt to run, even when Galt let go of her wrist so that she could dress. As soon as she'd done so, he took her hand and pulled her inside the inn. He took up three mugs and a cask of ale, and gestured for her to precede him into the main room.

"We can all use a drink of this ale," he spoke heartily to the innkeeper. "This boy and I have walked too far today to go another step. If there is food in this house he could cook it."

"There may be food." The innkeeper was indifferent. "I have not looked."

Galt stared hard at Athirra as he spoke. "Go and look, boy. See if there's something you could get us to eat. We're all cold and hungry. This good man's wife died today and he is blind. He can do nothing for himself or us. It would be good for us all to eat here. Are you warmed enough yet?"

Athirra's eyes widened, and she nodded. Even in the dim firelight, Galt could see she was a mess. The blood returning to her face and hands had them glowing scarlet. Returning to her feet, it made her clumsy. But her wits were not frozen and she could understand what Galt was trying to convey to her. And she was desperately hungry. Galt nodded at her and pointed to the back room.

There was food in the cupboards, and water could be pumped into a pail, right there inside the room. She made some shift to wash herself, her face and hands as cold as the water. She dried on the loose end of Teq's tunic. His clothes were not too bad a fit. She was a very tall woman, though slim and comely behind the grime. She found bread and cooked meat, bitter root and a basin filled with meat fat. She brought them over to the fire and spread the fat over the bread as she sliced it: then set the bread in a pan over the fire and the meat on top to warm through. The bitter root fried in the fat oozing from the bread. The smell was wonderful. There were wooden bowls and utensils still stacked on the tables. In a few minutes, she scooped out the food and piled it on three plates. They all three shoveled the food into their mouths without speaking. Galt had no trouble in eating his second dinner.

"That was good." Galt sat back from his plate and looked at Athirra. "You have a talent for cooking, boy." Then he clapped the old man on the shoulder. "I am Galt," he said, "and this is... Albet."

"Galt!" The old man started. "The Captain of the Watch?"

Galt grabbed Athirra's wrist even as he answered. She pulled against him, eyes wild, for a second, then gave up and sat still. "The same," he answered. "I am wandering about with this failed apprentice because I promised myself I would find a place to settle him before I slept, and I haven't done so yet." He laughed. "This boy is the most useless guard I ever took on. I pride myself in the picking of a good boy, but I was totally wrong about this one. He'll never make a guard! What is your name, old man?"

"I used to have another name, but they call me 'Corn'. They say I fell from the oak when it was young. The truth is that the innkeeper found me carving faces in the oak thirty years ago and took me in - to work off the damage, he said. I was always carving in those days. Carved all day long. Never did learn to cook. Couldn't wait to get back to the carving, and there was no innwife then. Innkeeper himself did all the cooking, even though he was an old man. They do say it was all that close work ruined my eyes. The carving. They've been getting worse for years now. When he died, he left me the inn. That day I renamed the inn and got me a wife. I was nearly blind even then, and I couldn't cook at all. She did it all. Now she's gone and I can do no more. I can hardly see which direction the firelight is coming from. Life is over for me. Well it's been good enough. Good enough." He sighed.

"Did she bear a child?"

"Aye, a boy. A good boy. Never made to be an innkeeper, though. Too restless. He's a hunter, Captain. Name of Chapra. Have you come across him? I sent word his mother died, but he's outside the walls. Too late to see her now. He comes around now and again. Now and again."

"Let me ask you straight," Galt said. "Could you use a boy to apprentice, Corn? He can cook. You just tasted it. And it would be doing me a favor to take him off my hands. Albet is a good boy, even if he is no guard. The inn would be a place for him. It's the only independent inn in the quadrant, isn't it? People like a change from the Guild places now and then. What do you say? Could you help me out? It would be better than dying?"

"Would it?" Corn asked. "I was fond of my wife. She worked till she dropped, caring for me and this place. She was never really well. Would an apprentice do as much? I owe her memory something. My death, I think. I had made up my mind to it."

"Everyone knew your wife was sickly, Corn. Albet here is young and fit, except for a bit of a cold." He grinned over at Athirra who was wiping her nose surreptitiously. "Would you look after Corn and the inn if I left you here?" He stared hard at her, making her look up at him. "A boy like you is too young to be abandoned by the Watch. But if you had a good place where you'd be warm and fed and could learn a trade, I could see fit to leave you alone. What about it?"

"I would," she answered clearly, and then mouthed "why?" at him.

"Is it a deal, Corn? Dying is a hard thing, all alone. The Captain of the Watch would be in your debt, and would stop by from time to time to see how you did."

"If the boy is willing, then I see no harm," Corn decided. "Starvation is a hard death, true enough, though I was meaning to. Wasn't I? You saw for yourself."

"Indeed I saw, and believe me, this is better. Shake hands, then, Corn, Albet. Now then, Albet will see you off to your bed. You are a fine man, and a strong man, and the Watch Captain thanks you for what you are doing for this boy. Now it is time you slept. This day has been too long already. When Albet comes back, he and I will talk before I go. That's a promise."

"There's only the room where the servies sleep - I have two very little ones - and mine," Corn faltered.

"Albet will sleep by the hearth tonight, and make a place for himself in the back room tomorrow. You must have done the like yourself. You can sleep well now, with a clear conscience. Everything is in good hands. Your wife would be proud."

"Well, I must trust the Captain of the Watch." The old man tried a small smile and got to his feet. Athirra took his arm. "Put water on to heat. You'll never get the grease off those plates with cold. My wife is - was - a particular woman," he said, prattling as he moved off. "The sleeping rooms are beyond the back. I can find my way. I don't need a light. The blind don't, you know. But there are candles somewhere. You can use one. Come and see which way I am going, then return to Captain Galt. He will be needing more ale."

Athirra returned with a candle as well as the water to heat on the fire, as Corn had instructed. She was not stalling. She was accepting and preparing. When she sat down at last, she sat across the table from Galt, composed.

"Are you really the Captain of the Watch?" she asked.

"I am."

"Then why are you helping me? Why am I not taken in arrest, isn't that the term? Surely a public whipping before I am sent to the meanest Pleasure House, is what I should be expecting." Her mouth twisted.

"Surely it is," he answered.

"Then why?"

"I told you outside. I am Teq's father. I am doing it mostly for his sake. He needs to believe there is some compromise in the world."

"Teq? Teq, the map' apprentice who talked to me at the Matted Vine as if I were a real person? That Teq? And a father. What is that?"

"Teq tells me - yes, that Teq - that you come from an Honor."

"Of course. Made captive by these noble Town hunters with the rest of the Honor hunting party. It was my first hunting party. We had many fish. We were careless because of our success, I suppose. Well. Here I am."

"And now you are a boy. Albet. Innkeeper's apprentice. In your Honor was there a Sieur?"

"Naturally. How else would we have been born?"

"The Sieur was the father of all the children in the Honor."

"Ah. Father. Sire. So you are the father of Teq."

"I was the Sieur in Teq's Honor. Marisel's Honor, far to the east of here. When I was conquered, Teq had not yet had his drumming, though it was close. Teq's true mother was beloved by me. Her name is Tarabeth. I named you Albet in her memory, to honor you and Teq. I urged Tarabeth to warn Teq to escape during the Challenge battle, that his life might continue. It was for her sake, though I liked the boy himself. He did escape. It chanced that he and I met again, and met another who knew of the Town. We decided to come here together. Thus I know Teq as my son, and he knows me as his father. We do not address each other so, but we know. I am his true father, if you like, and we are fond of one another. Respect one another. I am proud of him. Your rescue is for his sake, as his rescue was for his true mother's. Satisfied?"

"Yes, I see, I think. There is a closeness between you, as there was between me and my true mother, you are saying." For a moment Athirra's eyes teared. She ignored it. "But how does this bring the Captain of the Watch to release me from all punishment? I know why you would search for me. I am a miscreant. I must accept that you have helped me. But I must understand. I am unused to... debt."

"You must learn to accept this. That is your punishment, if you like. When you ran off, it was remembered that Teq had spoken with you often: inappropriately for an apprentice. He was blamed, particularly because he was also missing. It was supposed you had run away together. It happened that he had been in a fight in another part of the Town - for other reasons." Galt smiled a little. "It was at the same time as your disappearance. I found him, much battered, in his Hall. Barely conscious. I can go anywhere as Captain of the Watch," he said in response to her skeptical look. "He knew nothing of your escape, of course, but he was glad when I told him. Fiercely glad, I would say. Foolishly glad, hm?"

"I never thought of him. How could he be blamed?"

"His fellow apprentices had noted how he spoke to you. And you to him, I'm told. They reported it."

She hung her head. "I was wrong to allow it. It was just... it was such a pleasure to have someone to talk to... who spoke to me as if I mattered. Your -er son is very brave, Captain."

"Yes, he is. It is one of the reasons I am proud of him, and why I promised to find and aid you. I knew I would find you. You have surprised me by staying hidden for so long. You did well. Perhaps you are as brave - and as foolish - as Teq."

"It has been hard to do. I have been cold and hungry, though never so cold as tonight. I had no plan how to get out of the Town. I just ran blindly when, for a second, I had the chance. The humiliation of the Pleasure House was more than I could bear. I know how stupid I was to run away without an idea where to go, especially because of the season..."

"Well you are safe now. And so is Teq. His name is cleared because he was in that foolish fight on the other side of the Town. Those clothes are his, by the way. He had the idea of giving them to you because they have no Guild colors, and because he had thought about it, and realized you would never be safe as a girl. He's right, of course. Nor is there any way that I can think of to get anywhere, even if you managed to get outside the walls. Hm? You had better disguise the clothes in some way. It would not do if they were recognized."

"I believe I must thank you."

"I believe that you may - especially as my reputation will suffer sadly when I fail to find the missing servie. I shall have to stage something. Perhaps a drowning at the waterfall would do it. A suicide, when you believe you are found. What do you think? Do you like the idea? I shall tell Teq where you really are. He'll probably rush round. Don't even consider talking to him. I'll warn him of the same."

"I am not a fool, Captain. I understand the risk you are both taking. The suicide, of course, would stop the search. I have never seen the waterfall. As an apprentice I'll be able to go, and be properly appalled," she added dryly.

"No, I don't think you are a fool. You would be wasted in a Pleasure House. They should let women run them. You would do that well." He chuckled as she flushed with anger. "I will go now. You have a lot to do before you sleep. Cut your hair and bind your figure and so on. Perfect your disguise. You'll know how better than me."

They both rose and walked to the door.

"The food was good," Galt told her. "I ate it all, even though I had already eaten once. We take our rewards where we find them." He grinned at her again, determined she should learn to know she was being teased. "Lock the doors behind me. And find out what that innwife died of. I must be off to the Death House to discover that for myself."

"You fear disease?" Athirra sounded afraid, and then spoiled the moment by giving a mighty sneeze.

"It might have been from Corn beating her." Galt tried teasing again.

"Don't mock me."

"Well it would not have been a disease or the inn would have been quarantined at the time when she was collected. Don't worry. You are safe here with Corn."

"I hope you will thank Teq. And I do indeed thank you, most sincerely, Captain. For the rescue, and for talking to me plainly, and not as if I were a fool. I shall do as you say."

"Oh yes. Always," he said, and smiled down at her on his way out into the frigid night.

Chapter 20

In the middle of the morning, the door to the Mapmakers' Hall crashed open, making the smoke swirl all over the room, and Galt strode in. Competent Gaveril hid his annoyance at the interruption and hurried forward, nodding to Teq who had leapt to his feet, to close the door.

"How can we serve you, Captain?" Gaveril asked.

"I need another map of the Town. Do you have one on hand?"

"Why certainly, Captain. Do I charge this to the Watch?"

"No. I'll pay for it myself. I want one to keep in my own quarters. There we are, Competent. Thank you."

He exchanged credits for the map that Gaveril retrieved for him, and swept on to the door. It was cold in the Hall, in spite of a huge fire. Even though the matting screens were lowered over the open wall, rendering the place dim, it was still impossible to heat. He noted that everyone was bundled in so many clothes, it made bending over the tables to work, difficult.

Teq held the door open, waiting quietly.

"Well Teq. Keeping out of trouble?" Galt asked, gripping Teq by the elbow in passing.

"Yes, Captain," Teq murmured, retrieving the piece of paper Galt had managed to wedge into its crook.

It was several hours before Teq had the chance to read the message. "Late dinner at the Carved Oak. Tomorrow." The next day was a half day, so going across the Town for his dinner would pose no problem, so long as somebody else was willing to pay. He wondered what news Galt had for him.

Galt walked back to his quarters, many credits the lighter, but heavily laden all the same. For the past ten days he had been forced to put up with total silence from his new servie. He was tired of it, and determined to put a stop to it this day. It was close to the dinner hour and he was hungry and cold. He was in no mood for argument.

The woman sat on her cot, but came slowly to her feet as he entered. His quarters consisted of one room, but it was large, and she had contrived to partially screen a corner for herself. The place was immaculately clean. The fire burned well, and it was warm.

"Go to the kitchens and bring enough food for me as well as for yourself. We will both eat in here tonight," he bade her.

She bowed, and absented herself, walking stiffly upright to do his bidding. While she was gone, he got rid of his own outer clothing and undid the bundles he had brought. There was a warm shift with long sleeves, a warm cloak, heavy hose to put inside the cloth shoes, which were the servie uniform, along with their sleeveless shifts. On top of these he placed a good cord belt, and mittens.

The woman returned with the food, and put the pot in the hearth to warm.

"Those are for you," Galt said, indicating what lay on her cot.

She examined them one by one and something like a sob escaped her. "Is it allowed?" she whispered.

"Ah, so you do speak. After all this time I was beginning to wonder. Yes, it is allowed if I allow it. And I do, as you see. I want you able to go out and about without freezing to death. Now, let us begin at the beginning. What is your name?"

This time she replied. "Ibaren," she told him.

"Good. You already know my name is Galt. I am the conquered Sieur of Marisel's Honor. Here is my new life."

"I am the conquered Council Member from Gunnelda's Honor." Ibaren allowed herself a small smile.

"Then we rank with one another, and I am offering you a home in the Town. I am trying to save enough to buy a house, which you will then run. Meanwhile, this is what there is." He indicated the room.

"I have too little to do, Sieur."

"Call me Galt or Captain here, Lady, as I shall call you by your name. I am no longer a Sieur."

"Then, Captain, there is too little for me to do."

"It is a thing I wish to discuss with you, now that we are speaking. I need the help of a friend, and I need to know whether I may depend on you as a friend. May I?" The question came out forcefully. She had a variety of stares which were as intimidating as cold speech. She must have been formidable in Council.

"Why did you bid for me at that sale?" she asked.

"I didn't want you to go to Ruper - the man who bid for you first. You impressed me by your demeanor as beyond that. Truly the words were out of my mouth before I gave them thought. But you were not one who should go to such a place. He is the owner of a Pleasure House where, it is said, any perversion is allowed. You would have been servie to his women."

"Then I thank you. I am glad to be here rather than there. But please understand that I would still prefer to be at Gunnelda's Honor. Friendship would be to return me there."

"I am Captain of the Watch. I do not leave the Town. There is nobody in the Town who would take you there, even if they could. That is reality. How did you come to be captured?"

"Vanity. I was proving to myself that I was not too old to take part in the Great Hunt at summer's end. I was probably slowing them down. We were but one day from a successful return to the Honor when we were captured. No such thing had ever happened to any of our hunters before, so we were not wary."

"Not even by Wilders?"

"Wilders?"

"You've never heard of Wilders, have you? Where did your young men go after their drumming?"

"We never knew."

"How many days' march from here is Gunnelda's Honor, and in which direction?"

"South and east along the coast. Beyond the desert. Fifty or sixty days. So few escaped. The Honor will be nearly bereft of hunters. I blame myself."

"No need for that. The confraters are efficient. But so far away! Well, it only emphasizes the impossibility of your return. The Wilders are packs of men also seeking women. They do not attack the confraters, the Town's hunters. They are too well armed and organized. Better than any Wilders I know of. But you would never pass through them alone. Here is where you must make your life. Nor is there any point in burdening your thoughts with guilt. What is done is done. Do you understand?"

"I do. Thank you for being straightforward with me. I will stand your friend, Captain, if that is what you need. I understand, however, that you own me."

"Well, yes. I purchased you. There was no other means of rescue. But now I need you to help with another rescue."

"Of a woman?"

"Yes. She was due to have been sold into a Pleasure House, so she ran away from an inn to escape it. I have found her, and arranged for her safety, but there is the matter of accounting for her to my Chiefs. Will you help me?"

"Why do you do this? You are well situated and respected here. Why jeopardize your own position?"

"I was happy at Marisel's Honor. The life was full of restrictions, of course, but full of compensations too. Marisel is a woman of honesty and dignity, if a little rigid. My first matron a woman of incomparable grace and beauty." Galt was speaking slowly, picturing the people of whom he spoke. He wanted Ibaren to understand. He wanted fully to understand himself. "Her true son, Teq, escaped from the Honor and came here with me. He is a mapmaker apprentice, here in the Town. He befriended this woman when she worked in an inn."

"The woman who ran away, and whom you found?" Ibaren wished to be clear.

"That's right. Athirra is her name. A very handsome, and serious young woman. I have given her some of Teq's clothes and apprenticed her to a blind innkeeper under the name of Albet."

"You feel safe telling all this to a mere woman, whose utterings would be ignored, I am sure," Ibaren was quizzical.

"Do you think that I why I am telling you this?" Galt asked impatiently.

"Perhaps."

"It is true that you are dependent upon me, however much you wish it were not so. What I am trying to show you is that I am dependent upon you too. Do you understand? Now where was I?"

"This Albet is a supposed boy."

"Correct. However, Athirra is still diligently sought by my troops: the Watch. Where I need your help is in arranging for her to disappear. I have decided a fake suicide would serve us best. That's where I need your help. Are you with me?" Galt sat down heavily. "I really do need you."

"Do you have a plan?"

"I do."

"Is this help something an old woman can handle?"

Galt chuckled. "Yourself, you mean? It is something you could do. Oh, and I have here a map of the Town. It would be useful if you were to study it and learn where things are."

" I will help you, Captain." Ibaren smiled at him. "I believe you to be a good man, Captain. I will stand your loyal friend."

"Excellent," smiled Galt, rubbing his hands together. "Let's eat."

The following evening found them eating at the Carved Oak. Teq sat opposite Galt while they ate and talked of indifferent matters. Albet stood at the fire, and Ibaren sat in a corner. Albet had acknowledged Galt's arrival for Corn's benefit, but had ignored Teq. The two little girls who were the inn's servies, ran around serving up the meal.

When the inn was cleared of people at last, they sat in silence until all the plates and dishes were washed, and Corn and the little ones had retired. Albet made a beanbrew drink and came over to the table to join them. Galt beckoned Ibaren over and introduced everyone.

"You make a fine boy," Teq grinned at Athirra. "A pity you had to cut your hair, but the disguise is good. Well, you must have seen the shock on my face when I first walked in and recognized you. I had to look twice before I did."

"I thought the Captain would have warned you," Athirra answered. "Do you recognize your tunic, for which many thanks, by the way? I dyed it in beanbrew last night and dried it by the fire this morning."

"It's a bit streaky, but it looks different enough," Teq acknowledged. "It looks smaller too."

"It shrank," she nodded.

"Glad you're all pleased with everything," Galt interrupted, "but we can't spend a lot of time here, chatting. There are things which must be arranged. Athirra's suicide will be tomorrow evening."

"Suicide!" gasped Teq and jumped to his feet.

"Sit down, sit down." Galt pulled him back on to the bench. "It will be a fake suicide, of course, so that Athirra will no longer be sought and Albet can live on.

Now. Ibaren will help me with that. I want to be sure you two are out of the way. You must be seen to be out of the way. Conspicuously. Tomorrow. At the dinner hour. It is imperative that it is clear Teq had nothing to do with it, and if anyone should doubt Albet's reality, he must be visibly here. Is that clear?"

Teq and Athirra both nodded vigorously.

"It should be easy enough," Teq put in. "I can trip over somebody at the Matted Vine, or jostle someone's food elbow. There'll definitely be a challenge, if not a fight. Nobody wants to fight me any more," he chuckled. "They're beginning to call me Takeon Teq. You know, take on anybody. I usually win, you see."

Galt laughed and Athirra smiled. "You're growing big enough! You'll soon be as big as Galt. Er- the Captain," she said. "I can do something like that too: spill some food and shout at the servies, or something."

"If you too are taken care of, then Ibaren and I can do the rest. We have already been over the ground on the way here, and she knows what to do."

"Where does Ibaren serve?" Athirra asked, curious why this stately woman would be helping, and above all, why she came with Galt.

"With me," Galt answered shortly. "She will be running my household, if I ever get enough credits to have one."

"It is also my wish to help," Ibaren spoke quietly, smiling at Athirra. "Women should."

They all shook hands with one another, and then Galt urged Teq on his way. "The less time we spend together the better, now," he said. "If you think you are not being noticed, you can be sure someone is watching. We'll find a way to meet again soon."

Teq waved his hand as he slipped out of the door. It was not long before Galt and Ibaren followed him.

On the following evening, dusk found Ibaren following Galt out of the baker's market situated beside the waterfall. There were three buildings in this forbidding location, climbing behind one another along the path beside the falls. The path stopped abruptly at the pool which had formed half way down the falls, making two waterfalls, in fact. The area was always damp, with a thrown mist saturating the air. It was not a desirable place to have either shop or home. However it was cheap. Galt was making a great fuss about the quality of the baker's bread (which he had indeed sampled before).

Just as they emerged, the Watch could be heard approaching, as they did regularly at this hour, en route to going off duty at the Barracks, in this same quadrant. Galt stepped down the path to meet them, calling to Ibaren to wait for him up there. She stepped further up the path, to a cave, which was clearly visible to one side of the pool. Nobody ever went up there at this season. It was too cold and wet, but Ibaren stepped up there humming loudly.

Galt stopped the sergeant of the Watch and asked how things were going around the Town. The men fidgeted and looked down as the sergeant reported. They wanted to get off duty now.

Suddenly there was a scream from Ibaren and an enormous splash in the pool. It was just enough darker to make it impossible to make anything out clearly, as they heard Ibaren shout, "Captain. Quickly. Someone just jumped in."

"What?" he yelled. "A person?"

"Yes, Captain. Oh do come quickly. I can't see her."

"Her?"

"Yes, yes a woman, I think. I can't be certain. It was so sudden. I wasn't expecting anything."

Galt sounded incisive. "Sergeant, take a couple of men and get up there. That's my servie doing all the shouting."

"Right, sir. Come on then." The sergeant pointed at a couple of his men and sprang up the path, the men following.

"Over there," Ibaren told him, as soon as he reached her. "I was going to wait in the cave, to be out of the wet. The Captain told me to wait for him. When I got up here, someone rushed past me and jumped into the water."

"What made you say it was a woman?" the sergeant asked, as he directed his men to look around the pool.

"Just an impression, sir." Ibaren's voice sounded nervous. "It was perhaps the long hair, or the dress."

"Hm. See anything?" He called to his men. "Nothing, eh? Can't see nothing up here, sir," he called down to Galt.

"Nothing has come over the falls down here either," he called back, "or perhaps we were just too late to see anything. Was it really a person?"

"This servie up here seems to think so, sir."

"Have a look in the cave, then," Galt shouted back up.

Ibaren was standing well out of the way, clutching the bag of bread they had purchased earlier. By this time all the people had come out of the three shops, and were trying to find out what there was to see in the ever fading light.

"Looks like someone's been living in this here cave, right enough, sir," the sergeant called down to Galt. By this time he had lit a torch. "There are cloth shoe prints and some meat bones. And looks like a sort of nest of rags in one corner. I reckon it was that missing servie, sir. No wonder we couldn't find her in respectable places. She's been living up here. Who'd have thought?"

"Then, you think she jumped? Heard my servie approaching, I suppose. Any of you people see or hear anything these past few days? A woman on the path, or a light or fire in the cave? Anything?" Galt had walked a little way up the path and was talking to the building owners. They all denied it vigorously, and started to slip away back into their houses. They didn't like being questioned by the Watch.

"Nothing else to see up here, sir," the sergeant called. "All right if we come back down now? This path is a bit treacherous in this light."

"Yes, Sergeant, thank you. Come on down," Galt answered. "We seem to have our answers. We can't see enough now to be any use anyway. I'll come back here for another look around in the morning. You get on back to the Barracks. I'll go and report this to Chief Sedemp right away. He'll be glad to know the missing servie matter is cleared up at last."

"Yes, sir. Thank you, sir."

The sergeant came on down and led his men off smartly. There'd be something good to tell in the Barracks tonight when they got there. Big mystery solved, and by his corps.

"Can you get down all right, Ibaren?" Galt called up to her, "or shall I come and get you?"

"I'm here," she answered from behind him. "I followed the sergeant's torch down. It really is dark here at night, isn't it?"

"And wet," he answered, chuckling. "But all in a good cause. You get off now. I must go and report this at once. The Chief has been most concerned. Save me some supper. I'll eat in tonight. Very well done," he added under his breath. "I was almost alarmed myself. Most artistic arrangement of the cave, from what the sergeant told me. And in such a short time too."

"I had everything ready in a bag, which is now in with the bread."

"Ah. I had no idea you'd be so thorough. I was just expecting foot prints from your shoes. It was a mighty splash too."

"I threw a mighty rock."

Galt laughed quietly. "Thank you," he said. "Most sincerely. Well it's all settled now, eh?"

"For the time being," Ibaren said as she watched him walk quickly away.

Chapter 21

Winter turned into spring at last. Galt had been able to see very little of Teq, but he had eaten at the Carved Oak as often as he could get away at the dinner hour. He often stayed on after the customers had gone home, and chatted with Athirra. Sometimes with Corn and Athirra. It was becoming important to him to have these times. The driving ambition which had sustained him until he reached the role he intended for himself was now fulfilled, and he realized that he was lonely.

On the down side, his frequent visits to the Carved Oak were gradually noticed by his fellow captains. One by one they began to eat there too. Athirra's cooking was better than most, since she varied the menu and experimented with combinations of foods to interest herself as much as her customers. Gradually it was becoming more and more difficult for Galt to have conversation with Athirra.

He came grumping into his quarters one evening, having been driven to leave the Carved Oak by a party of captains celebrating noisily, and obviously planning to stay until Corn threw them out.

"There is no privacy anywhere in this Town," he roared at Ibaren.

"There could be," she said, very difficult to discompose.

"You think you know more about the Town than I do, woman?" he snapped.

"I know more about your circumstances, perhaps. You have saved enough credits to buy the house I found today. The wine merchant who owns it has found a bigger one that he wants to buy, but is afraid it will be sold before he can sell the one he has now."

"What makes you think I want to buy a house?" he grumbled.

"You said so."

"You're right," he sighed. "I just came in prepared for a fight, and you happened to be here."

"I didn't just happen to be here. I'm always here. I could use some privacy too," Ibaren answered him reasonably.

"All right. Tell me what is special about this house that you found."

"Apart from the price?"

"Yes, apart from the price."

"It is in this quadrant," Ibaren began, "so it is conveniently placed. It is the only house on a tiny side street, which must have been created just to accommodate this house. It is close to the walls on the other side. There is plenty of room, and the courtyard entrance, is walled and shaded with a great tree."

"How did you hear all this?"

"I was buying wine, and the merchant was telling everybody who would listen. I went past there on the way back here and it looks ideal. On the main street is a small house where bachelors live: probably Competents. The main thing that appealed to me, is that both Teq and Athirra would have a way to visit you without too many people noticing. That poor girl must be going crazy with the confinement to that one room. I know I am." Ibaren wondered if she should have said all that, but it needed saying, so she risked Galt's displeasure at the plain speaking.

He was silent for a while. "There are enough rooms?" he asked at last. "You'd need help in keeping it, if there were. That would be a problem if Albet were to arrive, and want to spend time there as Athirra. Have you thought of that?"

"I have, and I have a solution, but I didn't want to sound greedy." Ibaren smiled at him. "There's a daughter at the wine merchant's, who is simple minded. She is of an age to go to a Pleasure House, but nobody will take her. She's rather ugly too. They've never even given her a name. They call her 'Girly'. It seemed to me that she would be happy to remain in the familiar house. I could teach her to clean, if she doesn't already know how. And there would be no chance of her understanding or carrying tales about anything she might see. I don't think she'd cost you much."

"You are a marvel!" Galt said at last, and laughed at her. "You think of everything and then go out and find solutions. You even worry about my finances, which are not too bad. It is spring. Time for changes. I will go now and strike a deal with the wine merchant."

"Now?"

"Better than waiting until he sells the house in the morning."

He picked his cloak back up and swung out through the door, his step light as it had not been when he arrived. And then he was back.

"What about furnishings?" he asked.

"There are some problems you have to solve on your own, Captain," Ibaren laughed at him. "I can't do everything in one day."

He went out laughing.

It took a week, but at the end of it, they moved in. The house was charming. There was enough room, and more, to give a feeling of spaciousness, and yet it had a cosy quality. Girly turned out to be just as Ibaren had surmised. The merchant was more than delighted to be rid of her. He found her an embarrassment. Since his main reason for moving to the larger house, was that he wished to entertain more visibly, Girly would have been in the way.

There was a minor disturbance at a Pleasure House in the northern quadrant, the next evening, which Galt decided he ought to see to, no matter how minor. These were becoming more and more frequent, recently. Perhaps it was the confinement of the winter months, or the stirrings in the blood brought on by spring. Whatever the reason, Galt went, but the matter was settled by the time he got there.

"Don't even know what caused this one, sir," the sergeant told him. "Some of our own men was hanging around, off duty like. Not that they can use the House, but they moved off when we arrived. Just joked with us, you know, sir, and then moved along. All the same, it's happening too often."

"I agree with you, sergeant. Perhaps we should increase patrols for a bit," Galt said. "I'll talk to the Chief about it tomorrow, and see what's to be done."

Since he was already in the area, Galt stopped in at the Matted Vine. It had been some time since he'd seen Teq. It seemed to him that the lad was even bigger. He was a good looking boy and no mistake. It couldn't be long now until he made competent.

Teq was glad to see him. "I've been hoping nothing was wrong. ," he said. "It's hard to know how to find you. Everything well at the Carved Oak, still? It really irritates me that apprentices have no credits, and I can't choose to eat somewhere else."

"It's the very thing I've come to tell you about. News!" Galt grinned at him. "I know I've been threatening this for ever, but I've finally bought a house. Moved in yesterday. You can come and see me any time you can get away. Ibaren is for ever asking about you. She'll be in charge of the cooking, so come for a meal any half day. Next half day."

"That's marvelous. By the Sky I would love to go inside a real house for a meal. They say the food in the Matted Vine is good, but how do I know? I've hardly been anywhere else. Where's the house?"

"It was the wine merchant's. The one in a street by itself, up near the walls. In the center of the southern quadrant. Know it?"

"We mapmakers know everywhere. Yes. I'm pretty sure I know where you mean. It's only a couple of streets away from the Barracks. And not too far from the falls, right?"

"Quite right. We'll see you in three days, then. Come for dinner. Come as early as you like. Even if I'm not there, you can have a look around, all right?"

"All right. Tell Ibaren to expect me, and that I eat a lot."

Galt laughed and left. He hadn't eaten at the Vine because he wanted to go to the Carved Oak and give his news to Athirra, but now it was getting late. He hurried.

When he got there, the place had mercifully few customers. Albet sent word with one of the servies that he had some special food he wanted the Captain to try later, when the inn emptied out. Would the Captain mind having a mug of ale with Corn, and waiting?

The Captain would be delighted, he told the servie. Took the mug he was offered and walked over to the corner where Corn was keeping an ear on things.

It seemed that his son, Chapra, had made a visit that day, and had sat with him for quite a long time. He had given Albet the afternoon off. It was good of the young people to visit the old and bring news of the world. He had had a wonderful day, and now he was almost ready for bed. Would the Captain mind? Were the customers leaving yet? Galt told him that the last of the customers was just getting ready to go out of the door. The servies had all but finished cleaning up. He could certainly understand why Corn would want to be off to his bed. Could he call the servies to help him get there? And so he did.

It was really quite early for Athirra to be free. As soon as the old man retired, she went over and locked the door, grinning from ear to ear. Galt had never seen her looking so cheerful. And her smile was truly wonderful. He'd seen it too seldom. But then he was feeling pretty cheerful himself.

"Guess what I got today," Athirra greeted him. "I was so hoping you would come in tonight so that I could share it with you. You must have known I was thinking about you."

"Well, I didn't, but I think about you so often, that maybe our thoughts crossed."

They both looked a little startled at what he had just said, so he added, "show me," into the silence. She ran into the back room and came out with a fish on a plate.

"Have you ever seen a fish before?" she asked.

"Seen, caught and eaten," he assured her. "Where in the world did you find one in the Town?"

"Corn gave me the afternoon off, and oh it was such a beautiful day! I decided to go and visit the site of my suicide. I'd never been there. I climbed up that path on the side, to the pool, and saw this creature. Did I ever tell you that in my Honor we are hunters of fish? How could I resist? There's a quiet place, where the water rests, on the far side of the pool, beyond that shallow cave - my home?"

Galt nodded, grinning at her enthusiasm.

"I just lay down there in the shade, and trailed my fingers until he swam over to investigate, and I had him. Banged his head on a rock, and carried him home in a flap of my tunic. I must have looked silly. But here he is, and now I'm going to cook him for our supper."

"For our feast of celebration," Galt said.

"Oh? What are we celebrating?"

"I've bought a house," he said, and told her all about it as she prepared and cooked the fish.

There was a wonderful intimacy about eating special food in the empty inn. When they had finished the last bite, Galt helped her clean up in the back room.

"Come and see my house," he said suddenly. "I want to be sure you can find it. I got it so that you would have a place to go and be yourself. And Teq," he added, but didn't sound as if he was thinking of Teq at all.

"Now? Tonight?" she asked.

"Why not? I'll bring you back again afterwards. It's a wonderful night. There's even a moon. I can't think of a better time."

"Well you could hardly take me there during the day, it's true. Yes. I'd like that."

She donned a cloak, so that she would not be easily recognizable if they met someone, and they slipped quietly along the streets. It really was a beautiful night, and the gentle moonlight made even the harshest buildings seem lovely. He pointed out the route they were taking so that she could find her way another time, but when they got to the little street, he simply took her hand.

They tiptoed into the courtyard, being quiet so that Ibaren would not hear them and come to find out who was visiting.

"Do you want to see inside?" Galt whispered.

"No, let's save that for the daytime. I know my way. I should leave now."

"Sit for a minute. There's a bench under the tree. Will you?"

"Yes." There was something especially intimate about whispering.

He led her to the bench, still holding her hand, and they sat down, close together.

"Are you cold?" he asked.

"A little."

He put his arm around her, a little afraid that what he was feeling, was more than what she was feeling. He had not totally realized that he had long ago stopped thinking of Athirra as a waif he had accepted as a responsibility, for Teq's sake. Cropped hair, large tunic, bound bodice, none of it mattered. For him she was a beautiful woman and he wanted her to want him as he wanted her.

She did. As soon as he put his arm around her shoulders, she snuggled up close to him and laid her head on his shoulder. He could feel her trembling. Tentatively he reached out and lifted her chin with one finger. They looked at each other, eye to eye, for a long minute and then he kissed her. By the time he returned her to the Carved Oak it was morning, they were lovers, and Galt was almost dancing through the empty streets to his new home.

Chief Sedemp was busy by the time Galt finally surfaced the next day, and recollected his duty enough to seek him out. The Chief sent word that he was with the Dignus and would see the Captain on the following day. By then it was too late. Rioting had already begun.

It started off quietly enough, with the now commonplace call to a disturbance at a Pleasure House. But this time, when the Watch got there and found once again that the disturbance was being caused by green shirts, the Watch simply changed sides and joined in. The sergeant had to flee.

Galt was in the Barracks when the word reached him. It reached the rest of the men in the Barracks at the same time. He stood to muster his men and go to the scene, only to discover nearly all the men were gone. He was left with his sergeants, and a few of the older veterans.

He had hardly assimilated this when the Hunter and Guard Captains came bursting in. Their men were gone too. The walls were unmanned, there was chaos in the streets, and there was nobody left to deal with it.

The cause was the use of the Pleasure Houses. Ever since the last intake of women, there had been no shortage in the Pleasure Houses. So long as there had been a shortage, the men could more or less understand why the privilege of their use was limited to senior men. But they knew there was no shortage now, and they were tired of being deprived. The older apprentices joined in. They began by throwing rocks at the Pleasure Houses, but green shirt discipline prevailed. One of them, acting as leader, pointed out that there was no point in trashing the places they wanted to use. They found more leaders and a voice and marched on the Palace.

In the interim, the Chiefs had been to the Barracks to discover who was there and what it was all about. Chief Sedemp recognized that Galt had tried to warn him, but now it was too late for preventative measures. There were no men to man extra patrols.

The Chiefs decided to rally everyone who was left, and they reached the Palace not long before the mob. Sedemp had reasoned that they would come here in the end, and when they did there would be an answer waiting for them. Kambar urged that their answer should be a hail of arrows, and orders to return to work, and Fergin, who almost always did, agreed with him.

But Sedemp disagreed, and most of the Captains were with Sedemp, though they took care not to show it. Sedemp reasoned that the men were right. They needed women as much as the upper ranks did. There was no point in trying to enforce unenforceable and unreasonable rules. Especially as they had no one to enforce them. When the mob arrived in the square, he stepped on to the Palace steps to meet them, the other two chiefs reluctantly backing him up.

His policy worked. He promised there would be a revision of the rules within a week. If there were not, they were welcome to come again. In the meantime, the Dignus would consider their requests and come up with an answer, so long as they dispersed quietly now and went about their duties.

The apprentices were the hardest to coerce, but in the end the older green shirts got even them to disperse. By evening the streets were quiet again. The whole matter had lasted barely the length of an afternoon.

Within the week the rules had changed. Certain Pleasure Houses were designated for the use of Chiefs, Masters and Captains. Certain others were for the use of Competents and Sergeants. A few were named for the exclusive use of men of no rank and apprentices over the age of eighteen. Those apprentices were also to be paid a modest sum of credits, to be deducted from the amount they received along with their Competent's collar.

The incident of the riot was never again mentioned. The proclamation changing the rules was read aloud and posted, days before the requisite week had passed. There was once more order in the Town.

Chapter 22

A year passed in fair tranquillity after all the upheavals of that spring. Galt's house was used as he had hoped, as a meeting place for the people he cared about. Teq was there whenever he had the chance, and Ibaren grew very fond of him. She made sure he was well clad, giving him small items of clothing she had sewn, to increase the rather sparse wardrobe the Hall was willing to supply. In the middle of it all, they spent a lot of time talking. She was interested in his thoughts and doubts, and let him talk them through. And she educated him in the recognition and use of plants, which had been a specialty of hers in her Honor: which ones were of use as medicines, which for cooking, and which were poison. Galt occasionally joined in with these discussions with what he remembered from his Wilder days.

Athirra was there whenever she could get away. It was a rarer matter, because it was hard to leave Corn alone, and in spite of everything, his health was deteriorating. The two little girls who were the inn's servies were still very young, but were more help in keeping the place clean. It was just as well because Albet's cooking was getting well known, and the Carved Oak was becoming prosperous. She visited mostly when Chapra was off duty and able to be with his father. He was a pleasant young man, and seemed interested enough in the inn, but he was sharp-eyed and Athirra thought it best he should not spend too much time with Albet.

Galt was happy. He was pleased with his house. He was glad to spend time with Teq. He was truly fond of Ibaren and respected her wisdom. And he was in love with Athirra, a thing he had never supposed would happen in his life, much as he had loved Tarabeth. This was different. Athirra was someone he regarded as an equal, not one of a superior tribe of women whose needs he was required to serve, however he had been given the impression he was in command. It had not been so, he recognized. The Honor had belonged to the women. He was replaceable. Indeed he had been. Freedom from the traditions of an Honor had liberated both Athirra and himself and they had something new together. Crazy that such a thing should happen amid all the restrictions of the Town!

The first expeditions of spring were out now, hunting for game and women. It was the evening of a beautiful day that the alarms sounded from the walls, and Galt rushed over to see what was wrong. One of the expeditions was returning, with a small group of captive women, surrounded by every hunter they had, and carrying litters with three wounded. Wounded! There had never before been such an event. Chief Fergin had all the wall guards covering as far as they could with their bows, while Chief Kambar took a contingent of hunters out himself, to surround the returning party and see them safe inside the walls.

Not that there was any visible threat. The party was not apparently being followed. Whoever had wounded the hunters had not come after them. Nonetheless the whole matter caused an uproar, not least because they had no skilled healer in the Town. It was generally supposed that the women could deal with normal everyday ailments, and the captains could handle any accident that happened with a weapon. These men were more seriously injured than that, partly because their captain had judged it best to get his whole party back to the Town as swiftly as possible, and had not stopped to tend to them.

At the Barracks, what could be done for them, was done; but alas, one of the men died. One did recover, but the third, Chapra, Corn's son, had a wound in his leg, caused by an arrow, which had broken the bone. By the time it was seen to, the leg was irremediably misshapen. He would never again walk straight. He would never again be able to go out on a hunt.

But this was not the worst of it. The Captain in charge of this particular expedition was newly promoted and anxious to make his mark. He had been determined to bring home women, and win a name for himself with Chief Kambar, as well as the men. In his zeal, he had not hesitated to bring in the first women they had seen. And they were women who belonged to a Wilder pack. Honors who lost their women to capture, did nothing about it, other then mourn their loss. Wilder packs had such a hard time finding women of their own, that they were certain to come in search of them. Such an event would probably unite the packs and bring them down on the Town in force. The trail of the fleeing party would not be hard to follow. The Town which had hitherto been nothing but a rumor, would become known. It was a disaster.

The Chiefs spent the next day in consultation, bringing in their captains to discuss how they would best handle the situation. It was decided to do nothing yet, other than demote the overzealous captain. There were still two parties out in search of game. Better to wait until they returned and see if they had news of the Wilders massing. If there was no news, scouts would be sent to find what they might discover. If there was no uprising apparent, an expedition would be sent out in a month or two to garner game, but more as a show of force, to discourage the Wilder Packs further, from attempting to pit themselves against the disciplined forces of the Town.

That decided, they dispersed and went to their homes. Galt was not a little surprised to find a distraught Athirra waiting for him, all alone in the courtyard of his house.

"Whatever is the matter, love?" he asked her. "I'm sure it can't be so bad that no solution can be found. Have you eaten?"

"Yes. No. It doesn't matter. How were things at the Palace? Ibaren told me that was where you were. I can't stay. I made a stew and it is sitting at the back of the fire, with the little ones watching it; but I must get back in time to serve it."

"I'm glad to see you, even for a little while. Was there something special on your mind? Something you needed to tell me."

"No. It's all right. It can wait." She seemed odd. Distracted.

"No, it can't wait," Ibaren said, coming out to the courtyard with drinks and a plate of food for Galt, to tide him over until dinner. "It's important and you should know."

"There are really two things. Somehow that was why I had to come and tell you," Athirra began. "The first is that Chapra has been wounded. He won't be able to remain as a hunter. Had you heard about that?"

"Yes I had. Does that effect you?" Galt was puzzled.

"He will come home. To the Carved Oak. To live. I can't stay there. He'll want to run the place himself, for one thing. For another, it wouldn't take long for him to wonder why I don't shave. Hm?"

"By the Sky and the Earth. It never occurred to me. You are Athirra in this house, and I forget you are still being Albet there. Oh, my poor love. How could I forget such a thing? You said there were two things, though. Tell me the rest."

"I'm pregnant." Athirra stared straight at him, afraid of his reaction, but afraid not to see it.

"What? Are you sure? Oh, that's wonderful!" Galt's face lit up with a huge smile. He circled the table and sat down beside her, hugging her.

"Wonderful, is it?" Ibaren asked. "A pregnant boy? It would be a little hard to explain, don't you think?"

"But not a pregnant wife," he said reasonably. "There will be a wiving to arrange. I'll set that up. At once. Before Chapra moves in. Will that satisfy everyone? I know it will satisfy me. I have been at a loss how to arrange such a thing, but now that you are pregnant, there's no hazard."

"Well I don't see how you can do it," Ibaren said. "Even Captains of the Watch have their limitations."

"Do you trust me, love?" he asked Athirra. "Don't worry about the old lady, here. She'll just have to be amazed." He grinned at them.

"Of course, I trust you, if you say you can arrange it. You will arrange it." Athirra smiled at him, her wonderful smile. "Now I can breathe again. For a little while it had become difficult. Are you really pleased about the baby?"

"How could I not be? Not only will we have our own child, but it will bring my Athirra here to live all the time. Life gets better and better."

"Oh, you are definitely a treasure of a man. But then I knew that," she chuckled. "Now I have to go, or the stew will burn and the customers will starve, and

Corn will accuse me of trying to spoil things for Chapra. Corn is really happy about this, you know. I will have to tell him I have been offered a job somewhere else."

"Tell him you have a job as a cook in a private home, and he won't start worrying about the competition, or trying to find you," Ibaren suggested.

"I'll do that. And I could write down my recipes for Chapra. I'll tell Corn I'll do that. That would be fair don't you think? I must run." She kissed Galt and flew out of the door in the wall, bursting with excitement.

"And now all you have to do is create a miracle," Ibaren said sternly to Galt.

He grinned up at her. "Well I'll just do that. Am I to get any dinner tonight?" he asked her.

When she came back with his dinner, she sat down opposite him. "I shall be glad if Athirra takes over the cooking," she told him. "I'm an old woman, and this house is big. I know I said I could handle it, and I'm not complaining. It's just another reason I'm glad you're planning to perform this miracle."

"You should have told me," he said, worried. "It's possible that Athirra will feel less and less like cooking too as her pregnancy progresses. It's easy enough, though. There's just been another intake of women. I'll bring home another servie."

"Buy another woman?"

"That is the way of the Town, Ibaren, and a miracle I can't perform is to change a whole Town's customs. One thing I will try to do, though, is to buy someone who'll benefit from being here with you."

"You're a good man, Captain," Ibaren smiled wearily. "I was worried about Athirra and didn't see what was to be done. How are you going to make the transition from boy apprentice to wife?"

"Aha. That's my secret. I can't let you in on all my secrets, now can I, or you'd think there was no miracle at all?" He laughed across at her.

"Oh, very well. I'll just wait and see," she laughed back.

In fact Galt had been thinking about how he was going to manage it himself, and then he remembered Lombro. The man owed him a favor. This was the very time to call it in. He would see him the next day at the Distribution of Women, no doubt, and he could arrange it then. Meanwhile, he could definitely afford the extra call on his finances that a wife and the purchase of another servie would mean. In that he was fortunate.

The next day dawned in a vile mood, with pouring rain and a chilly wind. It was not summer yet. It seemed to be the last gesture of spring before it decided to let go and give way to the summer's heat. Galt went over to the women's barracks anyway, to see if everything was ready for the Distribution. The platform was up and the green shirts were in place, but there was not a buyer to be seen. While he was considering what to do, Chiefs Kambar and Fergin arrived.

"We'd better accept the reality of the weather," Kambar decided. "nobody needs new women so badly as to turn out in this. Send out your men, Captain, and announce that the Distribution will be held at the noon hour. With any luck the weather will clear up by then."

"Yes Chief," Galt replied. "Perhaps I should do something about getting some food for these women."

"We'll have to add it to their price, if I have to pay for a meal," Fergin said. "They should have been fed by their new owners."

"Whatever you say, Chief," Galt acquiesced. "Do you want me to get the food sent over from the Barracks?"

"No." Kambar decided. "The cooks at the Barracks have enough mouths to feed, and there aren't very many women, this time. Go to some independent inn."

Nothing loath, Galt took the opportunity to see Athirra. He sent one of his men over to the Carved Oak with the order. Albet would be glad to leave them with this little bonus. He was careful to say that Chief Fergin would be paying.

In the interim he looked over the sorry little huddle of women. They had already been sorted into groups, ready for sale. There were only two children, both very small, and four elderly women. All of them looked less plump and less vigorous than Honor women, as if they worked harder and fed less well. There were about eight or ten young women, gathered together. The children were crying quietly, and one of the young women walked over to them, glaring at Galt defiantly. She was small and dark and angry. In the poor light within the barracks, Galt stared at her hard. He was not certain whether he was looking at a child or a woman.

In fact, she had not yet reached puberty, though she was older than some who had. Her very smallness made her seem childlike, but her fierce expression belied it. Not that the green shirts who did the sorting had made a deliberate mistake. They had been swayed more by her spirit than her looks. Galt gestured to the sergeant to let her alone. It was better that someone care for these children and not leave them to cry.

About an hour before noon, Athirra herself arrived, carrying a huge basket of food, bowls and spoons. From her own time at the women's barracks, she remembered very well that they were given water to drink, and had mugs there. She nodded to Galt on the way in, thanking him for the order, and then set about feeding the gathered women. By this time, the little fierce one had gone back to join the young women.

Athirra fed the elderly ladies first, and then the children. She spoke to the young women as she served them. Galt could not hear what was said, but the guards moved in to stop the talk. This was an apprentice cook from an inn, and should not have discourse with women who might go to a Pleasure House forbidden to him. Galt did not stop them.

As Athirra left, he walked over to her and assured her that the bowls and spoons would be returned by one of his men.

"And I have not forgotten my promise," he assured her, murmuring quietly.

"Corn will submit the cost to the Chief as you instructed, Captain. Perhaps your man will carry it when you send him over. That short, dark one," she added under her breath. "She's not yet a woman. I asked her. She should be placed with the children. You have to see to it."

"Thank you Apprentice. I will see to it," he answered, as if referring to the bill.

As soon as she had left he instructed his men to prepare the women for the Distribution. It was almost noon, and although the clouds were still lowering, the rain had stopped. The wind was blowing the clouds into rags. The day should clear soon.

"Wait, sergeant," he called. "That one there." He pointed to the little one. "I don't believe she is yet a woman. Are you?" He directed the question to her directly.

"Not yet, whatever it matters to you," she answered rudely.

"Hm!" said Galt pondering. "I doubt if she will be an asset to an inn. I was intending to buy another servie from this group anyway. I think I'd better take her. Perhaps we can teach her something in my household before she is sold on."

The sergeant grinned at him. "Rather you than me, sir. She's a little demon all right. I noticed it before. Shall I put her up on the stage with the others?"

"Yes. I'll bid on her in the normal way. I don't want to deprive you of a proper price. That would not be right. Just see that she's offered with the children."

"Right, sir."

As usual the Distribution began with the children. The crowd of potential buyers was very thin. Just one innkeeper and a few of the Pleasure House Keepers. Galt noted that both Ruper and Lombro had come. Good. He would be able to talk to Lombro without going to see him at the Silken Veil.

The lone innkeeper bid on the two small children, and bought them unchallenged. When the little dark one was offered, Galt made his bid, and was astonished to hear Ruper call out a counter offer. Galt walked over to him

"Are you using servies in your House, now, Keeper?" he asked.

"That's no servie. She'd pleasure a man well. There are those who would pay very well for a child-like woman."

"But she is an actual child, according to the rules," Galt said sternly. "We cannot allow your bid for that purpose."

"Want her for yourself, do you?" Ruper spoke insinuatingly.

"As a servie, yes."

"Well, I'll tell you what, Captain." Ruper's voice became unctuous. "The minute she stops being an actual child, you let me know. I'll give you a special price for her, used or not," and he named an outrageous number of credits, which Galt ignored.

Galt didn't bother to answer. He was afraid he might say something unsuitable for the Captain of the Watch. Instead he walked back to the auctioneer and told him to disallow Ruper's bid, although the conversation had been loud enough for everyone to hear. He paid the higher price which Ruper had bid, plus the cost of the meal, as all the other purchasers would do, in order to still any arguments The Distribution moved on.

Ruper bought one young woman, and Lombro bought two. As soon as Ruper had left with his charges, and a limited number of the Watch to guard him, Galt walked over to Lombro.

"You remember the last Distribution, Keeper," he began.

"I remember it with gratitude every day, Captain," Lombro replied. "You need something from me?"

"I do."

"You need that young woman taken off your hands. You prefer she not go to Ruper?" he suggested.

"No, no. She really is a child, and I really need another servie. I am about to take a wife," he smiled. "No. I would like to talk to you. Once we get our charges home, we could probably use a jug of wine. Name the wine shop and I will meet you there."

"There's one next door to my House," Lombro suggested.

"Then that's where I'll come," Galt bowed, and left to pick up his new servie.

"What is your name?" he asked her, remembering how Ibaren had refused to answer him.

"My name is Bessindel," she said sullenly, then burst out with, "I suppose that man was right. I am to service your needs?"

"Wrong," he chuckled. "You are to help an older lady and my new wife. Now be quiet until we get to my house, and I give you into their charge."

Bessindel's fierce exterior shielded the frightened child inside. She was quite sure she was being punished for telling lies to her true mother in the Honor. All the girls her age had moved into the young women's quarters, and she was still housed with the children. She was certain she was old enough to hunt. She hated going out with the herd every day, and taking care of the little ones, though she was very good with them. She wanted to be a person of importance in the Honor, and felt it was more than time she started. So she had lied. She told her true mother that her courses had come, and she was ready to move. Her true mother was as ready as Bessindel was to have her daughter move on. Her late development seemed like a reflection on her true mother. She didn't question Bessindel's word too closely.

And so Bessindel had joined the hunt. She had been practicing with her bow, and she used her sling to keep the goats in order. She never had mastered the spear, but she was sure she would get practice now she was accepted as fully grown. The matter of being taken to the Sieur had never crossed her mind. Once she was out on the hunt and heard the other young women discussing it, her mind had gone cold. She was terrified. The Sieur was so huge, and so old...

But she was never to have to worry about him. She was off on a reckless run after a gumbuck, which she somehow thought she could bring down single handed with her bow, when she was caught by Wilders. They had rushed her over to a temporary camp where a few old women were waiting with a small group of young women, two of whom had children. They were told to keep an eye on her, and have a meal ready when the hunters came back. The women had laughed at her dismay. But not for long. Within two hours, they had all been captured and carried off by the Confraters. Captured twice, the first time she had left the confines of the Honor! And now she was again faced with the terror of a Sieur-like person. He had bought her. Why else? He said he didn't want her, but he was huge and he was old and she was terrified. It was her anger which got her through.

They got to a house and he pushed her gently ahead of him through a door and into a courtyard.

"Ibaren," he called. "I've brought you some help. At least I hope she'll be a help. She seems too angry with me to do anything other than snarl." He laughed.

Ibaren appeared, with Teq in tow. "It's a half day," she answered, when she saw Galt was surprised to see Teq. "So Teq has come for a meal. I can certainly use the help. Let's have a look at you," she addressed Bessindel.

"Tell the lady your name," Galt instructed.

"I suppose I'm for him, then," she said, indicating an astonished Teq with her chin.

Both Galt and Ibaren laughed. "Her name's Bessindel," Galt said. "I'm off to perform my miracle. I'll let you deal with this one." And he left for his meeting with Lombro.

Lombro had preceded him. "There you are, Captain," he said heartily. "I have taken the liberty of ordering wine. Please try this one. It is a favorite of mine."

Galt sat down and poured himself a mug. The day was still chilly and the wine went down very comfortably. "Let me tell you what I would ask of you, Lombro. It is a matter of the strictest confidence, so I hope I may rely on your discretion."

"Without any hesitation, Captain," Lombro assured him. "I have been waiting anxiously to be asked to perform some service for you. It makes me uncomfortable to have an unpaid debt."

"I hope you won't find this too onerous," Galt asked. "I don't think you will, but certainly if you can manage it, there will be no more question of debt between us."

"Just ask."

"I have decided the time has come to take a wife."

Lombro's face clouded. "Alas, Captain. None of my girls is pregnant. The first one, though. The minute I am assured that one is pregnant, I will have word to you on the instant."

Galt laughed. "No, but thank you. No. I already have the pregnant lady. What I need is to have her come from a recognized House. At the moment she does not, though I can tell you no more about the matter than that."

Lombro was puzzled. "The use of my House is open to you, Captain, but how... what. . ?"

"Don't worry about the how and the what. This is what I would like. Tomorrow night, I will bring to your House a lady, who will be veiled. She is to be seen by nobody. Simply kept within your walls overnight. The following day, I will come to you and arrange the marriage in the normal way. You will bring her out, still veiled, and I will lead her away as a wife. Is that something you can do?"

"Yes, of course, Captain. I am at a loss to know how... that is why..."

"As I said. The condition is that you do not ask. Is all this possible?"

"Yes. It is. I have a room within my own quarters which she may lock from the inside. I will bring food myself, and leave a tray outside her door. You have my word, there will be no betrayal of your trust. There will, of course, be no question of a money transaction between us." Lombro accepted the matter thoroughly. Curious as he was as to who this woman might be, he knew Galt would never even imply where she came from. Could she have been the wife of someone who died? Who had been ill? And she had been servicing Galt during that time? That must be it. Speculation on his apparent celibacy had been a matter of gossip among the Keepers and some of their clients for some time. But, who had just died? Hm.

"How else could she become a recognized wife?" Galt's question brought him back abruptly to the matter in hand.

"Very well, Captain. Let us say, you can pay me for a meal she might eat, and it will then be seen that credits change hands. We will count that as the cost of a wiving - though I will not have lost any of my women."

"Perhaps you will have tired of one you kept for yourself, though there will be no need to explain that unless the question arises. Certainly the lady will never be told that."

"As you say, Captain. I say again, you may have absolute faith in the confidentiality of this conversation, and what transpires in your wiving. I would like to congratulate you in advance. I am sure you already know she will be satisfactory."

"Yes, I know that. Thank you Lombro. Let us shake hands on the matter, and I will be on my way. I will knock at your door and ask for you tomorrow night after it is dark. Until then..."

Until then, Captain..."

Galt rushed off immediately and signaled Athirra to come and talk to him. She managed to slip over to his house for a few minutes before the dinner hour, although it was already late, and she could stay only minutes. He explained what she was to do, but would tell her nothing except that she would spend tomorrow night in a safe place. She had already given notice to Corn. In fact, Chapra had arrived that very day, and was already settling in. He had turned the two little servies out of their room, and told Albet to make a place for them where he had been sleeping. They were anxious for him to be gone, now.

Indeed the whole arrangement worked perfectly. Albet left the Carved Oak after breakfast the following day. Corn was too thrilled to have Chapra living there to do more than ask where the written recipes might be found, before wishing Albet well. The apprentice walked swiftly over to Galt's house, and was never seen again. When Athirra emerged after dark, she was once more dressed as a woman, though more richly than the little servie had been, and covered with cloak and veil.

The transaction with Lombro was completed without her knowledge. He merely led her out to Galt, with the usual announcement, he had made to the pregnant women who had been purchased from his House in the past. "You are now a wife. Go with this man and be a credit to this House and to your new status."

Athirra acknowledged this with a startled bow. She was still veiled, which was just as well, since it hid her still-cropped hair.

At the house, Ibaren had prepared a feast for dinner. Teq was to join them. It was to be a day when Athirra was honored. For the first time in her life, Athirra was to be the matron in her own house. For the first time in her life there were no feelings she had to hide. For the first time in her life she was truly happy.

Chapter 23

Teq spent the following morning in a state of agitation. For one thing, there was the feast. He was delighted that Athirra had become Galt's wife, and would be a permanent resident of his house. He was less glad about the new servie. They had sat at the table which Ibaren had set up in the courtyard, with Galt at the head of the table and Athirra at the foot, just as if they were joint heads of the house, or so it had seemed. It was nice. Ibaren sat on one side between Girly and the new one, Bessindel, and he sat opposite. Throughout the meal, the girl Bessindel had glared at him, as if he had done her some injury. It wasn't until he said good night and was ready to walk out through the door that she finally lowered her eyes. What did she think he was going to do to her? He wasn't even a member of the household!

Then there was the weather. He had awoken to one of those glorious mornings which are supposed to typify spring, but which are actually rare. The sun seemed to sparkle off everything, turning the most prosaic objects magic. It made him restless in the oddest way. He wanted to jump, and run and sing and quarrel with somebody, all at the same time.

And finally, as soon as he sat down to his work, it had dawned on him that two apprentices were missing. They were quiet ones, brought in from among those born and raised in the Town. But they had received their collars and were now Competents, whereas he, who had been apprenticed longer, was still just that. An apprentice. He could barely contain himself in the requisite silence until the horn sounded for nooning. It was a half day, so there was no hurry to get to his food. He approached the Competent and spoke as neutrally as he was able.

"When are you planning to set me my test to qualify as a Competent, sir?" he asked.

"Certainly not yet," Gaveril responded, gathering up his work.

"Is there a reason, why not?" Teq wanted to know.

"Yes. I said so," Gaveril smiled nastily.

"Then I request to see the Master. Now." Teq said firmly, mad enough to feel no trepidation.

"Very well, I will find out if he will see you." The Competent managed to give the impression that there was no chance that Master Kinnasen would. He was wrong. When he went to see the Master in his withdrawing room and gave him Teq's request and the reason for it, he was amazed to hear the Master agree.

Gaveril summoned Teq. "The Master will see you, Apprentice. Go in."

"Come in too, Gaveril, the Master called. Let us settle this matter. Now then Apprentice, you wish to take your Competent's test, I understand."

'Yes, Master.' I think I am more than ready. More ready than the last two who got theirs."

"I see. Gaveril, is he ready?"

"He is not, Master, in my judgment."

"For what reason? I know his work and it is good. Even very good. Hm?."

"He is a trouble maker, Master. He has never settled in here as an apprentice. Never made friends among his peers. Always treated me just bordering on disrespect."

"How do you answer that, Apprentice?"

"I do not think the fault is all mine, Master."

"Hm. And yet his work is ready. Perhaps he is ready to throw off the yoke of apprenticeship. He looks old enough. Let us test him, Gaveril, and then make the judgment. If there is any reason to believe he will disgrace this Hall... Well, let us see."

"As you wish, Master," Gaveril ground out.

"Good. Now what will you assign him? Has he made copies of the whole Town? Of the surrounding country? Hm?"

"He has, Master. I should assign him something new." Gaveril was thoughtful.

"But within the Town, of course. Is there anything?"

"There is the area of the falls, Master," Gaveril recalled. "It has never been properly mapped."

"Very well, Apprentice Teq. You have your assignment. You may begin on it tomorrow. Now you are dismissed."

Teq bowed to them both and bounded out of the room, hardly believing that he had just asked for and received what he wanted. And the falls would be a challenge, too. They really had never been properly drawn. He was ecstatic and could hardly wait until he had eaten before running across the Town to tell Ibaren or Athirra or Galt or whoever would listen.

Meanwhile Master Kinnasen told Gaveril to sit down. "Do you understand why I overruled you, Competent? I have never done so before, and I do not wish you to take this as a personal slight."

"It is as you command, Master. I am here to serve you," Gaveril said woodenly.

"True, but I had a reason, and it was your reason. That young man is an uncomfortable presence. I believe as you do, that his very being here is somehow upsetting to the good order of the Hall. He seems always on the point of breaking out. So we should let him go. And his work is really excellent. He will never disgrace our training in that area. It is simply that our lives will be calmer once he is gone. Do you agree?"

"Oh, yes, sir. I had not looked at it in that light. I merely had no wish to reward such a person, such an apprentice."

"Quite right. But I think my way will serve us best. Hm?'

"Oh yes, Master. I do." Gaveril went out, smiling.

The project itself promised to be fun. Teq took his tools to the falls the very next morning. Winter rains had swelled the waters, and they thundered down, wetting everything in the immediate vicinity. Teq walked up the path to the pool, measuring distances, unheeding of the wetting. He was enjoying himself.

Once he had measured the pool itself, and the famous cave beyond it, he clambered up to the top by the upper falls. There was no pool up there, and no path, but the way was not impossible to walk up, without any sense of actually climbing the rocks. The rocks were slippery with the constant wetting, though, so Teq took his time, noting down everything as he measured the route. It was easily noon, by the time he reached the top, and he cursed himself for not thinking of carrying his nooning with him. However, since he was there now, he decided to finish the measurements, and perhaps he could cadge some food from Ibaren when he got down. Galt's house was in this same quadrant.

The upper falls came over the top of the cliff at a sharp angle. In all the eons the waters had been falling there, they had eroded the rock, so that they fell as a curtain, fairly far from the face of the cliff. On a whim, he stepped behind them. There was no sign from below that such a thing was possible. More than that, there was no sign that a cave existed behind these falls. He had found another cave!

In the excitement of his discovery, he forgot all about hunger. He went carefully, remembering from his days at the Honor, that caves could house angry animals. He stepped in, sniffing. There was no feral odor. The ground underfoot was loose, dry soil, seeming to be the accumulation of ages. Nobody - nothing - had set foot in this cave before. At least since the Town had been occupied. What a find! He was certainly not going to include this on his map. This was his.

Cautiously, Teq worked his way inward. How deep did this cave go? The roof began to slope together, so that he was forced to stoop, and then to crawl, and finally, as he rounded a corner, to slither forward. But the cave did go on, and the air was surprisingly fresh. He was able at last to raise himself up, to crawl again, and ultimately, to stand. He was facing daylight. There was an exit. He had to struggle a bit to get through, but he did it. And he was outside. Out on the Western Mountains. Outside the Town. And nobody knew about this place! Nobody knew...

Teq stood there for quite a while, gazing across the enormous vista to the snowcapped mountains in the distance. The cliff behind him rose much higher than the place where he stood. The falls tumbled from its other side. He was part way down the slope of a valley.

He returned to himself and realized that somebody might come looking for him. He had better leave, get himself back down into the Town, if this place were to remain a secret. And of that he was determined. He would tell nobody. Not even Galt, as such knowledge might compromise him. Nobody at all!

In the Mapmakers' Hall, Teq worked hard on his test presentation. He sat at the table and pictured the day he arrived, when fat Bardon had been working on his. How long ago had that been? Three years? Nearer four? He completed his preliminary sketches from his notes, then drew a rough map. The finished product should be ready within the week. All the time he worked he hugged to himself the knowledge of his cave. The irony of finding a way out of the Town just when he was about to be able to go outside officially, was not lost on him. But a secret exit: who knew when it might come in useful?

He was almost ready to present his test to Competent Gaveril when he went over to Galt's house to spend his half day. Athirra was out buying food, and Galt was not due back until the dinner hour so he was chatting to Ibaren.

"The only thing about making Competent is that I am suddenly on my own. For one day after I ran away from the Honor, I was responsible for myself," he mused, "but I was much too scared of pretty much everything to think about that. Now, I am going to be given my first credits, and then it will be up to me to earn more, in order to live."

"Where will you live?" Ibaren asked. "Do they let you stay on in the Hall?"

"No. Never." He was vehement. "In any case I wouldn't want to. But I should be out now looking for somewhere. You're right. I don't even know where to start."

"Well I do." Ibaren chuckled at his astonishment. "I am a woman of many parts. Didn't you know that?"

"But what? Where?" he stuttered.

"Next door. I sometimes talk to the young men there if I happen to bump into them on my way in or out. They were worrying just the other day about not having a full house. The man who owns the place might charge them more for their rooms if he can't keep the place full."

"Which place? This one right on the corner of the main street?'

"Yes. That's the one," she nodded. "Why don't you go round now and see if they have a room free? It would be nice to have you close. Let me lend you some of Galt's credits so that you can pay for a week now and reserve the place if it's available."

Teq didn't say a word. He just leaned over and kissed her cheek as he accepted the credits she offered him.

He jumped to his feet and ran round there right away. He was fortunate in that one of the Competents who rented space in the house was at home. They had rented one room since Ibaren spoke to them, but there was still one empty. The three larger rooms upstairs were all taken, but the small room downstairs off the big entry room, which served for cooking, eating and entry, could be rented. The Competent told Teq where to find the owner, and he ran round there immediately to complete the transaction. He was immeasurably grateful to Ibaren for suggesting it. He had not planned that far ahead, and that far ahead was only a matter of days. The room was small, but he would be able to afford it. There was a bed, a table and chair, and hooks for hanging things. It was enough. He would pay Galt back as soon as he got his Competent's promotion credits. Meanwhile, he was beginning to feel liberated at last. The huge weight of his long confinement was beginning to lift from his shoulders. He felt incredibly light. Weightless. As if he might blow away in a brisk breeze.

There was little ceremony to making Competent. When he handed in his test to Competent Gaveril, he made sure to offer it humbly, saying things like that he hoped the Competent would find it good enough, and that he only dared to hope the Master might accept it. But he knew it was good: as good as anything Gaveril himself could do. Except, of course, that he had left out any indication of an upper cave!

At the noon hour on the following day, just before the horn blew for half day, Master Kinnasen awarded Teq his leather collar, and handed him his credits due. There were some solemn words about the reputation of the Mapmakers' Hall, and some polite applause from the assembled apprentices, but then the horn blew, and it was all over. Teq had no intention of eating this day at the Matted Vine. He ran up the ladder for the last time to gather together his few belongings, and he was off. Forever.

Although he didn't own much, he had to juggle his mapmaker's tools and his clothes, which he had wrapped in his cloak, and his weapons, now restored to him. He had his head down, and his arms full, when he heard a voice say, "Teq?"

A Competent he didn't know was addressing him. And then, suddenly, he did know him. "Vork?" he asked.

They both laughed, and would have clapped each other on the back - at least, they looked as if they want to - except that Teq was so laden.

"You're moving out?" Vork asked.

"I made Competent a few minutes ago, and I'm on my way to my new rooms, with everything I own."

"Have you eaten yet?"

"No. I want to eat somewhere on the other side of the Town from the Mapmakers' inn."

"Here, let me help you with that stuff," Vork offered, "and then I'll buy you lunch to celebrate. The truth is, I was coming here to find you, after all this time, and I was afraid I'd miss you completely. I almost did. This is great luck for me. Will you eat with me?"

"Of course. It's kind of you. And I surely do feel like celebrating. We'll have wine, and I'll buy that. Yes, a celebration. Thanks," he added as Vork moved forward to unburden him of some of his stuff. "I have a room in the southern quadrant."

"I live in the eastern quadrant," Vork told him. "Some of the other Builders' Competents and I have built a house to live and work in. It's quite near the Hall, so we get referrals of business all the time."

"How long have you been a Competent?" Teq asked.

"Just over a year."

Teq winced. "Ouch! Congratulations, though. My place is with three others, but none of them a Mapmaker. All different disciplines as it happens. You know, I came to see you, once."

"Yes, I heard. I'm ashamed to say I didn't tell a soul that I was the person this mad brown shirt apprentice was looking for, but I recognized you from the description. You've become a legend in the Builders' Hall."

"I've become a legend in the Mapmakers' too!" Teq told him dryly. "That little incident kept me from making Competent until now. They said I was a trouble maker. One thing, though. It did find me Galt, if not you."

"I know what happened to Galt, of course. Everyone knows the Captain of the Watch. I've never made myself known to him, though I've seen him a few times," Vork said.

"He saw you once, and told me you looked settled and happy. He was pleased. He'll be glad to know we've met again. Why were you coming to find me just now?"

"I am a person of little courage, as you know. I just never thought you would be pleased to see me after I failed to rescue you from my fellow gray shirts," Vork admitted. "Today I heard that the legendary Teq the Brown Shirt was to make Competent. I gathered up that meager courage and came here before I lost it again. I'm glad I did."

"Me too," Teq agreed. "Here's the place I'm moving into. Galt lives quite close."

"Yes, the Barracks are near here, aren't they?" Vork asked, looking around him. "I don't know this quadrant at all."

"I forget everyone isn't a mapmaker. I know the whole Town intimately, because I've copied the map over and over again," Teq laughed. "Just let me dump this stuff inside, and then we can go to the inn of your choice and celebrate. We have to celebrate this meeting as much as my promotion."

Vork still walked with the same tentative gait, as if he were protecting his burned feet. How he had managed this obvious level of contentment when his relationship with the confraters had begun in that hideous way, Teq did not understand. Perhaps everyone did not question everything the way he did.

They walked over to Vork's quadrant, where he had a favorite inn, and they spent the entire afternoon reliving the past few years as each had spent them. As the wine was flowing freely, the later confessions were more personal and totally forgotten by the time they parted. Teq stumbled off to Galt's house to tell them about his meeting with Vork. By the time he got there, however, he decided he needed sleep more than conversation, so he diverted into his new house and slept until morning.

The following night he was invited to Galt's house for dinner. The celebration continued, though somewhat more soberly.

"Where do you plan to seek your first assignment?" Galt asked him, as they waited for the women to finish cooking the feast.

"Like everything else, I hadn't thought about it. I was simply counting time until I was free of the Hall. Now, I suppose, I had better start looking around. The promotion credits won't last for ever," he confessed.

"Would you like to go outside the Town on an expedition?" Galt suggested.

"You know I'd love it above all things, but I'm newly made. Unproven. Would they accept me?"

"Mapmakers aren't very adventurous on the whole," Galt told him. "There's this expedition leaving to go into Wilder territory and show our strength. To avoid a confrontation over stealing their women. You've heard about it?"

"You've told us something about it, yes," Teq said. "Would that be it?"

"That would be it. Captain Jebend will be leading it. He's someone I know and respect. He's been telling me they could use a mapmaker. Would you like me to set it up for you?"

"I would love it." Teq didn't know how to contain his excitement.

"They'll be leaving in about a week. It wouldn't be a bad way to start off as a Competent, eh?"

"What's all this?" Athirra and Ibaren came out to the courtyard to bring the food. "We thought we'd eat out here tonight. Were you telling Teq your idea?"

"He just told me," Teq got up to help them carry the platters, as Bessindel appeared looking hot and flustered, with the meats. "I can't wait to go. To leave the Town again after all these years. Maybe it will be easier to live here, if I know I can leave from time to time."

"All very well for you," muttered Bessindel, crossly. "Some of us can't leave."

"Don't spoil his pleasure, child," Athirra chided. "This is Teq's night."

"My night. I think I may burst," he told them.

It was a night of laughter and kindness. Teq had never felt contentment like it since he had passed through the Town's walls. He wondered if this was an omen that his trials were over and done at last.

It wasn't.

Part 4
Faring Forth

Chapter 24

Teq had one more day in his cave. He had worked so hard every day during the past week, that the job was far along. He used a piece of the shale, which was lying around everywhere near the falls, as a digging tool. The dirt at the bottom of the cave was soft and easy to move. Some quite large stones were embedded in it, so he worked out a plan for containing the dirt behind a sort of dry stone wall at the wide mouth of the cave.

His aim was to deepen the floor enough that he could get through to the opening at the back, crouching all the way. By the time he reached the bend, he had given up on that idea, but even crawling forward was better than inching along on his belly. He was concerned that, should he need for any reason to use this exit from the Town in a hurry, he could bring along a pack. One never knew. It was all very well to say he could leave the Town now that he was a Competent, but not at will, and that was the rub. The exit itself was clogged with ancient vines, but these were comparatively easy to clear. He needed to feel that he would have a reasonable expectation of getting it out as well as himself.

But now his time for the project was suddenly limited. Not that there was any reason to believe that he would be unable to continue work in the cave after he returned from the hunting expedition. It was just that he wanted to complete it enough to be useful before he left. Because of this need for haste, Teq hit on the idea of throwing the dirt out of the rear exit, instead of dragging it back to the mouth. As a result, things went quickly, and it was still full afternoon when he got through.

The day before he was due to leave, he stood on a grassy ledge above a sharply descending slope, just outside the cave's entrance. In the distance he could see more mountains, as heavily treed as the ones on which he stood. They appeared to be an extension of the northern range, which stayed snow-capped throughout most of most years. The river, of which a branch flowed through the Town from the falls, ran along the higher ground behind him, in a gully it had cut for itself over the eons. The terrain sloped from the north almost imperceptibly, towards the south. One of its tributaries flowed down into the valley before him, watering it. Teq's mapmaker fingers itched to sketch what he could see, but he realized how foolhardy it would be to commit this view to a readable document. He turned and looked up, amazed at how high above him the crag reached. He recalled that vista of the Town he and Galt and Vork had seen when they first crested the hills at the far side of its valley, that day. It all seemed so long ago now. Living within the confines of the Town had cramped his vision. He breathed deeply and was intoxicated by the smell. It occurred to him that what he was smelling was freedom.

All very well, but he had to prepare himself to report to the barracks at dawn, with all his clothes clean. Reluctantly he crawled back into his cave and edged out through the falls, washing the worst of the loose grime off on the way.

When Teq reported to Jebend, the Captain was not yet out of bed. He sent a message that he intended to leave after the noon meal. He was taking a large force and he wanted to inspect them thoroughly before they left. It was his intention to move slowly through the countryside, the sergeant explained, making a lot of noise and a show of strength, along the way. He wished to cow the Wilder packs into fearing to attack, rather than force a confrontation. Teq was required to report for inspection just before the noon meal. He was to expect that all his gear would be checked.

Nothing loath, he took himself off to Galt's house to wait out the morning. Ibaren took one look at him and ordered him to unpack his possessions. His clean, damp clothing fell out of the dusty blankets.

"You thought that would pass inspection?" she asked.

"It's clean," he protested. "I washed everything."

"And wet. And wrinkled. I hope you take better care of your arms."

"Oh yes. I oiled my staff and my bow last night, while these things were drying."

"Hmph! Drying, you say," Ibaren snorted. "Well at least you know how to take care of something. Have you eaten?"

"Not yet. I expected to eat at the barracks, but the sergeant told me to go away and report back before the noon meal."

"Go to the kitchen. Bessindel will feed you while I do something about this gear. I am not sure why I bother. Possibly because the Captain recommended you and I don't want him disgraced. Go on with you."

Teq looking suitably chastened, strode off to the kitchen. He had been up most of the night preparing - which he thought he had done rather well. It had been so many years since he had gone on a hunt that he'd had to think really hard about his needs. It was hot summer, but it could get cool at night if they went high into the mountains, so he packed a coat and both his blankets. The thongs which held his pack together, were the ones he had taken when he fled from Marisel's Honor. He had no arrows, but his bow was in good shape and his staff fit his hand now, better than it had when he arrived in the Town.

"What do you want?" Bessindel interrupted his reverie.

"Breakfast. Ibaren sent me."

Bessindel sighed heavily and put a steaming mug of beanbrew before him. "Here," she said ungraciously, "I thought you didn't live here."

"I don't."

"Well why am I giving you breakfast, then?"

"Because Ibaren said to."

"I don't know that."

"What are you talking about? Why would I bother to lie about it?"

"To get free food."

"What are you so mad about?"

She slammed down a plate of food. "Oh nothing much. Just getting captured twice and sold like a slave, just when I was due to be a woman of the Honor. Nothing you could understand."

"No?"

"You don't know how perfect life in an Honor is."

"So perfect I had to escape before a new Sieur killed me, just because I was born a boy child."

"How did you know about that? How did you know to run away?"

"My true mother warned me."

"Hm! Eat that before it gets cold, now that you've got it. I suppose I can have mine now too." Bessindel sighed again. "I don't know the customs here. I can eat with you, I suppose."

"Well obviously. If we starved the women, there'd be nobody to serve us," Teq teased.

"Bessindel sniffed. "It would be terrible if you had to feed yourselves. But then I don't suppose you know how."

"Of course I do. I was alone when I ran off. I had to hunt and prepare and cook my own food for weeks. I was just about your age then," he said loftily, ignoring his exaggerations in the interest of teaching her a lesson. "You can sit and eat with me if you like."

Bessindel glared at him from her near-black eyes, but decided she was hungry, and sat down opposite Teq with her plate and mug. He was a big one, she thought. Big enough to make a Sieur one day. He had the same tawny look as Galt, the same easy way of moving, but without favoring one leg as Galt obviously did.

"Have you known the Captain long?" she queried.

"All my life. He was my Sieur. He's my father. He told my true mother to warn me to flee. We came here together when he was replaced by the new Sieur. We came to the Town together. He's looked out for me here. You're lucky to be in his household. You really don't know how they can treat women here. You listen to Ibaren and Athirra."

"Why should I listen to anyone? Why should I listen to you?"

"Because you're young, and bad-tempered, and too stupid to see things for yourself. Now, thanks for the meal. I'm off to see Ibaren where the conversation is better." And he got up and tramped off.

It was not just his words which made Bessindel throw the bread from her plate at his retreating back. It was the fact that he didn't seem to care enough to try to win the argument. Worst of all: she failed to hit him.

Ibaren had smoothed and spread Teq's things in the hot sun of the courtyard. She was beating his blankets against the wall when he got there. Teq had the grace to be ashamed.

"I should have done that," he said, taking them from her.

"You would probably have done it badly," she returned. "Now go and turn everything over so that it will dry on the other side. Stooping is hard for me. As soon as everything is dry, I will watch you fold and pack it. I have found an old pack of the Captain's which you can stow your gear into. It will be easier to carry than that bundle you had, though I grant you it was neat enough."

"Thank you." He walked over and kissed her cheek - a thing he had hardly done since he left Tarabeth to go to the boys' room in the Honor. Somehow it seemed right, and he was in the mood. "Where is Galt?" he asked her.

"He'll be sorry to have missed you. He was out at dawn. Some disturbance over in the North Quadrant."

It was mainly due to Ibaren's ministrations that Teq passed Jebend's rigorous inspection. He was grateful. He would have felt a fool if he had been inspected when he first reported to the barracks.

"Can you use these?" Jebend pointed to his bow and staff.

"I have not practiced with the bow in years, but I did all the hunting for our group on the way to the Town. That was more than three years ago," he answered. "I've had plenty of practice with the staff." Teq schooled his face to keep from grinning at his memories of broken apprentice heads.

"Good. You will be more useful than I had supposed. Report to the dining hall now. Before we leave, ask the supply sergeant for arrows."

Captain Jebend was quietly efficient. He had eight sergeants in his command for this excursion, with a total of forty men, plus Teq. A large group. Each corps moved out with its own sergeant in command. They mustered at the inner gate of the East Quadrant, and each corps passed through between the walls to the outer gate, separately. Wall guards called down "Clear", as the signal for the next corps to move out. Teq was unaware that Galt was watching the whole operation approvingly from one side. He wanted to see the lad away, but not interrupt his focus now he had started. Jebend had preceded them all, and instructed Teq to bring up the rear.

They mustered outside the walls in short order, crossing the valley at a jog trot, two corps running side by side. Jebend set the pace at first, then fell back to trot alongside Teq.

"We can walk now, Competent," he said as soon as they began to climb the hills on the far side of the valley. "The sergeants know to make camp just beyond the crest of the hills. "You keep up, I see."

"It's hard to stay fit when you're a mapmaker, sir," he answered. "I run around the Town every half day. It seems I have too much energy."

Jebend laughed. "There speaks a very young man. When we have cleared the Town Control Area, I shall hope to see you mapping the route. We shall no longer be running, so it will be easier." He smiled.

Teq smiled back, liking him. "The Town Control Area is this ridge of hills, I believe, sir," he said.

"Not any more. We have created a larger buffer zone in the years since you arrived at the Town. Just as well. It will give us better warning if there should be a Wilder attack. As soon as we reach camp, leave your gear and set off on a hunt for the pot. There's little game left so near the Town, but we take care not to hunt here for anything other than the first night out. Strict orders from Chief Kambar. There should be something. Let's see what you can do."

The pure delight of being alone in open spaces was nearly Teq's undoing. He took off, running. If he hadn't flushed a whole flock of doodly birds, he would have had to return to camp empty-handed. A lucky throw with his staff knocked one senseless, while he fumbled an arrow into his bow. The stupid birds' habit of rising straight up, then circling into the wind, gave him time to bring another one down before they flew out of range. It was less a matter of good aim, and more a matter of firing wildly into the flock, which got him his prize. He just happened to hit one. It sobered him. He stayed where he was to gut and prepare the birds before he brought them to the fire. He thought they would be better appreciated if he brought them in, ready to be plunged into boiling water or spit and balanced over the flames. He was not very proud of his offering and resolved to concentrate in the future. He needed to travel with this hunt to relearn his skill. That much was obvious. Learning from what Galt and Ibaren told him was one thing. Doing it was another. He resolved to look out for the edible and medicinal plants Ibaren had told him about as well. This was going to be a busy trip.

"You can eat with me," the Captain told him when he got back. "You've covered a good distance, quickly, and don't seem winded. I can use you for a runner if battle conditions arise. Captain Galt said you would be useful to me."

"Sorry about the poor contribution to the pot, Captain," Teq apologized. "I seem to be out of practice all right."

"Yes, well, it will all come back to you. We begin the morning with battle staff training. Be ready to join in. There will be practice with the bow on the following morning. Now, tell me about this famous fight of yours which brought you to Captain Galt's notice."

It was only at meal times that Teq spent any time with Captain Jebend. Otherwise he was assigned to one sergeant or another for the training bouts which always began the day. His skills began to come back to him. As he had promised himself, he watched the plants as he marched along, and began to be quite good at recognizing them. Fortunately his memory was good. He could hear Ibaren's descriptions in his head. At the same time, he was carrying out his main task of measuring and mapping the terrain as they passed.

They moved slowly. Apart from the training bouts, they made a great deal of noise, singing on the march, and creating cheerful chatter around the campfire, all at Jebend's orders. It was to warn off the Wilder packs with the size and discipline of their force. It seemed to be working. They saw no sign of Wilders at all.

The weather held good for most of the march. There were one or two days of steady rain. They were lucky that it was mostly light summer drizzle. The deadly heat and thunder of the week before did not follow them into the hills. Teq's gear remained enough to be useful. The coat helped to ward off the worst of the rain from his back, so even that came in handy. The pack kept his blankets fairly dry. He blessed Ibaren for thinking of it.

It was harder on the rainy days to measure the ground and make his maps. Not that he was trying for anything more than sketches. The finished product would be produced in his room in the Town. Nonetheless he concentrated so hard on getting the details, that it was more than a week before he recognized the territory. They had been marching along a route, slightly to the north of the one their group had taken to reach the Town.

They reached the edge of the forest, stretching mile upon mile to the east. As usual, groups of hunters set out to garner food for their supper pot. Teq set out on his own. He moved stealthily through the trees. This was good game territory and he wanted to come in with something worthwhile. He recognized gumbuck antlers trying to hide themselves among the trees. It was a smallish male. Teq eased around to his left, quite pleased that he could still move quietly through the woods. And then he snapped a twig. The creature's head came up, and it darted out of the brush ahead of him. There was one clear shot. He loosed his arrow just a second late, so that he wounded his quarry instead of killing it. The creature staggered, and then managed to keep to its legs. It set off due east, through brush and fern, blundering wildly. It was an easy trail for Teq to follow. He set off in pursuit, knowing the animal would not last long. It must fall down soon.

It fell into a canyon. Teq was so furious, that without thought he climbed down, and then back up, dragging the gumbuck corpse with him. He tied it to his staff, to carry back across his shoulders, pleased at last with what he could contribute. He was nearly back at camp before he realized where he had been.

That canyon had been the rift!

Chapter 25

"It doesn't seem right, sir," the sergeant said. "He seems to know his way around here, and he's always going off on his own. He does bring in his fair share of game, all right, and he's always scratching away at those maps of his before the light goes, but... . I just have a feeling, sir."

Jebend thought for a minute. "All right then, sergeant. Send a couple of scouts to follow him tomorrow. Not to do anything, mind. Just follow him and report back to me."

So, when Teq set off in the morning he was followed. Very silently. He had no idea. Not that he was considering the matter. For a day or two he'd thought of going south along the rift until he got a sight of Marisel's Honor. But then he asked himself what for, and could not come up with an answer. He could hardly go up to the walls and ask for Tarabeth. That would guarantee getting himself killed, if not her too. There was no point in bothering.

The camp remained where it was, on the edge of the forest. The main job now was to collect game to take back to the Town. They had been there for three days, which was about long enough to be in one place. They could not smoke the meat. They had to butcher it and cook it, and pile it on litters to carry home. The hunters took it in turns at hunting, butchering, cooking and building sturdy litters. Teq hunted every day.

On this last day he struck off to the northeast. He was trying to map as much of the forest terrain as was within reasonable reach of the camp. He followed the course of the stream where they were camped. As he expected, it took him to the top of the rift, round it, and then downhill to a wider, slower river. The rift was drastically narrower and shallower within the forest, than where he had known it so well on the plain. This was the end of it. When he reached the river, he crossed it by leaping from stone to stone. He had settled down with his back against a tree to sketch what he had discovered, when he was disturbed by a noise. He looked up at the point of an arrow directed at his eye. He jumped to his feet, swerving as he jumped. The aimer of the arrow took a step forward so that he could now see her clearly.

"Hulia!" he gasped.

"Who are you? How do you know my name?"

"I'm Teq. Don't you remember? Herding goats? Belleth's true brother? Tarabeth's true son? Surely you know me."

"Teq?" She sounded puzzled. "Really? But you're huge! As big as the Sieur." She laughed and put aside her bow. "You should be dead."

"I escaped during the Challenge fight."

"However did you know? Did any of the others escape? Did Mem? Salsi never stops talking about him."

"No. They were too little. Tarabeth warned me - at Galt's suggestion. But Salsi! Is Belleth all right too? Can I see her?"

"Well, yes. You can see Belleth. I've just been visiting her. That's why I'm up this way alone. She's just had a baby. And she's ill. Very ill, and when you're ill they banish you from the Pack until you get better. But Zolg came with her. He's one of her husbands, and a healer. They're in the cave. I can take you there if you want. Zolg says we can't get whatever she's ill with, though it's killing her. Sorry to tell you that. She has pain in her whole body, but the baby's all right. I came to find that out. I told her other husbands I'd let them know," Hulia explained.

"Wait. Husbands! Could you explain a little? I thought you all dead. I mourned you along with the rest of the Honor."

"Oh no. As you see. Come on. We can walk while I tell you. No Salsi and Belleth and me were caught by a Wilder Pack. The Far Forest Pack. As you know - I suppose it's the same for all packs - the Pack divides into groups. A few men share a fire and look out for one another: usually two to four men in our Pack, who are 'brothers', hm?" She glanced at him to see if he agreed. He said nothing, so she went on. "When they choose a woman from a capture, she marries the group. I hated it at first, because they kept the women confined to the camp all the time. Wouldn't let us hunt. They were afraid we'd run off."

"Didn't you want to?"

"Of course. At first. But then Chag, from our Pack, was the Sieur's Challenger. When he didn't come back, we knew he'd won and taken over. He would never have accepted us back into the Honor. We were married to his Pack mates, you see? And even if Marisel and the Council overruled the Sieur, he would never have accepted us to his bed. In the Pack we have husbands and children of our own."

"How did Belleth and Salsi feel?"

"Salsi is very passive. She mourns Mem all the time, but has four more children already. One each year. They make her happy. Belleth settled in from the start. She adores Zolg, and learned a lot about healing from him. She has two children. A boy back at camp, and now a girl. I have two also."

"Who's looking after the boy?"

"His other two fathers. Anyway, when I convinced my husbands I wouldn't run off, they put it to the Pack, and now any of the women who want to, can hunt.

From Honor Bound

I leave my children with women who prefer to stay in camp. Mind you, the Far Forest Pack is more enlightened than most as you can see."

"And I've been mourning you all this time, when you're all alive and married and happy! Did you ever get any news of Tarabeth, my true mother?"

"She's dead. We captured two more women from the Honor, and they say the Sieur killed her because she would not accept him. It all sounds very odd, but it seems Marisel said it was all right, so nobody objected."

"How could that be?"

"Well I don't understand it. Stand there. Zolg," she called out. "It's Hulia. I'm back and I've brought someone to see Belleth."

They had climbed while they spoke, walking steadily uphill from the river. There was a rockface before them, hung all over with woody vines. A thin trickle of clear water ran off the edge of it, to seep downhill to the river. A hand appeared between the vines, pulling some aside as if they were a curtain. A tall, dark, thin man came out.

"Who is this?" he demanded sharply.

"This is Teq," Hulia answered, "Belleth's true brother. This is Zolg, Belleth's husband," Hulia said to Teq.

"Teq!" a voice called from inside the cave, for it was clear that was what the vine curtain hid. "Let me see him."

"Wait," said Zolg. "Where have you come from? How are you here?"

"We are camped at the edge of the forest. I am a mapmaker. I was out sketching the terrain. Of course I knew I was near the Honor, but I had no idea that Belleth was even alive until I met Hulia." Teq answered him, smiling.

"Who are 'we'?" Zolg did not smile back.

"Oh, of course. I am with the Confraters from a place called the Town. We are only a group of hunters. Here for game. It happened that after I escaped from the Honor, Galt found me. We met someone who was heading for the Town and we decided to go too. Not that I like it so well, but we've been there ever since. This is the first time either of us has left the Town in all these years."

"Confraters!" Hulia shouted. "The ones who stole the women from the High Peak Pack? And I just assumed you were from another Pack, or were here to look for ours or something. Stupid, stupid. Why ever didn't I ask you. Camped at the edge of the forest? How long?"

"Three days."

She leapt up, then shouted over her shoulder, "I must go and warn the Pack. You stay here with Zolg. Thank the Sky and the Earth he had enough sense to ask you." Most of her words disappeared as she was off with a leap and a dash, swallowed by the forest in a blink.

"Let me see Teq," Belleth called again.

"I'm sorry if I upset you, but I really am all alone. I led nobody here. I couldn't have. I didn't know anybody was here. We're just here making a show of force to deter the Wilder Packs from retaliating for the theft of their women. Everyone agrees that it was a stupid thing to do. The captain in charge isn't out to capture anyone. Truly," Teq apologized.

"Hm." Zolg nodded, but ducked inside the cave to fetch his bow, as he gestured for Teq to enter.

Belleth lay in a dim light, but was unmistakably Belleth. She was nursing a tiny baby, who lay against her breast, sated and sleepy. Zolg could not resist passing a caressing hand over them both in a gesture of both love and ownership. Belleth caught his hand and squeezed it, even as she reached out her other hand to Teq.

"I can't believe it," they both gasped in unison.

"I was sure I'd never see you again," Teq grinned.

"And I was certain you were dead at Chag's hand. I was going to warn you to run away. I even tried once. How did you get away?"

"Tarabeth. Hulia says she was killed. I don't understand that. Her I never mourned, though Galt did. I just remembered her with such memories of kindness and grace. He loved her and lost her to the new Sieur, or so he supposed. He's married again, though, now."

"Tell me everything about yourself. You've grown so big. I don't think I would have known you."

"I'll go out and keep watch," Zolg interrupted them. "Don't take too long. This whole situation is making me nervous."

The brother and sister smiled at each other as he ducked out. "Look at that baby," Teq said. "Imagine you, a mother. What's her name?"

"Taza."

"Stay right there," said a voice as Zolg emerged. "Don't move. Those within come out, or this one is a dead man."

Teq shot out of the cave. "Who? What? What are you doing here?" he shouted as he recognized the scouts. "These people are no threat to us. Have you been following me?"

He was so angry he was almost incoherent. How would Zolg ever believe he had known nothing of this?

"Put down those bows at once. At once," he ordered. "This is Zolg. He is a healer, not a hunter. Inside the cave is my true sister who not only has a new baby, but is very ill. How could these people be a threat. Go away."

"That other one went off to bring a whole Wilder Pack down on us. She said so. Looked like a female doing it, to me. The Captain will want to know all about that, Competent, and how you just happened to meet all these Wilders here."

"Accidentally! I didn't know they were here. If I had, I would have asked the Captain's permission to meet with them."

"Yes, very likely, sir. You can tell it to the Captain when we get back there. Now, we'll all just move out, nice and easy. Leave the bows where they lay. That's right. We'll bring 'em along ourselves."

"My daughter is a newborn, and my wife is too ill to walk," Zolg limped forward. Teq as well as the scouts noticed his twisted foot for the first time.

"Healer, are you?" one of the scouts asked. "Couldn't heal that, eh? Or the wife? Still and all, a healer might be some use in the Town. We'll see what the

Captain says. Now then, Competent, you come along inside the cave with me, while we check out this story of the ill wife."

"Captain Jebend will have your head." Teq's fury was growing with every insult. Nonetheless he was pulled inexorably inside the cave by one scout. The other never lifted either his eyes or his bow from Zolg.

"Looks like you'll have to carry her, right enough, Competent. You're a big lad. Shouldn't be no trouble to you. Now, sir, we'll be off. Been here too long already. You lead the way, seeing as you're the mapmaker, eh, sir?"

There was no choice. Teq picked up Belleth, keeping both her and the baby well wrapped in their blankets. Once they were outside in the sunlight, he could see how ill she really was. She was as gray as old snow. Sweat beaded her forehead at the pain of being moved. Teq could see at once that what Hulia had said was true. Belleth was dying. She gripped her lower lip in her teeth to stop from crying out.

"It will be all right," Teq murmured fiercely to her, finally getting a grip on his anger. "I'll see that it is."

"Give me Taza to carry." Zolg limped forward. "She's just been fed. She'll sleep now."

"All right," the scout nodded. "Now, march!"

Captain Jebend listened to the scout, silencing Teq with an uplifted hand. He listened to Teq next, equally allowing no interruption.

"I ordered the scouts to follow you. The sergeants were suspicious of your wanderings. I do not have time to decide whether or not you met these people by rendezvous. Frankly, I don't see how you could have. But Chief Kambar can decide the rights of it when we are back in the Town. Meanwhile, we are not going to wait here and be ambushed by the Pack. Or Packs. Sergeant, strike camp. We leave in an hour."

"And my true sister, sir? She will be safe here with her husband and the baby. We can just leave them behind."

"I am not leaving people behind with details of our strength, Competent. Our direction cannot be disguised, but without the need for secrecy, there is nothing to impede our traveling with maximum speed. Besides, a healer will indeed be of use in the Town."

"But Belleth is ill, and Zolg is crippled, sir. They cannot travel fast."

"They will both be tied to litters and carried. You, Competent, can take your turn with the rest at carrying them. I am displeased about this. Let me hear no more from you until we reach the Town."

The whole journey back was accomplished at an alternate jog trot and fast walk. Meal breaks were brief. Camp was set only at sundown and broken at dawn. To add to the misery of the journey, by the second day they were accompanied the entire time by a damp, seeping rain. Nonetheless, they arrived back at the Town in less than a week. Captain Jebend sent scouts to warn the outlying guards that a Wilder Pack could be on their heels. Another ran ahead to alert the wall guards of their coming.

As they approached, they could see the three Chiefs standing on the walls, waiting for them. For the second time, Teq entered the Town between guards.

Chapter 26

They set up the tribunal in the great hall of the Barracks. Only the three Chiefs sat in judgment. The Dignus was not present. There were rumors that he was ill - ill enough to be dying. The only reaction to these rumors throughout the Town was speculation about who would become Dignus when this one was gone. It was too long since he had been a part of the workings of the Town for most of the Confraters to remember him. It was so long since he had appeared in public in any official capacity, that he was virtually invisible. The days of his glory, when he took the Town out of chaos and anarchy into the planned order of the present days were too long ago. Probably only Chief Sedemp retained any memory of the reason he had been made Dignus. He and the ancient men who sat in the inns and wineshops reminiscing to pass their days. Technically all Masters and Chiefs were eligible to become Dignus. That was how the Town's Constitution read. Actually, only the Chiefs had a real chance. They could command troops to their following in case of conflict. Order and organization were the politics of the Town.

But that was not the matter which was exercising Galt's mind as he stood in the same place where he had been elevated to Captain. Zolg and Belleth and the baby had been housed overnight together in the women's' barracks, for want of a better place. There was a detention cell for men in these very Barracks, but it was rarely used for any purpose other than letting the rowdies cool off. Judgments for felonious conduct tended to be summary and final. Execution or banishment were the punishments invoked most commonly. Having an outsider male as a prisoner was unprecedented.

Teq had not been held as a prisoner. As soon as they had entered the Town, Chief Kambar had heard what Captain Jebend had to say of the whole incident. Kambar made a small attempt to interest Master Kinnasen in his Competent's actions, but he signified that, since Teq had been on a hunting expedition, the matter was outside his expertise and Chief Kambar should deal with it. Kambar listened to Teq's side of the story, after he heard Jebend, and judged him no worse than foolish. He did, however, decree that on future mapmaking excursions with his hunters, Teq would be allowed no opportunity to wander off on his own. It was the fact that no other mapmaker was either willing or able to keep up with the hunters which worked most vigorously in his favor.

He therefore had the chance to tell Galt the whole story of his encounters in detail. The news of Tarabeth's death was more of a blow to Galt than he expected. He found it difficult to contain his reaction in front of Athirra. He closed the matter off in his mind, so that he might mourn her in private at a later time. That the female prisoner was Belleth, his daughter, nursing an infant and dying, appalled him. That she had been incarcerated in the bleak women barracks was worse. He was somewhat reassured by her apparent love for her husband, Zolg, who was not only a physician, but refused to leave her side. Galt was determined, though, that they should not remain there. In spite of Teq's protests, he did think that Captain Jebend had acted correctly in rushing them all back to the Town. There had been little choice, once Hulia had gone to alert her Wilder Pack. Anything else would have meant confrontation, which was the very thing they were out there trying to prevent. Galt felt that it was Teq who had acted incorrectly in not stopping her.

In case he would be needed as a witness, Teq now stood among the hunters facing the Chiefs' tribunal. Galt was there to speak on behalf of the prisoners. Both Ibaren and Bessindel were excited at the story of women from an Honor surviving well among the Wilder Packs. Athirra was more concerned with Belleth and the infant, Taza.

"Bring them here," she said. "We can look after them. This house is large enough, and here they could all stay together. She is married to Zolg, so even here in the Town, living in a house is acceptable. Once she gets better, Zolg can buy them a house of their own. Mind what I say, now. They are to come here. I will not permit them to put up with the Town the way I know it. I don't care what you have to do or say."

"Zolg can certainly earn enough credits as a physician. There is no other in the Town," Ibaren put in. "He could even take apprentices and become a Master, in time."

"I'll see what I can do," Galt agreed. "It would be the thing I would prefer. Among friends, they can adjust more easily to living here. What a mess!"

"You will succeed, of course. I have no doubt of it." Athirra kissed him firmly.

Captain Jebend's report of the hunt opened the proceedings. Next, the scouts who had been set to follow Teq, told their tales. The prisoners were brought in. It was the sight of Zolg limping on his twisted foot which recalled him to Galt's mind. Galt stepped forward.

"May I speak?" he asked.

"Is what you have to say distinctly pertinent to these proceedings, Captain?" Chief Sedemp queried.

"It is."

"Then, unless Chief Fergin or Chief Kambar objects, speak."

"No objection."

"Chiefs, you know I was once Sieur of an Honor," Galt spoke with all the earnestness at his command. He wanted them to attend to every word. "Shortly before I lost at Challenge, three young women of my Honor were lost on a hunting expedition. They were presumed either killed, or captured by a Wilder Pack. Competent Teq was also of that Honor. The young women he met on this expedition were two of those lost. This Belleth is therefore well known to me, as she is to the Competent. In addition, on the day I was bested at Challenge, I lay wounded in a field outside the Honor. The physician from the Wilder Pack offered me help and a place with the Pack. I refused. If I had joined him, I would have met again the three missing young women, because he was of the same Pack which had captured them. He told me his name. It was Zolg. Thus the physician is also known to me. I, therefore, request that these three be placed in my custody. They can remain in my house, while they learn the ways of the Town. My wife and my servies can care for this very ill young wife and her baby. The physician can earn credits at his trade, even as he helps in their care. The Town has a real need for his services."

There was a long silence as the Chiefs thought about what they had heard. Then they turned to confer together.

Chief Sedemp spoke. "As Guardian of the Confraters living within the walls of the Town, the disposal of the prisoners has troubled me. They have, in essence, committed no harm against the Town. I believe with my co-Chiefs, that Captain Jebend acted correctly in bringing them here. Yet their presence is awkward. Chief Fergin has been forced to double and triple the guard duties of his men to be watchful for the coming of the Packs, for they must surely come. Apart from their infirmities, these people cannot be released to an invading Pack. They have been within our Town. They know us now. We therefore agree that habilitation is the best solution. Where better than in a normal household of the Town? Your request is therefore granted, Captain Galt, and with it goes our thanks. It may, in time, be necessary to set aside a proper hall for the use of the physician. You may consult with me on that matter in a week or two. These proceedings are now concluded. You are all dismissed."

Galt enlisted Teq to help him carry Belleth's litter, while Zolg limped alongside. .

"I remember the encounter," he said to Galt.

"Good. I remember it with pleasure. A kind word was welcome, that day. My beloved Tarabeth, who was Belleth and Teq's true mother, had set up provisions for me, which I was anxious to retrieve before they were discovered. I also wanted to find Teq, here, if he had managed to escape. Otherwise, I might well have accepted your offer, especially had I known Belleth to be your wife. It is a strange world."

"It is that. And this Town is a strange place. Who were those men? What gives them a right to sit in judgment on their fellows?"

"We'll tell you the ways of the Town in good time. Here we are, now, at my house, with my women anxious to make a fuss over you. How goes it, daughter?"

"I am tired," Belleth smiled at him. "Isn't Taza a good baby? Our son, Zeld, was never so placid. I hope he is all right. He is only a little boy. He will miss us so much." Her eyes filled with tears.

"He has my brothers to father him," Zolg comforted her. "He is three, after all. Nearly old enough to learn to set traps. Eh?"

Ibaren had spent the morning preparing a room for their visitors, while Athirra and Bessindel cooked. Bessindel was learning to cook rather well, in spite of her early reluctance. When the party arrived, the women would not permit Belleth to set foot off her litter, but saw her disposed upstairs in her bed with Taza in a little box crib they had made ready, alongside. They fed Belleth there. Zolg stayed with her until she slept and then came downstairs to join the others in the courtyard.

"Thank you," he said simply. "She is comfortable. I had been dreading what might become of us."

"You are my family, as much as you were a family in the Wilder Pack," Galt assured him. "As much as we were a family in the Honor. We look out for one another."

They talked as they ate. They talked as they cleaned up. They talked as the sun set and hid their faces from one another. They talked through the whole of that night.

It was less than a week later that the alarm horns sounded. The expected Wilder invasion had arrived. Chief Fergin had reinforced his far sentries, who sent runners to alert the Town as soon as the first members of the Pack army were spotted. It was hardly an army. Not really. It was a group of men without apparent organization or cohesion. The men had been exhorted forward, as individuals, by the incensed speakers of each Pack. Individually they had agreed to join in, because they believed the cause to be just. Some came for the adventure. Some from curiosity - who were these Confraters who felt free to steal their women?

In contrast, the organization of the Confraters had never been more apparent. All the green shirts - hunters, guards and watch - marched together under the command of Chief Kambar. Because of the planned early warning, they were in place, ringing the heights which protected the approach to the Town, when the Pack first appeared.

All the young men of the Town, of all shirt colors, manned the walls of the Town under Chief Fergin's orders. Chief Sedemp, with the aid of the Masters, organized the remainder of the Confraters into their respective Halls, where they could be reached easily if they were needed. The women were kept within doors.

There was no confrontation. The matter was settled without an arrow being released or a spear thrown. Such a massing of organized forces completely unnerved the Packs. As their lines wavered, undulating this way and that, a few marched out in front. Chief Kambar and his Captains stepped forward to meet them.

"You have our women," a Pack spokesman said.

"We do," Chief Kambar agreed.

"And our healer," said another.

"Him too," Kambar nodded.

"Well we want them back."

"That is impossible," Kambar said firmly. "Once a person enters the Town, they do not leave it."

"If that was true, you wouldn't have been in our lands stealing our folk," said a voice. The Wilder Packs laughed.

"We ought not to have taken your women," Kambar told them. "We have as much trouble finding women as you do."

The Packs laughed again.

"We promise this," Kambar offered. "We will not hunt or raid in your direction again for two years. We will never again take any women from any Wilder Pack anywhere, so long as you go back now where you came from. If you do not, we are prepared to fight you with all the forces at our disposal."

"Let's see this Town now that we're here," one called. There was a roar of amused approval from the Packs.

"No," said Kambar.

"Well then... ." The spokesmen turned back to the Packs. They had heard what was said. There was no discussion. The men looked at one another. One by one they shrugged shoulders or shook their battle staves, but one by one they turned to go. It was clear even to the most warlike that they had no chance against the Town's army. Little by little the Packs began to drift away.

The green shirts followed them, keeping their distance, but marching shoulder to shoulder down into the valley and up the next rise. They remained in position, long after the last of the Wilders was lost to view. At dusk they turned back for the Town. That night they camped outside the walls, but no Wilders returned to raise an alarm among the sentries. The next day, they marched back inside, and the dreaded attack was over.

Teq was disgusted.

"You have to understand that Wilders are not like Confraters," Zolg told him. "We go and do things together when we agree to do so. Even then we don't all go. People who don't agree, don't go along. The Confraters do as they're told by their leaders, whether they want to or not. You didn't want to man the walls against the Wilders, but you went. Didn't you?"

"Yes, I went. I suppose I must be getting conditioned to the Town, just like I was in the Honor. It wasn't till I left that I realized how much I had taken for granted. Just accepted. Never thought about..."

"Most of us do. I was born among the Wilders. In an Honor I would have been killed at birth because of this foot. I don't know about here. It's because the Wilders accept everybody, whatever their differences, that I lived. I can't be sorry for that. It's something I admire."

"No, of course you can't object to that! I just wish I knew what was a good way to live. Excuse me for saying it, but the showing by the Packs yesterday was pretty pathetic."

Zolg nodded. "It did seem that way, and yet they got a good result from just coming here. Nobody was hurt. There won't be any more stealing away of people. You are just going to have to choose the best from each way of living. I'm glad we're here because it's better here for Belleth and Taza than a cave. That doesn't mean I won't miss the life of the Pack, my son and my brothers. Just making the best of what is. Do you see?"

"You don't know. If Belleth were not already a wife, it would be anything but better for her here. Well, you know, by now, she'd be in a Pleasure House. We have to be doubly glad you're here." Teq smiled at him.

"It's nice to hear, Teq. Thank you." Zolg smiled back and clapped him on the shoulder. "Let me go to Belleth now. I hear Taza crying."

All the same, Teq thought, I wish I did know the best way to live. Not that I can really change anything. But so far I seem to have been dissatisfied with everything. I can't go on like that forever.

Chapter 27

In two weeks, Galt's household had settled in comfortably together. Bessindel was not best pleased at giving up her room and sharing with Girly, but it was only because the luxury of a room to herself had been such a delight. The summer grew even hotter - the hottest of the three since Galt and Teq had lived in the Town - and the drains began to stink. Ibaren planted richly perfumed herbs in the courtyard, in the hope of counteracting the smell; but Athirra, now in her sixth month of pregnancy, found the weight of the mixed aromas oppressive and nauseating. The women did as little as they could, beyond wishing for a breeze. Bessindel, who was not permitted out without a cloak to cover her burgeoning woman's figure, never left the house.

Amid all this, Teq was delighted to receive a summons from Captain Jebend.

"I am taking a hunting party south, leaving tomorrow. When we have a full bag, I want to send the majority back and carry on with a small expedition party. A sergeant, six men, and myself. Chief Kambar wants the land to the Great Sea mapped. I have asked for you as mapmaker, Competent. Will you come?"

"Will I? I mean, yes, sir. Enthusiastically, sir. To escape this heat would be reason enough, but I should very much like to see the Great Sea."

"Good. We will leave early, before it gets too hot. Report to me here at dawn."

"Yes, sir."

Teq bounded off to share the good news with Galt, but found only a courtyard full of fanning women. They nodded and smiled at his news.

"Come tonight for dinner," Athirra said. "You can tell him then , when it's cooler. We bring Belleth down every evening now. Taza sleeps well, and there is usually a breeze."

Teq nodded and went to get his gear in order, including a dash over to the Mapmakers' Hall. His only reluctance in going on this long foray, was in leaving Belleth. He felt guilty that it did not stop him altogether, but the truth was that he found it difficult to spend time with her, looking so ill. She claimed to feel better since she had been so indulged in Galt's household, but Zolg assured them all that it was a temporary improvement.

"One day the pain will come back and will not leave again. We must make the most of what time we have."

The departure at dawn was accomplished with little noise. Only Teq and the sergeant carried a battle staff. The hunters carried bows and spears. Keeping the mountains on their right, they trotted south over the gentle hills where the Town herded their livestock, until the day grew hot. The Captain called a halt at a wide place in the river and ordered the men to sleep in whatever shade they could find. At dusk he sent out hunters to collect enough for their meal. As soon as they had eaten, they moved south again by moonlight.

In three days they had reached a great plain. It seemed as if huge herds of every beast known roamed before them. It would be less a hunt and more a slaughter, Teq thought. In three days more, they had amassed and butchered as much as they could carry. The morning after, the main body of the hunters left, carrying their spoils.

And the exploration party moved on south. They kept essentially to the same pattern of movement, sleeping away the heat of the day and the dark of the night. They moved at the early dawn and kept moving until the late dark. Although the massive hunt had scattered the herds on the plain, there was still plenty for them to capture for food on the march. The six hunters were more than enough to handle that. Teq amused himself enhancing their diet by again searching out the edible and medicinal plants Ibaren and Galt had described for him. His eye improved with the passing days.

It took a week to cross the plain. The area was already well mapped. Teq had been instructed to collect copies of maps of the region from Gaveril - much against his will. The request, however, had gone from Chief Kambar to Master Kinnasen so he had little choice. Teq found nothing in them to change. They were accurate and detailed, even to the bends in the rivers. The main river flowed from the continuing mountain barrier to the west, moving east and south. The river which flowed through the Town was its tributary. Another tributary flowed quiet and small from the southern hills which they were approaching, swelling the central river into fat sluggishness.

The party crossed the river upstream of where it was fed by its tributaries. In the heat of the summer, it was shallow enough to ford. Even in the center, the water was barely waist deep on the shortest man. They steamed dry during their afternoon sleep.

Mapmaking became interesting as they climbed into the southern hills. Maps of this region were bare sketches, without detail. Teq roamed wide, pacing his measurements and making his sketches, but Captain Jebend saw to it that he never roamed alone. Two men were detailed to accompany him all the time. Each day a different pair. Teq found their presence mildly irritating and mildly amusing. He had no true sisters to come upon in this direction, and he was not planning to strike out on his own. Where would he go? And why? All the people he cared about were back in the Town.

Once in the hills, the terrain rippled gently downward from northwest to south-east. The land underfoot became drier and sandier. They took to carrying water with them. The grasses became more scarce and more sharp-spined. Trees were few, stunted and alone. Finding shade for the midday rest became a matter of propping cloaks on their spears or battle staves. Even Captain Jebend, who owned the only tent, left the sides rolled open to allow for maximum shade and maximum passage of air. In the whole stretch of their journey they saw no signs of other people.

There came a day when the breeze was steady and smelled of salt. They moved a little faster, cresting the final sandy rise just as the sun dropped from the sky. Before them lay the Great Sea. Its immensity sucked the light from the darkening sky and sparkled it back at them from restless ripples on its surface. It muttered at them, grumbling a little and hissing a little in greeting. It was neither dark nor still, seeming to swallow all the dark and all the stillness of the night into itself, and send it back grudgingly. It is where the sun hides and where the moon comes from, Teq thought, awed in the deep quiet.

Only the Captain had seen it before. He smiled at the reactions of his party, and let them look their fill. "Impressive, isn't it?" he asked Teq. "I promise you, you can become used to it, like everything else. It is possible to move on its surface in vehicles called boats. Like the stretchers that we carry, only hollowed out. Deep. I have seen them far off. With the use of cloth tied to a pole, mounted in the center of these boats, they capture enough wind to push them along. I have tried to think how such a thing might be used on land as a means of carrying things, but cannot. There is always a wind on the Great Sea, and there lies the main difference. I would like to see a boat up close."

"Oh so should I," Teq agreed. "It would take a brave man to venture out on to that, though."

At the edge of the sea, the party turned east, walking the beach or the dunes, depending on whether the tide was in or out. Teq took careful measure of the way the land moved in and out, up and down, but to the Great Sea there seemed to be no end. There was no longer much game to fill their pots. The majority of the sea birds were inedible. They were lucky to come across the occasional bobbit among the dunes. There was endless fascination for Teq in the way the immensity of the ocean moved in and out of their way twice every day, ruled by some law he could not know. When they came to the place where the river reached the sea, it was only visible when the tide was far out, and then only as ripples cut in the sand. Such a trivial end to such an epic journey, Teq thought. He said nothing to the others, believing they would simply think him fanciful.

And then one day, the last of the grasses disappeared and there was nothing to the north, east or west of them but sand. On the southern side, the sea beat on relentlessly.

They saw sand in hills, sand in valleys, sand in loose, impossible slopes which they slid down and could barely climb.

"It is the desert," Jebend announced. "Nothing lives here but snakes. Nothing could. We turn back tomorrow. I think we will strike off to the northwest and see if we can map a different route back to the grasslands. You have no need to retrace the ground we have covered, Competent?"

"No, indeed, sir. There have been few landmarks to take note of for several days," Teq answered him.

"Good. Then we will camp here for the night and be off at first light."

Here, was a bowl surrounded by dunes, where a seepage into a cluster of rocks on the north side, provided the promise of fresh water. From force of disciplined habit, sentries were designated in pairs to keep the night. The nights were much colder, here in the desert, although there was no relief from the heat during the day. And the sky was dazzling bright. So many stars shone above them that the land ought to have been as bright as day, and yet the darkness below the crests of the dunes was unfathomable. Teq gazed upward thinking he could never sleep; but in fact his sleep was profound until the dawnlight woke the sky. He opened his eyes, looked up and gasped.

"Captain Jebend." He spoke with a voice sounding much steadier than he felt.

"I am awake."

"What do we do?"

"Get up, I suppose. All at once now. Sergeant Gard, the men are awake?"

"Four of them, aye, sir. I see no sign of the sentries."

"Neither do I. On my signal then. Up."

They had awakened to find themselves surrounded. At the top of the dunes in all directions, no more than an arm's length from one another, warriors stared down upon them. More awe-inspiring, even than the spears pointed casually in their direction from every hand, the warriors sat upon beasts. All the warriors were swathed in a thin cloth, which covered them from head to toe. Only eyes were uncovered and staring. Whether there was more than eyes to any face, was impossible to judge.

On the Captain's word, the party stood. As if at the same signal, a thin, ululating cry arose from the warriors. Somewhere. It was from one voice, yet it seemed to emanate from all directions at once. Simultaneously, casually, accurately each warrior threw his spear. The Captain's party was surrounded by an impenetrable fence. The hunters reached reflexively for their weapons. They were not there.

"What do you want with us?" Captain Jebend called. "We are not here to fight."

There was a ripple of laughter among the warriors. Two of the beasts parted for a moment and the two sentries were thrown down the slope to land outside the fence. Each was impaled through the gut on a spear. Each was mercifully dead.

"You have killed my men." Captain Jebend tried unsuccessfully to keep the anger from his voice. "We have done nothing to provoke you. What do you want with us?"

There was silence. Nothing moved.

"Someone must be in charge. Let him stand forth. Let him face me. Let me speak to him." Jebend tried again.

Again there was laughter. Nobody moved.

The sun moved. It rose fiercely and began its daily burning of the sands. The spears ringed the hunting party so closely, that they could neither bend nor sit. With difficulty, as the morning wore on, they managed, one after the other, to hook such of their cloaks as were within reach of their feet. They wanted to drape them on the spears to create some shade. But the least movement from any of them was greeted with a threatening grumble from the warriors. No words. Just menacing sound. They desisted. The warriors sat upon their beasts under the same sun, seemingly unaffected by it, arrows casually notched into their pointing bows. The beasts themselves showed little more reaction than the men on their backs. Here and there a head drooped or a tail flicked. That was all. The morning ached on. The men could reach no water. They closed their eyes against the relentless brilliance. Sweat broke only where contact was made perforce between one man and the next. It became difficult to continue standing, yet they could neither sit nor fall down.

When the sun stopped directly above them, bright hot as an anvil fed by the furnace of the sands, the beasts parted once more. A single beast, surmounted by a single tall figure, moved between them and began to descend the dune. They approached slowly, calmly, the figure swaying a little to accommodate the movement of the beast. At the bottom, they began to circle the fence of spears, looking the party over through a pair of unemotional, deep blue eyes. Teq thought of the night sky he had watched before sleeping. The figure gave him the same sense of insignificance he had felt looking at the remoteness of the stars, gazing down at their small party in the hugeness of the desert.

The voice, when it spoke, was female. It was rich and deep and securely used to command.

"Who are you?" she demanded.

The Captain's throat was parched. It took a deal of swallowing for him to be able to answer at all. "We are an exploration party," he managed, "come to see the Great Sea and the desert. We come from a place in the north called the Town."

"That is not what I asked."

"I am Captain Jebend. This is Sergeant Gard, and these four are hunters under my command, as were the two whom you killed. Not warriors. The young man is Competent Teq. A maker of maps."

"What are maps?"

"They are..."

"Let him answer me."

Teq swallowed convulsively trying to muster enough saliva for his voice to work. "They are charts, pictures," he croaked, "showing how the land -er flows."

"Ah. I see. Useful, I think. For warriors too." There was the hint of a smile at the back of the blue eyes. She circled them again on the beast. Slowly. "Ha!"

Jebend asked, "why do you attack us? Why have you killed my men. We have done you no harm, nor mean to."

"You have dared to bring arms into the precinct of the sacred spring. You have slept here and built a fire here, and defecated here. Just to approach it without my permission is death. Do not tell me you did not know this."

"On my honor, I swear, we knew nothing of this. We knew only that the spring gave lifegiving water. Please believe me. We intended no dishonor... How may I address you?"

"You." She pointed to Teq.

"We knew nothing, lady. Truly. We knew nothing of your laws. We did not even know of your people, the people of the desert. We have seen noone in weeks on our travels. We did not mean to offend, lady. Please, how may we call you?"

"I am Shamana, Priestess of the Spring, Princess of the Desert, Lord of my people through the will of the Mighty Mystery of Sky, Sea and Sand. In my hands is the life and death of my people. Yours also," she added, the suggestion of a smile once again at the back of her eyes. "Kneel before me."

In the cramped space between the spears, where they had not thought such a movement possible, led by Jebend, they knelt.

Chapter 28

It had been more than two months since Teq had gone off on his expedition and Galt was a little concerned. Parties rarely to never stayed away from the Town for so long, in his experience. They must be mapping an awful lot of territory. He missed Teq. His household was overwhelmed by women, almost like an Honor, he chuckled to himself. Belleth was beginning to fade. Her constant pain was a pain in his heart. Bessindel had learned a great deal about making medicines and administering them, from Zolg. It was a job Belleth had apparently done at the Wilder camp. What had been easier there, was the gathering of the plants to use in their making. Zolg was forced to go out with the herdsboys and the shorter hunting parties to find what he needed, and it was difficult for him to keep up. There was no question but that he would need apprentices, if he was to fulfill the Town's needs. Meanwhile, Bessindel spent a lot of time with Belleth, learning from her and administering to her. Ibaren divided her time between Athirra, now only a month away from birthing, and little Taza. Between them all they managed to keep Galt's household running, but only just.

As for Zolg, he was working at his healing arts as hard as he could, throughout the Town. He was furiously trying to earn enough credits to pay for a property of his own, where he could both live and have patients visit him. The constant walking around the Town to call on his patients was very hard on his crippled foot.

And the autumn rains had come. They were as excessive as the summer heat had been. Every afternoon thunderstorms roared up over the western mountains, deluging the Town, so that all business was forced to stop. The drains were swept clean, but they flooded over the streets and, at least during the first week of the rains, the resultant mud was an evil, stinking morass.

The river was overfilled too. The waterfall became so dominant that it poured down the pathway at its side and flooded both the baker's house and the one next to it. All three families living in that corner vacated their homes. New homes had just been built farther inside the quadrant and the families were able to move together. The Town compensated the first two, but the third building, which had been a wine shop, was sound and needed to be sold. It stood high and dry on a rock and was going cheap. Zolg decided to try and buy it. It was the biggest of the three, with an upper floor overlooking the falls. There was plenty of space downstairs for a workplace. One room had benches built in, where the wineshop customers had once sat to do their drinking. It held a counter and shelves besides, where he could stock and sell his medicines. The kitchen was sizable for preparing them as well as food, and there was yet another room downstairs where he could offer privacy if he needed to examine the sick visitors. Ideal. Upstairs, he could live, and even house apprentices, if he could ever afford any.

Galt went with Zolg to visit the wine merchant. He was so pleased to have the chance to sell the house, that he haggled very little over the price Zolg offered him. It also did no harm to be helpful to the Captain of the Watch. Zolg would not move Belleth. She was now much too ill to be in a place which offered so few comforts; but he spent every moment he could spare from seeing patients, getting the place ready.

Galt was with Zolg at the shop when his sergeant found him.

"Sir, there you are! Chief Sedemp sent me to find you. Most seriously urgent, he says. Wants you on the instant, he says, and I couldn't find you anywhere."

"Well, you've found me now. I'm on my way. Is he at the barracks?"

"Oh no, Captain. Excuse me. He's at the Palace. They say the Dignus is worse. All the Chiefs are there."

"Good gracious!"

"Let me know if you need me, Galt. Perhaps there's something I can do, at least to ease him," Zolg offered.

"Yes, I will. I'll suggest it to the Chief."

Galt hurried off. Rumors of the Dignus' deteriorating health were anything but new, but nothing much seemed to change because of it. If he really was dying, there might be an impact on the Town, but it seemed that lethargy ruled the reactions so far.

"There you are, Captain," Chief Sedemp greeted him at the door. The other two Chiefs stood close beside him, the tall, silent woman hovering behind them all. "We are all just leaving. We are told the Dignus needs his rest. Walk with me to my house."

Chiefs Kambar and Fergin greeted Galt absentmindedly, seeming reluctant to leave the Palace. However, Sedemp led the way and they followed, as happened so often. Sedemp and Galt walked ahead, the other two Chiefs coming behind, in close conversation with one another. Behind them the woman closed the door, a thing Galt had never seen before. The Palace door stood always open.

"The physician, Zolg, offers his services to the Dignus, Chief, if he could help," Galt ventured.

"Ah, yes. He is living in your household, still, is he not? How kind."

For the rest of the walk to the Chief's house they were silent, each occupied with their own thoughts. Once inside the enclave walls, where the Chiefs and Masters lived, they parted from the other two. It was a lovely place, the enclave.

Now, just at evening, when the day's storms had already rumbled past, a pleasant cool freshness left the evening breath clean. An arm of the river had been allowed to meander through the enclave, so that most houses looked out upon it. The banks were held by old trees, and though the streets were mud, there was grass along the verges which was pleasant to walk upon. Galt had been there rarely.

They walked through a passage into the Chief's large house and entered a central courtyard.

"Sit down, Captain. There is something you must do for me. If you do it well, the reward will be great."

"I am, as always, yours to command, Chief. There is no need for special reward." And Galt meant it. He had a true respect for Chief Sedemp, whom he had found to be both intelligent and subtle in his demands for the Town.

"Ah. Excellent. Think of this, then. How would you arrange to empty the Town of its people for a day?"

"All its people, Chief?"

"No. Just the Confraters and apprentices. The women are of no consequence."

"Perhaps a fire, or a threat of fire. No. They would be needed to stay for that and aid in fighting it. Hm! The Wilder invasion threat emptied the Town successfully. We cannot create an invasion, but perhaps a rehearsal. A drill. Would that serve?"

"Yes, I believe it would serve very well. Yes. I will suggest it to the Chiefs and Masters. We meet tonight to discuss the arrangements for the transition when the Dignus dies. Alas, his death is imminent. He has taken his farewells of us, but I think he will last the week. Perhaps a little longer."

"But will it seem strange to be upsetting the Town with this drill at such a time?"

"Why no. It is what we want. It is our fear that the Town will divide into factions, fighting one another to support one or another of us to become the new Dignus. The green shirts mainly, of course, but the apprentices would be all too eager to join in. The Chiefs and I have decided to disperse them under the command of their chiefs. This will keep order and the new order will be established without upheaval. It will be done when they return. Do you see?"

"How will the new Dignus be selected, Chief?"

"By the old. It is already done and witnessed. You and I and the witnesses are the only ones who know, and must remain so."

"May I ask... ?"

"You may speculate. Now then, tomorrow you may have your men start spreading the word regarding this -er drill. Make a plan. Let each Confrater know what route he must take to the walls. And the apprentices also, of course. Organize your Watch to get them there, before they leave to join the other green shirts on the hills. As soon as I send you word in the morning, be ready to begin."

"Yes, Chief. And the day?"

"One week from tomorrow. Horns will sound to start and end the proceedings. Dawn and dusk, will do. The people should all carry food for their nooning. Women indoors. Masters gather at the Palace. Questions?"

"None, Chief. It is clear."

"Good. You will hear from me in the morning."

Galt found the whole proceeding a little excessively precautionary, until it dawned on him that the idea was less to empty the Town of green shirts, and more to remove the other two Chiefs with their men. Clearly Sedemp had been chosen, since he alone knew who the Dignus had selected as replacement. It was hardly surprising, since he was virtually the only person the Dignus remembered, these days. No question but that Kambar and Fergin would be incensed at being left out. But, Galt thought, they were much younger and it would not be long before Sedemp ended his own years. They could wait. In his opinion, Sedemp was the proper choice.

If nothing else, Sedemp had always been persuasive. There was no apparent dissension at the evening's meeting, although Galt was required to keep a few of the Watch in the vicinity to ensure order, and the easy passage of the Chiefs and Masters to the meeting. He himself hovered near, but received no orders until the morning.

He conferred with Kambar and Fergin, suggesting the green shirts be allowed to vacate the Town at the drill's first warning horn. Confraters and apprentices would man the walls on the sounding of a second horn. Each would cover the walls in their own quadrant. They had been orderly during the Wilder attack, but this time there was no threat to the Town, and the whole drill took on a holiday air. For the apprentices especially, it was a day of freedom, and they cavorted on the walls as if they were at a game court. The Confraters grumbled mildly that they were losing a day's business, but since they were all losing the same day's business, it was not a serious matter.

The closing horn shattered the sense of holiday by sounding at noon. At the last minute, Galt had been instructed not to leave the Town, but to keep a contingent of the Watch at the Palace. The Watch were sent to muster the Confraters, and then the green shirts, to gather in the space before the Palace. Black cloths had been draped at the windows. The Masters were clustered in front of the door, facing the crowd. The green shirts arrived, and cleared a passage for their Chiefs to reach their peers. Once more the horn was sounded, so that the crowd fell silent.

"Be silent for an announcement," Galt called in a stentorian voice he had hardly been aware he possessed.

The silence was complete.

"It is time to mourn the death of the great man who began the Town. Our home." The voice of Sedemp had never seemed quieter. Never been more penetrating. "Our Dignus is dead. He has named me his successor before witnesses. There is a Dignus still. You have not been abandoned. His last thoughts were for you all. Us all."

There was the beginning of a murmur in the crowd. The voice continued as if the speaker heard nothing.

"In anticipation of the sadness we feel at the loss of our first great leader, the Chiefs and Masters and I have made plans for the ceremony which will mark his interment, here in the Palace forecourt, where he may be visited by you all. We have further planned for the investment of my own person as the new Dignus. Chief Fergin will tell you details of the first, and Chief Kambar of the second. May Earth and Sky bless us all in our time of grief."

This was the most dangerous moment. In calling upon the two Chiefs to address the assembled citizens, Chief Sedemp was essentially forcing their endorsement of his mandate as Dignus. If they said nothing now of their own claims, the moment would have passed.

"Be silent for Chief Fergin," Galt bellowed above the rising tide of voices.

Fergin was unquestionably the weaker of the two men. He stepped forward looking confused and uncertain. He cleared his throat, looking to Kambar and to his men. Kambar looked away. He would certainly not encourage Fergin to lay claim to the position. There was a pause. Fergin again cleared his throat. When he spoke it was simply to outline the funerary arrangements planned for the dead Dignus. There was a relaxing of tension among the Masters, less visibly in the crowd. The interment was set for the morrow.

"Silence for Chief Kambar," Galt yelled again, as soon as Fergin finished. The momentum had gone. The moment had passed. The crowd remained undisturbed, unaware of the potential upheaval. It was no surprise that the Dignus had died. Speculation on how his successor would be selected had never been a hot topic. It was outside the interest of most Confraters. It was far too long since the Dignus had impacted on their lives. He had been a historical, rather than a real figure, for almost a decade, never even appearing at Founder's Day ceremonies for the past three years. Apart from the partisanship of the green shirts, there were few who cared enough to show concern. Of the green shirts themselves, both Guard and Watch had accepted the decision. The Hunters could do little alone, even if they wanted to most passionately.

All of this was perfectly clear to Kambar as he stepped forward. He bowed solemnly to Sedemp, but whether because of his masterly handling of the transfer of power, or whether because of his new dignity, would never be clear. Kambar was terse and succinct on the process of the investiture. It would be the day following the interment. There would be what, in essence, amounted to a three day holiday, counting this one. The murmur the people were finally permitted to release was crowned by a cheer from the apprentices. The thing was done. As if to emphasize the finality of the matter, the first clap of thunder heralded the afternoon rains. The crowd dispersed.

The ceremonies were interesting enough to cause most of the Town to assemble in attendance at each. Wine shops and Pleasure Houses did exceptional business on all three evenings. Inns were heavily patronized since shopping for food was impossible for three days, and cooks had to make do with what they had. The break in the routine was welcomed on the whole; but when lives went back to normal at the end of the three days, that was welcomed too.

The day after it was all over, the new Dignus sent for an exhausted Galt. Order had been maintained at some cost to the Watch. Galt came from heaping them with praise and commendations. He resolved to request a bonus for each of them when he met with the Dignus.

His entry to the Palace was not the same as on that first memorable occasion. Tall young men guarded the entry way. An older man led him through the rooms and announced him to the Dignus. Sedemp sat at a table, not crouched before a fire. No young women shared the room. The silent one drifted in with wine for them on a tray, and then drifted out again.

Sedemp acknowledged his presence and told him to sit. To drink. "I sent for you to commend you, Captain Galt," he said.

"May I congratulate you, sir?" Galt responded. "There is certainly a new order in evidence here."

"Ah yes. Small changes at first. We will be working on certain codifications. Laws, you know. An order to things - even the way members of the Council and the Dignus are to be selected." He allowed himself a small smile. "Do you see?"

"See and applaud, Dignus. You show a farsightedness for the Town, I think."

"Well, thank you. What I want to do this morning, is settle the matter of the reward I promised you if things went smoothly during this troubling time. It is my opinion that your management could not have been bettered. I am pleased. The Dignus had been dead, you know, for two days by the time of the drill. It was necessary to be expeditious. I wish to reward you for your handling of all this, in a way which is now within my control. As the past Dignus named me, so I am naming you, Galt, as Chief. You will take over my old duties, and indeed my house, if you will. You must, of course, live within the enclave. There will be expenses involved in your duties, so sell your current house and keep the credits you raise to cover those. Clothes, and so on. I have called a Council meeting for tomorrow and shall announce it then, and present you with your metal collar. Be present, if you please. Shall we drink a toast?"

Galt was stunned. He had neither anticipated nor wished for such a promotion. But he was pleased. The more he thought about it: he was delighted. He trusted his own judgment more than most, and he felt he could contribute as a Chief. He realized he would now be the one to award bonuses to the Watch, no need to argue for it to someone else. Good. However, the best he could find to say to Sedemp was, "I am speechless, sir."

"Yes, yes. I was too. Now there is much for you to do. You must move in two days, so you had better take today to set your preparations in motion, eh? No rest for either of us. And congratulations, -er Chief Galt."

Chapter 29

Shamana climbed her mount out of the Valley of the Spring and the warriors rode down one by one to retrieve their spears. Without any apparent signal, the last warriors casually looped ropes round the men of Jebend's party and dragged them one by one to their feet. Others scooped their gear out of the sand on to the backs of the beasts. The whole silent group rode out of the valley in Shamana's wake, dragging the explorers behind them.

But the endless morning spent under the burning sun had weakened them. Without the use of their trussed arms for balance, they were unable to keep their feet. One after the other they fell. The warriors took no notice. They were dragged, recumbent, to the rim. Their mouths, eyes, noses were full of sand. It was in every corner of their clothing. Their hair. They lay at the bowl's edge coughing, spitting and blinking in arid misery.

Once more they heard the ululating cry. One by one, each was hauled up and slung over a beast's back, ahead of a rider. They hung from their stomachs, head on one side, feet on the other, like newly-killed meat. The only easement came from the wind of their passage, which was produced by a mile-eating walk, still in the uncanny silence. No warrior spoke to another. The terrain never changed. The sun blasted down on their backs.

By the time they had arrived somewhere, they no longer cared. Their eyes were shut against the unendurable pain. One after the other they were tossed to the ground. They lay without movement, certain they would find the ground was heaving beneath them with the movement of a beast. Certain they would vomit blood if they so much as twitched an eyelid.

And then they became aware of voices. People were murmuring. They felt around them with their fingers. They were lying on grass. Not sand. The rustling above them was the sound of wind riffling trees. They looked up. At trees. Certainly oddly shaped, but trees nonetheless. One by one they dared to stir. They tried sitting up. They could see a small lake of water, which suddenly made their thirst unbearable. They were still tied, but they could sit. They heard a grunt, and there was one of the warriors with a skin of water and a cup. He rinsed his mouth and spat. He offered each a tiny mouthful of water. The first man offered tried to swallow it, but the warrior struck his back so that he was forced to spit it out. The others did not try to swallow. They rinsed as they were shown.

Very little notice was taken of them. It was evening, and they were in a camp. Many tents were pitched on the farther edge of the green place, under more of the trees, not far from the lake. There were children about, and food was cooking. Warriors were everywhere. There was a curious stillness about them. They were fluid in motion or utterly still. No twitchings. No scratchings. No turning the head to talk or call to one another. In fact it was not they who talked. The people at the fires were doing the murmuring. They and the children. All were swathed, even the children, in the light clothing from head to toe. Among the warriors, only their curiously pale eyes moved, and they were everywhere.

It was a child who brought them food. A warrior walked over and rewrapped their ropes, binding them so that one hand was free to scoop up the meat and vegetable stew. There were nuts among the vegetables. Quite delicious, though they were not really in a mood to care. When they finished eating they were given a cup of water, and then rebound. Each was tied to a spear stuck upright in the ground. A warrior sat by each spear. The night grew cold. Their cloaks were taken from their packs and thrown over them. Trussed like packages, they shivered through the night. In all the time since the Valley of the Spring, not one word had been addressed to any of them.

Morning brought Shamana. Only her tall elegance differentiated her from any other adult. The covering robes frustrated all other forms of recognition.

"You will be fed now and then you will fight. Not these, I think." She indicated the four hunters with her head. "We have seen a sample of how such as these can fight. Their fate can depend on you. We will begin with you, Captain Jebend. The leader of these." She walked away before they could respond. Ask questions.

The party had been staked too far apart for whispered conversation. It would have been necessary to speak loudly to be heard. But talking at all seemed impossible in the middle of this silent multitude. Jebend and Sergeant Gard nodded with satisfaction, however, when they heard Shamana's words. It sounded proper to be doing something at last. To fight for their lives - they assumed it was for their lives, and those of their fellows - seemed most proper of all. Nothing seemed proper to Teq about any of this. This killing of people seemed to be a routine thing among all peoples. He wanted to know why. He wanted to know other things. Who were these people? What did they want? The talk of serving a Mystery was apparently self-explanatory to Shamana, but it meant nothing at all to Teq. What was a Mystery? Princess was a word he had heard. There had been some talk of a Wilder Prince once, and of a Princess among the Honor holders. But priestess was a word without meaning. If he was to fight for his life he would like to know why.

But conversation was rarer than water in this desert camp. A meal porridge with a sweet fruit mixed into it was brought to them. They were untied and made to stand and walk about. Another cup of water. And then the warriors began to form a circle around a level piece of ground. That looked familiar - like the Challenge. The hunters were again trussed against spears, but within the circle rim. Jebend, Gard and Teq were led forward, Jebend into the center of the circle. The other two were at the inner edge, between warriors. Separated from one another. Jebend was handed his sword and knife, and then left alone to swing them in his hands. Get the feel of them. The knife he tucked away into his belt, then stood ready.

A ululating cry and a warrior leapt into the circle, a long knife in each hand. The knives were of equal length, somewhere between Jebend's sword and his knife.

"Sa,sa,sa," the crowd began to call. After the complete silence of the past two days, so much noise was shocking.

The robed figure twirled and stabbed. Jebend parried, then made a quick, jabbing thrust. And in the stabbing was slashed on his sword arm with the second knife. He was an excellent fighter. Ambidextrous. Changing sword hands to thrust and parry and beat down his lightening opponent. Who was never there. Wherever he thrust, the warrior was gone. Wherever he parried a thrust from a knife, another knife stabbed, slashed, cut. He began to look grim. He was bleeding from a dozen places. The sun was beating its way higher and higher into a bronze sky. The whirling figure darted in and stabbed hard into muscle.

"Aah," Jebend cried out at last.

"Sa,sa,sa," hissed the crowd.

Jebend rallied his strength and drove a mighty thrust, drawing blood at last from his opponent's cheek.

"Sa,sa."

It was enough. The warrior turned into a cloud of sand, never there, and then always there. Jebend turned and twisted as fast as his failing strength allowed. But the warrior never tired, was always stronger. Until at last Jebend faltered, was tripped and fell.

Shamana stepped forward. "You did well, Captain. Nobody has ever drawn blood against my daughter. Come forward, Melansa. Remove your veil. You may have him. Live or die?"

The warrior stepped forward, not even panting, and removed the veil, unwinding the headpiece of the robes. Long and silky, her cloud of dark hair flowed down her back, waist-length. Her face was fine-boned, high-arched and proud. The eyebrows curved high. The cheekbones slanted up. The nose arched down. The lips smiled. Hers was a haughty beauty, her movements as elegant as her mother's. Blood dripped from a cut on her cheek.

Jebend gasped, "I have been beaten by a woman! I am looking at a female who has bested me in a fight. It is not to be born." The disgust was plain in his voice.

She moved so neatly, so sparely, it seemed she had not moved at all, but was suddenly there, on her knees before Jebend. Quick fingers plucked his knife from his belt, then his eye from his head.

"Sa,sa,sa."

Jebend roared in pain and clapped a hand to the socket.

"There Captain Jebend," her voice as gentle and mellifluous as her mother's. "You see me not with one eye. Would you choose to see me not at all?"

Into the silence the only sound was that of Jebend groaning.

"Leave him alone," Teq shouted. He knew Jebend would not beg, and if he did not speak, the other eye would follow the first. He could not bear to see this continue. Jebend was beaten, in pain, desperately injured and humiliated. They were at the mercy of these monstrous people.

"Well?" Shamana's question was asked of her daughter.

"I have seen my future child by a one-eyed man. I will keep him," Melansa answered. "Take him to my tent and attend him. Tie him. He is angry and a valiant warrior."

"Attend her also. You should return to see the next fight, my daughter."

It was belatedly clear to Teq that there were as many female warriors as male. It had simply not occurred to him before. He seemed to go through life being suddenly struck be revelations about what had always been before him, he sighed. Some of the spears were built lighter than others. All were fashioned from a light metal and not wood. It was as strong as wood, this metal. Stronger.

The warriors retired into the shade, leading their charges. The sun was still on the rise, nearly overhead now. They settled to sleep.

When the sun was past its zenith, they gathered again in the fighting circle, after one more cup of water. This time Gard and Teq were led forward together. Gard was a broad, stocky man of middle years, hard and weathered. He had been born and bred in the Town, a veteran of the game courts and a sergeant among hunters, his rank well earned by strength and experience.

"Looks like we're to fight together, Competent. Back to back against all comers, then sir, whatever the weapon."

"Back to back, sergeant. Glad to have you there. Looks as if they're bringing us our battle staves. Good luck, sergeant."

"Good luck, sir."

The battle staves were handed to them, and, like Jebend, they were given time to get the heft of them in their hands. They had been given one another's and they swapped them, without any restraining movement from the ring of warriors. As soon as they stood back to back at the ready, two warriors sprang in to the attack. They were using their spears, but using them as staves. It was apparently a form of fighting with which they were unfamiliar. Teq and Gard had the pair knocked unconscious in short order, only mildly disconcerted by the ring of metal against their staves.

"Sa,sa,sa."

Two more leaped into the fray. They had learned quickly from the two before. They fought well. Neither Teq nor Gard was tiring. They beat the next pair to the ground, though it took longer and required more skill this time.

"Sa, sa, sa."

Two more. This pair was much more canny. The match was even. Their tricks were not the practiced moves of Teq and Gard, they were fresh. New. Adaptive. Clever. And fast. They were terribly fast. Now Teq and Gard were tiring. They circled, back to back, never budging from that resolute support. Round them the warriors flashed, circled, spun, jabbed. And then suddenly, one reached in and tangled Gard's legs, just as the pair was making a steady turn to the left. He stumbled, and lurched forward and fell. Right on to the point of the still outthrust spear. He died at once.

Teq whirled and straddled him, furious. He felt now as if he was working with fighters who moved at half speed. He could see the thrusts and jabs coming from both warriors in plenty of time to counter them. He had time and more to parry them and thrust on his own. He could almost see their thoughts.

"Sa, sa, sa."

With a mighty jab he knocked one warrior on the point of the jaw, and on the same follow through, caught the second full in the stomach. Both fell, poleaxed.

"Sa, sa, sa."

Shamana walked up to him. He did not know he was roaring, circling still, spinning his battle staff threatening all comers.

"It is over," she said, in what seemed a gentle voice. "You have conquered. That is good. All your men will now live."

Teq stared at her, dazed. Speed was returning to normal. He gave a cry and knelt by Sergeant Gard.

"That was an error," Shamana said. "An accident of combat. He fought an excellent fight. He will be treated with honor. Give me the pole now. Give it to me. Come."

Teq looked blank. She eased the battle staff from his hand. He yielded it to her, panting. Bewildered.

"I will take this one," Shamana announced. "Take him to my tent. Divide the others as is due. They have fought well, these ones. The Mystery is honored."

Hands lifted Teq and led him, unresisting. Others picked up Sergeant Gard and carried him away. Somehow it was evening and fires were being stoked. Stars poking holes in the night sky. Heat being leached from the air. Teq began to shiver. He was led to a tent, stripped, washed and wrapped in clothes. He heard Shamana's voice, or Tarabeth's, perhaps.

"Sleep."

And he did.

Chapter 30

Teq woke in the middle of the night, sobbing. For the first time since he had been very little, arms held him. He was cradled and petted until he went back to sleep. He neither knew why he was crying nor why someone was there to comfort him. He was not even surprised. Just eased. Somewhere in his heart he had been crying all his life and it was over now. There was someone who cared. About him, himself. About his hurt.

The next time he woke he was aroused, and again there was someone to take care of him. He was wrapped in arms as warm as summer, as large as his heart. Roused more. Hugged. Climaxed and again, feeling eased, slept.

The third awakening was in real time and in dawnlight. He opened his eyes and he could see around him. He was in Shamana's bed and she was beautiful. She was large and she was elegant, even in her sleep. The cloud of her hair was lighter than Melansa's. All that was sharp-edged in her daughter was rounded and softened in her. There was a bigness and a calm in the way she lay, breathing gently with her lips curled into a smile. Propped on an elbow, he watched her sleep with wonder. Without thought.

As if she felt him watching her, she woke. Eyes heavy with sleep and lips smiling with pleasure, she reached for him and closed her mouth over his.

"Shamana," he said.

"Hush", she answered and loved him again. This time he was awake and aware. Her hands handled his body and his own knew how to respond, to pleasure her. She hummed and murmured in her throat as his lips found her secret places. When they were spent, she wrapped him in her arms, and held him safe and soft for a long time.

"Well, then. I will see to food," she said at last. "Don't move. Don't speak," she added when he opened his mouth. "We will speak when we have eaten. Cover yourself lest I take you again. You are beautiful."

He blushed, fully aware of his circumstance for the first time. There was something of pride and something of horror in the awareness. She was a monster princess of monstrous people who had killed his own. And he was loving her. She was their leader. And she had chosen him. Teq. A mere boy. No, he thought. Not a boy. I really am not a boy any longer. I have fought for my life and that of others, and I have conquered. And I have made love to their leader. I'll never be a boy again. I am a man.

"Yes, you are a man." Shamana came back into the tent bearing a tray.

"Did I speak?" asked Teq, embarrassed. "I was not conscious of speaking out loud."

"I can hear the thoughts of some people, some times. I heard yours then. I am a priestess."

"You can? Everyone's? Everything?"

"That is not what I said. Listen to the things I say. I mean only what I say. Some thoughts. Some times. Melansa also. She is a priestess like me. Not all my children bear the gift. She will priest this tribe after me. Here is food. Eat. Drink."

Teq got up from the bed and discovered aches and bruises he had been aware of only peripherally during the morning's enjoyable exercise. Now they were stiffening. Walking over to reach for his clothes had him sharply aware.

"Ow," he groaned. "Where are my clothes?"

"Taken for cleaning. Here, then." She wrapped a cloth around his loins, and led him to a pile of cushions before a low tray table. Food steamed in bowls. The jug contained wine mixed with honey and hot water. The food was again the meal porridge, but the fruit was different and there were nuts in the mixture. They ate side by side, then she rubbed an ointment into his bruises, caressing his limbs back into torpor. His body was rousing again.

"No," she said. "Ask your questions. You shouted questions in the night. Now I will answer."

His first questions shamed him, that he had waited so long to ask them. "Jebend?" he queried her. "The men?"

"Of the men, two are happy and two are reluctant. The happy ones are the young ones. They were not virgins. They enjoyed the beds of the warriors who chose them. The older two enjoyed themselves also, but they do not wish to. It makes them uncomfortable that the women chose them. That the women who chose them are warriors. Perhaps we will keep the young ones, I am not sure. But not the others."

"What do you mean, keep? And what of Jebend? The Captain?"

"Keep means allow them to stay as warriors. As members of the tribe, if they wish it. The Captain has a fever. He lost much blood and stirred his body into frenzy with anger. It will take time for him. There is some infection in his wounds. The healers are with him, and Melansa. He will recover and then he will father a child for her. As you will for me. My last."

"How can you know such a thing?"

"I am a priestess. We have each seen it. We see into the future. Some things. Some a long way off. Some close. We knew you would come to the Valley of the

Spring and violate it. The tribe was a long way into the desert. Far into the interior. We could not ride fast enough to be there to stop you."

"How would you have stopped us?"

"Turned you back to your own land. We would not have had reason to kill you. But once you had damaged the valley, it was too late. It was necessary we offer you to the Mystery, so that she might choose your life or death. Some of you she took. Some she spared. Great is the Mystery and all Her choices."

"What in the name of Earth and Sky is a Mystery?"

"A Mystery!" She smiled at him. "I am Her priestess. She sees us. She knows us. She has chosen the People of the Desert as her own. She describes Her needs through her priestesses. She is not the only Mystery, of course. There are those of the Mountains and the Plains and the Seas also. Do you not know these?"

"I have never heard of such a thing. I have lived on the plain, near the rift. I have journeyed through the hills and woods. I have lived in the Town in a great valley. I have walked across the plains to the sea. I have never heard of a Mystery."

"Then you have not listened. One day you will know the Mystery of the Mountains. I will bear you a daughter who will be a priestess. She will be able to hear. I will send her to you in the mountains. Let me see. I will name her Teksana, after us both, eh? When she is old enough, I will send her. I shall not forget. Don't you forget. She will come along the beach to find you, and you will make her priestess to your people."

"You are talking nonsense. At least nonsense to me," he added quickly when he saw her face. "I do not live in the mountains. I live in the Town which is in a valley. What you say cannot happen."

"It will."

"My home is among the people I know. I have no wish to leave them. And you know we do not have a daughter. How could we?"

"We will work on that. Drink more of this wine before it cools too much. It will help to ease those hurts."

"I should visit Jebend."

"He is in excellent hands. Aren't you?" she asked, pushing him back among the cushions, and reaching again for the ointment.

"Mm," he said, feeling weak and loving it.

Shamana led him from her tent three days later. His limbs felt supple and strong again and his head was clear. He felt whole.

"Come," she said. "I would like you to teach my warriors how to fight with this pole. First there is something to show you. These piles of stones among the trees, are to show respect for the warriors who have fallen. This pile is for your Sergeant Gard. We have taken his weapons and distributed them among the warriors he honored by fighting them. Here is his pole. If you wish, you can allow those you teach to use it in his name."

Teq thought a minute. "I believe he would be pleased by that," he decided. "We'll use it. And Jebend?"

"Recovering. It is better not to disturb him yet. You will see him in a few days. Two or three. Now. Here is your pole. Teach these."

There was no sign of the other four hunters of his party, either. It was already late in the day. The worst of the heat had burned off. Dressed once again in his own clothes, Teq felt more in control. Himself, only more so. The sense of his manhood stayed with him. He began to exercise with his battle staff and warriors gathered round to copy his every move.

"It is a battle staff," he told them.

They nodded. "Battle staff."

"Here." He threw Gard's staff to one man of a build similar to the sergeant's. Somehow it was obvious to him now, which warriors were men and which women. He could not imagine how he had ever been confused. "Fight me," he told the man.

A hit was met with a "sa,sa,sa" and he realized that it was approbation. Applause. It was a goad too, as it had been the other time. It urged greater effort. He grinned when he heard it. Sa, sa, sa, yourself, he thought.

Part of the next few days he spent teaching the battle staff, and part in learning to throw the light metal spears. The nights he spent with Shamana. He caught no sight of either the Captain or the other hunters.

And then Shamana announced there would be a feast that night. Melansa came to the tent to speak with her mother.

"She is very beautiful," he said, when she had left. "Nearly as beautiful as you."

"Is she not? Her father was a huge man. A man from the seas. Priest to his own tribe, which is why I chose him. It is why Melansa is such a powerful priest. We had two children, he and I. A son also, who is now with his father. Satisfactory was it not?"

Teq looked sullen and she laughed. "Tonight you will see us dance for the Mystery," she promised. "You will be intoxicated. You should know that I am already pregnant with your daughter, and Melansa with your Captain's. It is good, is it not?"

The feast was huge. Dish after dish was brought. There were fish from the seas. Teq thought of Athirra and was homesick. He thought he could see the hunters sitting among the warriors. At least two of them. The older ones. Bens and Rogin, if he remembered correctly. He was drinking a great deal of the wine. It was heavy and unwatered. He was unused to so heady a brew.

The moon rose, three quarter full, and lit the water in the lake. A flute began to play, thin and reedy, and then another. Somewhere a drum began, a throb, not a beat. Shamana rose from his side and Melansa glided in from somewhere behind him. The ululating cry and then the women moved. They moved in a way Teq had never seen, as if they were the music. They moved in rhythm and swirl and beat to blind the eye to the fact that they were the movers. They moved more to lead the heart, to stir the loins, to spark the breath. They dipped, and turned and swayed, always apart yet as if they were reflections, one of the other. Their feet turned to drums, their fingers clicked.

"Sa,sa,sa."

Teq found himself hissing the odd words along with the warriors. The dancers quickened their pace and began to clap their hands: one two three; one two three; one two. The watching warriors, the old people, the children clapped in unison to the rhythm they set. They were more vivid than the music now. Louder, more involving, more heart wrenching.

When the music slowed to a heavy, voluptuous pace, the dancers slowed with it, as if it dragged them there. The drum beat was the heart beat now. Teq's mouth was dry. He did not dare to blink, to miss a movement, a ripple of their fingers. It ended with Shamana in his arms. They were in her tent and he did not know how they got there. It was the longest night and the deepest of love making, they had spent. Richer. Fuller. More potent. Total.

He woke in the cool of the morning and there was no longer a tent. Nor Shamana. He sat up and his head was full of pain. The light hurt his eyes. The tents were gone. The whole tribe was gone. Not possible. He had to be dreaming still. He closed his eyes tightly and opened them again. It was true. He lay under the same trees where they had spent their first night, tied to the spears. The rest of the clearing was now empty. But no. Wrapped in cloaks, as he was, lay three more figures. He pulled himself to his feet, wincing as pain lanced through his head. There were Rogin, Bens and Jebend, pale and with a patch over one eye, but certainly Jebend.

He explored further. Their packs and weapons lay neatly piled to one side. An arrow had been picked out in stones, pointing off to the northwest. A great basket filled with porridge lay ready with their gear. It was still warm. There were two large bags of water and a small cup. That was all.

After eating some of the porridge he began to feel better. He rinsed his mouth with water and spat it out, then drank some. He thought he had better rouse the other three, but said nothing until he had handed them some porridge and some water. They looked as dreadful as he felt when they woke. Perhaps the wine had been drugged to make them sleep. Or the porridge to help them wake. Whatever the answer, they felt better once they had eaten.

Teq climbed to the rim of the green place, where it rose a little, not really expecting to see any sign of the People of the Desert. They would have vanished as totally and as silently as they appeared. But he was rewarded. Far away to the east there was a plume of sand in the sky, stirred by their passing. Why did I never ask about those beasts, he asked himself? They were out of sight all the time we were here and I forgot about them. How could I have been so careless? We could have learned to ride them. I would rather be going, like the tribe, on the back of a beast. I bet it beats walking when you're not hanging upside down.

"What do you see?" He heard Jebend's voice calling to him.

"Their dust, far away, Captain."

"The other two men? Surely they have not been killed too."

"Gone with them, I expect, sir," Rogin answered. "They was talking about how they liked this life: the fighting and enough women and all."

"Not you?" the Captain asked.

"Nah. I got children at home. Sons," Bens answered.

"I got one on the way," Rogin said. "I want to get on home. These people is weird. Not my kind anyway."

"You, Teq?"

"It's been interesting. I learned all sorts of things." He turned away, blushing, as the Captain cocked an eyebrow at him. "I learned about things I'd never even heard of: like the Mystery, and the Men of the Seas, a little. We talked a lot, sir. I asked a lot of questions. I just forgot to ask about those beasts, and I could kick myself for that," he added. "How are your wounds, sir? Are you healed? They wouldn't let me come near you."

"I am healed - except for the eye, of course. I too have learned a lot. Women seem to make good warriors, and to be capable of intelligent thinking. Maybe just these women, but it surprised me. I considered staying with the tribe."

The men grunted in surprise.

"I was shamed by losing my eye. And by losing my men. Too ashamed to feel I could be acceptable in the Town. I am still. I am no longer who I was. I can see change in you too, Teq. Perhaps these people have changed us all a little."

"They have that, in some ways, sir. Quite an experience, I'd say," Teq answered.

"I'd like to be getting on home, now, sir, just the same." Bens sounded a little surly at all this talk of change. "Seems we've been away a good long time."

"Yes. We must go home. I'd suggest we take the day to check our gear and supplies. We'll all feel better for not being too hurried about it. We'll set off at evening, in the cool of the day. Agreed? The moon is with us, as I recall."

"Aye, sir. Whatever you say, sir. Is there any more of that porridge stuff, Competent?" Rogin grinned.

Teq carried the basket over. "We may as well finish this before we start work. Then I'm with you, Captain. We can go back to the plan you proposed, what seems like a lifetime ago: go home by the northwest route, and I can map it as we go."

"Yes. A lifetime ago, I agree," Jebend sighed.

"I'm beginning to think there's more than one way for time to pass, like more than one way of going," Teq agreed. "It's been a very long time."

Chapter 31

They walked through that night and rested through the following day. Nothing moved in the desert heat but the occasional snake, whipping out of their way with amazing speed, and some rather large and very ugly insects. They didn't talk much. All four were occupied with their own thoughts. Both Teq and Jebend had been given a spear of the lightweight metal, left with their arms. The tip of the spear was somehow fused to the shaft. They knew so little about the working of metal. One family of men in the Town knew how to work both copper and tin, but this was some other metal that they did not recognize. The family of smiths kept their secrets to themselves, so other than the sons and brothers of the smiths, nobody knew a thing about metals. These spears would certainly be intriguing.

By the second night the dunes became less steep, and the sand seemed firmer. The morning saw them on the flat with rocky hills on the horizon, thrown into relief by the rising sun in their rear. They decided to try to reach the hills before the sun got too high. On the flat, there would be no shade to weather the heat of the day. The sandy plain was dotted with scrubby vegetation, and the hills, when they reached them, were split with deep defiles.

"We had better try and get through this before it gets dark," Jebend decided. "There will be too much shadow thrown by the moonlight. The footing will be treacherous. We won't be able to get through this tonight."

"I could scout ahead and see if any of these defiles cuts through," Teq offered. "I suspect we'll have to go over the top, though."

"Don't waste your time on the defiles. Try for a reasonable route across the top. Take one of the men with you," Jebend agreed.

"I'll go, if you like," Rogin suggested. It was noticeable on this journey back, how much less regimented the small group had become. On the way out, Jebend gave orders and Sergeant Gard saw them implemented. Now, service was volunteered and accepted. Suggestions were made and agreed to. Teq supposed this method would not work very well with a large group, but it was useful to listen to everyone's ideas. To take advantage of everyone's experience.

Apart from disturbing a nest of gourd snakes, they found a route to the top without difficulty. Teq sent Rogin back to bring the other two up, while he scouted a decent camp site where they could spend the rest of the day. It was already uncomfortably hot. He thought he might also scout out a way down, with luck. Once the top of the hills was crested, he found that stunted trees grew up there. They could camp under them for shade. And he could see far out across the grassy plain, where the river wound wide and gentle. Far off to his left, there was a glint from where the sun sparked off the sea. Away and away across the friendly plain was the dark smudge which was the mountains of the west. He found a crack in the rock going down the side of the hill, which looked from there as if it went all the way to the bottom. Teq wedged his spear into the top to mark the spot and went back to guide the others to the place he had marked for their afternoon rest camp. There was just enough water left to last them until morning, and enough food to allow them each one solid mouthful now, and again before they set off in the morning. They settled down and slept.

"I noticed an odd thing, Captain," Teq told Jebend. "The river sweeps close by these hills before it turns to the sea. Just here. It seems to arrive very broad, and then leave narrow. I find that odd. It's wide again by the time it gets near the sea - which is as far as I can see it. This is a sharpish bend here. I'd like to explore that when we get down out of these hills."

"First things first. We have to get down there. But when we do, no doubt we can all use the chance to clean up and drink enough. I'll send the men off to hunt for food, and you can explore all you like. I hereby declare myself the evening's cook," Jebend smiled at him. "Glad to see you haven't lost your mapmaker's curiosity."

The trip down was frustrating. Twice they had to turn round and climb back up when the track they were descending dead ended in an impassable cliff. Even so, having started at first light, they were on the level plain not long after noon. Of them all, Jebend was the one who had suffered most at the hands of the People of the Desert. His strength was by no means fully restored. He had lost some of the sureness of his authority, as if it had been plucked from him with his eye. There was a sadness in his face, as in parting from some precious thing for ever. Well, of course, he had. But the sadness seemed to be draining the energy from his body along with the vigor of his mind. He seemed glad enough to potter about making camp while he sent the other three about their business.

They had reached the plain on the north side of the river. They would not have to ford it later. It seemed to Teq that this was a good thing. It was running fuller and faster than it had been when they had forded it before. It must have been fed by some heavy rains which never reached the desert. Of course it might have meant that the ground sloped steeply in the river bed, but that was not apparent on the banks. Certainly they sloped sharply down to the water, but Teq interpreted that to mean that the spring flood ran deep. There was certainly a race in the water here. Maybe it was just eager to get to the sea, he chuckled to himself as he marched along its edge.

They had found a tree to camp under fairly soon after reaching the plain, so it was not far to the hill face. Just over a hump in the land. It was really a cliff face here. As he stood on the top that morning, searching the shadows for the lie of the land, he formed a fancy that this line of hills, curving away to the northeast, would join up with the great rift of his birthplace. It seemed very probable. He would examine other maps when he got back to the Town to see what they showed.

Abruptly he was faced with the cliff. Not so, the river. Shallow enough to make its dark mouth nearly invisible, there was a cave. Half of the river tumbled into it, where jutting rocks formed barrier enough to send half on its way to the sea. But where did the cave half go? On the other side of these hills, the desert was barren and waterless, so it didn't simply flow through. Could it be flowing under the ground? Teq pulled off his boots, slid down the bank and dangled his feet into the river. The tug of the current nearly pulled him in. Crabbing back up to the bank, he crawled forward to peer into the cave. He could see nothing in the black dark, but he could hear a familiar roar. Magnified. Echoing. It was the roar he knew from the waterfall in the Town, but more. Much, much more. What a discovery! A river underground. It had to be this river which watered the green place where they had camped with the People of the Desert. He trailed his fingers, and his arm felt the mighty tug of the water. He'd better warn the others. Pulling on his boots, he raced back to the camp.

He got there just as a stripped off Jebend was about to step into the water.

"Stop, Captain," Teq yelled. "Don't get into the river."

"What have you found? Monsters?" Jebend shouted back.

"No sir, but the current is terribly strong. Much more than it seems. It could easily drag you underground."

"Under water, don't you mean? Come now. You have found monsters," Jebend grinned, really amused by Teq's alarm. The truth startled him even more. He insisted on seeing for himself.

By the time the two hunters returned with a bag of succulent birds, the other two had found a rocky pool upstream where they could bathe safely; and a place where the water tumbled over rocks and they could easily fill their water bags.

As they traveled north, there was a noticeable cooling in the weather. The last full day on the march was spent in the chill misery of a fine, cold rain, which penetrated inside clothing and turned boots soggy. They were almost at the outer edge and just out of sight of the area patrolled by the Town's guards, when Jebend called a halt.

"It looks to me as if the sky is clearing at last," he pointed out. "With any luck the night will be dry. I don't think, though, that we can get all the way there before the Town gates are shut for the night. Let's stop early and dry out. We will be able to go the last bit in better order. What do you say?"

"I was hoping to get home tonight, sir," Bens grumbled. "I'd like to get home."

"We'll have to report in before we can go home, anyway. They might even put us in custody until the Chiefs are ready to hear our story. Better to get that over with first thing, when we're not all exhausted," Jebend persuaded.

"Reckon that's right, sir," Rogin said. "I'd rather look a bit clean like when we report. I feel a right mess now."

"Aye, that's right enough," Bens agreed grudgingly. "We'd best see if we can find something to eat, then, and some dry wood. We'll need a right good fire to dry all our gear."

"Over that rise there's a pretty dense copse of trees, according to my map," Teq told them. "Could we camp there, sir? Better chance to find dry wood where it's been under their cover all day."

They managed a roaring fire, which both dried their clothes and cheered them up. There was a good meal and a good sleep, so they set out in the morning thoroughly refreshed. It would have taken a wild stretch of the imagination to call them neat but at least they were clean. They approached the Town in good order, marching in step, heads up.

As soon as they were recognized by the outlying guards, Jebend sent one of them ahead to warn the Town of his party's arrival. He dreaded reporting back. Of the party of nine who had set off into the wilderness under his command, he was bringing back only four. He had lost a sergeant and two hunters to death, and two more hunters to desertion. On top of that, he himself was returning maimed. It was obvious to him that Chief Kambar would not accept a one-eyed hunter. What else could he do? He had always been a hunter, interested in the challenge of understanding his quarry and the discipline of the green shirts. He was unable to picture himself in any other role. He tried to see himself keeping an inn or a store, and the picture would not come clear. He fit in nowhere but where he was, and where he was he could not stay. He knew what he must expect. There was no changing the fact that he had been bested in battle by a woman warrior. Nor that he had a changed picture of what a woman was capable of being. Nothing could be as it was. He knew he must suffer his fate in silence, and worry about his future when this day was over. He straightened his shoulders and answered the challenge at the gate.

"Jebend! We thought you lost. Welcome back." The Captain of that day's guard had come to the gate to meet them. "I can't wait to know what's been happening to you, but I suppose I must." He looked at the bandage over Jebend's eye and looked away again quickly. "I am instructed to take you all straight to the Palace, no less. The Chiefs will meet you there."

As for Teq, he was content to go unnoticed, or at least, unremarked. He wanted to get this part over with, and hurry round to Galt's house to see everyone and tell them his adventures. Well, almost all his adventures. How many details he would recount about his stay with Shamana would depend on the company. He wanted to tell Galt everything, but probably not Ibaren or the other women. Probably not.

Since Teq had never before been to the Palace, the signs of the new regime meant nothing to him. He looked about him in interest, as they were led through the building and into a room with a blazing fire. Raised on a dais was a chair for the Dignus. Other chairs were ranged around the walls, but the party was left standing before the empty chair. A door to one side opened. Teq watched Chief

Sedemp enter. He walked to the great chair and sat in it, which was momentarily surprising. Three Chiefs entered behind him. Kambar took position on Sedemp's right. Fergin and Galt - Galt! - arranged themselves on his left.

Sedemp spoke. "Welcome home, Captain Jebend. Men. Much has happened here in the Town in the time that you have been away. I can see that much has also happened to you, and we wish to hear about it in detail. That is why we invited you here. But first we must inform you that, here in the Town, we lost our beloved Dignus. I am now Dignus. Chief Galt has been elevated to the tasks I once performed. Your journey has been long. Much longer than anticipated. It is evident that it has also been arduous. You may place seats for yourselves before us."

As Bens and Rogin turned to gather up two chairs each, a man materialized from the side door and placed chairs for the Chiefs. As soon as they were all sitting down, he reappeared with cups of wine for everyone. Bens and Rogin looked at each other, eyebrows raised. This was more of a reception than they'd been expecting. They relaxed a little in their chairs. Jebend looked down. It was to be a long session, then. Teq could think of nothing else but Galt, the Chief. He caught his eye, and Galt smiled at him warmly, but made no attempt to walk over to him. Abashed, Teq contented himself with smiling back. It seemed that this was not the time or place for congratulations.

"Now, Captain. Begin," the Dignus commanded. "Tell us in your own words all that has happened. In particular, we are eager to hear what happened to the rest of your party."

Jebend told them everything, as concisely as if he had been pondering the wording for days. Perhaps he had, Teq thought. Teq was particularly relieved that he omitted to mention his own sharing of Melansa's tent, and Teq's sharing of Shamana's.

"Would anyone care to add anything?" the Dignus asked.

"The Captain took care of us well. Stuck by us. Led us carefully," Teq blurted out, seeking for words to describe the conflicts Jebend had faced after his battle with Melansa, and finding none. He fell silent, fully aware that he had added nothing to the tale. And yet he had, minimally, tried to convey that the party had remained a party of the Town, in spite of everything.

"Aye," Bens muttered.

"He did that," Rogin agreed.

"Anything else?" The Dignus looked amused. "You, Competent. Did you actually make any maps during this epic journey? This was the reason for the expedition, after all."

"Oh I did, sir. Well, sketches. Not finished maps. Not yet. I have all the information gathered, is what I mean. It will take me a while to produce finished maps. I gathered information both going and returning. I have made at least one discovery, also. Possibly two."

"Discoveries?"

"I believe I know how the rift was formed, and why the green place blooms in the middle of the desert, sir. The Captain is witness to the last."

"Ah, so this aspect of the expedition might be termed a success. What is your opinion?" Sedemp turned first to Kambar, and then to the other two Chiefs.

"Captain Jebend acted properly. We are hunters. Not warriors. Nonetheless, he posted sentries in strange territory, and made use of scouts. These things are in accordance with regulations. The death of the two sentries does not lie at his door," Kambar said thoughtfully. "Nor does the death of his sergeant. It would seem that he was incapacitated after a valiant fight, when the sergeant was killed. The Competent also seems to have fought well. On these issues there is no blame. As for the hunters, they fulfilled their duties well, and in particular demonstrated loyalty by not going off with this desert tribe as their colleagues did. It is my ruling that they may remain with us as hunters."

"As for the hunters, I agree," Fergin nodded. "But were Jebend's judgments wise? Was there a reason to penetrate the desert, for example?"

"We shall never know if there were signs which Jebend missed when he decided to enter the desert region," Kambar decided. "The purpose of the expedition, however, was to explore and map. This appears to have been accomplished in greater detail by this decision. We will not be able to judge how well it has been mapped until we see what the Competent produces. All of this indicates that neither Jebend nor the Competent is due any punishment by failing in their duty. However, there is no need to belabor the matter since we cannot use a one-eyed Captain of the Hunters. Nor should it go unnoted that this Captain seems to have modified his notions of the place of women in society. But perhaps I read too much into this."

"It is axiomatic," said Fergin, always ready to follow Kambar's lead, "that a Captain of the Guard must be far-seeing. He is not acceptable to me in that capacity. Galt?"

"For myself, I have been hoping and waiting for Captain Jebend's return, Dignus. It has always seemed to me that, along with his competence as a captain, he has the very qualities of open-mindedness and tact, that are needed for the Captain of the Watch. To that end I have made no move to fill the post I vacated. It had been my intention to request his release to that post from Chief Kambar, on his return. There is no problem for the Captain of the Watch in having only one eye. His job is in keeping the peace and not in seeing any great distances. In reading faces, not movement. So, Dignus, with your permission and that of the Chiefs, I would like to ask him to report to me in that capacity in two days' time, ready to go to work. It has already been too long for the Watch to be without a captain."

Kambar looked surprised, but raised no objection. Fergin merely nodded his agreement.

There were a few moments of silence while the Dignus appeared to ponder the matter. "I have considered what you have all said. I am in agreement that those in authority performed their duties as diligently as they knew how. What they know how to do may need some reconsidering. It seems there is some need for warrior training among the green shirts. We will discuss this at a later time. There will be no punishments, then. Just a welcome back in the fullest sense. So,

Captain Jebend, would you find the position Chief Galt has offered you, acceptable?"

"With all my heart, sir. And my thanks to Chief Galt for the offer. I have been
sensible of the fact that losing an eye diminished my usefulness as a hunter and
a guard. I could not see... I am... I am deeply grateful for the opportunity to retain
my rank. The Chief can expect my very best."

"Anything to add?" from the Dignus to all of them in general.

"Them warrior women was fierce fighters, sir. In them robes you couldn't
never have guessed they was women." Rogin got to his feet, very red in the face,
but with a stubborn look to his mouth.

"That's true, sir. Can't blame the Captain. He fought hard." Bens rose, more to
support his comrade than his captain.

Teq rose silently to stand with them.

Once again the Dignus looked amused. "So noted, men. The Captain will not
be blamed for his inability to recognize the gender of the warrior. Now, you must
all be anxious to get to your homes. You are dismissed."

The four men stood as the Dignus and the Chiefs left the room. The same man
was waiting to lead them through the maze of rooms and out of the Palace. Once
outside, they found there was nothing to say to one another. They clapped each
other on the shoulder in an awkward gesture of farewell, then set out in their various directions.

"Teq."

He turned at Galt's summons, watching him hurry with his familiar limp, from
the grounds of the Palace.

"Chief Galt, eh?" said Teq, grinning broadly. "I can't go away for a minute but
you're going up in the world." He pumped Galt's hand. "I have so much to tell
you, other that Jebend's bald account. Shall I come straight to the house, or shall
I wait until evening when everyone's free to listen? How is Belleth? And Athirra?
Is there a babe yet? You can't know how worried I've been."

"Slow down, lad. Why do you think I ran after you, even if my dignity does-
n't allow for it now." Galt grinned at him. "Ay, lad, it's good to see you. I've been
worried myself, as the weeks kept going by with no sign. Come this evening.
Here. I don't suppose you have any credits left, and I know you'll have a lot due.
Take this now and buy yourself some food and some new clothes. Oh, and I've
moved. I have to live in the enclave now. Chief Sedemp's house came with the
job, so to speak. We moved Belleth very carefully. She came to no harm, but
she's sinking, lad. She'll be very glad to see you tonight."

"Moved! I've been dreaming about talking to you all at your house. It's odd to
think of you all somewhere else. Do the others like the new house?"

"Oh it's very grand. And very quiet. It's nice in the enclave. Athirra likes it.
Oh and no. No baby yet, but any day now. You'll like the house. I'll send Ibaren
to fetch you, so that she can show you the way. Be sure to be ready. They'll never
forgive me if you're late. Just before dusk, eh? We'll see you, then."

"Of course I'll be ready when Ibaren comes. I'm dying to see everyone. Tell
them to be prepared for tall tales. Until evening, then -er Chief."

"You look good. You look grown, though I suppose you really aren't any taller. Grown up, perhaps. That must be it. I'll see you tonight."

Galt hurried off and Teq stood watching him go. Moved! There was something devastating about that. All the time he'd been away, thoughts of home meant Galt's house. He hadn't realized how much his life centered there. Without the house next door, his own place no longer seemed his own. Stupid, thought, but he was really shaken. He was delighted, of course, to see Galt chosen as Chief, but... Ridiculous that he should be so shattered by such a small piece of news! And good news at that.

All the same...

Chapter 32

It was as if the whole world had changed. Teq had gone on the expedition to the Desert a boy, and come back a man. The boy who left had a home he looked forward to returning to. A place where he was safe, and welcomed, and even loved. The man came back expecting the same, and found everything different. Was it him? Had he changed so much? Was it the fact that Galt had moved his household inside the enclave where everything was unfamiliar? The truth was that even just visiting Belleth was terribly hard. She was so weak, and she seemed to save all her strength for Taza. She had been overwhelmingly glad that Teq was safe, when he first came back, but beyond that she could do very little now but smile at him. And that took effort. She was in constant pain in spite of everything that Zolg could do for her.

Then there was Athirra. She was so near her term that, not only was it hard for her to move about - and she truly was enormous - but she was also irritable. She tried not to complain, you could see that, but her patience had almost ceased to exist. Both Galt and Ibaren were loaded down with increased duties, which left only Girly to do everyone's bidding. Bessindel was little help outside the sick room, where she had taken on the care of Belleth, and to a certain extent, Taza. Teq felt that he was in everyone's way at Galt's house nowadays.

So he spent a lot of time thinking about his life. His future. He was busy most of the day making the maps of his Desert journey, but they, even with enough fair copies, would be finished in time. Obviously Jebend would no longer be in charge of trips of exploration, now that he was Captain of the Watch. Who else would ask for Teq as their mapmaker? True, mapmakers were not exactly clamoring to take the risk of an excursion into the unknown. Teq's own two major trips were held up as examples of why not. Besides, the green shirts were a superstitious lot, and preferred not to travel with him. He was regarded as bad luck.

Teq's thoughts kept returning to the cave he had discovered. Suppose he were simply to leave the Town. To go into the Western Mountains and start afresh. Yet again. How would he live there? Find shelter? Build shelter? Would there ever be a chance of coming back if he failed out there? He had many skills for survival, but perhaps not enough. For instance it would be impossible to survive in those mountains without adequate housing. That was the first thing. He needed to know how to handle that. He had, of course, earned a lot of credits while he was away not spending any. He could start to use them to gather together things he might need. If he decided to go. Somewhere, always in the back of his mind, he remembered what Shamana had told him: that he would end up living in mountains. Silly of course. Imagine claiming to see into the future! While he was with her it had seemed plausible. But now... However, it would not hurt to plan a little, regardless of belief in Shamana's predictions.

His first thought was of solving the shelter problem. He remembered Vork. If you know someone who has the skills you need, you're half way to learning them. In the meantime, access to the cave was much easier, now that Zolg's was the only dwelling actually overlooking the falls and his cave. Zolg's place was now about ready for occupancy, and he had already started his healer's work on the premises. Most days, Teq arrived there when the work day ended, carrying wine, so that they could both relax a little, and stretch limb and mind. His own little room was cramping. The other three Competents who lived upstairs were not noisy. They worked outside the house. But as soon as the sun was past its zenith, the light began to go in his room. And the days were growing shorter. The constant strain to see his work until the work day ended, was an ever increasing annoyance. The room had never seemed small when he could go over to sit in Galt's courtyard next door whenever the mood took him. Now there was no place to go. And he got restless. Zolg's house had become his new destination at then end of the day, and Zolg seemed glad enough to finish his work with a little chat over wine.

"It is good to see you here, Teq," He said. "I miss my brothers. We were always three together. Always. Now there are women everywhere at the house. Galt is so busy all the time. I miss the talk with another man."

"Do you hate being here? In the Town, I mean," Teq asked him. He had noted that Zolg was no longer wearing his hair dressed high, Wilder fashion. He was beginning to look like a Confrater, even to dress like one.

"Not really. I am trying to settle in here. And I am busy. I have two apprentices now, did I tell you? I have been given special permission by Chief Fergin to take them with me when I leave the Town to gather the herbs I need. It is more than enough exercise for this leg of mine. One of them is older. In a year he will be ready to become a Competent, I think, and I can send him out on his own. Even send apprentices with him. I shall be glad enough of that."

"You've learned the ways of the Town quickly," Teq told him. "It took me much longer. But then, I didn't want to learn. I felt trapped here when I was an apprentice."

"Survival." Zolg grinned at him. "When you're crippled you have to learn every detail of everything quickly. Knowledge can make up for physical weakness."

"There's something I'll tell you, then." Teq poured them both more from the wine jug. "Someone ought to know about it, and you're well placed in this house. I've kept this a secret, even from Galt, up till now. I'm afraid that it might be awkward for him, if he knew. Perhaps not. Anyway I'll tell you."

"Are you sure you want to tell me? You won't regret it?"

"Yes, I'm sure. It's because of Belleth and Taza, really. Things may change before she grows up, but suppose she doesn't want to enter a Pleasure House when she's old enough. There's no hiding her. Everyone knows you have a daughter. I just think there should be a choice. You know Athirra's story, don't you?"

"Skies preserve me, I haven't thought of it. I know you told me when we first arrived that it was lucky Belleth was married and I was with her, but really I forgot all about it. And it never occurred to me about Taza. There must be a way I can get her out of the Town before then and back to my Pack. What can you tell me? Is there a way?"

"You're supposed to say 'fraternity preserve me' here," Teq chuckled. "More wine? I've found an unknown way to leave the Town. That's my secret."

"You have? Nobody else knows? You're sure?"

"Very sure. I more or less made it myself. It was there, but not big enough for a man to get through. I enlarged it so that now it is."

"Where is it? Where does it lead? But then there's no way to cross that huge valley. No Teq. It doesn't help. I could carry Taza out when I search for herbs, come to that. She's small enough. I could get back to my camp through the hills, once I got up into them."

"How? There are far guards posted all round the valley and beyond. You'd never get away, and if you tried, they'd know you wanted to and they'd guard you. Especially you, with that foot. Forgive me, but you couldn't travel fast enough. My way out leads into the Western Mountains. Nobody goes there. No guards are posted. From the valley they're about impossible to climb. That's why the Town was built up against them at this point. There's no danger of approach from that side."

Zolg though a minute. "But then what? She's just a baby girl."

"She'll get bigger. I don't know what then. I haven't thought everything out yet. I might go there myself. I'm thinking about it. I really am. The Town has too many things about it I don't like. The way they treat women, for instance. It makes me angry. Galt has rescued four already, and we haven't been here four years yet. The place makes me restless too. You can't just leave whenever you feel like it. I don't know when I'll be allowed out again."

"Well if you were out there with a place for Taza to go to... That's different. Mind you, there's time before I have to be worrying. Where is this place?"

"In a cave behind the top falls. Nobody knows about it because nobody ever goes there. The cave has a back exit which opens on to the mountains. At least it does now, as I told you. I found it when I was assigned the falls area to map for my Competent's test. How's that for irony?"

Zolg laughed. "I can see that buying this house was useful in more ways than I knew. No other place overlooks the way up there. Don't you worry. Even though we've finished a whole jug of wine between us, I'll remember not to betray your secret. It's important. Thank you for telling me. I won't even tell Belleth. Thinking about Taza's distant future would only worry her. She's much too ill now to think so far ahead." He sighed. "I can't bear to lose her, yet I can't bear to see her suffering as much as she is. I must go home. Thanks for the wine, Teq. Will you be over this evening?"

"No, I don't think so. I was there at the noon meal. Kiss Belleth for me."

"I will."

Teq was enormously cheered to have told someone his secret at last. Even to have talked about his own thoughts of leaving. It all sounded less far-fetched now. And he trusted Zolg. A man who'd had to protect himself from his childhood on, didn't give up advantageous information lightly. He didn't know how he knew that, but he was sure. Since he'd got started on all this, he might just as well go now and look for Vork. They could have dinner together if he was free, and Teq could sound him out a little.

He found Vork just about to sit down to a meal in an independent inn near his home: the Fatted Fowl. He was on his own and was delighted with Teq's arrival. He was bursting with news and dying for an audience, but it was late and all his friends had already eaten.

The food at the Fatted Fowl was limited to fattened tame birds, which sounded very bland. But the birds were cooked in many different ways, so that it smelled very good. Ibaren despised the birds and wouldn't cook them, so everything was new for Teq. He was pleased he'd come. He chose the meat wrapped in a pie with chopped vegetables. He was quite content to munch away and listen to Vork's news.

"I'm going to be rich," Vork exulted. "I shall be able to afford a house and a wife, in less than a year!"

"Good for you. What's the cause of all this wealth?" Teq asked through a mouthful of food.

"The Town has just given me the contract. Me! My design was chosen by the Master and submitted to the Dignus himself. Credit will be levied from each household to pay for it and I am to be paid the sum I asked for. Think of it! Of course I knew my design was good. I worked really hard on the details. I am a man of substance!"

"Congratulations. Let's drink a toast to you and then you can tell me what you're talking about."

"Oh sorry. Yes of course. Drains."

"Drains?"

"You surely remember the stink from the drains last summer." Teq nodded.

"Well, the new Dignus did too. He had the idea of getting our Master Builder to find a solution. The Master gave the job to all the Competents to solve by last week. And he chose mine. It was just confirmed. I've only just left him. That's why I was so late for dinner and couldn't tell anybody. I'm so glad you happened along. I was dying to celebrate."

"And your housemates knew where you were and didn't want to celebrate with you, eh? Jealous, perhaps," Teq guessed. "What's your plan?"

"Covered conduits from every street, out under the walls to a drainage field: a sort of swamp. I'll have to make that first. The Dignus even spoke of making a Master of Drainage - me - if I get this right. The covered conduits would hide the smell. Pipes would be set up in each house for them to empty the slops into. Water from the river would be pumped into the conduits to keep them flowing. A wind pump, I think, if the force of the river itself isn't enough. Then there would be one huge pipe to take the outflow from each quadrant, down to the sump area. The swamp. I'll put it in that sort of dell place at the edge of the Western Mountains. Do you understand?"

"Most of it. I'd like to see the plan you made. I'm guessing it will be sort of like a map. I can read any map and understand it, better than I can from hearing it."

"By all means. As soon as we finish here, if you like. Come home with me and I'll show you."

"I'm paying for this. It is your celebration. Let's go then."

Vork's rooms were piled high with scrolls of paper - just like the Mapmaker's Hall only not so tidy. Good old Competent Gaveril would have a fit if he saw this mess, Teq thought. What he said was: "you must have a plan for every kind of building here."

"Several of some," Vork grinned. "Over there is a whole bunch on strengthening the Town walls - as if they needed it. Those piles are plans for every type of house in every kind of material. And here is what you came to see."

Teq was really interested. Vork showed him all his ideas, and explained them as if he were making a presentation to his Master. Teq asked intelligent questions, and really got involved with the plans. It seemed to him that Vork could use a good map showing the gradations of the ground outside the walls, so that he could get his gradients right. He suggested it.

"Well, I'd love one, but I couldn't afford it. I'm not rich yet." He sighed. "It would surely make siting the sump much easier. It would indeed. Perhaps the Master or the Dignus would buy one."

"Better than that. I can make you one. There isn't one in existence now, but the measurements are all known. It would be no problem to pull them together for you. You can pay me with copies of your plans. How's that?"

"I can't let a copy of this one go yet. I'm always afraid someone would steal an idea from me. It's probably silly, but I can't be too careful with this many credits at stake." Vork sighed again.

"Oh I don't want that one. I understand that one already. How about plans for simple houses. I'd really like to know how the building of one is planned. Could I have copies of some of those?"

"Of course. Yes indeed. Those have already been used. Nothing to hide there. But are you sure? It doesn't seem fair swapping old used plans for making a special new map?"

"It's no problem for me. I can gather the information together and have a map ready for you in a week. How about that?"

"That would be marvelous. How about if I buy you dinner at any inn of your choice?"

"Good. I'd like to eat at the Fatted Fowl again. The food was really good. There, then. One week from today."

"Done. Look, go ahead and choose the plans you want while you're here. Sort through that pile and take whichever ones you want. Those are all copies, the ones with the red cords. The yellow ones are new stuff."

Teq left with three, well-pleased with his bargain. He hadn't had to explain his real reason for wanting to study how to build a house, and yet he had come away with exactly what he'd been looking for. He'd do Vork proud, with an excellent map, in great detail. Fair was fair.

Once he had read and understood the plans, he thought one of them much too complicated. He considered discarding it, but on second thought, he bundled them all up with extra copies of all the maps he could lay his hands on, and took them up to the cave. He was going ahead with his idea of gathering supplies too. He'd already bought blankets and clothes and shoes; weapons and pots and durable foods. He had done everything but confess to himself that his decision to leave was already made.

During that week, he finished up his maps of the journey to the Desert and presented them to Master Kinnasen for the Dignus' approval. If they were approved, he would be due a lot more credits. He had been paid so far, only for the time spent on the expedition. Just like Jebend and the hunters. The professional fees were still to come, and he knew they were well earned. Like Vork, he had worked really hard on the details. He knew the maps were good.

Teq had looked forward to his dinner with Vork, and he was not disappointed. The food and the wine were both excellent. The two men were delighted with one another, and stayed to eat and drink late. Teq walked home with a tremendous sense of well-being. The bargain had been fair - though Vork still did not know why Teq was pleased with what he got. They were still friends after all this time. He'd enjoyed himself.

The night was crisp and bright. Sound carried well on such a night. It was almost chilly enough for the first frosts of autumn, though still too soon for those. Memories of the desperate heat of the summer still lingered in the walls. Very few people were about. Maybe the chill was keeping them within doors. It was too early in the season to build a fire in his room, Teq reflected, though a fire always made it seem much nicer.

He had just reached his house when he heard screams and shouts. They seemed to be coming from over near the falls. Anything to do with the waterfall always alarmed him. He started out towards the noise, deciding he'd better know what was going on. He could hear pounding footsteps. One person was running towards him, whom others were chasing. He got to the corner of his building and the quarry cannoned into him, knocking the breath out of his body. He grabbed and held on.

"Let me go. Oh, please. Let me go," said a familiar voice.

He gathered in a huge breath and looked down to see who he was holding

"Bessindel!" he gasped in astonishment.

Chapter 33

"Teq? Help me. They're chasing me." The voice was undoubtedly Bessindel's, although it was too dark to see her well.

The old Teq might have asked, "Who's chasing you?" or "why would someone be chasing you?" The new, decisive Teq grabbed her up and swung her back around the corner. She had time for nothing more than an "ulp" before he had her inside his house and the door shut, his hand clapped over her mouth.

No sooner done than the footsteps pounded around the same corner and then charged on past. Then came to a stop.

A male voice shouted, "Lost her, by the Sky!"

"Can't have," shouted another. "Look around you. Any open doors? Any shop she could have run into?"

"Can't see any. Better wait till the Keeper catches up. Who was that girl, anyway? Why are we chasing her?"

"Beats me. He knew her all right. Someone he wanted to buy from another Keeper maybe."

"Don't know. Here he is now."

"We lost her, Keeper. Somewhere around here."

A third voice, breathless, but showing authority, "Did you check that alley? It seems to me the Watch Captain who bought her lives down there."

"Captain of the Watch, sir? Captain Jebend, sir?"

"No, Galt."

"But he's a Chief now, sir."

"Oh, that's right. Well look down the alley anyway. She might belong with the house. Keep checking."

"You want us to knock on their door, sir?" The fist voice sounded incredulous.

"Yes, of course. She could be hiding there."

"It's where I was heading," Bessindel whispered, panic in her voice.

"Ssh. Don't speak. Don't move," Teq hissed.

There was some light in the kitchen from the cooking fire. Objects inside the house were becoming visible to their adjusted vision. They could hear the men clump off to Galt's old house, sold, now, to a merchant. The new owner would be none too pleased to have strange men knocking on his door in the evening hours looking for a servie; searching through his courtyard.

Bessindel was trembling violently. Teq put his arm round her and held her against him to still her shudders. Gradually she ceased to tremble. He put a finger over her lips and led her past the furniture in the main room, to his own. There was only the bed and the chair at his work table. He pushed her down on to the bed and walked quietly over to the window to close the shutters.

The sound of the men returning was, therefore, less clear. Eventually they moved off, however. Teq went outside to look around to make sure.

"All clear," he said when he came back in. "Now, what was all that about? Why would anyone be chasing you? And why are you out without a cloak? It's cold."

Bessindel burst into tears. Exasperated, Teq went and found a clean cup and brought her some water.

"Have a drink," he said. "Here." And then more kindly he sat down beside her on the bed and pulled her over to weep on his shoulder. "Sip some water." He handed her the cup when she quieted down, and she took some.

"I'm sorry. I never cry. I feel so stupid." She hiccuped a little as her sobs died away entirely. She sniffed mightily and drank some water before she told him: "I have no idea who he was, but he seemed to know me. It was my own fault. I ran out without remembering I am supposed never to be seen without my cloak, because there was nobody else to go. I just didn't think. I ran. And that man saw I wasn't a child, in spite of the fact that I'm wearing servie clothes". She looked down at her well-developed figure in acute embarrassment. "I was running you see," she finished lamely.

"What did he say to you?"

"He shouted, 'That's the girl I wanted. The little one. ' Then he grabbed me and tore at my tunic. He was wearing some rich stuff. Some long tunic, and a cloak with fur trimming. I'm sure I've never seen him before."

"Perhaps Galt will know what it's all about. But what was the rush? Why are you out running about?"

"Oh," she wailed. "I should have told you that first. I'm really sorry. It's Belleth. She's worse. Really much worse. Ibaren was doing what she could for her and Girly had the baby so that she could try to feed her something, and Galt was out, and Athirra can hardly move, and so I went. I ran to get Zolg. I was going to look for Galt. And you. I told Zolg where I was going and I had just left him when that man grabbed me, and then I got away and ran and the only place I could think to go was the old house. I don't know my way about the Town much."

"Slow down. Well, I see why you were out. Are you up to walking now?"

"I couldn't. I daren't. Can I stay here till morning?"

"You'd be much harder to see in the dark, but you can stay if you like. I must go. I must see Belleth. Is she..." He paused, not wanting to say the word. Then"... dying do you think? Tell me the truth."

"Yes, I think she is. That's why it was important. Athirra wanted to go, but she really can't get about any more. She's as big as a house."

"I know. Look, you stay here then. Go to sleep if you like. Are you hungry?"

"No. We had dinner."

"Well sleep then. I'll look for Galt if he isn't already there. I'll be back later. Don't leave the room, though. Three other men live upstairs. Just stay quiet, and you'll be safe."

"Thank you, Teq. Thank you for rescuing me." Tears started up in her eyes again, and Teq found himself wanting to hug her, instead of leaving. He had better leave at once, if he wanted to go at all. He grabbed up his cloak and went out, closing the door on her. He set out at once for the enclave.

Galt was already home. It was the only sense Teq could make of what was happening there. The house was in an uproar. Taza was crying, and Girly was just looking at her helplessly. Galt was pacing. There was no sign of anybody else.

"Can I go up and see Belleth?" Teq decided that a direct question was the only way he would get Galt's attention.

"Oh. Teq." Galt focused on him with difficulty. "No. No. Zolg is with her. He'll let us know when we can see her. It's Athirra too. She's having the baby. Now. Ibaren is with her. I was never around when children were born in the Honor. Didn't even know when it was happening. I don't know what to do."

"You could look after Taza and keep her quiet. You could try to get her to sleep. I'll send Girly up to help Ibaren. She might be some use there. She's none here. She's used to doing what Ibaren tells her," Teq suggested, taking control.

"Good. Good idea. I can't find Bessindel anywhere. Where is that girl when we need her?"

"She went out to get Zolg, and you. She did find Zolg and me. She's safe for now. I'll tell you about it later, but she won't be here tonight.

"Won't?"

"Can't."

"Oh well. I suppose you know what you're talking about. Here, girl. Hand me that baby. She usually heeds me." Galt took her from Girly's hands, glad to have something useful to do.

Teq sent Girly upstairs to Ibaren. She was back in a minute with orders from Ibaren, for him to get lots of water and heat it. By the time he had three large pots filled and on the fire, Taza was asleep and Zolg came down to fetch them.

"She's as comfortable as I can make her," he told them. "She's awake and aware. Come up and see her while you can. She won't last the night." He turned away from them, his eyes full of tears. "I'll be up in a minute," he said.

They crept up the stairs together, father and son, desperately aware of the muffled cries coming from Athirra's room.

"What a night!" Galt said.

"Hello," Belleth spoke sleepily. Zolg must have given her a dose of something powerful to ease her pain, because she was smiling. She looked as if she was resting in a place of peace, somewhere a long way off. "Athirra's having the baby, isn't she?" she asked.

"Yes she is," Galt told her.

"Perhaps you'll have another daughter to replace me," she murmured. Barely audible. "That would be nice for you, wouldn't it?"

"Nobody can replace my Belleth." Galt knelt down beside her, taking her hand and stroking the hair back from her forehead.

Belleth just smiled at him. "Is Teq here?" Her voice was weakening.

"Here," he said, and clasped her other hand. "You don't want to leave us. You've only just come back."

"Oh, I do. Yes, I do. I can't keep on. Too much. Too much. I'm glad we all met again. Glad we had a chance to say goodbye. Zolg?" Her gasping voice ended on a wail.

"I'm here." He had come back up and was standing in the doorway.

Teq got up and crossed to Galt's side. "We should leave them," he urged.

They both kissed her and moved quietly out of the room, as Zolg lay down on the bed beside his wife and took her in his arms. Galt was crying. Teq had the irreverent thought that the whole world seemed to be crying tonight. He wanted to cry himself, but everyone appeared to be depending on him. So he didn't. It was better to be there in case one of the others, whose need was so much greater than his own, needed him. It might have been a silly fancy, but he stuck with it and waited with Galt until he was calmer.

"Let's get out in the air," Teq suggested.

"Good idea. This kitchen is stifling," Galt agreed. They walked out into the courtyard, and sat down to wait for news, in the long shadows cast by the setting moon.

Girly found them there. "Ibaren says, 'come, now. Big surprise.'"

Once again they tiptoed together up the stairs. The house was suddenly overbearingly quiet. Teq walked over to Belleth's room, and Galt went to Athirra's.

Zolg was covering Belleth's face. "She's gone," he said bleakly when Teq walked in. "She stayed long enough to hear the news. She wanted to. I'm glad she did." He sat down on the bed, put his hands over his face, and finally, he too wept.

"Twins!" Teq heard Galt roar. "Twins!"

Once again, torn between holding the head of a weeping soul and rushing off to the next thing, Teq did the latter.

Ibaren grabbed him outside Athirra's room, just as he heard Galt say, " What a clever girl you are. You have given me both a son and a daughter."

"Leave them together," Ibaren told Teq wearily. " She needs him now. You'd do well to pour everyone a cup of wine. I'm too tired to do it and I don't even know where Bessindel has got to. Is she in bed in all this todo? Just when I need her the most..."

"Don't worry about her. She's safe," Teq said again. "Tell me where to find the wine and I'll make sure everyone gets some. Come on down and sit by the fire. You need a rest now, more than anyone."

One by one they all gathered around the kitchen table, warmed by the fire which Teq had stoked. One by one they sipped at the wine and felt the better for it.

"To lose a daughter and gain a daughter all in the same night is more than I can take in," Galt said, at length.

"Belleth knew about the babies before she died," Zolg said quietly. "She was glad of it."

"You could name the new baby Belleth," Teq suggested.

"No. There's only one Belleth. I could call her Belletha."

"What will Athirra think?" Zolg asked.

"She will like it. We'll call the boy Gath, for Athirra." Galt looked pleased. He took another sip of his wine. "Those are good names. I'll ask Athirra what she thinks as soon as she wakes. But they are good names."

"Yes they are," Zolg agreed.

"Yes they are," Teq nodded.

"She'll like them," Ibaren predicted. "Now let's all go to bed. There's been quite enough for one night. We can talk again in the morning."

"Do you want to stay here tonight?" Galt asked Teq.

"No. I'd better get home. I'll be back in the morning. I'll tell you Bessindel's story then."

They looked at him, puzzled, but too weary to ask him to explain. He must get home to her. Little Bess. Sleeping in his bed. He walked along with his head down, glad of the chill in the air which kept him from falling asleep as he walked. The whole Town was asleep. Far away he heard the tramp of the Watch on their rounds. By the time he reached his front door, he was so tired, he didn't think he could have walked another step.

He crept in, afraid to wake anybody. The kitchen fire had all but died down. Embers glowed and gave off enough light for him to get through to his own room without bumping into anything. He pulled off his tunic and shoes and crept on to the bed. Bessindel made a very small hump in one corner. He was much too tired to worry about it. He tucked the blankets around her, pulled his cloak over himself, and fell into a profound sleep.

The morning light was dim. The shutters were still closed. It was enough to see by when he woke, lying uncomfortably rigid on the narrow bed. He opened his eyes on the pillow, and found Bessindel, lying with her eyes open, watching him. She was wrapped like a package in the blankets.

"Did I wake you?" she whispered. "You looked exhausted."

"It's all right," he said, suddenly very aware of her closeness.

"I need to relieve myself and I can't get up. Sorry," she said.

He jerked out of his cloak and rolled off the bed, landing on the floor with a thump.

Bessindel grinned, hard put to it not to giggle out loud. "Where do I go?" she asked.

"Oh. Yes. Look, you'd better wear the cloak in case anyone sees you. I should have brought yours with me. I didn't think. Sorry. Come on, I'll show you." He pulled on his tunic. "Don't make a sound."

They crept through the kitchen and she relieved herself where he showed her and then he did, and they crept back inside again. Thumps from upstairs let them know the other Competents were stirring.

"I came in very late. I'm sorry I slept so heavily. I'll make us a hot drink. It's cold," Teq shivered.

"That would be nice, but I'll make it."

"No you won't. Nobody must know you're here. Take that cup and go back to the room. I'll make a jug and bring it in."

She had barely closed the door when the first young man came clattering down the stairs.

"Were you talking to someone?" he asked Teq.

"Yes. Myself." Teq grinned. "I'm too stupid in the morning to remember how to boil water unless I tell myself what to do."

The young man laughed and used some of the water to make his own drink, as Teq staggered off with the jug, a cup for himself, and a loaf of yesterday's bread.

Bessindel was back in bed trying to keep warm. She beckoned him over.

"What happened last night?" she whispered.

He glanced at the door. She pulled back the covers and gestured for him to climb in beside her. He didn't move. He was rooted to the middle of the floor. He sipped at his drink, and she at hers without saying a word. The cloak lay on the floor. He put it on the bed as an extra cover, still standing in the middle of the very small room. She beckoned again. He climbed into the bed. Who was he trying to argue with? She snuggled up beside him.

"What happened last night?" she asked, right into his ear.

He took her head into his hands and laid it on the pillow. He lay down beside her, and speaking into her ear, he told her. She wept when she heard about Belleth dying while she was not there to be with her. They had become such good friends. So Teq took her into his arms to comfort her. And then he kissed her. Very hard. And then she kissed him. Very hard. And he made love to her. Very slowly. And they slept.

When they woke, they looked at each other for a long time, not speaking. His hands began to caress her and she smiled. Loving it. Loving him.

"Little Bess," he murmured.

Chapter 34

In the general movement of the noon hour Teq got Bessindel home. She wore his sleeveless short coat and his cap, and walked a pace or two behind him carrying his maps. He had to belt the coat around her waist to make it short enough so that she wouldn't trip over it. He dirtied her face and feet with soot from the fireplace. They both laughed so hard at the picture she made that they had to wait until they could compose their faces before they dared to leave. She had to walk barefoot as her women's shoes would have stood out like a horn blast proclaiming her gender. As it was, given her smallness and her short hair, she passed casual inspection as a boy. Even Ibaren, who was the first person to see her when they entered Galt's house, had to look at her twice before she recognized her.

"What's this?" she asked. "What happened to you?"

"This is something we must all talk about," Teq answered for her. "Let her go and clean herself up before we do. Is Galt in?"

"He's upstairs with Athirra and the babies. Zolg's here too. We will be eating in a minute and Athirra insists on coming down for the meal," Ibaren told them. "Galt has suggested we bury Belleth this evening in the great garden of this house. Zolg likes that idea. He is preparing her. All three babies are asleep at last, so Girly is just about to put the food on the table. We've certainly needed you." Ibaren turned to Bessindel "Get on and clean yourself up and then we can all hear this tale. I'm worn out with those babies." Ibaren sat heavily down at the table.

Bessindel ran off without a word. By the time she reappeared with Teq's coat and cap in her hand, the meal was on the table and everyone gathered round it.

"Now tell us where Bessindel has been, while we're eating," Ibaren urged.

"Bessindel had better tell you herself," Teq replied. "I've brought her up to date on what's been going on here."

"Such a lot!" she began. "After so much, what happened to me seems trivial. I am so sorry that I was not here for Belleth, Zolg. Let me help you now."

"Yes. Thank you. You can help me after we have eaten," he nodded.

"Athirra, twins! I know you needed help too. You must be exhausted. Are they beautiful?"

"They are marvelous and we could have used your help. I am unable to think of a reason why you should be excused for this defection. Things were at crisis here when you left. They would hardly have improved quickly. Belleth, at least should have been able to command your loyalty. I am extremely displeased. I repeat, you were needed here. Ibaren has done everything. Now where were you?"

"Hiding at Teq's."

"Hiding!" Galt spoke at last. "Why?"

"Some man saw me just after I left Zolg's house and set his men to catch me. He actually did grab me himself and tore my tunic, but I got away from him. I just ran. I was heading for the old house when I bumped into Teq. He took me into his house and saved me."

The look Bessindel exchanged with Teq was not lost on Athirra. Oh ho, a romance, she thought! They could hardly have chosen a more inopportune moment to discover one another. She was not displeased that they had. She was sure Galt would not be either. All the same, there had better be some excellent reason for the absence. Who could this mythical man have been? Who knew Bessindel? She wanted to be fair, but on a day like yesterday, there was little excuse for this hiding. Athirra was prepared to give vent to the anger which she was containing.

But she asked, "What man? Did he say anything that would identify him"

"He said I was the little one he'd wanted," Bessindel answered.

"And he knew Galt had bought her," Teq put in. "They knocked on the door of your old house to see if she'd run there. We heard them talking outside my window. Bess was too scared to risk coming out again. He had those two bullies with him. So I left her hiding in my room when I came here. There was too much happening for me to tell you about it last night."

"Quite right," Ibaren agreed.

"I would never have heard you, Teq," Galt said. "You did right not to mention it. I do think I know who the man might be, though. What did he look like?"

"It was too dark to see him. He must have seen me in the light from Zolg's house when I was coming out, but I just didn't notice him until he grabbed me. He was wearing a cloak of some rich stuff, and the cloak was trimmed with fur. That's all I can tell you about him. I felt the cloak when he had his hands on me," Bessindel remembered, with a shudder.

"Well, Galt. Does that tell you who he is?" Athirra asked. She turned to Bessindel. "You went out without your cloak, I'm guessing." Bessindel nodded, looking ashamed. "It's not as if you haven't been told," Athirra added, not yet ready to release her ire.

"I think it was Ruper," Galt said.

"Who's he?" Teq asked for all of them.

"The least desirable Pleasure House Keeper in the whole of the Town."

"That's right," Teq recalled. "His men did call him 'Keeper'. But why would he want Bess?"

"His clients are the odd ones. The ones who find their pleasures in odd ways. When he first saw Bessindel at the Distribution she was still a child. Just. He thought his clients would like a child to use. He offered me a huge sum of credits for her as soon as she grew past the age to be a servie. He kept at it, every time I saw him. He never forgot her. It's the main reason I bought her in the first place, to keep him from getting his hands on her. It's why I told Athirra and Ibaren to keep her off the street. But it's been a year now and I'd nearly forgotten about it."

"We have kept her in. We wouldn't let her out without a cloak," Ibaren defended.

"Why didn't anyone tell me why?" Bessindel wondered.

"When you offered to run for Zolg, I never thought of it. I'm sorry," Athirra told her, shifting in her seat to try and get comfortable. It was acceptable. Galt knew about this man. He ought to have told her the whole story before, but at least there was a real explanation. Athirra was fair minded, even on this day, when her body ached with the fatigue of birthing her twins.

"Are you all right, love?" Galt asked her solicitously. She smiled at him warmly, loving him and forgiving Bessindel completely. She nodded. Content. "You were starting the babies last night. No wonder you didn't remember the cloak." He smiled back at her and took her hand.

"The question is, what are we to do now?" Athirra worried. "The damage is done. He's seen her. Do you think he'll come here after her?"

"Not into the enclave," Galt said, "but he'll stop me to ask as soon as he sees me. I'll tell him she ran away, perhaps. I'm not sure what I'll say. Let me think about it. Meanwhile she'd better stay in the house."

"That won't do for ever," Ibaren said. "We can't keep her indoors for the rest of her life."

Into the thoughtful silence which followed Teq said, "I think I know what to do. She can run away - really run away - and never come back, and I know where."

"But we need her. There are three babies and this big house," Ibaren complained. "And we'd miss her."

"We'll all miss her, but one way or another we've got to lose her." Galt said. "And don't worry about the load of work. I'll buy two to replace her. I would buy one for the babies anyway, and buying two will simply reinforce that she's gone, the way word travels round the Town. I'll set the Watch looking for her, just the way we looked for Athirra. That's the easy part, but only if Teq can take her where she won't be found. Tell us your idea."

"It's a place I found. A way out of the Town. I told Zolg about it. It's near his house."

Zolg nodded. "I climbed up there one day after you told me. I couldn't go all the way on this foot. It was much too hard for me. I did see the shadow of the cave, though. Once you know it's there you can see it. Nobody saw me. I went very early in the morning, and I was back down by the lower pool before anyone else was about."

"What good's a cave?" Athirra wanted to know. "You don't mean the one Ibaren set up to look as if I was living there, surely? Where I was supposed to have killed myself? Everyone knows about that one now. I caught a fish there once," she added with a smile for Galt.

"No. Not that one. Higher," Teq assured her. It's at the top of the upper falls, behind the falls, actually. I found it when I made the map for my test. It has a back exit to the mountains. Nobody else knows it's there."

"Well I believe you," Galt told him, "but I don't see how it will help Bessindel. It's getting on for winter. She can't live up there."

"Not alone. It's been in my mind ever since I got back from the desert, to leave the Town for good," Teq said slowly. Earnestly. He wanted them to believe him. "There are too many rules in the Town. Too many things I don't agree with, like this business with Bess. Why do we have to hide her at all from this awful man? Because she's a woman! I can't picture living the rest of my life in this place. I've been stocking the cave for a while now, with things I'd need to start life in the mountains. I didn't want to do anything while Belleth was so ill, or say anything while Athirra was waiting for the baby - babies," he grinned. "Anyway, Bess and I could go together. I even got plans on how to build a house, from Vork."

"You told Vork?" Galt asked incredulously. "He'd inform on you in a minute. . Nobody's more in love with the Town and all its ways."

"No, of course not. I did him a favor and told him plans fascinated me the way they were like maps. He gave me some old ones."

"There is another thing," Zolg put in. "What is happening now to Bessindel could happen later to Taza. Even Belletha. Teq and I talked about the cave as a way out for them. We'd have to plan it, of course. Know how to reach him and so on. We wouldn't lose touch with him, and there'd be a way out for anyone who needed it..."

"He's right!" Athirra was vehement. "Think how I reacted to going to a Pleasure House. We have to keep Bessindel from this Ruper. And the girls! We must have a plan. Teq's right. Zolg is right. I can't believe I never thought of it. Listen, Bessindel, I still have the breeches I wore when I was a boy. We can outfit you properly. You'll look like a hunter again. Ha."

"Nobody's asked Bessindel what she thinks yet, unless Teq has? What do you think about all this?" Ibaren asked.

"I can't believe it! It's wonderful. I could lead a normal life again. I hear you talk and I begin to dare to hope."

"It would be just the two of us - at least I don't think anyone lives in the mountains - we'd have to go with care. But we can make life as normal as we like," Teq smiled.

"We could start a new Honor," she burst out.

"Oh no we couldn't! New ways for a new place. I won't take you if you want to go by those old rules. The Honor was just as dangerous for me as the Town is for you. More. They planned to kill me because I was a boy. Oh no. None of that." Teq was completely serious. "Equal partners or nothing."

"That's fair," Athirra said.

"It is," Bessindel agreed. "I was just remembering how I was happy in the Honor."

"Belleth was happy among the Wilders," Zolg reminded them. "You should remember our ways."

"We'll be something like Wilders ourselves to start off with," Teq agreed. "But, they are not an organized society. They were too easily beaten at the walls. Each Wilder had an opinion, as I recall. It was a mess. Though probably a happy mess." He smiled.

"I've been dreaming about escaping from this vile Town," Bessindel butted in. "I've been thinking and thinking to find a way out of here."

"I didn't think at all. I just ran," Athirra confessed. "If it hadn't been for Galt and Teq I would have been dead by now, one way or another. Now, I'm happy here. But you must escape."

"Does the idea of starting in a new place frighten you?" Ibaren asked Bessindel. "You know you cannot go back to your Honor, no matter if we could get you there, don't you? You would not be acceptable to your Sieur and Council after all this time. There'd be no proof of the purity of line, do you see?"

"No, I didn't know that. You were on the Council, weren't you?" Ibaren nodded, and Bessindel smiled defiantly. "In any case, going to a new life doesn't scare me. You may as well know I'd go anywhere with Teq, just because he's Teq."

"Aha!" said Galt. "Love is it? What says Teq?"

Teq was blushing furiously, but he reached for Bessindel's hand. "Shall we join?" he asked her. "I would like it if you would be my wife."

"Yes. Oh yes, if you want to."

"We can take care of that," Galt laughed. "Now all you have to do is get her pregnant and buy a house and then you can stay here. I'm sure it could be arranged. I did it for Athirra and me."

"No. Definitely no." Teq was vehement. "I want to go anyway. I wanted to go before ever this came up."

"Thank the Sky for that," Zolg said. "I could see my Taza's escape route disappearing."

"All right, it's settled then," Galt decided, just as the first wails from upstairs let them know that first one twin, and then the other, had woken up.

Athirra got up to go to them, and Ibaren went with her. "Let me know what you decide," Athirra charged them.

"You can take your wiving oaths this evening. We want to bury Belleth before we have our dinner. A closing for her and for Zolg," Galt told them. "Your ceremony can make a new beginning after our meal. I'm afraid it won't be a feast, alas. Now I have some things to take care of."

"I'll walk with you." Teq got up and went to Galt's side. "I'd better tidy my place up and sort my stuff, if I'm setting out for a new life any day."

Galt had a plan in mind he didn't want to announce yet - until he saw if it would work. He was delighted to bump into Captain Jebend talking to a corps of the Day Watch very soon after he parted from Teq.

"Come with me, if you would, Captain, and bring along a couple of your men. I believe your presence will deter a problem before it arises," Galt told him.

"You have knowledge of a disturbance brewing, Chief?" Jebend asked.

"No. It seems I have been robbed, and I want my property returned with the minimum of fuss."

They walked on in silence, and ended up, to Jebend's surprise at the sign of the Wicked Woman - Ruper's Pleasure House. It was the middle of the afternoon, when the people of the Town were busy about their business. There was no activity at the Pleasure House. Galt knocked at the door. When it was opened by one of Ruper's men, smiling a welcoming smile, Galt demanded to have Ruper come out to him.

They were kept waiting, an arrogance which almost made Jebend enter to fetch the keeper out. How would this man dare to keep a chief waiting? Galt held him in check and Ruper finally appeared. It was Galt's intention to have this conversation on the street, with witnesses. Storming into the House after Ruper would have served Ruper's purpose and not his own.

Galt attacked immediately Ruper appeared. "Where is my servie? Word has been brought to me that you chased after and captured her last night, after I sent her to fetch the physician, Zolg, to my house. I want her back. Now."

"Why, Chief! Whoever would tell you such a thing?" Ruper asked.

"That is none of your concern. Produce her at once, or I shall have these men search your House."

"But I do not have her, Chief. I do not." Ruper was beginning to sound anxious.

"At least you do not deny that you know who I'm talking about, or that you caught her. Sold her to someone else, have you? Who?" Galt demanded.

"No, Chief. In truth I did not capture her. Truly. She escaped me. She ran off."

"All right, Captain. Send these men in to search for her. She is very short of stature. Dark-haired. Just come to womanhood and due for the next Distribution. To take her without payment is theft. If you do not give her up freely, when we find her we shall have you up before the Tribunal of the Dignus." Galt sounded furious.

"Indeed, Chief, I do not have her." Ruper was becoming frightened. He had not fully considered the night before that Galt was a Chief. He was beginning to be glad she had escaped him. "You are all welcome, more than welcome, to search my humble premises. I saw her, I grabbed for her, she ran away. My men gave chase and lost her. I could only assume she had run away from your household. I recognized her, of course. It was my intention to capture her and return her to you, Chief. Theft of a valuable woman? I would never dare to think of such a thing! If you or your men find anything, anyone, they would like to sample during your search, they are all free of charge to you, naturally."

"Be careful what you say," Galt boomed, "or I shall have you for trying to corrupt the Watch, let alone a Chief!"

Galt and Jebend entered the House and cast an eye over the women there. Ruper's men were produced from the night before. They swore they had captured noone. The women swore that no new woman had arrived at the House last night. Galt and Jebend retreated, threatening dire repercussions if Ruper were later found to have lied.

"Thank you, Captain, for your help," Galt said to Jebend after they left the Wicked Woman. The child must have been terrified. Now, who knows where she has run to? I actually believe that idiot was telling the truth."

"I'll keep my eyes and ears open, Chief," Jebend assured him. "If someone has her illegally, I'll hear about it eventually, I'm sure."

"The worst of it is, that I sent her for the physician because my wife was birthing. Having twins, in fact. Now I am short-handed in my household, all because of this missing servie, and I don't know where to find a replacement. Two, in fact." Galt sighed.

"Congratulations, sir. Twins indeed! Perhaps I can help you there, with your problem," Jebend offered. "A weaver in the south quadrant has died this morning. His wife and daughter need housing. Would they do?"

"Of good character?" At Jebend's nod, he added, "excellent! Show me where to go and who to pay. My household is in an uproar."

The woman, Hulid, seemed eager to leave. There were two sons and they would be squabbling over the home. One already had a wife and a cloth shop. The other, a weaver too, worked at home, but he was the younger son. Both would want the House, Hulid told Galt, and she had no intention of acting as a servie for either of them. Looking after a Chief's children would be a step up in the world. The daughter, Ulda, was about eight and trained to cook. She could help Ibaren in the kitchen while Girly did the cleaning. Athirra should be pleased with him. Galt was satisfied, and paid the sons, letting them squabble over who got the actual credits. Hulid and Ulda would be at Galt's house in the morning.

The burying of Belleth was saddening for them all. She had been with them a short time, but had been gentle-natured and helpful with her knowledge. They had loved her, and they would remember her kindly. But they could not be sorry that her pain was over. Even Zolg, in his misery at losing her, could not have wished her to live on with the pain she was suffering. He wept, but it was for his own pain, and that would pass. They buried her with full but calm hearts.

Galt cheered them at dinner by reporting that Bessindel's disappearance was well taken care of. The Watch would seek her. She would not be found. It would be assumed that some Pleasure House Keeper had found her and stolen her. Unless she were recognized by a member of the Watch, that Keeper would go uncaught. As this was the assured outcome, everyone could breathe more freely, and even chuckle about Galt's attack on Ruper. It served him right, they all agreed.

After dinner Teq and Bessindel made their vows to one another, and Ibaren produced a special cake she had found a moment to bake, as a celebration. There was wine to go with it, and their spirits lifted. That night Bessindel was to slip home with Zolg. She could hide in his living quarters, where the apprentices never penetrated, until Teq came to claim her, and fetch her to the cave.

All that now remained was to devise some way for Teq to disappear. He was better known and it would be harder. But Galt felt he had an idea for that, too.

Chapter 35

Because of the death of his wife, Zolg became the most fierce advocate of arranging a disappearance for Teq. His whole life was now centered on seeing that Taza would never be faced with commitment - sale! - to a Pleasure House. In this Athirra was his most vigorous ally. On the pretext that she was unwell after the birth of the twins, she and Ibaren often visited Zolg's house to discuss and plan. But talk as often as they would, they could come up with no plan that would work. Teq was too well known. He had been fairly distinguishable as Galt's protege ever since the dramatic battle with the gray-shirt apprentices. But more, the excursion with Jebend had been discussed in every inn and wine shop. Details of the journey became better known as Bens and Rogin told the story. The valor of all four of them - Jebend and Teq as well as themselves - grew with every telling. The tale had given them many a free meal or jug of wine. The one-eyed Captain of the Watch was already well known to every person in the Town. The young mapmaker Competent was pointed out wherever he went.

Galt had the rudiments of a plan in mind, but it would require getting Teq outside the walls. As a chief, he himself was far too visible to arrange it. He was at a loss to know how to get his plan implemented. He would go to Zolg's house, ostensibly to collect Athirra, and join in the futile discussions. All their planning had now to be done at Zolg's. The presence of Hulid and Ulda made it too risky to talk sedition at home.

With all the activity centered around Zolg's house, it became harder for Teq to slip up to the cave. His marriage to Bessindel made him wish to spend more time with her, but they feared that if he spent too much time there, somebody might spot his interest. Of course his connection with her was unknown in the Town, but they had both been frequenters of Galt's house. No suspicions could be allowed to arise.

In the meantime the Watch continued diligently to seek for clues about Bessindel's disappearance. Jebend felt that he owed it to Galt, since he owed Galt his position as Captain of the Watch. And Bessindel herself swung between ela-

221

tion at her continued freedom and despair that her escape with Teq would never really happen. To keep her occupied, Zolg taught her more about herbs and remedies: an education which had begun with Belleth. He had her tending his concoctions during the long daylight hours spent in his living quarters. She amassed an equal stock of the remedies she prepared, for herself, as her contribution to the new life she was beginning to doubt that she and Teq would ever share.

The solution to getting Teq outside the walls came in a rather unpleasant way. The Guard manning the walls at sunrise one morning, nearly two weeks after the birth of the twins, saw a scene of apparent carnage among the distant herd. Chief Fergin was informed, and he sent a group out under one of his captains to find out what had happened. They found the gnawed corpses of most of the herd, but worse, they found the bodies of the herd boys in the same state. The captain concluded that wild predators had come down out of the Western mountains and attacked the herd - a thing which had never happened before. He speculated that the depredations of the Town had so thinned the game in the area, that there was no longer enough for the wild predators to eat. Whatever the cause, the threat of it happening again had to be dealt with.

The runner who reported back to Chief Fergin did so by shouting his message up to the wall where the Chief waited. The captain had sent him to ask for reinforcements to build a pen for the herd over towards the friendlier western hills where both animals and herders would be safe. They also needed to round up the remainder of the terrified herd. The word of the attack spread through the Town like quicksilver. Galt called on Teq on his way to the Palace for the immediate conference.

"Glad I found you in," he said to Teq. "You've heard the news, of course. I can't stop now, but I just came to tell you to get a rope. A long one. Twice the height of the walls, if you can. Get it up to your cave. I'll see you later at Zolg's."

Teq had no time to do more than nod that he had heard the news, and that he would do as he was asked, before Galt was away.

The glimmerings of Galt's plan began to take shape in Teq's mind. He decided to use what remained of this busy day to finalize his own preparations, once the rope was found and purchased. He dropped in at Zolg's on his way down from the cave to make sure that Bessindel had heard the news.

"I don't see how it helps us," she sighed. "I am getting to the point where I'm ready to walk out of this house in full daylight, find your cave, and just leave, Watch or no Watch. ."

Teq laughed. "It really does help," he assured her. "One thing, though, how good a hunter are you? Were you? I realize you must be out of practice. If there are predators in these mountains which would like to eat us, it would be useful if we were both able to protect ourselves."

"Of course I'm a hunter!" She was disgusted. Then she thought for a moment and told him the actual facts. "I was never any use with a spear, though," she confessed. "I'm not strong enough to throw well, and I'm too short of reach for a decent thrust. But I'm very accurate with the bow and the sling. Very Exceptionally! My eye is very good." She laughed at the look on his face. "You don't know how lucky you are to have me as your wife," she teased. "I'm a treasure."

"As well as beautiful," he added solemnly. "We shall do all right, you know. We really shall. How can we lose, what with your treasure load of skills and my brains..." He ducked as she threw a slap at him.

"I'm well prepared, at least," she told him. "Athirra has brought me warm clothes and good boots. We have so much stuff already that we shall need a stretcher to carry it all. It will never fit into our packs."

"I planned to store things in the cave and come back for them once we've found a place to settle. We'll want to come back to the cave routinely anyway so that we can make our plans with the others to rescue the girls later, oh and just to keep in touch." Teq had been considering all this for a long time.

"I've been thinking," Bessindel said tentatively. "If we keep rescuing girls, we'll need to bring in some men too; unless you were thinking of setting up another Honor with yourself as Sieur..." She grinned at him.

"You know how I feel about that," he answered her with a hug. "No more Honors! "I've thought about that too. Zolg tells me that Wilders respond to drums - because of the drummings in the Honors, you know. They want to see what kind of youths are out looking for Wilder Packs. They gather when they hear them. I thought I could make a drum, and set it up where the hills rise to join the mountains - eventually. Only the most adventurous Wilders would come that far. We could check whoever comes, and invite some to join us. It's too early to worry about it yet, but I think something like that would work."

"It's a good idea. But then, there might be people in the mountains already."

"You've really been thinking about this, haven't you?" Teq was delighted, and impressed. "I'd thought of that too."

"Not much we can do till we get there and look around," Bess said. "Now tell me what you're doing to get us out of here!"

And he told her.

With the general upheaval going on in the Town, Teq was able to take the last of the personal items he felt he would need up to Zolg's house. There was enough left behind to create the illusion that he still inhabited his house. When it grew dusk, he carried the stuff up to the cave, and risked taking Bess with him, carrying her supplies. They made the trip safely up and back, and found a very agitated Galt waiting for them.

"Did you get the rope?" he asked as soon as Teq walked through the door.

"Yes. I took it up there earlier." Teq grinned at him. "I think I know your plan."

"Well, if you know that, you know we'd better set it up now. It should be light enough. The moon will still be almost full tonight, and there's not much cloud about. Come on, then. It's not something you can do alone. Anyway I'm dying to see this cave of yours. We're expected for dinner at my house, and you still have to volunteer, so we'd better get on with it."

"Volunteer?"

"Of course. You mean you hadn't heard that the hunt will be volunteers only? Naturally every hunter will want to go. How often have we had the chance to hunt killer beasts? I'd like to go myself."

Teq kissed Bess goodbye and followed Galt out of the house. From then on he led the way. The older man still had the stiffness in his leg. It was getting stiffer as the years passed. There would soon come a time when this climb was beyond him. Still, he was more agile than Zolg by a long way. One day, he thought, he'd show this place to Athirra and she could be in charge of getting the young girls to the cave.

Once they were fully inside the cave and could not be seen from below, Teq struck a light. In spite of his excavations, passage to the rear was not easy, especially since the cave was now crammed on both sides of a narrow passageway, with supplies.

Galt gave a "hrrumph" when he saw them. "You don't intend to do without much that the Town can supply you with, do you?" he chuckled. "Have you left anything behind at all, so that your rooms don't look abandoned?"

"Oh yes. I thought of that. My oldest clothes, and my fanciest, are still there. I'm leaving a map I'm copying on the table, and of course I won't make the bed. Everything here is new. Even the weapons. I'll take the tried and true ones with me on the hunt."

"I should have known I could trust you to think carefully." Galt clapped him on the shoulder. "Now, is there any need to discuss what we're doing, or can we just get on with it?"

"It wasn't until you came by and told me to buy a rope that I worked out your plan," Teq confessed.

"Let's get it done, then," Galt said. "Lead on."

Getting through the cave was a real trial from someone of Galt's bulk. And he wasn't as young and flexible as he used to be. Once they were outside the going was not much easier in the moonlight, but they managed to find their way. Teq scouted ahead. There was a massive outcropping of bare rock which bulged southward from the mountainside which rose above the cave's exit. Thin trees grew here and there, straight and sturdy, as if sheltered from the bitter force of the winds by the weight of the mountain. In the moonlight the trees threw moving shadows which murmured in the chill breeze. They followed the line of the outcrop round, and found it looming over the outer edge of the Town's south wall, which had been built to lean right up against the mountain itself. Between the top of the wall and the outcrop, the mountain leaned inward on the ascent, so that the outcrop formed an overhang at that point. Without a rope the climb up the mountain would be impossible. From this point southward the ascent was even more formidable, being made up of sheer cliff. How the predators would have come down to reach the flock was beyond Teq's imagining.

While Teq worked out a way to ease round the outcrop to a point just above the Town's wall, Galt was tying knots at intervals all along the length of the rope. At the end of the rope he tied a rock. When Teq returned he had him rub dirt into the rope to make it less visible against the rockface.

"Now that's about as invisible and climbable as we can make this thing," Galt said. "Let's get it secured and drop it over the edge. It had better be long enough!"

They chose a tree which seemed rooted strongly enough to outlast eternity, and tied the rope to it. Teq carried the weighted end on his shoulder as he eased perilously around the outcrop for the second time. With a silent blessing, he threw down the rock. The rope snaked after it just as the moon dipped coyly behind a cloud. Teq waited for the yell of the Guard if one had happened to be at this end of the wall, and the rope had hit it, or snagged on it; or even the thump of the rock hitting the ground if they were lucky enough that it reached that far. He heard neither. Even here, the din of the waterfall outshouted all other sound. But there was no apparent alarm. He had to trust that nothing had gone wrong.

"We'd better hurry, lad," Galt said as soon as Teq rejoined him. "This took more time than I thought. All well?"

"All well, I think," Teq answered. "Can't tell much over the noise and with this poor light. But then conditions would be the same for the Guard, even if they had been there."

Galt chuckled. "It's the dirt we'll hear about if we don't hurry and get washed in time to eat. Don't worry about Bessindel, lad. I'll see she gets safely to the cave tomorrow night. After that we'll all just sit around and worry until we hear from you again. Don't forget about us in the excitement of your new adventure, eh?"

They ate a sumptuous meal, without any recriminations from the women about either their lateness or their dirt. After the meal, Athirra and Ibaren walked Teq to the gate.

"You be sure to take care in that wild place," Ibaren admonished him. "You two may have been hunters once, but you're not used to the wild any more."

"We'll take care," Teq promised as he kissed her cheek.

"We haven't set up any plan for signaling," Athirra said. "Galt will take me up there soon, and I'll work something out. We need a plan whereby you can signal us, and we can signal you. Don't forget. Come back soon so that we can work it out. Be sure."

"We'll do out best. If you don't hear, you'll know it was because of something we couldn't control. Now don't start worrying the minute we leave. It's going to take weeks of exploring, probably, before we decide where to settle. You know that." Teq squeezed her arm.

"How will we know you got safely away at all?" Athirra asked suddenly.

"If I don't make it to the cave, Bess will go back to Zolg's house. Then you'll really have something to worry about." He laughed. "It will work. You'll see. You've quite enough to worry about with this family you've produced. Don't spare us a thought. We'll be fine. It was a memorable meal. Thank you both. We'll be in contact soon. I must get going and volunteer or I'll be too late and then the whole thing fails." He kissed her on the cheek too and was off.

As soon as he left the enclave, Teq started to run. It really was very late indeed.

He reached the Barracks just as one corps of the Guard was going off duty and another starting out.

"Who do I have to see to volunteer for the hunt?" he asked the departing sergeant.

"Chief Kambar's still here, Competent," the sergeant told him. "He may have enough, though. You can ask him."

"I've come to volunteer for the wild beast hunt, Chief," he said loudly as soon as he got to the table where the Chief was sitting, surrounded by his captains.

"Who are you? Oh, Competent Teq. Why do you want to go?" the Chief asked him.

"The chance of a lifetime, sir. I've just heard about it. I've had my head down, working until I went out to eat. I came to volunteer as soon as I heard. There'll never be another hunt like this one."

"We hope not," Kambar agreed dryly. "You'd be much better off on the other hunt. We're outfitting two. They're off to the hills to muster game. The winter hunt will be a little early. We don't want to lose the Town's meat to these predators."

A hunter captain leaned forward and whispered into Kambar's ear.

"Ah, yes, of course," Kambar said. "The game hunt will be going into the hills where you are not permitted to go, right? No, Competent, we can't send you on that hunt."

"But the wild beast hunt is to the south, isn't it, Chief?" Teq was trying desperately not to sound desperate. He had to go out with the wild beast hunt or all plans were void. Then what would they do?

"What do you think, Captain?" Kambar looked at the man making notes on his left. "Do we need an extra man there?"

"We're sending so many after game, we could use someone, yes, Chief," he answered. "This Competent seems eager, and I hear he is a good hunter and fighter."

"Very well, then, Competent. Report here at dawn. Bring bow and spear, water bag, food bag and a blanket. We may be gone more than a day. I shall lead that hunt myself. Get a good night's sleep."

"Yes, sir. Thank you, sir." Teq bowed and left.

Altogether things were pretty good. He was delighted they did not plan to return to the Town each night. He would have a much better chance for slipping off, with or without sentries, at night. But Kambar himself in charge? That was something they had not counted on. The Chief had eyes everywhere, and everyone would be especially alert to impress him.

Well, his chance was now. He was committed. By this time tomorrow, he'd know whether or not the plan had worked.

Chapter 36

Kambar split his force into two parties. He was to lead a small group, all agile young men, along the cliff and through Vork's sump, south as far as the falls which began the Great River. Their task would be to seek a path up into the Western Mountains. The second group under Captain Haupt, was to go to the site of the carnage and follow the spoor of the predators. It was deemed most probable that the two groups would meet at the spot where the predators had emerged from their mountain fastness.

To his disgust, Teq was assigned to Haupt, on the principle that he and Jebend had gone that way before and knew the territory. He had hoped to go with Kambar's party and have a chance to examine the cliff face for possible points of entry to his new home.

The place where the herd had been attacked was much trampled. It took Haupt and his hunters a long time to distinguish the marks of the predators. At last one of the older men found a clear print of a hind foot in some muddy ground behind a large rock. The beast must have stood there, watching the herd, his front feet on the rock and his rear feet on the ground. The print was big - much bigger than that of any animal they knew. It was the mark of a soft pad. Clawed. The claw marks dug deep, as if to give purchase to the animal when he gathered himself to leap down from the rock among the herd. Now that they knew what they were looking for, they found the marks of a second animal among some rocks to the northeast. Next, to find out where they came from: search for tracks in and out of the area.

The creatures had devoured their prey on the spot, though the amount of damage they had caused seemed to belie that. The attack on the herd boys must have been because the boys bravely charged the beasts, in defense of the herd, with nothing but their lightweight spears as weapons. The boys had been mauled, but not eaten, as the first reports had implied. Only four animals had been eaten thoroughly. Why, then, so many dead? Great flocks of carrion birds hovered eagerly in the sky, waiting impatiently for the men to get out of the way and let them resume their meal. Had the beasts been providing food for the birds? Such a partnership was unknown. Other scavenger beasts, perhaps, since scared off by the activity of men? Teq had another one of those insights which seemed to have plagued him all his life: as hunters they ought to know more about the other hunters in the land. They should be as aware of the other creatures which preyed on the game, as they were of the game itself. Why had no one, Honor, Wilder or Town dweller ever turned their thoughts to these beasts? He vowed to learn about all the creatures who shared the mountains with him, if he ever managed to set up a home there.

By the noon meal break, Haupt decided they would have their answer once they found the beasts. They must concentrate, therefore, on discovering and following their trail. Half a dozen men were assigned to carry the pathetic remains of the herd boys back to the Town. The rest set about finding the trail of the predators.

It was the same older hunter who found their trail. The creatures had traveled among the rocks, leaping over muddy ground where necessary, seeming to be aware of the need to avoid leaving tracks. Haupt and most of the men had been casting westwards towards the mountains in search of the trail. The actual route, both in and out, led to the north and east. The sun was setting by the time Haupt was thoroughly convinced that their way led to the very hills in which the winter hunt was taking place. Not unreasonable, Teq thought, since they would also know that was where game was to be found. So they had not come out of the mountains.

"Not much more we can do now until daylight," Captain Haupt told his men. "We'll camp here for the night. In the morning our two swiftest runners will go to warn the main hunt. Chief Kambar should be informed tonight."

"I'll go," Teq volunteered swiftly. "I know this territory well, and I'm under ban not to go into the hills."

"Yes, very well, Competent. That's a good idea. Are you sure you can find your way?" He was also under a ban not to go off by himself, but fortunately Captain Haupt seemed to have forgotten that.

"It's not dark yet, and there will be a moon later. In any case, the Chief's party will be lighting camp fires, which will be easy to see from a long way off," Teq answered with confidence.

"In that case it's probably better to wait until they are lit. I can write a report for you to carry in which I will have formulated more detailed plans," Haupt considered.

"Better to go now, sir. I can tell the Chief what you have in mind. You will probably want time to think out your report, and you will want to send another man in the morning to find out the Chief's wishes. I expect the Chief would want this news immediately." Teq was trying to sound as if his only wish was to save all parties from trouble. His own desperate need to be off must not appear in his arguments. With any luck at all, he would avoid Kambar's hunters completely. The first they would hear about the change in direction would be with the arrival of Haupt's report in the morning.

"Very well, Competent," Haupt said again. He had reached the rank of captain some years earlier. He was devoted to Kambar and had followed him slavishly through all their lives. With each promotion of Kambar's, Haupt had gained the next place below. When Kambar was made Chief, Haupt was promoted to Captain, a rank just beyond his capability. It had not mattered until now, because he had been at Kambar's shoulder, ready to carry out all his orders and insist his bidding was done. Alone, he was as easily swayed by Teq as he had been by Kambar. He let Teq go off alone without a thought, his mind fully occupied with the structure of the report he would write for Kambar. By the time he remembered to post sentries, Teq was long gone.

Teq loped off in the evening light, heading directly west towards the mountains. He was perfectly visible to the sentries of both camps, as well as the Guard on the Town walls. The distances were not very great. He paused at a high point, catching his breath and scanning the ground for his best route. He hunkered down to eat and drink from the supplies he carried, aware that he had a long, hard night ahead of him. By this time Galt should be at Zolg's house, getting ready to escort Bessindel up to the cave. No problems there. It was cramped in the cave, but Bess was so small, she would have plenty of room to stretch out and sleep the night away. He'd be with her long before dawn. He could not believe how well events had played into his hands, allowing him to get to the rope with the whole night before him. The only question was whether the rope was long enough to reach the ground, but he had measured with care, and there ought to have been enough of it.

Ahead and to his left was a patch of scattered trees. Far beyond them, to the south and west, the campfires of Kambar's party were beginning to wink in the increasing darkness. He jogged towards the trees. By the time he reached them it should be full dark. He would then be able to change direction and make straight for the Town walls unseen. Easy!

Galt was indeed with Bessindel at Zolg's house, pacing up and down in extreme agitation.

"I have just come from the Palace," he told them. "Chief Fergin has convinced the Dignus that the only easy access to the Western Mountains is where the walls join them. He's right, of course. The Dignus fears that the beasts, crazed with blood lust, will climb down there, enter the Town, and attack all the citizens. Madness! The Guard on the walls is to be doubled, with the extra men posted just there: at the junction of the Town walls with the mountain. Just where Teq will be climbing the rope. It is insane. No wild creature would willingly enter such a place as the Town, with its smell of fire and man! But they will be posted there all night! With lit torches! I did not dare protest overmuch, in case it would be supposed I had some other purpose - which of course I have. Now I am at a loss."

"Exactly where Teq will be making his climb!" Zolg gasped.

"Exactly! Besides that, it is right beside the falls where Bessindel and I must go in a little while. We'll never make it there and back unseen. We must delay leaving."

"No." Bessindel was adamant. "If Teq does get through and I am not there waiting, he will not know what has happened to me. He will come down here, and then he will be caught. We will have to plan all over again, and now is the right time."

"But there is not enough time before the Guard is posted."

"No time to get there and back. There is time for me to get there alone. Then nobody will be coming back. I have little to carry. We took it yesterday. There is no need for you to go with me. I am dark. My clothes are dark. The falls are loud. I will not be discovered if I go alone." Bess was certain.

"She's right," Zolg agreed. "Let her go. She can slip back here if Teq does not come, but if he does... She's right."

"I agree," Galt nodded. "I don't like it, but I agree. You are a brave woman. Look after Teq as he will look after you. I shall miss you both." He hugged her quickly. "I will go to the walls and see what I can do there. Take care."

Bess gathered her few belongings and kissed Zolg. "I cannot thank you enough for putting up with me, and for teaching me so much. All things willing, I will not be back again, but you will be in my thoughts, as will the others, all my life."

Zolg walked outside to check for passersby. The Watch marched by and the sergeant waved to him. He watched them go, then beckoned to Bessindel, blowing her a silent kiss to speed her on her way. She slipped by him, a shadow in the dark. She climbed the route by the falls, her way lit enough by the light which always gleams off moving water. At the first pool she paused and looked around. It was true that more men than she had ever seen there were gathered on the walls. A contingent carrying torches was walking along the wall, heading in her direction.

A fish jumped in the pool and startled her. She remembered that Athirra had told her about catching a fish here. She grinned, cheered, and started to climb again. The upper falls were above the level of the walls, but the light from the torches could well reach all the way up there. She had to be behind the curtain of water before they arrived at this end of the wall.

And hurrying, of course she slipped and fell, awkwardly, with one arm twisted beneath her. She cried out in pain, her voice lost in the voice of the water. She had also skinned her knees. She rocked quickly back on to her heels, afraid of leaving a sign of blood on this upper route. When she had gathered herself together, she reached over and dipped the sore arm into the icy water to still the pain, and dripped water off her hand on to her grazed knees. Everything hurt. She wanted to whimper with the pain, but there was no time. She thought of all the salves she had carried to the cave, but had none with her. The thought made her grin again. Catching her lower lip between her teeth, she pulled herself upright and started to climb.

Just as she reached the upper falls, the torch bearers reached their position. They waved their torches around as if to defy the threatening dark. Bessindel froze beside the falls - so near to her destination - trying to become a shadow in the rock. In moments the Guard was called to order. It must have been Galt. Someone, whose voice she could not hear, had apparently ordered them to use their torches to illuminate the walls themselves. She could hear a sergeant shouting at his men, but could not hear the words over the thunder of the falls. Not that she cared! She pushed her throbbing body behind the waters and slipped into the cave. She eased around the corner until she judged it safe to strike a light, and did so. She built up a pile of their packs to create a wall and make doubly sure not a glimmer would show outside, through the waters. She could not bear to wait here all night for Teq without a light. She found her salves and dressed the wounds on her knees. She was fairly sure the arm was twisted and bruised, but not broken. But it hurt. She hurt all over. She pulled some blankets together to form a bed, and then she sat down on them and cried.

Renewed by the way food he'd eaten, Teq decided to sprint toward the walls as fast as he could move, as soon as he left the shelter of the trees. He was far off from Kambar's men, who did not expect him anyway, and out of sight of Haupt's. The only direction from which he might be seen was the Town walls - and it was now dark. He wanted to be certain he was under the walls by the time the moon rose. Once under the walls the chances of being visible to the Guard were almost none. And no Guard was ever posted at the junction of the walls with the cliff, where he would make his climb.

He had not allowed for the nervousness of the Guard. Just before he actually reached the walls he heard a shout.

"There, sergeant."

"Fire."

Teq fell flat on his face as a flurry of arrows was loosed in his direction. They fell all around him.

"Hit anything?"

"Can't tell."

"Nothing moving out there now."

"Something was moving this way. I know I saw something."

"Me too."

"One of them beasts looking for more than goats."

"All right. All right. That's enough. Keep a sharp eye. If there was anything we scared it off. Don't light that torch. Spoil your night eyes. Leave the torches for them as is at the mountainside. Back to your posts. Sharply now."

Teq took a deep breath. That was close. One of the arrows had actually nicked his ear. Too close! He pulled the arrow out of the ground and stuffed it in with his own. It was marked with blood. His ear was dripping blood still. Ears will bleed. He took his water bag and clapped it up against his ear to stop the bleeding. No question but that he'd been careless. Too sure things were all going his way. He stayed close to the ground and wriggled his way over the last yards to the wall. It was not far, but it seemed to take forever, between moving on his belly and keeping the water bag on his ear. The ear had stopped bleeding by the time he was able to sit up, panting, with his back to the wall. He hoped he had left none of his blood visible on the grass. He did not know that his Bess had been having the same thoughts about her own blood, very little earlier on that same night.

There was a paling of the sky. Moonrise already! He had hoped to be half way up the rope by now. He still had to follow the wall round soundlessly, and then find the rope. Maybe the moon would help him. No time to worry about it anyway.

It was a cloudy night. Much more cloudy than the thin wisps of the night before. Teq crept forward in every shadow, and froze when the light of the moon beamed cheerily down. At that speed, it was past the middle of the night when he finally reached the cliff. The adrenaline from being shot at had long since leeched from his body, leaving him with a sore ear, and legs stiffening from his long run. He was also cold. The heat built up when he was running had chilled into sweat as he crept through the long grass at the wall's edge.

The grass was even longer at the cliff face. He and Galt had done far too good a job of darkening the rope. It was indeed invisible. He patted the stone of the cliff face and the wall, groping for anything that could possibly be a rope. Not even a vine! He moved over to the junction where the wall met the cliff and sat down on a stone, head down, hands hanging between his knees. Teq talked to himself sternly. He reminded himself of the reason he was there; of all the people who had helped him; of Bess waiting for him even now. It was the thought of Bess that finally got him going again. He straightened up, stretched, back against the cliff, and felt a knot in his back. He reached back and grabbed it. It was a knot in the rope. He was sitting on the actual stone they had used to weight it!

It was enough to set him upwards grinning. The rope reached all the way to the ground. It was long enough. It was invisible, sure enough. The plan was working. The climb itself was not hard. The knots in the rope gave him good purchase for hands and feet. Placed as he was in the angle of wall and cliff, there was plenty of support to keep it steady. He could place a hand on one or the other if the rope wanted to swing. He clambered swiftly upward.

When he hung just below the edge of the wall, he heard a cough. He froze. Then a voice - surely it was Galt's - saying: "I would suggest, sergeant, that the men are better off without those torches. They spoil the night vision."

"All due respect, Chief, but Chief Fergin wanted us using them, as beasts is frightened of fire, he says."

"I see."

Torches then, on the walls just here. That's what they'd been talking about when they shot at him. Why hadn't he taken that seriously? Teq hung on the rope, a mass of indecision. Carry on up, and hope he could get all the way unseen, or go down and have nowhere to hide come the morning? Galt had obviously heard about the torches and come along to see what he could do. But the sergeant was determined. Now what? He was so close to the top of the wall he could hear the men breathing over its rim.

He was dithering. Teq knew he was dithering and was helpless to make a decision. At last he heard Galt's voice again.

"Captain! How are things going?"

Another voice spoke. "Farther along they thought they saw a beast running through the grass a while ago, Chief. They shot at it, but I don't suppose they hit anything. Scared it off, whatever it was. Could have been nothing at all. Everyone's jittery. How are things, here, sir?"

"Quiet. Very quiet indeed. It's hard to see much with the glare of these torches, although the sergeant very properly pointed out that wild beasts fear fire." Galt's voice again.

And then the other. "You're right, though, Chief. They do spoil the ability to see at night. Chief Fergin has found the same at the northern wall. You'd better douse those, sergeant. Leave one lit in the sconce, and pile the others beside it, so that you can light them in a hurry at need. I can relieve you now, Chief, if you'd like."

"That's all right, Captain. Why don't you take your men along the inner rim and I'll watch here over the wall, for a bit."

"All right, sir. I'll take a few and leave you a couple."

"Thank you, Captain." There was a pause, the sound of marching feet, then Galt's voice again. "You men space yourselves ten paces from me and from one another. I'll take the cliff edge. Good."

The sound of feet moving off was Teq's signal to start climbing again. Good for Galt. Come to the rescue again! He would be within inches of Galt but a good ten paces from the others. But his fingers had cramped from hanging there so long. Cautiously he let go with one hand and allowed the blood to flow into the fingers; and then the other. It hurt, but they were alive again. He pulled himself up another notch. Warm hands reached out and grabbed his.

"I'd no idea you were so close," Galt murmured, his voice soft enough to mingle with the constant rush of the torrent. "Don't speak. On your way. Good luck."

For that one moment, Teq had time to loosen and shake each cramped leg, his hands grasping at the rim of the wall. And then he was climbing again, stiffly, but moving. He fell on his face over the lip of the cliff and edged forward, mindful of the overhang above his head.

There was still much to do. The clouds had thickened during the climb, but he needed light to ease safely round the outcropping. His fingers felt raw and stiff, but he rubbed at them and flexed his feet. When a break in the clouds finally came, he was ready to take advantage of its light to make the perilous journey round its edge.

With failing energy, Teq managed to heave the weighted rope hand over hand up the cliff, muttering to himself in fear lest it bang against the wall. At one moment he felt a double tug on it, and knew that Galt was easing it past. Signalling him an all's well. The rock wedged under the overhang. He had to crawl back over the same ground to shake it loose. In the end, he just untied it and left it there. The moon had set, and dawn was already a whisper in the sky by the time he had the rope untied from the tree and coiled.

He pulled it over his shoulder, and tottered the last steps to the cave, just as the night's clouds greeted the dawn. It suddenly started to rain. A deluge. Good. All traces and tracks would be washed away. His last worry was over now. When he reached the slit of an entrance to the cave, he was glad of the guiding light from Bessindel's lamp. He dropped the rope inside the entry, too tired to carry it any further, and then was forced to get down on his hands and knees to creep forward under the low part of the roof.

"I'm here," he said, still kneeling and looking over at the pile of blankets where she was curled, hugging her arms round her knees.

"Oh Teq. It's morning. I was trying to tell myself it was time to go back to Zolg's, but I knew you'd come. Oh." Bessindel tried very hard not to laugh at him, kneeling like some great, shaggy animal, dripping water all over the floor. And then she lunged forward and hugged him fiercely, as hard as her sore arm would allow. All her tears had long since been wept and forgotten.

"What a night!" he chuckled, her laughter infectious, hugging her back. "How was yours? No, tell me later. I am finished." He crawled a mite further and then fell beside her on to the blankets, laughing still, now that the tensions of the night were over.

"And famished," he added. "Climbing is hungry work."

"My night was horrible," she smiled, "But I don't care now. Let's eat and then sleep. I have food ready."

"And to think I was going to do this alone!" He sighed and kissed her long and hard. "You are a wonder, my Bess."

"So are you," she whispered, serious now. "Nobody else could have planned and carried out all this. You've saved me, you know."

"I've saved me, and cleverly found someone to go along. That's where I'm clever." Teq rolled on to his side and looked at her.

"Come on. All this has addled your brain. You need food and sleep."

"Let's do that then." Teq lay back wearily against the blankets. "Let's eat and then sleep. Then we can start having a new life."

Part 5
Mountainhome

Chapter 37

It was the column of smoke which first attracted their attention. Teq and Bessindel left their laden travois, in the hollow where they had spent the night, and crept up to where they could see what was happening. They were on a high, bare hill, and the way down towards where the fire was burning was fairly steep. Bessindel gasped at the sight before her, and then clapped a hand over her mouth, as if she could be heard. It was such an astonishing sight! Teq laid a restraining hand on her shoulder, trying to size up what they were seeing.

There was one aspect at least of the sight before them which was not new to Teq. The Great Sea, sullen and gray, was beating against the sandy shore below. Since they had been traveling directly west for more than two months, he had not expected it to be there. According to his maps, the Great Sea lay to their south. Either it curved around the whole of the land, or here was another of them.

However, that was not the cause of their reaction. For the first time since they had left the Town, they were looking at people. What was more, they were looking at people under attack. Two long boats were drawn up along the shoreline, and surly men were attacking the group of villagers below. Both groups were few: less than twenty in either. It was clear, however, that this was yet another group of men out to capture women. Worse, they had apparently set the houses on fire. The villagers were running back and forth trying to fight them off and put out the fires, while the marauders were taking their time to cut out the young women they wanted, who seemed scarcely more than girls, and herd them aside from the rest. The whole attack and defense was taking place in comparative silence. It gave the watchers the sense that they were looking into another world entirely. They would have expected shouts and screams, not to mention the clash of arms.

Bessindel threw Teq's hand off. Without a second's hesitation for thought, she jumped up, fitted an arrow into her bow with all the aptness of one who has killed food on the hoof for a long time, and shot. The arrow flew true. One of the boatmen fell, with an arrow in his throat. There was nothing else for Teq to do but join her. They rained down arrows until at least seven had found their mark, killing or maiming their targets. The villagers waited for no more, but used the confusion to attack with a ferocity which bespoke their anger. The remaining boatmen rallied to their leader, ready to charge up the hill, but he ordered them back to the boats. They obeyed with apparent reluctance, picking up their companions, and fighting off the villagers with seeming ease. A few pushed the boats into the Great Sea while the fighters scrambled aboard, each group handling their weapons against the villagers as the others got to the boats. They were gone. Bessindel sent a last arrow after them, which missed. Teq held her arm so that she could do no more.

"Enough," he said. "We had better get down there, now that everyone knows without doubt that we are here."

"Oh, Teq, I'm sorry." She looked up at him. "I just get so angry when I see men grabbing women. I suppose it was silly."

"It was silly. Who knows if the villagers are going to be friendly?" She looked so contrite that he added, "I'm sure they were glad of the help. We'd better go and see if we can help with the fire now. We don't look very threatening ourselves, and the use of our arrows is going to incline them to like us. It'll be all right. Come on. Better to show ourselves right away."

Bessindel's eyes teared up at the rebuke, but she felt good about routing the invaders, so she said nothing. Just nodded. They left the travois where it was, and started down the steep hillside.

The travois was a tool they had made use of from the start. That first night in the cave was warm enough, but as soon as they set out the next day, it was apparent that they had chosen the wrong season to run away. Who in their right mind would choose to leave the safety and comfort of the Town when winter was coming on? The only positive side that Teq could think of, was that everyone in the Town would think the same. It would be assumed that Teq had been attacked and eaten by the predators. It would occur to nobody to search for runaways.

They got no farther than the opposite side of the valley, before they realized how cold it was. They were lucky. They might have been several days' travel along the way before the cold struck. They talked about it, and decided that they had better go back and get all their supplies, if they were to survive in the mountains. There was too much material to fit into their packs. So little of the accumulated necessities could reasonably be abandoned that they decided they had better find a way to bring everything. They cut two saplings for a litter. It was the conventional way to carry excess burdens. The only problem was that Teq was very tall and Bessindel was very small. With Teq going uphill first to bear the heavier weight, the ends of the poles went right over Bessindel's shoulders, missing them entirely, and trailed on the ground behind her. She had to duck out from underneath, and run behind picking up everything that slid off the litter. Apart from that, the dragging poles did very well. They stopped to tie everything on, and the poles got crossed. That seemed to work even better. Going uphill, Teq discovered that an extra binder tied across his forehead helped to ease the burden on his shoulders. They had made the first travois they had ever seen.

It was because Teq had become their beast of burden, that most of the hunting fell to Bessindel. There was no time to stop along the way. It was important to kill their meals as they traveled. Teq was certain, that if they could but cross the mountains, they would find a sheltered place to build a home, which would see them through the worst of the coming winter. They did not want to dally along the road.

"Over the top," he called to her, " in an hour. Not more."

"I'm going ahead," she called back. "I can't wait to get somewhere." And then, "Oh, no. Teq, come and look."

"As fast as I can," he panted. The final slope was really steep. "Oh, Skies preserve us!"

The vista before them was of range upon range of mountains, sweeping in rock strewn billows as far as they could see. Whereas they had been traversing deep valleys, and ever higher climbs, what was now before them was a very shallow dip, followed by a higher range, and on and on until the snowclad peaks to their north and west gleamed brightly in the winter sun.

"On or back?" Teq asked at last. He lay where he had fallen when he unhitched the travois and dumped it on the ground.

Bessindel was crying. He knew by now that Bessindel cried easily, and crying comforted her, in spite of her protests to the contrary. It no longer tore him up to watch it. He let her cry for a while before he interrupted with his question.

"Which would be worse?" she responded. "How far have we come?"

"Three weeks, isn't it?"

"It must be."

"And no people."

"Not one."

He got up and walked back to the summit. "Bess," he called. "Come and see if I am seeing what I think I am seeing."

"What?"

"Come and look," he called impatiently. "Are we being followed?" he asked, "or am I imagining it? Is that - look, there, - someone or something on our trail?"

"That isn't a person," she spoke thoughtfully. "I wish I could see better. Too much shadow. It looks like a beast. Something walking on four feet, not two."

"That's exactly what I think too. You know we never found those predators before we left, though they did seem to come from the hills, not these mountains. Probably a silly thought."

"Hm." His Bess might cry a lot, but she didn't lack for resolution. "It's probably nothing of the sort, but we have left a fine trail," she said. "I think it would be better to go on, though. There's plenty of game back there. No reason for a predator to be looking for us. All the same, they scare me."

"I agree. Better to go forward, build big fires, and not worry about it. Let's get going , then. We can be over the next top before dark. Change of view, at least."

Bessindel laughed and picked up the end of the travois. "It's getting lighter. We've used up a lot of the journey food. Perhaps I can take it for a while."

"If we ever reach flat land, you can. Meanwhile you'd better find us our supper."

Nothing much changed the pattern of the days. At night they heard creatures roaring and howling, now. Something they had neither of them heard in their Honor or Town days. It seemed much wilder, the deeper they got into the mountains. And colder. The huge fire they kept burning at night served two purposes now. It staved off the bitter cold as well as unwelcome visitors.

They took turns watching through the night. As the days went on and on in their sameness, Teq decided to call a halt each noonday, as Jebend had, so that they could sleep a little while the day was at its warmest. Since they had no idea where they were going, they likewise had no idea how long it would take to get there. No point in wearing themselves out. It was on these midday halts that they were able to make love and remember who they were. The nights were for talking and then for enduring.

On the last night in the highest heights, one of the predators came near the fire. That day snow had fallen. They were heading for a pass, which ran like the back of a gumbuck, from the snowclad mountain heights to their right, to the lower, craggier hills to their left. There were no trees near where they stopped that night. They had hoped to have crossed the pass before nightfall, but the going was stonier and more difficult than they had yet encountered. The gleanings of wood were meager, and they were not able to make the mighty fire they had become accustomed to. The blaze was puny, and constantly in threat of being blown away. As the night drew on, it began snowing again. The wet whiteness hissed in the fire. Bess drew closer to the warmth, wishing that Teq would wake up. She could hear things moving in the dark. She'd never been scared like this before.

And then she saw a huge, hairy paw, claws extended, reach out towards the haunch of goat she had been planning to have for the morning. Finding game up this high had been hard. What this creature had been doing on a crag at noonday, apparently watching them approach, she had not stopped to query. She shot it. It had been a good dinner. Apparently something else wanted it too. She screamed. The creature snarled and withdrew, and Teq leaped up from his blanket, his battle staff in his hand.

"What? Where?" he yelled.

"Teq. Oh, Teq. I am so scared. I think it's gone. It wanted the remains of the goat. Sorry about the scream, but I couldn't help it. Really, I couldn't. Oh, I am so sorry to wake you. You need your sleep. It seems to have frightened it off, though."

"What was it?" Teq walked round their camp at the very edge of the firelight. "Can't see a stupid thing," he grumbled. "Too asleep still, I suppose. Shall I throw it the rest of the goat, or put it on the fire?"

"Cook the thing. It's hard enough to find food at all this high up," she decided. She was crying from the fright of the invasion. "I'm not going back to sleep now, anyway. You can if you want to. I'm sure I shall be all right."

"No, I'm awake too. Let's eat now, and get over that pass early. I want to get lower. If the snow has started, we're too high anyway."

"Oh, yes. Let's," she agreed, her sobs lessening now that she knew he was going to stay awake.

Unfortunately, there was another pass beyond that one, and another beyond that, before they could begin to descend. And the snow continued. There were no more noon halts. They had to hunt for shelter early, and hunt for food, and hunt for fuel, before they dared to make any kind of camp. The predators were getting bolder. There was no more game, but they found a coney the first day, and birds the second, and they managed to make them last nearly a week, along with the remains of the goat. The snow made the climbs difficult, and the descents treacherous. And their boots were wearing thin.

"My feet hurt," Bessindel complained. "I want to stop and use the goat hide to mend my boots."

Teq laughed. "I want to stop and do all kinds of things. I want to stop pulling this stupid load, which seemed so important in the Town. Is all this stuff really necessary? What have we got all these medicines for?"

"If we didn't have them, they'd be just the thing we needed," Bess retorted.

"We could dump them here, and find them on the way back."

"If the burden is too much for you, I'll take it. You can find us food for a while. Especially now when there's not a thing to hunt," she snapped, starting to cry.

"Oh, no, my lady. Why should you be burdened, when you have this man to serve your needs? Allow me to find you food AND carry your medicines. You wait here for me to return. Or simply lead so that I may follow." Teq was grunting all this in short bursts through his teeth. The terrain was all rock, and there was no place which did not drag back at the ropes on his head. The fallen snow hid every hazard from view. There was no relief.

Bess stamped her foot. "What do you want from me?" she sobbed.

"Stop that snivel, at least," he grated back.

Bess sat down in the snow and sobbed. Out of all patience, Teq dragged on and left her there. He was pushing through snow which was nearly knee deep, and did not even have the energy to stop and look back at her. The gray of the afternoon grimmed down. In seconds, when she wiped her glove across her eyes, he had disappeared from view. Her anger gave way to fright. She jumped up and hurried forward to follow the deep track of the travois. And then she heard his cry.

It sounded like "Aaaaaah..." and dwindled to nothing.

She pushed along, as quickly as she could. He might be horrible, but he was all she had in this wilderness.

She heard a cry again: "Bess, take care."

But it was too late. She was over the top, and sliding down the same slope. She fell in a heap on top of him. He caught her. There had been time to unhook the travois and turn to face the slope. He started to laugh, as she thumped down on top of him. "I think we're over the top," he said.

"I think you're right," she gasped angrily. "Is this a tree, we're lying against? Could there be wood here for a fire? Oh, Teq. Are you all right?" She got no answer but his laughter.

He pulled her to her feet. "If there's a tree here, there will be more below. Come on, girl, let's see if we can get out of this snow."

In two steps, the white mist dispersed. It had been a cloud, damp and cold and dense and full of snow. They were over the top indeed. And they could see. Not far, but enough to know that the ground was sloping downwards. They went on down, and surprised two coneys. Supper. And found wood. Fire. A little further and there was the sound of water. Camp. It might still be early in the day, but they decided they deserved a rest. While supper cooked, they made love, barely remembering the quarrel of earlier in the day. They just knew that they were safe, and together and out of the terrifying mountains.

They spent two days there, sorting out their belongings, and drying out and reckoning how long they had been on the march, before they traveled on. If it was more than two months as they both agreed, no wonder it had snowed. It was nearly Winter Long Night. They had believed they would have found an idyllic home place and built a shelter by now - at least in their dreamier planning. If it hadn't been for the threatening predator and the howlings, they might have stopped somewhere. They knew really it had been better to explore. Better to find out what was in these mountains. Better to find out if there were other people.

And now they had found them. Very slowly Teq and Bess went down the side of the hill towards the people below them, who were still trying to put out the vigorous fires.

Chapter 38

"Those men disappeared on the gray water plain. What is it?" Bessindel murmured to Teq as they descended the steep, grassy hill.

"It is the Great Sea. They traveled in boats. I have seen it before when I went with Jebend's party."

"The beginning place?"

"The same."

"It is a place of awe." Bessindel was a little frightened.

"It's all of that," Teq grinned in agreement. "Now. Will you talk or will I?"

"You talk. I have not met strange people before. I'm much too scared, now I have time to think."

"I didn't do too well last time. I ended up fighting for my life and those of my men."

"Well, if you have to do that again," Bessindel smiled, doing her best to encourage him, "you'll probably have a better chance of winning than I would. In any case, women were being captured here. It may be another place like the Town."

"We'll soon find out." They stepped on to level ground, grassed in the same coarse way as Teq had met by the Great Sea before. Below them still was the sand and the Great Sea.

Two elders, a man and a woman, sat on a log at the edge between the two. Nobody at all was watching Teq and Bessindel come towards them, which Teq thought very odd. The people were busy, pulling at the edges of the burning huts, and throwing the pieces on to the sand, where the smoldering cinders died. There was almost nothing left to salvage from the remains of the huts themselves. They must have lost everything, but they showed no emotion, made no sound as they worked.

Teq walked up to the elders, Bessindel at his back. "We greet you. May the Sky be thanked for the saving of your young women this day," he tried.

The two did not look up, but the woman called, "Ocham."

A young woman looked up from among the workers. She brushed her black-ened hands against her leather skirt, and walked over to them. The woman said, "Speak to these."

The young woman was calm. She was of medium height and of slim though sturdy build with long, straight hair of a shade so pale as to be the color of the sand, glinting in sunlight. Her eyes, set very wide apart, were large, and of a deep, silvery gray-green. Her serene beauty made Teq think of Tarabeth, his true mother. She looked them over with care. "I am Ocham," she said. "Where have you come from?"

"I am Teq, and this is Bessindel, my wife. We have come from the other side of the Mountains."

The old people gasped. "Then you are true People of the Mountains," Ocham bowed. "You are the first we have met. My brothers and I were born in the Mountains, but our mother and father were Sea People. In all the time they lived in the Mountains they met no others."

"Neither have we," Teq agreed. "We are not really Mountain people ourselves. At least, not yet. We mean to live there. We were simply exploring when we came to the end. To the Great Sea. And saw the men attacking your village."

"Why did you fight them?" Ocham asked.

"They were stealing your women." Bessindel spoke for the first time. "We could not see that and not help." It seemed to her like a really silly question.

"How did you know they were marauders, though? Pirates? Not true Men of the Sea?"

"We didn't." Teq answered.

"Would that have made a difference?" Bessindel was indignant.

"Of course. The Men of the Sea are entitled to the young women. But they had already been to collect them. These were pirates. They were taking the young girls. We thank you for your help. It was an unusual thing. I have not known such an attack in my lifetime. I do not know why the Men of the Sea were unaware. Not here to prevent it."

"But you, yourself. You did not resist capture?" Bessindel asked.

"I? Oh, I am known. They would not have taken me. I was fighting the fires," she answered calmly.

"I don't understand." Teq was puzzled. Why would any group of men not want a woman as beautiful as Ocham? He could hardly voice this, but he wanted to know.

"Why they would not want me?" She smiled at them.

They nodded, both equally curious.

"I am not truly a Person of the Sea. Neither are my brothers. We were born in the Mountains. The Mystery of the Sea would not find us acceptable. My broth-ers will not go and join the men, when they are old enough. The villagers allow us to dwell among them, but we are not of them."

There seemed to be nothing to say to this. Teq was at a loss. He decided they had better simply leave these people alone. Obviously the elders would have no part of them because they had come out of the Mountains, even if they had saved their lives. He was not very pleased with them, but at least they were not being attacked. Considering his experiences with the People of the Desert, he felt that to be something of value.

"We will collect our arrows, then, and be gone," he said. "Is there any further way in which we may assist you?"

"Oh, yes. Please do take your arrows. The Sea will take these," she said, pointing to the corpses of the invaders.

The elders spoke again, this time the man. "Ocham," he said.

She bowed to Teq and left them to gather up their arrows. Before they had set out, ready to climb up to the abandoned travois, however, she was back. "Where are you going?" she asked.

"We have left all our possessions a short way up there. We are going back to them," Bessindel answered. "Why?" What business had these graceless people to question her and Teq? They had barely thanked them for the undoubted rescue of the young girls. She was extremely irritated by them.

"We ask that you come with us. We will be leaving very soon now. The marauders will be back, of course with more men. They do not like to be thwarted. But it is almost Winter Long Night, in any case. We would be in our winter homes by then."

"We'll find a place for ourselves, but thank you for offering," Teq answered courteously.

"There is nowhere safe in the winter storms, unless you are far into the Mountains. You do not know this place, I think. The sea gales begin soon. They blow very far inland. Without a stone house, you would not survive. Above the places where the gales reach, there is snow. Very deep. Nothing lives in that snow."

"Stone house? House of stone?" None of Vork's plans allowed for anything but timber in the building of houses. That would be difficult, Teq thought.

"Nor is there time to build one," Ocham assured him, "one man alone. Your only chance of survival is to come with us. The elders ask that you come. You fought to save us. We would like to save you."

"But you survived in the mountains, and you were a child then, " Teq protested.

Ocham smiled. "It was early spring when my father was thrown ashore by the Sea Mystery, more dead than alive. My mother elected to save him from the Mystery's fury, so she took him to the Mystery of the Mountains. He was a very beautiful man, she told me. They built their stone house in the summer, both working together. My mother was bigger and stronger than you." She smiled at Bessindel. "Even then, they barely survived the first winter. Believe me, you would not survive without going all the way back to where you came from. We do not ask why you came. We are grateful for your help. We wish to help you."

Teq looked at Bessindel's doubtful face and made up his mind. "You know the region. We do not. We will accept your help. Will there be time for us to go back and get our belongings?"

"If it is truly not far. I will send my brothers to help you. You will travel with us, of course. The Mystery would reject you otherwise."

"What does she mean about the Mystery of this and that?" Bessindel asked Teq as Ocham went to summon her brothers.

"I'm not all that clear myself. I know what they told me about the Mystery of the Desert and I didn't altogether understand that. Just do what they say and we can ask more later."

"Are you sure about going with them? I'd rather be on our own. We've done all right so far," Bessindel grumbled.

"Completely sure. Either the sea or the snow would kill us if we tried to make it on our own, and that seems stupid, when there is help to be had. No, we must go with them. On top of all that the pirates will come back, and if we have survived the weather, they will kill us. We killed them. There is no choice."

Ocham walked up with two youths, one just a boy. "These are Doban and Royar, my brothers." She introduced the older boy first. He looked a lot like his sister, although Royar looked subtly more like the other young boys around the place, with darker hair and eyes more gray than green. "They are both experts at working with wood," Ocham said proudly. "They will help you with your belongings. Please show them where. You can stay with me and start loading, if you prefer." She turned courteously to Bessindel.

"I'll go with Teq," she answered shortly.

"As you wish."

Doban was as calm and spare with his words as Ocham, but Royar skipped a little as he went with them back up the way they had come.

"He is unused to coming this way. I apologize for his excitement," Doban said gravely. "He was very small when our mother died and we came down to the Sea. He remembers very little."

"How did she die?" Bessindel asked. Teq tutted at her nosiness, but Bessindel stared at him defiantly and moved closer to Doban.

Doban didn't seem to mind. "She was killed by one of the great cats. She was bringing home game during the hungry time, and it wanted what she had caught. They fought for it and the cat won. We found her when we searched. She had told us to come here if she died. In the spring, we did."

"What of your father?" Bessindel was ever curious.

"Lost in the snow months before. We never knew."

"That is very sad. We ourselves are not very used to a group of father, mother and children with no other adults," Bessindel explained. "I can see where such an arrangement presents danger. You needed more adults until you were grown."

"We were in the hands of the Mystery. It is obvious that our parents were rejected by both Mysteries." Doban spoke as if this was completely comprehensible. Bessindel looked at Teq and shrugged. He shrugged back. "We hope it is not so for my brother and sister and myself," he added with his unruffled calm.

By this time they had reached the place where the travois lay. It was not far. The column of smoke which had alerted them was still drifting in the sky, tattered and torn by the briskness of the breeze from the Sea. Soon there would be no sign of it.

Royar was delighted with the travois. "This is a useful thing. You could attach it to a carry easily."

"Carry?" Teq asked. "I have pulled that through the mountains."

"It is a hard way to travel," Doban commented. "We will take it with us, just as it is. I believe it will fit."

Bessindel was gathering up their blankets and pots. There was no time wasted in stowing them neatly. It was a thing they had done so often, they didn't have to think about it. The load was balanced and secure in short order. Teq lifted the wider end as usual, but Doban picked up the other.

"It will be faster to carry it, rather than drag it, I think," he said.

"True," Teq agreed.

"The fire is out. I have all our weapons. We're ready," Bessindel said. "Lead the way." She looked at the bouncing Royar.

He grinned at her cheerfully, quite delighted with the brief outing, and fell in at her side. "This way," he announced, moving off at a slightly different angle from the way they had come.

It was no time before they were back at the shore, but around a curve of land from the village itself. Four boats were drawn up out of the water, three of them already full of people. Ocham stood by the smallest. Royar ran down to join her. "We're back," he announced unnecessarily.

"Good," she smiled. "Load up."

Doban guided Teq in the loading of their travois on to the boat. The poles jutted out before and after, but balanced well, and were propped inside the confines of the boat itself. Teq was delighted at the idea that he was to travel in a boat. It was not a wish he had ever thought to have fulfilled, when he had expressed it to Jebend all those months ago. The craft was pointed sharply at either end and there were three flat boards sitting in the middle. Ocham had taken their bedding blankets off the travois, and made two soft places at either end. She indicated those now. "You two sit there," she said.

Already the other boats were being pushed into the water by the young boys. In each, an elder and three of the older children, boy or girl, were taking up their own boards. They were using them to propel the boats through the water. Casting his mind back, Teq realized that the men they had chased off that morning had done the same thing. It looked simple enough. He looked around for Bessindel. "Come on, Bess," he called.

"No. Not me. I'm not getting in that. I'm not going anywhere on the water. The Great Sea may not like me," she added to Ocham. "You'd better go on without us. We'll just walk along beside the Sea and meet you later."

Ocham laughed. "That is not possible. We are going to a place which can only be reached by Sea. Please do not fear. It is really a safe way to travel. The Sea is most kindly today."

"No. I will not get in that. We'd better just stay here, then. We'll take our chances. Just take the travois back off. We'll be just fine. Don't worry about us."

"Don't be silly, Bess. Of course we must go. We have already discussed this. Come on, now." Teq was slightly aggravated. Surely they would not have to discuss every matter over and over again.

"No. You can't make me. You go. I'll see you in the spring." She started to cry. Bess knew he would never leave her. As he walked towards her she added. "You'd better get our stuff."

"I won't be parted from our things, or from my Bess," he smiled at her. And then he picked her up in his arms, holding hers trapped at her sides, and carried her to the boat. "Where do you want us?" he asked Ocham.

"In the bow. The front," she answered, grinning. "Royar, in. Push off," she shouted to the impassive Doban.

Bessindel screamed and fought. Teq freed one hand and clapped it over her face. "There, there, don't look," he murmured. "Turn your face in to me. There. You're just sitting in my lap with your eyes closed. This is wonderful. We're not walking. Just relax, my Bess, I'll look after you. See how gentle the Sea is."

And they met their first wave. It was not big as waves go, but it was the first wave either Teq or Bess had ever met. It slapped the boat and wet them. Teq grinned in surprise.

Bessindel gave him one horrified look and was sick. There was not a moment during the rest of that journey when she was not either being sick, or trying to be sick.

For Teq, his own food was fighting against the smell of Bessindel's offerings. He was trying to enjoy the experience of traveling in a boat. His heaving stomach would not allow it. He tried very hard not to resent Bessindel's reaction to the water. Her misery was genuine. In the end he succeeded because she looked so desperately helpless, and needed him, if only to care about her. The other three, after one startled laugh from Royar, looked to their work, guided the boat, and seemed not to notice the difficulties of their passengers.

It was a noteworthy way to meet the Mystery of the Sea.

Chapter 39

The boat journey suspended them in time. The weather was remarkably fine. Although the waves seemed enormous to the two visitors, their hosts assured them that it was unusually calm for the time of year - undoubtedly what had prompted the pirates to attempt the raid today. Bess lay with her head hanging over the side, retching and wretched. Teq learned to rise and fall with the sway of the boat, but was so distressed by his wife's poor state that he had little time to enjoy the unusual experience. Meanwhile, the other three paddled tirelessly, and kept station behind the boats which had preceded them.

By early afternoon, the sun little past its meridian, they were rounding an enormous headland. It had loomed before them almost from the outset of their journey. However hard the paddlers worked, it seemed to get no nearer, and then all at once it was there above them. The cliff reached to the clouds. From their position below, their insignificance was humbling. Threatening. The beating of the waves, battering at the lower cliff had done their work through the ages. It was scooped out below the distant top, and pitted with ledges where birds clung, laughing at the puny boatloads of people fighting to pass by them. Bess was unable to see any of this. Perhaps it was just as well. Terrified as she was of the sea and traveling on its surface, the sight of its true power would have driven her into a swoon.

As it was, Teq was a little troubled by her. The way she had not hesitated to kill the pirates, not even for thought, was reminiscent of the sureness of the women hunters at the Honor. But reminiscent also, that they had been at least consenting partners to the killing of the boy children. Only he, it seemed, felt there was anything amiss in killing people. True, the pirates were the aggressors, and he had joined Bess in killing them, but it bothered him that he had done so. What had he become? Killing in the desert was different. He was personally trying to save the men of his troop. And actually he had killed no one. He knew there had been little choice this morning, and Bess should be admired for her prompt desire to help. It was either that, or stand back and watch the villagers abducted. But he was troubled.

And then Bess had shown absolute panic in the face of the unknown Sea. Of course, considering the effect it had on her, she had been right to be fearful. This was his Bess who had climbed the cliff to the cave and waited through the night all alone, for his sake. Well, her own too, but she had not hesitated. The Bess who had escaped from her attacker in the Town - and then cowered in his room when she knew Belleth was dying. Stop this at once! he told himself. Here is your poor little wife, helpless in your arms, and you are thinking these dreadful, disloyal thoughts. All the same, he feared she would make a poor leader. She seemed always to react to her feelings of the moment. To think nothing through. To consider no consequences. It was just that she was so young. He knew that. Time would mature her, as surely as it was doing with him.

Before the short winter afternoon was well begun, they rounded the headland. Before them was a deep gash let into the cliffs: a sort of narrow valley, with one end open to the Sea. Teq could see why they had been told that to go overland to reach this place would be nearly impossible. The cliff they had rounded was backed by higher and higher hills. But the farther end of the inlet was a deeply grassed and gentle slope. Three rivers slid down its banks to feed into the Sea. As soon as the paddlers took them within the walls of the inlet, the Sea was kinder. Glad to receive the water offerings from the Mountains, no doubt. Even as they watched, Teq recognized the phenomenon of the receding tide. Each move of the waves fell lower and lower on the slope of the grassy hill, revealing a beach of sand below it.

The outgoing tide was hard on the paddlers. If Teq had known how, he would have offered to relieve Royar. The youngest boy was visibly tiring. As they approached the banks, they could see people gathered, and beyond them, houses - yes, made of stone - built hard up against the cliffs. There were animals milling about also: the common herd beasts, and something larger, taller and longer-necked. One house was very large indeed, and lay in a narrow space between two of the rivulets, gentling down to the Sea. On the central land, which was broadest, there were many smaller houses, all built to follow the terrain, so that their backs were against the stone walls. One house stood alone, close to the tumbling falls of the third stream, but on the farther side from the main village. It was towards the beach below this, that Teq's boat was aiming.

They beached, and Teq stepped first into the shallow water, carrying Bessindel still. He laid her on the soft grass, then turned to help the others drag the boat high and dry. While they unloaded, Teq was standing beside Ocham. Her nose twitched against the sour smell of his clothes. He looked down to find her laughing at him.

"You would like to wash, while we finish unloading, I am sure." She spoke gravely, but her eyes still laughed.

"Where?" he asked, grinning back.

"In the fresh water, close to the beach. We drink from the water higher up."

Without another word, Teq grabbed the bedding from the prow of the boat, and went to stand, fully clothed in the frothing waters of the river. The water was freezing cold, but oh, so fresh. He laughed out loud as he lay in it, letting it beat down on him. Ocham and Royar to laughed with him. Bessindel rolled over and sat up, curious to know why they were laughing. Now that she was certain the ground beneath her was no longer moving, she felt completely well. She wanted to shout at Teq, or at somebody, for submitting her to all that misery, but her own smell was too vile. Standing warily, she walked over to the river. She stepped in and lay down with Teq. He reached out and pulled her to him, and all sign of her resentment fled.

They pounded the bedding clean, and came out, shivering, to spread it and their clothes on the warm grass. Ocham and Doban were walking up the hill, the boat balanced upside down on their heads. Royar followed carrying the paddles. The travois with their clothes and possessions was unloaded and lying near. Teq and Bessindel pulled dry clothing from the bundles, and spread their wet clothes to dry; then they followed the others to the small house on this side of the stream.

The house, when they reached it, proved to be two levels high. The under part had a wide-open door, where the others had gone with the boat. They walked in after them, and found themselves in a wide barn.

Royar skipped over to them. "This is where we keep the animals when the snows come. The hay we harvested last summer is up there." He pointed to slatted shelves slung near the ceiling. A ladder stood in the corner. Slatted boards had also been made into dividers, so that there were several divisions within the barn. More stood propped against the wall. "We use those to make pens," he added, seeing where Teq was looking.

"Can we make a fire anywhere?" Bessindel asked. "We have the means. Shall I go and look for wood?" She was still shivering.

"That would be very good. We have nothing with us, due to the fire. There is some journey food in the house above, but that is all," Ocham agreed.

"We have our weapons. We can look for something for supper," Teq suggested, glad of the chance to move about too.

"I will come with you," Doban offered. "I can show you which way to go. The other families will be taken care of by those here, but we must fend for ourselves. Your help will be most welcome."

They ran down to the beach and grabbed up their weapons. "Are you sure you feel up to this?" Teq asked Bessindel. "We can manage with just two of us if you don't."

"I want to get as far away from the sight of that Great Sea as I can. Never again. I will never travel on it again. Nothing in the world could be bad enough to make me. If you ever pick me up against my will like that again, I shall be your enemy for ever," she said fiercely. "I am not joking. I knew. I said I would not go on it. But it is over now. You did not know. Let us get on with the hunt."

"Can you lend me a weapon?" Doban came down to ask. "Everything of mine was burnt in the fire. Tomorrow I will make more, but the day is already far gone. We should hurry."

"Which weapon do you prefer?" Teq asked, more than a little startled by Bessindel's attack, but deciding it would be better to ignore it. She was undoubtedly still feeling badly after her experience on the water.

"I am better with a bow," he answered, "but I am not sure that my reach is as long as yours."

"Try it," Teq offered.

"Good. I can manage. Follow me up this way."

Teq picked up the spears of the Desert people. He had not used them on the crossing of the mountains because Bess did all their hunting. He was eager to try them now.

They did well. It was so close to evening that the animals were coming out to feed. They managed no large animal, but had enough small ones to make at least two meals for them all. Teq found some wild roots to go along with them, and dug them out with his spear. It had not been much use otherwise. They gathered wood as they returned in the heavy dusk.

Ocham had lit two fires, using wood that was stored at the house, and what she could pick up from the shore. The fire in the house was clearing out the smoke from the old soot in the chimney. The one out of doors, was drying their clothes, propped round it on sticks. Royar was gathering bracken to pile for their bedding. Blankets and winter clothing for the three homeowners had been stored at the house, so all had not been lost in the village fire. It was a good thing. With the coming of night the damp chill was enough to penetrate through the skin, and make pimples stand up all over it.

While the food cooked, they moved their gear into the house. The chimney had finished smoking and a small fire was drawing well. Teq examined the stone walls. They had been made by piling boulders, so that they rested on one another as if in agreement. Chinks between them had been filled with mud, renewed over and over again, so that it was packed hard, and little air slipped through. There was a narrow door on the side farthest from the open water, and a shuttered window-slit opposite. The door was doubly thick, as was the shutter. It wasn't until he looked at it from the outside, that Teq realized there was a second shutter out there, which was fastened with rods which could be pushed deep into the wall itself, on both sides. The house was built to withstand really severe weather. He could see now from the strength of the structure built to survive the winter that attempting to live through it in a tent would have been laughable. He went inside and told Bess about it, where she was plying a broom to sweep dust and cobwebs from the walls.

"I told you I had forgiven you. I cannot comment on your judgement in coming here, but perhaps you are right. But there is no privacy. We will be living so close with these people all winter, we will never be alone. Kiss me now. Please. " She laid aside her broom and put her arms around his neck. "Oh, Teq. Will we ever be alone again?"

He didn't bother to answer her, just held her close and kissed her thoroughly. Everything was all right between them. And he was certain he had been right to winter here. Just so long as she could be content here too.

They were hailed outside to eat. There had been no time for food since morning, and frankly, it would not have been welcome when they first landed. But by now they were furiously hungry, and ready to eat anything that might be put before them. They looked around and saw fires lit at all the other houses. There was a warm sound of laughter coming across the water, and the good smell of food.

"Why is your house so far separated from the others?" Teq asked as he filled his mouth and prepared to fill his stomach.

"They are the true Sea People, as I explained," Ocham said, in some surprise. "This is the Home Place. We are fortunate that they allow us to be here at all. So far the Mystery of the Sea has not rejected us. Until Royar is full grown we do not wish to move back to the Mountains. So we have a house here, and we are safe."

"I really don't know what you mean by the Mystery of the Sea," Bessindel said. She really wanted to know, and she thought she had better ask.

"No, I don't really know either," Teq agreed. "I have traveled to the Desert and the People there followed a Priestess who said the Mystery of the Desert spoke to her. I didn't understand that either."

"There is a Priest with the Men of the Sea. He speaks with the Mystery. We, of course, do not. But the wishes of the Mystery are clear. It is through the Priest that we learn what to do. What the Mystery wants from us. If we are rejected, that is clear also. We cannot always know why." Ocham was trying to explain as simply as she could. "We will not risk the Mystery rejecting Doban and Royar. They will not go and learn the ways of the Sea with the other men. The Sea rejected our father. He was cast ashore close to death. We never knew why. Our mother rescued him and cared for him, but the People sent them into the Mountains for fear of angering the Mystery against them all."

"Did the Priest have nothing to say about that?" Teq asked, remembering Shamana's power among her people.

"He is with the men, not with the village."

"You said there was a Mystery of the Mountains. The Priestess of the Desert told me that too, I remember," Teq said.

"The Mystery of the Mountains rejected both of them too, but allowed us to be born there and come out of the Mountains safely. We were very afraid. All three of us quite young. I had a dream, that I should bring my brothers to the People of the Sea, so I did that. The People were in their Sea Village and allowed us to stay, though not to mingle with them."

It was all beyond Bessindel's comprehension, and she snorted. "It seems to me that you did very well by your brothers to bring them to safety out of the Mountains. It cannot have been easy, Mystery or no Mystery."

"Thank you. You have been there yourselves. You know what it is like." Ocham smiled. "It was very early spring when our mother was killed by the great cat. The going was not hard, though we were hungry after the winter. It was why my mother had gone hunting. Royar does not remember. Doban and I carried him."

"Your father had not been lost for long, then?" Bessindel asked.

"No. Just that winter. It was a sad time. But as you see, we are all well. We believe that the Mystery of the Mountain wants us to come back, so we will go."

Doban got up and stretched. "Come with me," he said to Teq. "We must go into the house and divide the sleeping quarters, and I am ready to go to bed. Are you? Royar is already sleeping." He nodded over to where the younger boy had curled up near the fire.

It seemed as if Doban was prepared to talk more now that his sister had told their story to these strangers. Or perhaps it was because they had all gone hunting together. Either way, he was less reserved. Accepting them more, as Royar had done from the beginning.

"Bessindel and I are husband and wife. We sleep together," Teq explained as they walked to the house. "I hope that causes no difficulty."

"Oh,no. None. Is that usual?" he asked. "I recall that my father and mother did."

"Where are your husbands and wives?" Teq asked. "I have seen only elders and the young."

"There are wives wintering in the long house," Doban told him. "If they are pregnant, the Men of the Sea bring them here to wait out the birthing."

"Where are they?"

"The Men of the Sea? Oh, I do not know. They have a place somewhere, besides their ships, but we will never see it, and we do not talk to the wives."

"How do they get together, the Men of the Sea and their wives?" This was really puzzling Teq.

"In the springtime, the Men come to the Sea village and collect any young girls who are become women, of course. Didn't we tell you? There are other villages beside ours, along the coast. The women are eager to go with them, naturally. It is always hard for Ocham. Ever since she became a woman, though she says nothing. This year I would have gone with them myself. They take us when we become men also. It is hard to have no place with them. To be rejected. We will be glad to go to the Mountains when we are sure Royar is old enough to be safe. The Men will come and collect the wives in the spring who have birthed. The others will come back with us to the Sea Village and they will take them from there when they have had their babies. It is safer."

"Aren't you curious? Don't you want to sneak off and follow them?"

"Of course I do," Doban answered fiercely, "but what is the point? I would never get there. The Mystery would see to that. I have learned patience, as has Ocham. It is not easy, but we endure. Here, help me with the dividers." He showed Teq where they were propped. "Royar and I sleep here. You and Bess, isn't it?, can make a place over there. Ocham likes to be near the fire over here. Good."

It will do, Teq thought. It will do. But will we do, not angering any Mysteries through the very long winter?

Chapter 40

The feast of Winter Long Night came upon them all too fast. They had not really had enough time to hunt and prepare for the winter. They had been fortunate in that the really bad weather had not yet arrived. Indeed the day of Winter Long Night was beautiful. The weather was clear, with a high ice-blue sky free of clouds, and very little wind. They did not follow their usual pattern of hunting throughout the morning and butchering the kills during the afternoon. That morning they prepared special food dishes which would take all day to roast in ground pits, or boil gently at the back of the fire. Teq had made a special effort to gather as many roots as he could along with the hunting of game. They used some of these in their cooking. Royar had found a patch where wild berries still grew, and he gathered enough for a handful for each of them as part of the feast.

The focus of the Long Night celebration, was the rising of the sun the following morning, however much it was often obscured by rain or fog. Although it was no longer a matter of terror, their ancestors had viewed this longest night of the year as a time when they feared the sun might never rise again. That its life-giving rays had disappeared from the world for ever. Therefore it was a night of vigil, with story telling, music and song, keeping each other awake and on watch throughout the night. And it involved the lighting and maintaining huge fires in a high place: the more the better.

While Royar gathered his berries and Ocham and Bessindel saw to the cooking, Teq and Doban gathered wood. There was a substantial forest near to the top of the rise behind their houses, stretching high into the hills. It was the main source for the game they hunted as well as the wood they burned.

"I am looking forward to the tales you can tell. It will be something new to the feast," Doban told Teq. "Since we eat apart from the others, as always, our stories are very old to us now."

"But they'll be new to us," Teq said. "Do you have the cleansing before the feast? We've done that wherever I've lived so far."

"Oh, yes. Ocham will be preparing our clothes while we're away. Royar always fights us when he has to take off all his clothes and wash. You can help me with him this year. He's getting big."

"Perhaps he's big enough to act grown up about it," Teq laughed. "I hope Bess is getting our stuff ready. It's time we wore our winter clothes. It's getting very cold at night - especially tonight, if we don't go to bed."

"Your clothes are not made like ours, I've noticed," Doban said.

"I've noticed the same thing about yours - apart from the leathers, of course. How are yours woven?"

"We have two needles to weave the spun wool together, don't you? We spend part of each winter day doing it. Since the wool is taken from the carries and goats during the spring, we spend all summer spinning it, on and off. Mostly during the evenings while it's light," Doban explained.

"That's not the way we do it. In fact we had been worrying about how to make our cloth in the Mountains. In both the Honor and the Town we had looms where the spun wool was woven into cloth: great big things on a frame. It's hard to explain."

"I like the result. Do these looms make different shapes for clothes for different people?" Doban wanted to know.

"No." Teq started to laugh, then though better of it. "The cloth has to be made into clothes once it's made. Do your needles?"

"Yes, they do."

"Well, that's much more efficient. I must learn how to do that. You could write down what to do, so that we won't forget."

"Write?"

"Make the shape of words on leather. Do you do that?"

"I don't even know what you mean," Doban puzzled. "If it is how it sounds, though it seems impossible, that would be a very useful thing. I've seen you making pictures on leather whenever you sit by the fire. Is that what you mean?"

"Not quite, but almost. I am making pictures of the way Bess and I traveled through the Mountains, showing everything I saw, and how far one place is from another. That's called a map. It is what I do -er best," he added. He did not want to get into the whole system of earning a living in the Town just now. I am talking about writing, which uses symbols to show sounds, so that anyone can read the same thing every time they read what is written. It's not so hard. Bess and I can teach you all during the winter, in return for learning how you weave. We'll be busy."

"Perhaps Bess can show us how to make medicines too," Doban thought. "Ocham has said she wants to know."

"Of course. And I'll show you mapmaking. These aren't as good as they should be, because I rarely had the chance to make any measurements. I had to guess at distances, and they can be deceptive."

They were both pleased with the plans for learning they were outlining, for spending the long winter days when they would all be confined together in so small a house. Teq did not realize how much all five of them had been secretly dreading it until now.

When they got back, it was time to begin the fire on the hilltop,and carry Royar off to the stream to wash. The women had both washed already, and were wearing their winter finery. Royar looked at Teq and decided that wisdom was the better part of valor. He did not fight the washing, but acted as if he thought a strip and soak in freezing water, in freezing weather, was a great way to spend the last of the daylight. By the time the three of them had rubbed each other dry, they had rubbed themselves into a glow of warmth and well being, and they were ready to eat.

Ocham was across the stream, talking to one of the elder women. She came back, smiling. "They are going to allow us to use their smoke house," she announced. "That will make all the difference in being stocked for winter. We owe it all to you two," she told Teq and Bess. "They do not approve of killing, but they appreciate that you saved our young girls for the Men of the Sea, and they want to show some token of their thanks. All our summer preparations were lost in the fire, and since there will be five of us to feed instead of three, they have seen our need. Not that there are not five of us to gather the food instead of three," she added hastily, "but it will help a great deal. Now, help me to carry the food up to the fire."

The feast was sumptuous. Bess had used all the skills she had learned from Ibaren and Athirra to make her part of the food. Ocham made things which were new to Teq and Bess. They ate and talked and ate again and talked again, until they could eat no more. Then Doban pulled a pipe out from inside his shirt, and Royar a tube into which he blew to make hollow humming sounds.

"Wait," Teq cried. "If we are to have music, I will make a drum."

"Oh, let me," Bessindel put in. "I was learning to be a drummer in my Honor. I remember most of the rhythms."

They hunted among the wood pile where Doban remembered he had put a hollow log he found. Teq ran down to the house to gather a partly-cured goat skin and some binders to stretch over the hollow. It was crude, but not as crude as the one Galt made so that he and Vork could have their drumming, so long ago. There was music now at the other fires, but faint. Doban started to play and Bess supplied the rhythm as Royar put in accent notes.

Ocham began to dance. Teq remembered the dance of the two priestesses in the Desert, and how it had worked on his mind. He watched her move. There was a different sort of grace to her. More rhythmic. Less seductive. But less stylized than he remembered his true mother's dances to be, with her formal and civilized grace. Ocham had a wildness in her, which she had never before shown. Teq was enthralled. Who would have guessed that either of them, Doban or Ocham, could produce this heady recklessness? The music soon left the formal. Soon left the ditty far behind. There was a mad beat, madder than the heart in the recklessness of the hunt, growing faster and swirling higher and lower in notes Teq had never known the pipe could produce. And Ocham matched its wildness. She danced like a spirit of the night, her pale hair gleaming in the firelight; her arms flung up to the Sky, leaping and spinning in a near frenzy.

Teq could not contain himself. He leapt up and joined her, moved by the same spirit which had snatched him up in the rite of his Drumming. His feet beat the turf. He leaped high enough to cross the fire, landing again as if he were a creature of the forest, of the Mountains, able to move without bending twig or grass. He caught Ocham by the hand and spun her. She widened her hands and spun on and on around the fire, and stopping before him, where she beat a rhythm on the ground with her feet to match the wild beat of the music. Bess followed with her drumming, increasing the tempo, driving the dancers to faster and faster stepping, until she stopped. Suddenly. And Doban stopped with her. There was one moment when they were all caught in a web of the music. Transformed into other than themselves. Teq and Ocham stared at each other, frozen exactly where they had landed, face to face.

And then Royar laughed and the moment was broken. "That was the best ever," he said. And they all laughed and agreed, although there was some small trouble in the laughter. Something more than they knew had happened there this night.

And the sun did its part by rising clear and bright in the cold of the morning.

"We must hunt while the weather stays good," Ocham announced.

"I'm tired," Royar complained.

"We all are. I'll tell you what," Ocham offered. "Let's take the boat and go fishing today. Would you like to come?" she asked Bessindel and Teq.

"Yes, I'd like that," Teq said, as Bess said, "I told you I would never get in that boat again."

Ocham laughed. "Don't worry. Royar and I will go."

"I'll come too," Teq announced. "I really do want to know how to catch fish, and how to make the boat move."

"Then I will go hunting with Bess, if she will have me," Doban offered.

"That will be good," Bess agreed. Don't come complaining to me if you've been sick," she grinned at Teq.

He grinned back and kissed her. "Let's be off before we all feel how tired we are."

He found his day fascinating. Royar woke up as soon as he realized he could teach Teq how to throw a net and haul in their catch. Ocham showed him how to paddle, so that it was not necessary for Royar to do more than laugh at him when he made a mess of it at first. But when he learned the technique, Teq marveled at how they sped through the water, making nothing of distance.

"It would be wonderful if we could do this across those Mountains," he said. "I can see why your people worship the Mystery of the Sea. This is a gift beyond gifts."

"But the Sea is an angry master too. Unforgiving. It does not do to make mistakes. To forget to respect the Mystery. The Sea can kill as easily as you crush a bug," Ocham warned. "Do not think you know all about the Mystery now that you can paddle this boat near the shore. There are places on the Great Sea where no shore can be seen, they say. Then you must ask the Mystery of the Sky to help."

"I will show nothing less than total respect. I think the Men of the Sea must start learning its ways from birth," Teq agreed.

"They do."

They reached their beach with a full catch and no sign of the other two. When the catch was emptied on to the river stones, and the boat rinsed and carried to the barn, they found the results of Bess and Doban's hunting, stacked there on the travois, with no attempt made to butcher it.

"Something must be wrong," Ocham said, hurrying to stash the boat. "Let's get into the house. Royar," she called, "you work on those fish. Come on," she said to Teq, hurrying inside.

What they found was startling but not chaos. Doban lay on his bed on his back, naked from the waist down. Both hands were clasped over his rigid member. Bessindel knelt beside him, apparently unaware. Teq took in at a glance that Bess was fully clothed and relaxed the anger which was growing in his mind.

The second look showed the front of Doban's legs rubbed raw, from the top of his thighs to his ankles, one of which was red and swollen to twice its normal size. Beside Bessindel was a bowl of dirty water and several rags. The water steamed gently in the cold air. The fire was dying down. In one hand, Bess held a pot of ointment, and with the other was liberally slathering the raw places on Doban's legs.

"Oh, Ocham," Doban said weakly, blushing the painful red of the fair skinned.

"Are you all right?" she asked.

"He's fine," Bess answered, "though he had better not try to walk far on that ankle for a few days. It's not broken."

"Can you tell us what happened?" Teq asked. "If you're too busy, we can wait."

"No, no," they chorused, and Doban went on. "I was stupid, although it didn't seem so. A gumbuck had broken a leg. The one that is in the barn. I threw a spear at it, to make sure it was dead. It was lying in the water. It must have jumped down to drink, or something, and the footing just there is very poor. The leg was wedged and had snapped."

"Very poor footing," Bess put in, almost smiling.

"It seemed too good a chance to waste, especially as we had already turned for home. We had a lot. The water was deep, so I took off my trews and jumped down," Doban continued.

"And suffered the same fate as the buck, I see," Ocham grinned.

"Well, almost. My ankle is not broken, but I fell and slid on the small, sharp stones by the river. At first I did not know I was hurt. The water was so cold it numbed me. Bess threw down a binder rope, and we hauled me up and then the gumbuck. Then I stood up, and my ankle wouldn't hold me, so I fell down, and Bess noticed I was bleeding. I fell in the dirt, and the cuts got dirty." He was speaking very quickly now, aggravated with his part in the tale.

"And then we had the problem of getting home," Bess put in.

"I could walk then, so we hobbled along, with me leaning on my spear and on Bess. I was like an elder," he grinned.

"We made it, but he could not go back, and he was worried about all the game we'd abandoned," Bess went on.

"You should not have worried about it. We could have gone for it later," Ocham assured her.

"Well, we did," Bess said. "And then I remembered the travois. I put it together in the barn. Doban put on water to heat and then lay down, as it told him to, staying off the ankle."

"I could have gone," he muttered.

"No, you couldn't," Bess said, as if she had said it many times already. "I just dumped the travois in the barn and came back to settle these cuts. They were full of dirt, and Zolg says that can be dangerous. So I washed them."

"And that really hurt," Doban said. "But this ointment helps."

"Now we must bandage the ankle, and he will do."

"As soon as he is covered," Ocham said, laughing.

"You were very brave. Both of you," Teq said, smiling. "And I agree, a blanket would be a good thing. Must keep the man warm, hm? I'll go and see to the haul you brought in, before it gets too dark. How clever of you to use the travois, little Bess," he said, and bent to kiss her hair, because he wanted to go away, and examine these feelings of resentment for Doban which were troubling his mind.

"She was wonderful," Doban said. And the worshipful look in his eyes as he watched Bess work, bothered Teq even more.

This promises to be a long winter, he thought.

Chapter 41

Teq was used to waking up in the morning and finding Bess was already gone from their bed. He was not used to hearing her cry out. He leapt from his bed and ran to the door, naked. He was not yet accustomed to sharing their sleeping quarters. He turned back to snatch up his clothes, only to bump into Ocham, also naked, also responding to the call. They both froze where they stood. Both blushed in uncomfortable awareness. Both realized they were, in truth, freezing, and broke to run for clothes.

"What is it, Bess?" Teq called as he dragged on his boots.

"Nothing," she called back. "I slid on the steps, that's all. I fell down, but I'm fine. It snowed. Everything is covered. It surprised me."

He went out to join her, immediately followed by all the others. Doban rushed to Bessindel to ask if she was all right.

"Oh, yes," she told him, smiling at his concern. "I'm sorry, though. I vomited where I fell down. I was on my way to the latrine, but I couldn't hold it in."

"Vomited!" Teq was worried now. "Are you ill?"

"Ill? No," she laughed. And then seeing his face still puzzled. "I'm pregnant, silly. There should be a baby late in the spring."

"Baby," he said, trying to keep the dismay from his voice. "But we have no home, yet. Nowhere to take him."

"Or her." She grinned. "We will have by next winter. It's all perfectly simple. Though she won't belong to any of these Mysteries, Sea or Mountain. You hear that?" she yelled. "You won't own my baby."

"Bess, be careful," Doban said, worrying for her. "The Mystery is jealous of his own. His own place. Don't you understand that?"

"Not mine," she chuckled. "This baby is mine. She will be an Honor child, brought up to respect those ways. I don't understand all this about Mysteries. And I don't want to. Really, Doban, there is no need to look so worried. Is there, Teq?"

"I don't know about that," he said. "I have been more places than you, you see. That's probably why I honor the ways of the place. The Priestess of the Desert could see what was in my mind, and it was true. She said she could see the future, sometimes too - if the Mystery of the Desert showed it to her. Ocham knows the Mystery of the Sea and the Mystery of the Mountains from her experience. I respect that. I respect them."

"Did you hear that?" Bessindel yelled again. "The father of the baby respects you, even though the mother does not. Does that satisfy you?" she asked him, sounding bitter.

"What's the matter, Bess?" He was concerned. "Did the tumble hurt you?"

"No, it didn't, but you seem to care more about what Ocham says than what I say. Why is that?"

"Come," Ocham said to the boys. "Let us go and prepare some breakfast. The fire will need stoking, Royar. Help me with the dividers, Doban." And she led them away.

"I have heard it said that women get silly when they are pregnant," Teq said firmly. "How can I say other than what I think, and why would that have anything to do with Ocham or you?"

"But it's what she thinks." Bess started to cry.

"Possibly, but it's not the reason I think it; any more than the reason I don't agree with you is because you think it. Don't be silly, little Bess. It's very cold out here and you fell down all alone in the snow. Let's cover up the place where you vomited, and get back into the warm, eh?"

Teq wrapped her up into a warm hug, and wiped the tears from her cheeks in a now familiar way. Then he cleaned up the snow and led her inside, carrying some more wood.

Ocham smiled at them brightly, and pointed to where water was heating for beanbrew. "We had best eat something as well," she said. "There's a lot for us to do today."

"Just tell us what needs to be done. There are four willing hands here," Teq assured her. "Is it because of the snow?"

"Yes. Not so much that it has fallen as that more is on the way. That was a light fall. The next may be a blizzard. It is time to open the pantry, bring the food from the smoke house, and gather enough wood to last for weeks. We are far behind with that."

"I'll open the pantry," Doban offered, "and clean it out for the food."

"I'll get the food. Who will help me?" Ocham asked. "There is a lot."

"Hadn't I better bring in the beasts?" Royar asked quickly.

"Oh, of course. We own three carries and some of the goats," Ocham explained to Teq and Bess. "The mother goats and kids, at least, need to come into the barn, and the carries need to also. We depend on them for their wool, as well as their strength; but they can't forage in the snow. Do you know these animals?"

"I've never even heard of carries," Bess said.

"Nor have I," Teq agreed, "though I've noticed the long-necked beasts among the herds over yonder. Are those carries?"

"Yes," Royar put in, "and I take turns herding them all during the spring."

"I used to be a herder too, when I was your age," Teq grinned at him. "You won't be needing help there. I volunteer to go in search of wood. I'll take the travois, and should be able to bring back a big load. Bess could help you, Ocham, if she wouldn't mind."

"Of course," Bess agreed, liking the way he suggested it. "But where is the pantry?"

"Let me show you." Doban was eager. "We have a place hollowed out in the cliff, which we can reach from inside the house. Once it freezes outside, the food stays fresh in there. I shall clean it out, and line it with bracken, and help you stow the food you bring."

"Yes, we'd better collect some fresh bracken first. Would you mind, Bess?" Ocham asked. "Oh, look, the water's boiling. We can have a brew and then get on."

"Of course, I'll help with the bracken. We might even freshen the beds," Bess agreed, good natured again. "You'd better bring a lot of wood," she told Teq, "then you won't have to go back up into the forest again for the whole winter."

As soon as they had broken their fast they scattered about their tasks. Bess was curious about going over to the other side of the stream to the main part of the village. She half hoped that she might meet some of the women who came from the long house, so that she could ask them about their pregnancies, even though Ocham told her they always kept apart. She might find a way to sneak over there, and just talk to them. Meanwhile there was a lot to do. She barely noticed as Teq trudged up the side of the hill with the travois on his shoulder, on his way to fetch their wood.

There was about an hour of daylight left when they heard a thumping on the floor of the cabin.

"Royar must have all the animals in. We'd better help him settle them," Ocham explained. "There is a trap here in the floor. When the snow is really deep, we can get down to the animals from here, without going down the outside steps. It's quite useful."

"I'd like to see that, and meet these carries," Bess offered. "Have we finished here?"

"Yes," Doban said. "All the food is stowed away. If you're going to help Ocham and Royar," he smiled at Bess," I'll go and see if Teq can use some help getting back."

"Good idea," they agreed.

Doban was glad enough to get out of the house. It was true the skies were lowering over the hills, but he was still glad to breathe some fresh air, having been stuck what felt like half inside the mountain all day. He got to the forest, knowing where Teq would have started, and followed the signs of his activities. He must have worked hard. There wasn't a twig or branch left ungathered. He found the place where Teq had cut down a sapling or two, without attempting to cut them up; and almost immediately came upon the travois, fully loaded, with the load bound into place. He called Teq's name. There was no answer, but then sound was quickly swallowed in the forest. He turned to the four corners and called again. He heard nothing. Walking in a circle, six paces from the travois, he walked, calling all the time. Nothing.

It was getting very dark. There was no point in the pair of them being lost. He would have to come back with torches, and help. This was very odd, but he was not alarmed. Teq was experienced on the mountain, after all: just as experienced as Doban was himself. He pulled his knife and cut an arrow into a tree, showing the way he was going. For some time, the white of the new cut bark would be visible in the twilight. He decided to blaze a trail all the way home, which would be useful to Teq if he was disoriented, and equally useful when they came back with torches. He hitched the travois up on to his forehead, as he had seen Teq do, and started to drag it home. No point in losing all this wood, he grinned to himself, even if the collector of it had gone wandering off. Perhaps he had seen a gumbuck, and decided to bring it home for supper. He would be glad enough not to have to manage both buck and travois, Doban was certain.

But even as these thoughts cheered him, the first snow began to fall. Doban trudged home through an ever-increasing blindness of the stuff. Had it not been for his familiarity with the terrain, he might well have become lost as the last light was snatched from the sky by the weight of the clouds. He followed the stream, dragging his burden, and came at last to the barn, where a torch had been left burning for the benefit of the wayfarers. He pulled the travois inside, and dragged shut the doors of the barn. If Teq had not made it home before him, there was no chance of his doing so now. Doban climbed the ladder into the house to discover which.

Teq was not there. He had been lured from the laden travois, just as Doban had supposed, by the sight of a straggly looking gumbuck plunging through the forest. He assured himself that he could easily get it home with him, if he tied it on top of the piled wood, and the fresh meat would make a welcome addition to the winter larder. He chose to ignore the threatening snow clouds, and followed his quarry, all but silent on the forest floor. Whether or not it had preceded him down the same hazard, or had managed to skip aside, Teq did not see the loose edge of a chasm, until he had missed his footing, and lost his balance. He had never before ventured so far inside the forest and had not known the chasm existed. He was falling, and the grabs he made at trees in his path were to no avail. He was falling to his death. He ran the gamut of disgust at himself, terror, panic and resignation in less seconds than it takes to name them. He had time left only for regret, as he tumbled out of control to a depth still unseen in the failing light.

And his passage was halted. He had the sensation of being caught on wide wings. Of being laid gently on to a grassy ledge, while he gasped to gain his breath and his reason. Reason told him that he was dead, and that the sensations he was feeling were those of another life. There might have been a ledge in his path, but so gentle a landing was beyond all logic. Beyond all hope. As he lay on his back, face exposed to the air, the first snow flakes began to fall, nudging him into opening his eyes. The top of the cliff was beyond his eyesight, though whether from height or disappearing light was impossible to judge. But exposed he was, and that was snow falling. He sat up. No dizziness. He looked around him. The mouth of a cave loomed conveniently in the cliff. He wondered briefly what fierce denizen of the forest might have chosen it for a winter home, but decided that he must risk death by predator, if he was not to die from exposure. Gingerly he edged away from the brink and crawled within. It was dry, and empty and contained a ledge of rock which he could climb on to and nestle down, safe from the winds which would come through the entrance.

Teq lay still on the ledge, beginning to shiver from the shock of his fall. His life consisted of a series of escapes which involved difficult climbs and the use of caves, he reflected. The thought came unbidden. What strange spirit had attended his birth?

And a voice answered, "I did."

The voice was more in his head than a sound heard. Teq waited in case a sound which he might identify was repeated. Something which would sound like a repeat of those two words. Nothing came. There was just the deadening silence of the snowfall. Perhaps his first reaction was the proper one, and he was dead. If so the afterlife was a remarkably uncomfortable place, albeit providing shelter from a storm. Teq stood long enough to remove his cloak and wrap it more securely around himself, then he snuggled back down on to the ledge, trying to compose himself to wait out the snow. Until that was past there was no exploring his position for chance of escape. He had better sleep. Indeed he had exerted himself vigorously in the pursuit of a winter's supply of wood, not even stopping to eat. He had not actually thought to bring food with him, and thinking of it now made him realize just how hungry he was. No point in thinking about food. He burrowed down as best he could to keep out drafts, and in time slept indeed

The snow storm lasted two days. Teq slept and woke, chilled but not frozen. Always waking with the sensation that he had been warmed in some manner while he slept. Hunger was another matter. There was no chimeral sensation of food. There was no food at all. He did his best to turn his thoughts from it, sleeping as often as possible, but on the day he awoke to find the storm over, he was lightheaded with hunger. He crawled to the ledge, and looking over made his head swim. He reached out for a handful of snow to wet his mouth, and tried to ponder his plight. A shaft of thin sunlight penetrated to his cave and he looked up.

Before him was the image of a person, neither man nor woman. No, not a real person. It was much too large. It stretched from the depths below him to the heights above.

Staring, he asked the question without true thought: "Who are you?"

"I am he that saved you. I am the Mystery."

"Of the Mountains?"

"Who else?"

"Why? Why me?"

"I have chosen you to people my Mountains. For this I have saved you. Many times," the voice added. Not that it was exactly a voice. More something Teq seemed to be saying to himself, inside his mind. And yet the figure was before him.

Teq thought for a minute about what he was hearing, or thinking or whatever it was, and decided that he could not have saved himself. The Mystery must be real. It was an awe inspiring thought. He was afraid now. The Mystery was greater than he had ever considered. It had said it was there at his birth. How could that be? There was so much... so many times... He had been saved again and again against the odds. "Thank you," he said simply, "for saving me." He thought for a minute. "I had decided to live in the Mountains," he considered he had better say.

"No, I decided you would live in the Mountains. You and the others."

"Ocham and her family?"

"Those."

"But I cannot get up or down from this place. I will die if I don't eat."

"It is only because you have not eaten that you can hear me."

"What can I do to ask you to save me again? There is nobody else, and I do not think I can save myself from here."

"You cannot. But I have chosen you and I will save you."

"What must I do?"

"Now, nothing. But you must not waver from your purpose. If you waver there will be a price. The price to the Mystery is always high. Remember this. We shall not speak again."

"But how will I know what you want of me?"

"You have always done what I wanted of you. I have not interfered. In the future, others will speak with me. Your daughter will come. She will know me."

"I will do as you wish. As you command."

"Do you believe in me and in my brothers and sisters?"

"How could I not? Here I am," Teq answered, and this time, for some reason out loud. There was again the sensation of wings and of flying. He lay face down in a drift of snow. There was no sign of a chasm. At his side was the rigid body of the gumbuck.

"I heard a voice," said someone quite close by. It said, 'here I am'."

Another voice called, "Teq," and this time he recognized Doban.

"Over here," he called. "I'm here."

The muffled faces of Doban and Ocham appeared through the trees. "You are alive," said Ocham, and there was joy in her voice. "We thought you must be dead. Bess is mourning you. Crying her heart out, but I thought we must make some push to find you."

"I'm glad you did. I am so hungry I could eat this buck by myself. Are we far from the house?"

"No, just beyond where you left the travois," Doban answered. "See here are the marks where I blazed the trees to lead you home."

"Well, let's get back there." Teq rose to his feet rather unsteadily. His mind was working furiously. Already his experience was becoming unclear in his mind.

"But what happened to you?" Ocham asked. "Doban said he came to find you and called your name."

"I'm really not sure." And Teq wasn't. "I followed the buck, thinking it would be good to have fresh meat. I must have stunned it, or something, and fallen beside it. I may have tripped when I hit it. I woke beside it. It must have kept me warm under a blanket of snow. It's dead now, in any case, after saving my life. How long has it been?"

"Two days," Doban told him. "We really did not see how you could survive."

"I won't much longer, if I don't eat soon," Teq smiled feebly.

"Come on. Let's get you home. And that buck. It will still make us fresh meat," Ocham said. "Lean on us. You must be weak."

"Yes, you can explain it all to us once you've eaten." Doban hefted the buck. "Tell us the whole story then."

ˈ But I really don't think I can. I don't know what I know, Teq thought. Was that true what I just said? I remember wings, and a huge man, and a voice. I think. Or was I just delirious? Dreaming? I don't suppose I shall ever know.

But there he was wrong.

Chapter 42

The winter was well and truly upon them. And it was hard. The first time they experienced a gale from the Sea, Bessindel fell into hysterics which burst forth freshly with each terrifying gust of wind. Her nervousness conveyed itself to the animals below, who stamped about restlessly, snorting or bleating according to their nature and adding to the general sense of panic. Royar caught the fear from her too, although he had been through winter gales all his life. The little house could not contain the quota of terror it was being asked to bear. Teq tried to calm Bess, and so did Ocham, but her fear was real and deep, and the panic in her heart blinded her eyes and ears to all they could do. In the end, Teq remembered the willow bark brew in their kit and poured some of it into her resisting mouth. It settled her a little, so that she was able to climb into their bed with Teq's arms around her, burying her head under the blankets, to endure until the gale had blown itself out.

From that time on, whenever the signs of a new gale became apparent, as well as bringing in the hobbled goats, and closing both parts of the shutters, they dosed Bessindel and pushed her into bed. Royar was sternly chastised by his sister for giving way to fear, and he was able to revert to the more stoic endurance displayed by the others. In spite of the mud filling the chinks in the wall, the double shutters, and the banks of snow outside, too much wind whistled through the house during a gale to allow the little lamps they burned to stay alight. Their only entertainment was to sing songs or tell tales, or play on the instruments they had made.

For the rest, they exchanged knowledge as they had planned to do. The supplies were sparse, but then so was their exercise. It was the rare day which allowed them to venture outside. On such days as those, the high, pale sky crackled with ice, as did trees, river and everything in sight. A mere flicker of sunlight could set the whole valley sparkling and twinkling enough to rival the distant stars.

Teq learned the ways of the carries as well as he had known the goats. Bess determined to teach Doban and Royar how to read and write. They used charcoal from the hearth on pieces of flat stone they had taken from the beach for the purpose. It left Teq to instruct Ocham. He found her quick and eager to learn, without any of the joking and merriment which accompanied the others. Doban was devoted to Bess. Every whim or fancy had to be fulfilled at once. As she grew larger in her pregnancy, month by month, Teq found himself indulging her too, even though it left Ocham with an unfair load of the cooking and making. He could not persuade Bess to learn how to weave the spun wool on the double needles, which all the others handled so swiftly, but Teq learned, and thought it valuable. The resultant shirts were heavy and warm, and had a good feel to them. She did teach Doban the drum rhythms, though, because she did not need to hunch over for the task, so long as the sticks she used were long enough.

Apart from the weight she gained, Bess felt well in her pregnancy. The sickness had passed, and she felt energetic in her mind. She planned the house she wanted in the Mountains, far from the sounds of the Great Sea. She made Teq unroll the plans of the houses Vork had given him, and fell to comparing one with another. Ocham found this equally fascinating, and begged Teq to show them the maps of the Mountains through which they had passed also. He showed them, although he was not very proud of their rough inaccuracies. The maps of the Town baffled them. They could not conceive how so many people could be together in one place, and not fight.

They did not fight, that winter, though they came close to it time and again. There were days when Bess was certain Teq was in love with Ocham and did not care for her at all, fat as she was. There were days when he was equally exasperated with her 'pandering' to Doban's infatuation with her. Ocham grew irritated with her brothers because they were not running to do her bidding at the first call. Teq grew irritated with Royar's giggle, and his idea of setting traps for all of them, laughing wildly when they fell into them. The winter went on and on.

But spring did come. They woke one morning to hear the snow dripping from the eaves above them, and the odd splashing hiss in the fire. Out of doors was a mess of mushy melt, but there was a smell of sunlight in the air, and the wind no longer froze the breath in the body.

One day the river broke free of its icy guards, and from then on gushed louder and fuller, until it was flashing past them in a heedless frenzy to be at one with the Greatness of the Sea. And the day came when Teq and Ocham and Doban dared to venture out to seek fresh game. The trees of the forest were dancing in their new finery, moved by the spring breezes, wanting to be seen and peopled by the torrents of birds building nests for their future families. The three of them could not be anything but delirious in their happiness.

Royar turned the beasts out to forage, along with the wild of their kind. Bess was now too large for any of this, but she aired the house and shook the bedding and swept the dust of winter out into the winds.

The hunters came back with very little. Like the rest of the villagers whom they saw distantly about the same tasks, they did not wish to unpeople the forest by interrupting the cycles of birth and growth. But all the same, the meal they had that night felt like a feast. It was cold at night still, but the freshened house felt new, and the tunes they played seemed to be the result of months of practice, not just the same old stuff played over again. It was time to begin thinking about the future.

The problem was Bess. They could not move into the Mountains now, until the baby was born. There was no question of persuading her to get into the boat and travel on the Sea to the summer camp, where the People of the Sea would be going. It was necessary to decide what all of them would do.

Ocham volunteered to find out when the village was moving. "They usually go before all the babies are born in the long house, so they leave some of the elders to help with the birthings. I'm sure they would help Bessindel too."

Teq came right out and said what he was wondering. "What about you? What about the three of you? What are your plans?"

They looked at one another, as if they had already discussed this, then Ocham spoke again. "We would like to come into the Mountains with you, if you would allow it. We have only been waiting until Royar was strong enough, and I'm sure he could travel now. It seems to us that the Mystery sent you to us, so that we could travel together. Of course, you may not agree." The three looked anxious. It was not as if the winter spent in one another's company had been trouble free.

"Bess?" Teq asked.

"Why not? I will be less use as a hunter with a baby to care for. If Teq is pulling all our goods on the travois, it means he has to keep stopping to find food. I'd be glad of your help."

"And if it fits with your plans, then so would I," Teq agreed.

"You wouldn't have to pull the travois. The carries could do that," Royar said.

"You plan to bring animals?" Bess asked.

"We have three females. We own them," Ocham explained. If we were starting a new homeland, I could exchange the pregnant female for a male. Then we'd have the makings of a herd. They're very useful. And a few goats wouldn't come amiss, would they?"

"A flock would slow us," Teq considered, "although they'd be really useful when we settle somewhere. It took us more than two months to get here. Our plans, which we have not explained to you, call for us to make a home not too far from the Town. That means we have to go all the way back. With the animals, it could take more than three months, and then we have to build a place to winter, for us and the animals."

"I don't think it would take that long," Doban put in. "I know I haven't traveled over the terrain, but there will be more of us to handle everything. For instance, if two went ahead each day to hunt and prepare a camp site, the others could come along slowly with the animals. And it wouldn't hurt Bess and the baby. She could come as slowly as she needs to." He blushed a little as he always did when he used Bess' name.

"That's true," Teq agreed. "That makes it sound possible. When could we leave?"

"The baby isn't due for two months. Right at the beginning of summer," Bess said flatly.

"We could leave as soon as it's born, if Bess traveled on a travois. We can build another one, and make it comfortable," Ocham suggested. "Walking from here instead of the summer village, it is fairly slow getting into the high Mountains."

"That would get us settled before autumn. There should be time to build and to get together enough supplies to see us through the winter."

"At worst we could creep into the Town and get supplies there, I suppose," Bess said. "Galt would not refuse us. Nor would Zolg."

"These are people you know elsewhere?" Ocham asked.

"They helped us to escape from the Town. We want to be able to take in any other people who want to escape too, later on. They are my family," Teq explained. "They would help us, I'm sure, but I really don't want to have to ask. We ought to be able to do this alone. It's why I left."

"I thought you left to rescue me." Bessindel sounded petulant.

"That's why I left THEN," he grinned, and hugged her.

"Is it agreed then? Are we to travel together, as soon as the baby is born?" Ocham asked. "If so, I'd better start asking to make exchanges, and looking for elder help in the birthing."

"I hope you'd do that, anyway," Bess sighed.

"Well, of course. But we need to know the elders' plans."

"It's all settled for me, and I'm glad you'll be with us," Teq assured them.

"Then, let's get on with it," Doban said, smiling contentedly. "I'll go and find good saplings to make travois out of."

"And I'll go and get our pregnant carry, so that Ocham can show her to the village. It's a fair bargain: two for one," Royar affirmed.

Once the elder women who were to stay behind, agreed to help deliver Bessindel's baby, it was a great weight off Ocham's mind. She was sure that none of the others had thought of it, but not one of the five had ever delivered a baby child, though they'd all helped with the animals. She was very concerned about it, partly because Bess was so small and thin. She looked as if she would not deliver easily. As the days passed, Ocham took the advice of the elders and saw to it that Bess walked every day, but she was irritable, so they all stayed clear of her for fear of rousing her temper. It was better for her to be calm.

The time came for the main village to leave. They had sold the boat for journey food and extra bedding. There was no changing their minds now. They were committed to the Mountains. The women from the long house never came out on to the village side of their house, so they were invisible to Bess. The more she thought about them, the more curious she became. Why were these Women of the Sea not available to her to talk to? Why could they not gossip together about their pregnancies? It would be less than two months until the baby came, and she was getting anxious. She no longer felt as well as she had during the winter. She was heavy and awkward, and the baby kicked her so hard, it seemed as if she were trying to kick her way out through Bess' stomach. The others were sympathetic, but none of them could know what she was going through. She blamed Teq really. He should not have allowed her to become pregnant until they were settled. Even traveling on the travois, caring for a new baby on the journey would be hard. Perhaps they ought to stay right here for another winter.

They were all out now. All four had gone into the forest to gather wood and hunt. It was a glorious spring day. Somebody should have stayed with her. You never knew with babies. It might come early, and here she was, all alone. Bess decided to go and visit the long house. There were only a few elders left in the village. Who could stop her? The rivers were very full with most of the ice melted, but at the lowest point they could be crossed, she was sure.

Bess set out feeling as gleeful as if she were going on a new adventure. They'd be surprised when they came home and found her gone. She dressed in her warm coat, because all the frost was not yet out of the air. She carried her boots, certain she would have to wade across the river. But when she got there, it was much too wide to cross after all. She would cross higher up instead. It was maddening! She put on her boots and walked higher up the stream to where it was narrow, but running very fast. There. That place looked as if she could make it across. There were stones she could step on, placed close enough together to cross dry shod. Bess was not used to the way the spring melt changed the river. She came from an Honor where the difference between the seasons was very slight. It annoyed her that she could not depend on the familiar.

"You see," she muttered, "you Mountain Mystery. You can't even control the things on your own Mountain. You can't do anything right. You can't control me. I don't believe in you. I shall cross this river of yours anyway. Bah to you!"

She stepped on to the first stone, and it was easy enough. The next was farther, but not a problem. Only two more and she'd be across. The third proved her downfall. Literally. It rolled when she stood on it, and she was not sufficiently balanced in her bulbous shape to recover. She rolled with it. She fell, face down, in the river, which was so cold that it snatched the breath from her body, before she could shout for help. With a huge effort, she rolled on to her back, and scrabbled back to the first stone where she had stood safely. She dragged herself on to it, and managed to kneel. And it was when she waited there, kneeling, gasping, that the first contraction rippled through her body. It hurt. It was so unexpected and so overwhelming that she screamed. She was terrified. The baby was coming! It had to be. What was she to do? She could not stay there, kneeling on a rock in the middle of the river, having a baby. All alone, she got into a sitting position and then stepped into the river. It was deep and strong. She did not dare to let go of the rock she had left in order to get to the bank. She was in water up to her thighs, and the pull of the water was terrifying. She screamed again, grabbing at the rock with both hands.

Ocham and Royar arrived, running, in response to the first scream. They got there just as she sounded the second. They were appalled. But Ocham was not easily daunted. She dropped the bundle of wood she was carrying and tore free the binders that held it together.

"Run," she said to Royar. "Bring the others as fast as you can."

He didn't say a word, but was off with legs flashing, and eyes startled wide.

"Now," Ocham said to Bess, "everything is going to be just fine. I am going to step over to the rock and take your arms. We'll get back to the bank together. Just to be sure, we'll tie you to me. You'll be quite safe. You're all right now."

It was not quite that easy. Ocham got Bess tied to her wrist, but getting back to the bank meant Bess had to let go of the rock, and she was in too much of a panic to do that. Ocham had to pry her fingers loose one by one, and then pivot her around, so that that hand felt the ground of the bank, before she would loose the other. Pregnant, little as she was, Bess was no light weight. Ocham was strong, and she was desperate. Bess had already been in the freezing water far too long, although it was only minutes since Ocham and Royar had arrived. Inch by inch she managed to drag Bessindel out of the water. She pulled off her own clothes and Bessindel's, and had Bess wrapped in her coat and boots by the time the next pain hit. Bessindel screamed a third time. She grabbed hold of Ocham's hand as if she would climb along it.

Royar returned with Teq and Doban, running, panicked themselves by the third scream.

"Bess, my Bess what is it?" Teq begged.

"She's having the baby. She fell in the river," Ocham said, herself shivering by this time. "Get her to the house and the fire. Royar, run to the village. Beg the elder ladies to come and help."

Teq picked Bess up in his arms and cradled her close.

"Here," said Doban. "You need this." He offered Ocham his coat. She struggled into it as she ran along beside Teq, still tied to Bess at the wrist.

"A knife," she said to Doban. "Cut me free."

They got to the house just as Royar plunged back across the river, laying down branches so that the elders could cross the river at the shoreline. He was baffled as to why Bess had tried to cross anywhere else during the spring flood. Women were odd, he supposed, when they were having babies. Why had she tried to cross at all? He helped the elder women across. Three of them had come, carrying bundles. He explained as they crossed how Bess had thought the baby would not come for another month or two, and she had fallen in the river. The elders looked grave but said nothing.

At the house, Doban was building up the fire and setting water to heat, as Ocham directed him. Ocham was setting a bed up near it, with plenty of cloths nearby. Teq was stripping Ocham's coat off Bess, as she screamed again, and lay moaning, holding on to him in a death grip.

The elder women looked in, and one of them called, "Ocham."

Ocham looked up and came over to them. "Thank you for coming, Mothers," she bowed. "It is serious, I think."

"Get these men out of here, and then we will see how serious it is. We have brought everything that is needed, including a birthing stool. Now hurry along."

"You must go. All of you," Ocham told the men. "The elders will look after her now. There is nothing more for you to do." And seeing the bleak look on Teq's face. "Go and bring in the game you killed. We'll need food later. Help him," she said to her brothers, knowing they needed direction now. "I'll be here," she assured Teq. "I'll help her, but without these elders, we don't know how. They insist the men leave."

Teq nodded, kissed Bess, and dragged himself out of the room. He retained enough sense to thank the elder women, bowing to them as they came in to take over.

But the last sound he heard, as he headed away from the house, was Bess screaming his name.

Chapter 43

Teq stumbled away into the forest until he was out of sight and sound of the house where Bessindel was struggling. His mind was in a torment and he needed to be alone to sort out his thoughts. He could not lose the thought that Bess was irresponsible. She acted like a spoiled child, daring things which were foolhardy, and refusing to do things which were necessary. Life in an Honor did not normally create that kind of willful behavior. There were too many matrons who held authority over all the youngs to allow any one of them to get away with anything. Perhaps it had been different in the Honor where she grew up, but it seemed improbable. Even her enthusiasms: teaching Doban the drum rhythms, for example, were carried out with no thought for how they might impinge on others.

Above all, Teq hated himself for thinking these things. Especially now when she was in such need. He had watched the patience and humor with which Ocham dealt with her brothers, and he found himself dealing with Bessindel in the same way. He did not need a baby sister, to start life over again in the Mountains. He needed a wife. A partner. How had he taken a wife? Thoughtlessly. He was the one to blame. There was no reason why he could not as easily have rescued her without wiving her! He was the older. He should have recognized the temporary worship she accorded him. The same thing that Doban was feeling for Bessindel, he realized. She was a child in truth. And now, she was fighting this terrible fight to bring another child into the world. He groaned. He was to blame. He did not love her as Galt and Athirra loved one another. They depended on one another. They respected one another's concerns. Athirra gave considered opinions, allowed herself to be angry when it was called for, laughed with Galt, worried with Galt. They cared for one another. All Teq had wanted was to take care of Bessindel, he thought, after that first time in his bed. He had never considered how he liked her. He had not even known that he needed her to care for him too.

Well, too late to think about these things now! They would be together always, and he must hope that having a baby to look after would make Bess grow up. Had he? Had he really become a man? The way Ocham had become a woman to be respected and admired for herself? He found his mind dwelling longingly on Ocham's serene beauty, and he was ashamed. On the other hand, the fact that she was nursing Bessindel at this moment, made him feel secure. She was so dependable. And she was not fractious: in constant need of reassurance. Whatever needed to be done she would do. Win or lose, she could accept reality and deal with it. She did not rail at the Mystery of the Sea for not accepting her and her brothers. She planned how to live with that circumstance and survive. Not like Bess, who ranted at the Mystery of the Mountains, simply for being there. He sighed. Enough of this. He had better gather up the game which they had killed, if it had not already been stolen by other predators, and get back down to see what was happening.

Doban had stayed near the house in case he should be needed to run errands, but he sent Royar off to gather in their animals. Once the baby was born, they would be moving into the Mountains in very short time. The screams and cries coming from the house were terribly upsetting. No wonder Teq had been sent far away. Ocham must have known how bad it would be to listen to. Nobody considered his own feelings with regard to beautiful, tiny Bessindel. Quite right! It was better he should be there to serve.

Inside the house, Bess had been stripped and wrapped loosely in a cloth, tucked just under her armpits. The fire was hot, and the house close. The five women sweated in the loud misery of the room. Bess cried out yet again. Blood was pouring from her. Not just water. The elders muttered about a dry birth and looked grave. One burned herbs in the fire. The aroma was intended to soothe. Another chanted with a sotto voce monotony which irritated as much as it calmed. Ocham wiped the sweat from Bessindel's brow and smiled at her encouragingly. Bess was sobbing wildly.

"It is a first baby," Ocham murmured to her. "They say these always take longer to come."

"Press down now," said the third elder.

"I can't. I can't," Bessindel screamed. "Leave me alone."

The hours passed. Nothing changed. The spasms continued to rock Bess, but no baby appeared. Day became night. Ocham heard the boys moving around in the barn. She opened the trap door and handed down journey food to Doban.

"Nothing," she said, in answer to his unspoken question. "Nothing, yet."

Bessindel's screams became less strident. More weary. More groan than scream. Her tortured body gave more blood. The elders could do nothing to staunch it, through the passage where the baby must come. Finally, they heaved the limp girl up on to the birthing stool, hopeful that gravity would help her. They had to support her limp body, one on each side, rubbing her stomach as her back arched in spasm after spasm. The baby would not come.

Morning arrived. Ocham called to Doban to bring them fresh water. She hoped its bright chill might give them new strength. It did not. By this time, Bessindel was hardly conscious, even during the racking heaves her body was still making, trying to expel the child. And then there was a massive convulsion. They could no longer hold Bessindel upright. She collapsed forward, completely spent, as the little dead baby was thrust into the waiting hands of the elder. With the after-birth came blood. Gushing out in great gouts. Soaking the cloths they had made ready. They could not stem it.

Ocham covered Bess, and wiped her hair away from her face. She called to Teq.

"Come in now. There is no baby. Come and see if you can call Bessindel back. She used all her strength. Come in."

Teq approached her warily, feeling huge and clumsy in the fetid room. The smell of blood was everywhere. The tiny, red-stained bundle near the hearth must be his child. Bess did not look like Bess. She looked shrunken and old and dried up. He was shocked. Was this a normal thing at a birthing? Surely not. The women of the Honor never looked like this. They would come to the hall on the first day to show off their new baby. They looked plump, and smiling, doting on the infant. Even after birthing twins Athirra had not looked like this. Something was very wrong here.

"Bess," he whispered. "How is my Bess?"

Slowly she opened her eyes. Slowly she smiled at him.

"Teq," she said, her voice scarcely audible. "It's over, thank the Sky. But, I don't want to die."

"You will feel better, little Bess," he promised her fiercely. But his fierceness was wasted. She had died. Her life's blood had simply flowed out of her, and taken her spirit with it. It was over indeed.

Teq sat on, clasping the small hand of his little wife, not recognizing her death. It was Ocham who came and led him away, as the elders moved in to clean Bess up. Ocham took him outside, shaking her head at the inquiring looks of her brothers. She led him up the side of the stream and into the quiet of the forest. She sat him down, and took his head into her lap, and covered him over with his coat.

"There, now," she said. "There. She is at peace now. You must find your own peace now too. There. Rest now. Speak to the Mystery of the Mountain in your heart. You will find your direction there. Don't say a word."

He didn't. He cried. All the thoughts of yesterday came crowding back into his heart and he was ashamed. His Bess was no more. There was no baby. All for nothing. All they had done together was for nothing. He had led her to her death.

"No, you didn't," said the voice in his heart. "She did it all herself. She did not want Me. She did not want you either. She had better start again."

"What?" he asked.

"She will have another chance as another person, another time. It is My wish. You have to go into these Mountains now. Bring your new family. Find the place I have set aside for you. Remember this when you wake."

"What?" he said again, but this time he did not mean it. He understood. He slept, there with his head in Ocham's lap. And as he slept, she slept. Carrying all their pain had exhausted her. Her brothers found them there and shook them awake

"The elders say it is time to come," Doban told them quietly. "We had better do as they say."

Teq woke, completely unembarrassed to find himself within Ocham's arms. The dreariness of his loss pained his heart. He felt numb. He looked at Doban, and saw a reflection of his own misery in the boy's face. He went and put an arm around him. Together they all four walked together back to the house.

With the help of the elders, they buried Bessindel and the baby in a place between Sea and Mountain, where she belonged only to the land itself. The elders led them in chants to set her rest in quiet. They wept as they covered her body, hiding her from the sights she had hated.

"She will be happier to be hidden," Royar said unexpectedly, and they all agreed with him.

"Yes, she will."

"She will not be lonely," Doban said. "She has the baby."

"I will plant some flowers here today," Ocham offered. "They will hold the ground against any storm, and smell sweet for her."

"There is nothing I can do," Teq mourned.

"You can remember her. Tell tales of her, as long as you have a hearth," Ocham said.

Somehow that made him feel better. He was able to go to the elders and thank them for all they had done and all they had tried to do. Ocham gave them dried fish from their larder in payment. It had not occurred to Teq. But then they were gone, across the river again, Royar accompanying them as before. It was noon.

"We will eat, and then we must sleep, Ocham decided. "It will be better if we leave at once. Tomorrow."

"Yes. Why not?" Teq agreed, driven more by lethargy than resolution. "I do not think I can sleep in that house, though."

"No need. We will set ourselves up in the barn tonight, and be on our way as soon as we have packed up," Ocham resolved. "We must not stay here any longer. We must go now. At once."

They did as she bade them, almost as if it were the first night they were camping on the journey. They cooked the newly-killed game, and loaded the remainder for food on the route. After a night's troubled sleep, they were clumsy getting packed and loaded, but they managed to get themselves far enough to have no sound or smell of the Sea in their noses before they made the first night's stop. They were on their way.

The pattern of travel that they had discussed worked well for them. Each day they would start by discussing their route. Teq was counted the leader in that area, so he must consider the ground, and the likely pace of travel for the animals, and decide how far they could expect to go. Then two of the older travelers would set out to find food and a camp site for the rest of the party. Much to his disgust, Royar was always in charge of the little herd, while Doban shared the chores of hunting with Teq and Ocham. Teq resumed his pattern of measuring terrain and marking his maps when they stopped for the evening. Right from the beginning, they did not demand too much of themselves, but concentrated rather on learning the Mountains, and where the valleys led. It meant that they did not always travel directly east, as they had traveled directly west on the outward journey. In fact, Teq saw to it that they followed a different route wherever possible.

The Mountain passes directed their steps in many cases, although it was sometimes possible to consider a pass which was higher and easier, rather than always aiming for the lowest heights. Pulling the travois had constrained Teq on the previous journey. Using the carries slowed them, but made their lives more comfortable. It was also comfortable to have camp made early in the day. They hobbled, rather than tethered their flock, and generally made a great to do with drums and music around the camp fire to discourage wild predators from coming to check them and their animals out.

"You know," Teq told them one evening, "the People of the Desert rode on their beasts. They didn't only use them to carry their possessions."

"Were they the same animals? Were they carries?" Doban asked.

"No. Their faces were the same, more or less, but they were a different shape. They were taller with longer legs, but shorter necks. I wonder if these beasts could be trained to carry us."

"They might. I could try," Royar offered.

"It's probably better to wait until we settle somewhere," was Ocham's opinion. "We don't want to unsettle them on the journey."

"I'd guess they'd do better if we trained them when they were young," Doban suggested. "If we wait until they are comfortable, and breeding..."

"Where do they come from? I mean the wild ones," Teq asked.

"I don't know. I always assumed they were a gift from the Mystery of the Mountains," Ocham told them.

"Me too," Doban agreed, "though I don't know where I got the idea. I've never seen wild ones."

"Perhaps we will as we travel," Teq thought. "We should look for them. Why not have the hunters range a bit farther afield and explore? Would you mind if I was one of the hunters every day from now on? I would really like to make my maps a bit more complete. Not that we won't be able to explore once we've settled, but we may not have any reason to come this way again."

"I don't mind," Doban said. "What about you, Ocham?"

"No, I don't mind. I like having the maps. Once we settle down, it will be like reliving this journey to look back at them, and there is no particular hurry. We've only been traveling a little over a month, and it is still spring. We'll have plenty of time to do our building before winter."

So that's what they did. The long slow rise to the Mountains proper, from the settlement by the Sea inlet, had given both them and the animals time to adjust to their travel pattern. Before they came to the high Mountains, they abandoned the travois, and loaded all their essentials on the carries, the goats and themselves. Since there was plenty of forage, even on the heights, they had no trouble with the animals. If the footing on the rocky places was a little hard on the carries with their soft feet, the two who remained with them led them along the easiest route. The goats had no trouble anywhere. It was another month before they spotted a herd of wild carries, in a valley far to the north of their route. They were running away from one of the huge Mountain cats which had visited their camp on the outward journey. They were probably the same species which had caused all the havoc when Teq was fleeing the Town. It made them realize that the Mountains were not going to be totally benign, quite apart from the weather.

They never spoke of Bessindel. Ocham felt that she must be part of their lives and could not properly be ignored in this way, but that the time would come naturally, and did not need to be forced. At least not yet. It was sufficient that they were all dealing well together and going where they needed to go.

After they sighted the wild carries with their attendant predators, Teq directed them further towards the south and east. The year turned into summer and still they had not come to the edge of their Mountains. And then one day they found their place. Ocham was traveling ahead with Teq, while Doban and Royar followed with the flock.

Ocham saw it first, but said nothing until Teq came up with her. She just halted where she was, and waited for him. He had stopped to kill a male gumbuck. They were careful to kill no nursing mother at this season of the year.

"Oh," he said and stood still beside her, looking down. "You are quite right. This place is perfect. Of course it's the place where we must settle."

"I didn't say a thing," she protested, laughing.

"You didn't have to," he laughed back, putting an arm around her shoulders. "This has to be our place."

They were looking down a wooded slope to a great lake. Calm and silver. As they watched, a fish leapt up in its middle. Two rivers fed into it from the north and the east. Another led out from it, falling away southward, flowing down through a flower filled meadow. At the farther edge, the lip of the meadow rose, but the river cut out a path through it in a gentle waterfall. The opposite side of the lake's bowl was steeper, than the wooded slope to the north and west. It climbed to a rocky top on the eastern side, where a flock of birds was nesting noisily. That river tumbled cheerily down the rock face.

"That must be the outer edge of the Mountains," Teq told her. "I'm sure we have come far enough. If not, my maps are hopelessly wrong."

"Do you think we could go down there to camp tonight?" Ocham asked.

"Why not? I'm carrying our supper. Walking through the wood, we'll gather enough to make our fire. Where should we camp?" He wanted her to choose.

"Right over there. On that big, flat rock by the river, sticking out over the lake. Right where we should build our house," she answered, with no doubt at all in her mind. "It is the strongest place. And the safest. It would endure for ever."

Chapter 44

The days settled into a new routine. They had studied Vork's plans for houses and decided to make a sort of mixture of the stone house and one of his. Since it was so early in the year - barely summer - Teq felt they had plenty of time to build well, and make a little more space for themselves. He wanted two houses, connected by a walkway, all built over a huge stone barn. The houses themselves would be made of wood, with stone chimneys on their outer sides. It was quite clear to him that stone had made much better chimneys, without the constant fear of fire which had always worried his living spaces in the past. The huge barn would provide space for an ever-increasing herd (he hoped), as well as storage. The wild grasses of the meadow could be harvested for winter fodder, and a good many roots could be dug and dried. Ocham insisted on a smoke house, and she also wanted the boys to make a boat, so that they could fish on the lake.

It was too much for one summer, but if the barn was warmed, there would be no reason why they could not work on a boat during the winter. Having work to do would take some of the tedium out of the snow-bound days. They decided to concentrate on the houses and barn. Once again the animals were hobbled, so that they would not stray outside the meadow, but there was plenty of grass to keep them happy there.

The work was hard. Ocham left the hefting of the stones from the tumbled scree slope to Teq and Doban, who was growing bigger and stronger with every day. She mixed the mud to fill in the chinks. In the long evenings they would go into the woods to select and cut trees for building the cabins. These would be left for Royar to clean and shape. There was no time for conversation. By sunset, they were all too tired to do more than eat whatever stew Ocham had flung together, and tumble into bed.

When they estimated it was Summer Long Day, Ocham called a halt.

"We will have a feast, and celebrate," she announced. "We deserve it."

"Too much to do," Doban worried. "We can't stop now."

"Teq?" she asked.

"Either way," he said. "It doesn't matter to me."

"I want a rest," Royar announced. "This is all too much work."

Ocham laughed. "Quite right," she said. "Tomorrow, then. Who knows when Summer Long Day really is. It's probably past."

They washed their clothes as well as themselves, in the morning. All but Teq knew how to swim, so Doban volunteered to teach him, while Ocham set the baked meats going. The smoke house was not quite finished, but they had racks set up, and she decided to smoke some meats to see how well it worked. If they caught any fish, it would be just enough to cook and eat. Without a boat they would only be able to cast a net from the shore of the lake, and probably not get much. She called to Doban to try it. Since he and Teq were already wet, they launched it together, wading out before they flung it, and dragged it back to the land. There were not many fish indeed.

Nobody was watching Royar. He decided he wanted to contribute to the feast. At least that was his rationale for doing what he had been dying to do ever since they got there. He wanted to climb the cliff after birds' eggs.

It was an easy enough climb to start with. Only the birds that raised two families in a season would still have eggs, and Royar had noticed some callow birds which did that, fishing in the lake. Apparently they liked fresh water fish as well as Sea fish. They were fierce birds, and he knew he would only be able to snatch their eggs if both parents were away from the nest. He resolved virtuously not to take all the eggs from any one nest - all this as he was scaling the easy part of the cliff.

But it became more difficult the higher he got. He began to wish he had waited for Doban. They usually climbed together. Doban normally went first, with Royar roped behind him. Of course he was much too big now to need a rope, but a companion was a different thing. He had spied a ledge near the cliff top, when he was lower down, which seemed to be where a lot of birds roosted. He was sure he would be able to reach the callow birds from there. Always supposing he could get to the ledge! He was beginning to doubt it. A piece of shale crumbled under his hand. He kicked hard with his foot to get a better hold in a crack, and that gave way too. In spite of himself he let out a yell of fear.

Doban heard him. He and Teq had just come ashore with their net wriggling with a few fish. He looked up and saw Royar hanging by one hand.

"By the Sky," he muttered. Then called, "Royar. Hold on. I'm coming." And ran.

Teq looked and saw Royar too, and sped along behind Doban. Ocham looked up and saw. She dropped what was in her hand and ran for the meadow. It was in her mind that she could scramble up the scree slope in half the time it would take the others to climb up to him. Up there, their own hold would be too precarious to be able to render him much help.

Teq noticed where she was going. She was always the one who was able to think clearly, in a crisis. She never panicked, he thought. She always did the most useful thing without wasting a second over it. He could see that climbing up behind Doban would be no use at all. Doban's presence would reassure Royar, but he wouldn't be able to get him down from there. He stared up. Royar had found another hand hold, but he was frozen, paralyzed against the face of the cliff. Teq ran to the place where they had dragged in yesterday's wood and undid the extra long binders they had made for the purpose. If he climbed up after Ocham, perhaps these could be used to haul Royar up, or let him down to a safer part of the cliff. He ran, long-legged and strong, climbing fast behind Ocham. At the top he was not far behind her.

There was another cry. He had not realized until now how silent they had all been since Royar's first shout. This cry had come from Doban who was climbing too fast, and had himself slipped a little.

"Think, Doban," Ocham called to him. "You are a good climber when you think. Royar needs you. Be careful."

She was leaning over the cliff edge just above them. Teq got there and looked over.

"I can't get down," she said.

"I can. I'm taller," he told her. "See that ledge. I'll bet that's what he was heading for. A bit farther along here, I can see a way to reach it. From there, I can reach him, I think. Take these binders and throw them down to me when I ask."

"Good," she said.

Royar began to slip. He gave a wailing cry, punctuated by the cries of the wheeling callows, by this time back from the lake and trying to drive these intruders away from their nests. One of them swooped down at Teq, where he clung to the face of the cliff above the ledge, screaming its anger.

Doban found a spot where he could wedge himself in tight, reached up, and got his hands on Royar. At full stretch, Doban could place a hand on Royar's buttocks, and press him back in to the wall. If they were ever to leave that spot again, Teq would have to get them. Royar was too precariously perched to find a way to start down. Doban would not be able to sustain that position for long. Teq roared at the swooping callows, and eased his toes on to the ledge.

He was at the narrowest point. Flattening himself against the cliff, he eased sideways, shuffle by shuffle, until there was a place wide enough for him to turn around.

There. To his right the ledge widened even further. There was a spot where he could sit down, and brace his back against the cliff. He peered over the edge. Royar was below and a little to the left. Not too bad.

"Ocham," he called.

"Here," she said immediately. "Right above you. Can you catch the binders if I throw them?"

"We can but try."

"I have a better idea. I can lower them to you. Wait," she said. "Now."

The binders came floating into view, just within his reach. He dared a small jump and caught them in his outstretched hand. "Got them," he called.

There was no place on that windswept ledge to anchor the binders. They would be long enough to reach Royar, but it would mean he would be hanging, a dead weight at their end. Nothing for it but to find a way to brace himself. There was a lip of well anchored rock a the edge. That would have to do. He lay on his stomach and looked over.

"Royar." He spoke quietly, calmly. The boy was alarmed enough. "I'm just above you on the ledge. Do you know where?"

"Yes," the boy hissed between tensed teeth.

"Good. I'm going to dangle a binder rope. Take your time, but see if you can grab on to it."

"All right. What then?"

"Then twist it around, both wrists if you can, and hang on to it. I'll haul you up."

"I can't."

"Of course you can. Look how far you got on your own. Doban is holding you. You're quite safe." Teq wished he could feel as secure as he sounded. "Here it comes. Got it?"

"Yes." Royar sounded astonished. "I've got it."

"Now wind it tightly round both wrists, and hang on to it. Let me know when you've done that."

"Thank the Sky and the Mountain it's long enough," Teq thought.

"Ready," Royar called.

Teq sat back against the cliff and braced his feet against the rock he had noted. "Let go with your feet, now," he shouted, and felt the weight of the trusting boy, pulling his arms out of their sockets. "I can't do this," he thought.

"Oh, Teq. Thank you. Neither of us could have held him," he heard Ocham say from above him, and he got another burst of strength he had no idea was there.

"Haul away," he shouted, and began to pull steadily, hand over hand. He could feel it when Royar began to have enough confidence to help with his feet. Before he lost the use of his arms completely, a small, scared face appeared over the edge, hands turning blue from the tightness of the binders, preceding him. One last heave and Royar was on to the ledge. They fell against each other, panting.

Teq drew in a great breath and called up to Ocham. "He's fine. How's Doban doing."

"He's climbing down. He seems all right."

"It was all right up to where Doban came," Royar said in a small voice.

"After birds' eggs were you?" Teq grinned at him. "For the feast? We'd better get some before we go down, then. What do you say?"

The pair of them were rubbing away at their wrists to restore their circulation. Teq had suggested the eggs because he wanted Royar to feel strong again. He was not all that sure himself how they would get to the top of the cliff, let alone rob nests.

"Wait there," he heard Ocham call. "I'm going for the ladder. Doban and I can bring it up and get you off that ledge." It was the very last thing they had made the day before.

Great idea," Teq called back. "You are the best of ladies." He heard her giggle. "Now. Let's see what we can do about those eggs before they get back," he said to Royar. "You did bring a bag to carry them?"

"Of course I did," Royar answered with scorn, his confidence fully restored with the challenge. "The nests are over there, at the fat end of the ledge."

"You grab and I'll hold you," Teq told him. "No more than four, though. One each. Those parent birds will be furious, so we have to be quick to hide them."

"I know that." Royar was watching the parent birds swooping over the lake. They had apparently decided the intruders were not a threat after all. "Come on. We'd better do it."

There was no point in chiding Royar. The lesson of the cliff was potent enough. He was rather ashamed at having to be hauled to safety from his adventure.

"Those cliffs are harder to climb than I would have guessed," was all Teq said.

"Mm," Ocham agreed. "We'd probably better decide not to go climbing alone in future. Do you think?"

"Seems right to me," agreed Teq. "Doban? Royar?"

They nodded, Doban grinning a little as he recognized that his brother was being handled.

"Good, then," said Ocham. "Let's get on with the feast. Oh, good. Eggs."

So there was fish and there were the eggs, and plenty of food to feast on. A day off was valuable, and gave them time to appraise all they had accomplished so far. They ate, they laughed, they praised themselves, and then came time for the music.

"I can't play the pipes and the drums," Doban said. "Bessindel..."

"Yes, Bessindel," Ocham said. "She taught us a lot. Perhaps, Royar remembers the drum rhythms." She looked over at Teq. "Or would you like to play them?"

"I'll do it," Teq answered, "Royar can too, if he'd like to. I want to play for Bess. She ought to be here with us."

"Let's begin then." Ocham nodded to Doban and pulled forward the drum. Royar took up his hollow tube.

They began to play. Doban started with a solemn melody that Teq had not heard before. Ocham sang along with it. It was a gentle, melancholy air, the music full of tears. Teq hardly beat the drum at all, just an occasional punctuation. The tune changed. Gradually, with great skill, Doban raised their mood. There were tears in their eyes, as if they could allow them now. As if the time of mourning for Bessindel was properly here at last.

The music stopped. "I loved her. I miss her. I wish she were with us now." Doban spoke with his head lowered, his voice choking, unable to bring music from his pipes.

"I thought she was fun," Royar agreed, "but she would do just the opposite of what people told her to. I'm sorry she died, though."

Teq smiled a little at Royar. "I think I hardly knew her," he said, "though I had known her the longest. I think I saw a person who was not there. Not the real Bess. I loved the person I saw. I hope I loved the person she was." He stopped because he was crying. "She cried a lot," he added. "I hope our tears for her can reach her wherever she is."

"She is here, the Mystery would see to it that she knew we were well and thinking of her. I'm certain of that," Ocham said. "I wish we could have saved her from that fall, that's all," she sighed.

"The Mystery spoke to me, I think," Teq told them. "He told me she caused her own death. None of us did. And that she would have another chance. At another time. Does that make any sense? Perhaps I just made the whole thing up. It was just as soon as she died. I'm not sure I was in my right mind then."

"But the Mystery was," Ocham assured him. "There have been times when I thought He/She spoke to me too. In my mind. Not in words. I'm never sure whether or not its real either. But I think so."

"I've not heard anything at all," Doban said. "But sometimes I feel comforted or warned or something, and I wonder how I could have known whatever... Do you know what I'm talking about?"

"I do," Royar nodded vehemently. "I know. Of course it's the Mystery. Who else could it be? Is there anyone else around? Huh?"

Ocham grinned. "You're right. We must say our thanks for the comforts and the warnings. The Men of the Sea have a Priest who speaks to the Mystery. It would be nice if we did."

"If it's all true, then maybe something else is too." Teq said. "When I was with the People of the Desert, their Priestess told me she was going to have my daughter. I was there less than a week, and I didn't really believe her. Or perhaps I did. I don't know. She told me I would live in the Mountains, and she would send me my daughter to be our Priestess, when she's old enough. She would be about a year old now."

There was a stunned silence in response to this. Nobody knew quite what to say. And then Doban took up his pipes again, and began to play a more cheerful tune. Teq beat a rhythmic tempo on the drums, and at last, Ocham rose to her feet and danced. They increased the pace, until Teq was leaping about in between playing. Finally Royar grabbed the sticks from his hands, and Teq leaped up to dance alongside Ocham. The feast was a celebration. They had come far and achieved much. Royar was saved and they had at last talked Bess into the open. They could allow joy into their lives.

They danced in the moonlight, whirling and tossing, apart and together, until they were too much together, and they fell nervously apart.

Chapter 45

The first chilly autumn rain drove them inside to sleep in the completed houses. Everything was stowed into the barn, and even the animals came inside willingly. They knew better than the humans that the wind would blow nastily, and the rain seep slyly into sleep. But the wind found every chink in the wood. It sought them out wherever they tried to sleep. They were miserable.

"This won't be any good when it gets really cold," Doban said to Teq the next morning, as they sat outside to get warm in the thin sunlight.

"No, it won't, and yet we followed the plans exactly," Teq answered.

"Didn't you say the Town was full of people?" Teq nodded. "Then they must keep each other warm."

"That's true," Teq grinned. "Not only the number of people, but the number of houses. Still, that doesn't solve our problem."

"I think I know what to do," Doban said. "We'll need more trees cut. We built the houses with the wood going sideways. If we put another layer inside going up and down, that should take care of it."

"Sounds right. Lets' do that," Teq agreed.

"Do what?" Ocham asked, joining them with a jug of beanbrew to refill their mugs as well as her own. Doban explained the plan to her.

"We'll have to get on with it," Teq said. "I was planning to leave about now. I must get to the Town and let them know that we're here. We need to work out a way to let us know if they need us, too."

"I didn't know you were planning to do that," Ocham said quietly.

"I always have had that in mind," he answered her. "We aren't too far away from my cave - the way in. Probably about two days. I'll be back again in six or seven days at the most, but the project can't wait that long."

"We only need to do the sleeping house before winter. The other one can wait," Ocham suggested.

"Oh, but they're both sleeping houses, aren't they?" Teq looked at her in astonishment.

"Are they?" she asked shyly. "Which is which?"

"It doesn't matter. Either one for men or women."

"Is that what you meant? Men in one and women in the other?" Ocham was furious. She snatched up the jug and went back to the barn.

"Whatever did I say?" Teq called after her.

"Take no notice," Doban said. "I've noticed the women get touchy sometimes."

"But it must be something. Perhaps I should go after her."

"No. Listen. You help us cut down the trees, and Royar and I can do the rest." Doban was confident. "We are better woodworkers than you are anyway. Bring us back some of that woven cloth like you have. That will cheer us all up, eh?"

But Ocham was furious. She was mainly furious with herself, because she had really believed that Teq meant one house would be for her brothers and the other for them. It was a dream which had been growing in her. She wasn't sure when it began, although when her mind drifted, she always pictured them dancing together. Even the dancing on Winter Long Night haunted her, even though Bessindel had been there, and Teq was already mated with her. But by Summer Long Day, Bess was no longer there, and she had been sure that Teq looked at her in a special way. The very thought made her breathless. And there were all the things they had done together; all the things they talked about; all the plans...

He had mislead her. How could she have guessed that he would be so unkind? And now, he was leaving to go to this Town, where he would obviously find another mate. He had no thought of her at all. How could she have betrayed herself just now? She had tried so hard not to let him know how she thought of him. She tried to treat him like one of her brothers, but it was impossible. In every decision, every crisis, she turned to him first. Had she dreamed that he always seemed to turn to her too? He was so kind. So funny. So eager. So strong. And good to look at! Just what she would have dreamed of in a mate. Well, so would any other woman. No doubt whoever he brought from the Town would feel the same. At least there would be time for her to fit in. All winter. He expected Ocham to live with her in one house, while he spent the winter with her brothers in the other. Well, she would have something to say about that. An unmated woman could live with her brothers if she pleased. Let him move in with his new woman right away, for all she cared.

The atmosphere got no better during the next few days. Teq tried to suggest a feast or a celebration for having managed so well, but Ocham would have none of it. There was no time for frivolities, she said. Certainly they were busy, felling the extra trees. Royar was enthusiastic about helping Doban on his own. He knew he could do it. Ocham was left to settle their possessions, get bracken together for their beds, and gather reeds to sift over the floors. They had already used the reeds from the lake as roofing material, and that, at least, was working very well. The long binders tied them down, and not a drop of water got through.

On the day when Teq set out, Ocham did not even appear to wish him well on his journey. He took one of the carries to heft his bundles: not so much on the trip out as on the trip back. The other female carry was already pregnant, and so were some of the goats. Their village was already increasing. Doban and Royar walked with him through the woods, heading north, and Ocham sat by the hearth and wept. When the boys returned they would never see her tears, but she knew it was the end of the peaceful times together, and she mourned their loss more than she had mourned losing her home by the Sea.

Teq knew roughly where he was, if his maps were accurate at all. He had to go north, bearing a little east with the lie of the range of mountains. The home place was fairly high up, but the eastern edges loomed higher. At some point he would have to climb. The second day it rained. The trees, which had been a riot of autumn color only the day before, now seeped greyness at him, and matched his mood. He dreaded going back into the confines of the Town, after the freedom of the Mountains. Of course, it was more comfortable: none of the houses leaked, and on days like today there was no need to go hunting in order to eat. All the same, he could never go back. He was looking forward to seeing the people, though. He wanted to see Galt, in particular, but he also missed Ibaren and Athirra, and even Zolg, who had become a good friend. But then he also missed Doban and Royar and Ocham already. He felt as if he would never be as comfortable with anyone else, as he was with them. Perhaps it was because they saw him as a man, where even Galt would always see him, partly, as the boy he had been.

There. Didn't that look familiar? It was not yet evening, but seeing through the rain was difficult. He had been sure he could not miss his cave, but now he was not so certain. He climbed a little higher, dragging the reluctant carry. It was a year since they left. Only a year! Could things have changed so much? Grown so much smaller?

Yes, they could. It was his cave. He tethered the carry and crawled in. Suddenly he was back more than a year, digging at the earth. Excited by the idea of it. Excited that it was a gateway to the world beyond. And now he knew where it led. Now he lived in the world beyond! He crept to the entrance, peering through the curtain of the falls. He heard the marching steps of the Watch clearly enough, but the tumbling waters seemed to obscure all other sounds. He decided to wait until dark before he appeared. It was possible that the houses behind Zolg's had been repaired and someone else was living there by now. Better not to risk being seen.

As night closed the Town into its quiet, he slipped out from behind the curtain of water, and stood in the shadows looking down. It occurred to him to wonder how he was going to get into Zolg's house without being recognized. He had spent so much time with Zolg during that last year, that the apprentices would know him at once. His apparent death by the predators would be known. His return would cause a sensation.

He walked down to the lower pool from where he could see better. It was drizzling still and visibility was poor. Gradually he could make out a number of people coming and going at Zolg's door, presumably coming for treatment at the end of the work day. But he did see another thing. Zolg had had a stairway built alongside his house and the one behind, stopping at a landing where there was a

door into the other house as well as one into his living quarters. Teq waited for
no more. He ran down to the stairs and climbed swiftly to the living level. He had
knocked on the door and heard someone moving to open it, before it dawned on
him that this would most likely be one of the apprentices. He just had time to
clutch the sides of his hood, and hold them together with a hand across his
mouth, when the door opened. In the sudden burst of light he saw - Ibaren!

"What are you doing here?" he gasped, astounded.

"And who are you to ask?" she answered coldly, peering into the darkness.

He stepped forward, pushing her before him into the light. "Ibaren," he said,
hugging her. "Don't you know me?"

"Teq! By the Sky, it's really you. You've come home. Oh, my boy, you don't
know how much we miss you. How we talk about you. Are you home to stay?"

"No. No, of course not. How could you ask? I've been 'dead' a year. I could
hardly come back to life now. And I wouldn't want to. I've done what I intended, and it's wonderful."

"Wonderful, is it? I can't say I don't envy you. I'd as soon be living in some
'out there' myself. Oh, but you don't know, do you?" she asked. "I live here now.
I came to look after Taza. There were enough people to run Galt's house, and
none here. Then, anyway. But what am I doing? Come into the warm. Get out of
those wet clothes. Let me look at you. Supper's almost ready. Would you like
some?"

"That I would, and yes, and yes. Does that answer all the questions?" Teq
laughed at her. He followed her into the living room where a fire blazed, and a
bubbling pot smelled tantalizing.

"How's Bessindel? You didn't leave her out in the cold, did you?" Ibaren took
his coat and hung it by the fire, where it steamed gently.

"She's dead, Ibaren. She died in the spring. She fell just before she should
have had a baby, and we lost them both."

Ibaren stared at him, shocked into silence. "Oh, Teq. Oh, you poor boy. You've
been alone all this time. Why ever didn't you come back to us. If you knew how
we miss you..." she said again.

"No. Well, no, I haven't been alone. We had met some people, by the Great
Sea. One family - a sister and two younger brothers - wanted to live in the
Mountains too. They were coming with us. When Bess died, we buried her there,
and came on without her. Just the four of us. We've built a place to live, only
about two days from here. I left them there and came to see you all. That's about
it."

"Are they good people? Do you like them? Are they strange and unfamiliar to
you?" she asked.

"They are wonderful people. Much better than me. And how can you ask if
they are strange, when we all came strange to such a strange place as the Town?"
He grinned at her.

"Oh, Teq," she hugged him close. "Isn't it just like you to count them better
than you, when nobody could be. Nobody at all."

"The same goes for you," he told her, smiling down at the familiarity of her warm face and gray hair. "I've missed you more than anyone, except Galt. How are things here with Zolg?"

"They have been good. The baby is perfect. Such a dear one, she is. But Zolg is going to marry again. He has found a woman, very gentle and sweet, he tells me. She has just told him she is pregnant, so he can buy her from the House where he has visited her. She is so shy, and the House so poor, he believes the child to be his. Few other men go there, he says. I am happy for him, but they won't need me. This place is very small. I think I had better go back to Galt's where they don't need me either."

"I need you," Teq blurted out. "Come back with me. Ocham would definitely be glad of another woman around."

"Ocham is the sister? Are you sure she would?"

"There is so much to do. If you could just cook, it would spare hours of work for other things."

"I'll think about it," she promised. "But you. How long can you stay? We must get word to Galt and Athirra. You could not leave without seeing them."

"Of course not. I need some supplies too. Mainly clothes. And I want to set up a plan with Zolg and Athirra to signal us if you need us."

"Two or three days, at least then. I'm going to make you up a bed. You can use mine, and I'll go in with Taza. I usually sleep there, anyway. You sit here and get warm." She bustled away.

She was back before any time had passed at all, Teq thought, and then realized he had fallen asleep by the fire.

"I'm going to take supper down to the apprentices," Ibaren told him. "Zolg will come up then and we can all eat. No don't move. I can manage."

In a few minutes Zolg's halting step could be heard on the stair. "Ibaren tells me I have a visitor," he called as he approached, "but did not tell me who. Teq! Teq! We had almost given you up for lost. It has been so long. It must be a year since that night. All Galt could tell us was that you did get away. I know Bessindel got away from here. And then nothing. But here you are. Wait. I have some wine. There could be no better time to open it. And then you must tell us everything. Or have you already told Ibaren everything? There is so much to tell."

"Ibaren said you will take another wife."

"Yes. The day after tomorrow. It is arranged. Oh, Teq. You don't mind? It is not that I have forgotten Belleth."

"How would I dare to mind? Your life goes on. There is Taza to raise, and now another one, I hear. And Zolg, Bessindel is dead. One day I will mate again myself, I am sure." As he said it, a vision of Ocham sprang into his mind, so vividly that he gasped aloud. "Ocham," he said, wonderingly.

"What?" Zolg called from where he was hunting for the wine.

"Nothing," Teq answered, absolutely stunned by the thought of her. He knew now and completely that life in the Mountains meant life with Ocham. For a very long time it had meant nothing else. Nothing less. The boys too, of course. But

Ocham. Ocham with him. Ocham to talk everything over with. Ocham to laugh with. Ocham to plan with. Ocham to love. Why had he not seen it before?

Ibaren returned. "I told those young scamps to fetch Galt and Athirra here as soon as they have eaten," she said. "It seemed to me that Teq might as well tell his story once, when we're all together. Meanwhile, we can eat."

"Is Taza asleep?" Zolg asked. "I would like Teq to see her."

"She's asleep, but he'll be here a day or two. Time for everything."

But now, Teq could hardly contain his eagerness to leave. He wanted to see Ocham again, more than he wanted to eat, or to rest or anything at all. It was when he was in bed, after all the excitement of that long evening, that he remembered how cold she had been to him before he left, and he was afraid she would not have him. Then what would he do?

Chapter 46

Athirra arrived alone. They had finished eating, and while Zolg cleared up down-stairs, Ibaren checked on Taza and tidied up. Teq seized the opportunity to slip back up through the cave to settle his carry. He found she had discovered the cave, and by folding her legs neatly under her, could shelter in comparative com-fort. Teq removed her tether and hobbled her legs, to allow her freedom of move-ment when she needed to eat or drink. He covered her with a blanket, and toted down to Zolg's house, such things as he had brought along.

Athirra came in just after he returned. "What urgent business brings me to you at this hour, Zolg?" she asked as he helped her up the stairs. "Oh, Teq. Oh, my. Oh, what a wonderful surprise! We had really feared you lost. We should have known better. What a miserable chance that Galt was called out tonight, just before we got Ibaren's message. I left word for him to join me here. Let me give you a hug."

She was pregnant again. Not so huge as the way he remembered her from before the twins, but round and matronly. She looked settled and contented. Being the wife of a Chief was a long way from the servie of the Matted Vine. Once Ibaren had everyone settled again, Athirra explained that Captain Jebend had sent for Galt to go to the house of the Smiths. They were normally very quiet people. The metalworkers preferred to keep themselves apart, more easily to guard their secrets. Athirra didn't even know how many people lived in the house.

"We are impatient to hear Teq's story, but thought it had better wait until we are all here." Ibaren told Athirra. "We've been trying to catch him up on all the news of the Town over the past year."

"Really, it's not much," Athirra agreed. "The twins are healthy and getting to be a handful, and as you see will have a brother or sister before the year is out. I do so like this idea of families knowing one another, and being together. You already know Zolg's news, and that Ibaren deserted us for him." She grinned fondly at Ibaren.

"I'm thinking of deserting Zolg for Teq. This house will need no more than one housekeeper, once Zolg is married to Tilla. Teq will tell us more soon, but he says he could use the help of an elder."

"Teq, you thief. How could we bear to lose Ibaren?" Athirra cried.

"How could Ibaren bear to continue in the Town when the wide spaces beckon?" he grinned back. "I am sure our need is greater than Zolg's."

"I expect it is," Zolg agreed, "but that doesn't mean I want to see her go. And forgive me for asking, but how am I to explain her departure?"

"I'm an old woman. Say I caught some disease and died of it," Ibaren suggested. "Cover me with red spots for a day, when I go shopping. I'll come back and succumb. How about that?"

"It's actually a very good idea," Athirra agreed.

"Perfect," Teq nodded.

"What about my reputation?" Zolg protested.

"Even the best of healers cannot heal everything, surely?" Teq said.

"Well, no," Zolg agreed. "Not everything, of course. And there are diseases with red spots."

"I know that!" Ibaren said. "That's why I suggested it."

There was a mighty crash of the door down below. "Stay where you are," came Galt's voice. "Zolg, are you up there?"

There were heavy footsteps on the stairs, and the door was flung open before Zolg could reach it. Jebend stood there, holding it open while Galt came past him into the room carrying a young girl.

"Where do you want her, Zolg?" Galt asked, looking up for the first time. "By the Sky, Teq!" he cried, nearly dropping the girl.

"Teq?" Jebend said, bewildered. "How could that be?"

"Ah," said Galt. "Ah. There is much to talk about here, but first things first. This is Jussy, the daughter of the Metalsmith. She has been badly beaten. She was knocked unconscious just as I arrived at Jebend's summons. I brought her to you. Now, Zolg. Where?"

"Put her down on the table, and let me look at her," Zolg limped over there, concern wrinkling his brow.

"Good," Galt agreed, doing so. "Now, Jebend. Go down and send the Watch about their business, then come back up here. Not a word about Teq, mind. And make sure those apprentices aren't eavesdropping."

"Yes, Chief," the startled Jebend agreed, bowing and leaving them.

"She is coming round," Ibaren announced. "How bad is she, Zolg?"

"There is not much beyond bruising, I think, although her ribs may be broken. Let me bind them before she wakes fully, then she needs to sleep."

"Put her in Ibaren's bed," Teq suggested. "She had already made it up fresh for me. I can just as easily sleep in here."

Ibaren slipped out and returned with bandages and a drink which she mixed with warm water from the fire. "I've learned a lot from Zolg," she said.

"As soon as I train one of you women you go and leave me," Zolg smiled as he worked.

"Yes, I see you haven't brought Bessindel with you," Athirra said.

"That's part of the tale I will tell you, now that we are all gathered."

"As soon as this poor child is settled, I'll mull some wine," Ibaren promised, "then we can talk in comfort."

"What will you do about Jebend?" Athirra asked Galt.

"Tell him the truth, what else?" he answered her. "I think Jebend will be sure to understand. His experience in the Desert effected him profoundly. And Teq was with him there."

"We became good friends," Teq put in. "I shall be glad to deceive him no longer. Here he is now."

When Zolg finished with his binding, and Ibaren had made Jussy drink her potion, Galt carried her into Ibaren's room, where the child settled in to sleep.

Ibaren and Zolg bustled about settling everyone down with their wine. "Now," said Galt, "to the telling of tales. Let me begin by explaining to Jebend the events of last year. It is possible he may not forgive me, because I deceived him and sent him on a wild goose chase all over the Town looking for Bessindel. He needs to know the why of it all as much as the what."

Where Galt left off, Teq took up the tale. The only time they interrupted him was when Athirra and Galt learned of Bessindel's death.

"She was such a silly girl. So young. I always feared she would never grow up," Athirra sighed, "but not in this way. It is so sad."

"She was silly and impulsive and very selfish, but she did enjoy the idea of adventuring, even if she would never understand the hardship it must involve," Ibaren agreed. "She was never good enough for Teq."

"No, indeed," Athirra said. "Not at all. I was afraid he would find out how shallow she was and tire of her, when there was nobody else to turn to."

"It sounds to me as if she kept up very well," Galt said. "It must have been hard for you to lose her, Teq."

"Very hard, at the time. But there was much to do, and the Mystery helped."

"You met the Mystery?" Jebend interrupted in spite of his feeling of being the outsider in this family group.

"Not the same one we heard about in the Desert. This was the Mystery of the Mountains, and I am not sure if I would call it a meeting. Not even an encounter. Just a voice in my head. Ocham knows what I mean, and even Doban and Royar a little."

"So you believe there is such a thing?" Jebend pressed.

"How could I not? It claims to have led me to the Mountains. And there I am."

"You understand this, Jebend?" Galt asked.

"It was something we never discussed after the Desert. People in the Town would have called me, at least, insane."

"You shall tell me about it later," Galt assured him. "I need to understand. But go on, Teq. What did you do after you left poor little Bess?"

They were astounded by the news of the carries. They were delighted with the description of the lake and the houses that they had built there.

"You have done well, Teq. I am extremely proud of you," Galt told him. "I even envy you a little, though the Town is where I belong, now."

"And I," Athirra held out a hand to him.

There was a sudden, loud moan from the room where Jussy was sleeping. Zolg hurried in to her. He came back, saying that she was crying out in her sleep. "What is her story?" he asked.

Jebend answered. "The Smiths, the Master Metalworker and his family all live together. He had the knowledge of metalworking from his father. It is a secret they guard with great jealousy. It is known only to the Master and his sons. He has four sons, all grown men, and one daughter, Jussy. She is the youngest. Apparently it is the custom for the youngest child to work the bellows, to make their fire, where they work, very hot. Today, it seems, she revealed that she had learned the secrets - simply let drop some remark. As a girl she was supposed to be too stupid to understand. It is a secret only for men, of course. The Master was overwhelmingly enraged. He beat her. Because of her screams, neighbors alerted the Watch. The Master would not allow me in, so I sent for the Chief. Him, he could not deny. While we waited, they beat her again. Her cries were terrible. The Chief came quickly, and burst in on them, with us behind, just as we saw one of the sons kick her in the side. The Chief said nothing. He simply picked her up. Then he said, "you will not be needing this child, Master, I see. I will take her to the healer."

"She has learned our secrets. She will not dare to speak them, on pain of death," the Master shouted.

"You have seen to it that she cannot speak at all," the Chief said, and we all marched out and came here.

"What is to be done with her?" Athirra asked. "She cannot be made to go back there."

"I could apply to the Dignus," Galt said doubtfully. "He might allow her to be sent somewhere else."

"Never," Athirra said. "She is only a woman. Her Master has control of her."

"But even the Dignus would not allow the beating to continue," Ibaren gasped.

"He might enjoin the Master to refrain from beating her, but he would send her back, I'm sure," Jebend answered.

"Let me take her," Teq suggested. "Surely that was part of the idea of my going. And certainly of my returning: to give some place for helpless little souls like she is, to go."

"Another red spot disease?" Ibaren asked.

"Red spot disease?" Galt was bewildered. They explained.

"Why not, after all," Zolg said. "I've been thinking about that. We are going to have to have some explanation when the time comes for Taza to disappear. Why not start now, and create the story of the red spot disease, which is mostly fatal. I mean," he said, warming to his subject, "what about when Belletha needs to go? Both twins could catch the disease, but Gath could survive and Belletha 'succumb'. What do you think? I could isolate such cases in the house behind here, that I'm preparing as a house for the very sick. It's so that I can keep an eye on them without wandering all over the Town," he explained to Teq. "Those that 'die'..."

"Would have to be burned in the heights above," Ibaren suggested, "and handled by no one but Zolg and any person in whom we might confide over the years, because the disease is catching." She finished triumphantly. "You, might confide," she amended. "I'm going with Teq and taking that child with me. Anybody not agree?"

Jebend was stunned by all this open discussion between men and women, with even his Chief participating. But he was a man who had already been alerted to the fact that women were not a lesser species, in the Desert. He knew they were warriors. He knew they ruled as Priestesses/Princesses in the Desert. He was also aware somewhat of the hearsay of the Honors, where women ruled indeed. Why would this surprise him? He smiled. He was pleased. Yes, he had been a little disturbed when the Chief revealed to him how he had been deceived over the matter of Bessindel, but he knew the reason. If you accepted the basic premise that women might have rights, then everything else followed. Why not? If they were people too, they had rights too. He recognized he was having more fun than he had enjoyed since the days when he first realized he had been accepted as a green shirt. "How would you make the red spots?" he asked.

"That's easy enough," Zolg answered. "Vegetable dye."

"It would be too difficult to transport Jussy," Galt said. "That beast of yours doesn't carry people, does it?" he asked Teq.

"We thought we'd try and train them to do that, but we haven't yet," he confessed.

"You'd need a stretcher," Galt thought. "I'm sorry, Ibaren, but if you have to walk for days over rough Mountain terrain, when you haven't been outside the Town for years, you're not going to be up to carrying half a stretcher. I'll have to go."

"No!" Athirra was firm. "I won't lose you to those Mountains. You can't."

Jebend blinked. "What about me?" he asked diffidently.

"No, I thank you. It will have to be me. Think about it, my love," Galt said to Athirra. "I carried her. I caught the disease. Now I do intend to get over it and return, but you will have to leave me here with Zolg. I could not bring the disease into our own house, to infect our children. I will return, and come home from here. It all makes sense. You, my dear, can go home and weep and wail and rail as much as you like. Jebend will tell the men and even the other Chiefs with a straight back and a disapproving stare. Everyone will be afraid, especially when Zolg pronounces Jussy 'dead'. My recovery will make everyone glad again. Even the Master Metalworker will be grateful that Jussy died without revealing his secrets. Joy all around."

"Well, it does make sense," Athirra admitted, "though I can't like it."

"I also want to see the home place you have made, my Teq," Galt grinned at him. "We can set up our system of signals while I'm there. And above all I want to meet this new wife of yours."

Teq blushed, mad at himself that he was still doing that. "Ocham is not my wife," he said stiffly.

"Not?" Athirra asked, laughing.

"No. At least not yet. At least, I'm not sure if she'll have me," he stammered.

"Don't embarrass the man," Ibaren interrupted. "He has to buy gifts before he leaves, and tell us what he needs to take back with him. I shall go and do his shopping for him tomorrow, appearing in public with a few, very obvious red spots."

"I'll go with you," Athirra said to Galt. "I'd love to see the place."

"Not this time," Galt was firm. "We need you to cover our tracks. Zolg and Jebend can't do everything. You can come here every day to 'see' me."

"And I shall visit you to inquire each day, if I may," Jebend suggested.

"I know you're right," she agreed, "but I would love to go. Nothing will stop me next time. How long will it take?"

"Carrying the stretcher, possibly more, but on my own, in the rain, I made it here in two days," Teq answered.

"Then it's settled, which is just as well because it's nearly morning," Galt said. "We should be ready to set out the day after tomorrow."

"You had better all get out of here if I have to paint three people with spots, and then get up and do a day's work as if nothing had happened," Zolg said dryly.

"Nonsense," Athirra got up to go. "You've been up half the night with your patients, and they are too infectious for you to leave them. Let the apprentices cope."

"I'll escort you home, if I may," Jebend said to Athirra. "My family will be thinking some disaster has happened in the Town to keep me out all night."

Galt kissed Athirra and took her to the door. He shook Jebend by the hand. "Thank you," he said. "I hope I am forgiven."

"You are my Chief now and always, sir," Jebend answered. "I am proud to serve someone of such great compassion and understanding. I have learned a great deal here tonight. You have my promise of silence and of loyalty."

"Thank you, Captain. And you have made many friends."

Teq shook Jebend by the hand also, really glad to have him in this small, closely bound group. Of which he was only peripherally a part now, he realized. From now on he belonged to Ocham. If she would have him...

Chapter 47

Ocham had done all her crying. She had reached the conclusion that she had been acting like any foolish girl who reached the age to be taken by the Men of the Sea, and fell down practically worshipping at the feet of the first one to step ashore. The Men of the Sea were forbidden to Ocham. Teq was the first man she had seen who could be available to her. She had fallen at his feet. She resolved that when he returned - if he returned - she would treat him as she would any companion in the village. He would be a little less to her than her brothers, and a little more than a total stranger. The thing that consoled her was that she was not at all sure that he had understood what she meant when she had betrayed her feelings for him. She need not feel foolish in front of him. The fact that all these resolutions left her feeling bleak was understandable, she decided. After all, the chances of another man coming her way were slim. Nobody else lived in the Mountains.

Nonetheless, she was completely calm when, after eight days of Teq's absence they heard his hail.

"Did you hear that?" Doban asked coming out of the second house they were relining. "That must be Teq returned."

"I'll run and see," Royar offered, popping out behind Doban. Without waiting for an answer, he was off. The thickness of the wood prevented them from seeing far enough to tell. It occurred to Ocham that his was probably not good. Someone or something could get quite close before they knew. Then again, the woods were the width of the lake away from the houses. There really wasn't much danger, if any.

Ocham ducked inside to tidy her dress and her hair. Not that she was doing it for Teq's benefit, but she had been working hard, and preferred to be neat if she was to be seen.

Royar came tearing back. "There are three people with Teq," he announced. "One is an old man, as big as Teq only thicker. Then there is an old woman and a young girl on a stretcher."

"What?" she said, stupidly.

"Teq says to prepare a bed for the young girl in the women's house, and please to heat some water. And is there any food or should he go hunting?"

Ocham shook herself. She had no idea what this was all about, but she was not going to be found lacking in hospitality. She went inside the finished house to light the fire and spread blankets over one of the fresh beds she had been preparing. By the time she reappeared, the party had arrived.

"Teq. Welcome back," she said with massive calm. "In here with the stretcher."

Teq was quite pink in the face - she assumed from the exertion of carrying the stretcher -and stuttered his greeting. "We're here," he said unnecessarily. "This is Galt, my father, and Ibaren and Jussy on the stretcher. Ocham," he said to Galt, "and Doban, brother and sister to Royar whom you met."

"Yes, quite," said Galt, trying hard to remain solemn in the face of his son's discomfiture. "Do you think we might put Jussy down before we go on with the niceties?"

"I am delighted to meet you, and delighted to have arrived," Ibaren spoke to Ocham. "Do you mind if I sit down? I have not walked so far in years and my feet are refusing to hold me."

"Please come in," Ocham offered. "There are stools inside, in the other house, or beds in here. We have not quite finished building yet, so we are not as organized as we might be." She had not yet made out why all these people were here, but she was determined not to ask.

"What about food?" Teq asked Doban. "Bringing so many people, I had better go hunting, hadn't I?"

"No," Doban chuckled. "You won't be able to run off as easily as that. Royar and I went hunting yesterday, since you weren't back yet, and we got a gumbuck. Ocham butchered it this morning, and it is already roasting. It's the easiest thing when you don't have much time, eh?"

Galt had picked Jussy up and carried her indoors, and Ibaren had gone with Ocham to see her settled. "Don't worry about so many of us," she said to Ocham. "I'm here because Teq said you could use an elder, and I wasn't needed any more where I was. And Jussy is here because we are rescuing her. Galt just came to help carry her. He'll be going back as soon as may be."

Ocham smiled politely. "You are all welcome," she lied. "Are you comfortable?" she asked Jussy.

Jussy was. She was in a house peopled only with women. She was warm, and she was lying on a bed which didn't move. "Oh, yes," she murmured, opening her eyes and looking up at Ocham. "I hope I am not a nuisance."

Ocham saw her bruises for the first time. "Oh, you poor thing!" she exclaimed. How did you get so hurt?"

"Her father and brothers beat her for not being stupid," Ibaren answered dryly. "I told you we were rescuing her. She may stay, may she not?"

"Of course. Teq has already told you so. Oh, yes. He is quite right. I am glad to have an elder here to counsel me. It is a luxury I had not looked for," Ocham answered, her voice sincere and her eyes seeking Ibaren's. "You are both truly welcome."

"Good. Then let's give this child a sip of water and let her sleep. For myself, I want to enjoy this beautiful day without having to walk about. And I'm quite a useful cook. I'm not just here to talk for my supper." Ibaren smiled at Ocham, liking her for her caution and her calm. This is a strong one, she thought. Much better for my Teq. It is a bonus that she is beautiful too.

Galt was giving orders to Teq. His father, Teq had said. Well, that would account for the authority. "Unload that beast, Teq. Perhaps one of these two young men would show me around. I am already impressed with what you have done."

"I will," Doban and Royar chorused.

"Both, then, unless your sister needs you?" Galt raised his eyes at Ocham in query.

"Please. Take them. I will show Ibaren."

And Teq was left abandoned, unloading the carry. It had not been a simple journey. Ibaren had gone shopping as she promised on that first day, and the artistic spots Zolg had painted on her caused a lot of remarks, and later several visits to Zolg.

He answered, sounding worried. "I have another child upstairs who is suffering from the same, as well as Chief Galt. I did not realize Ibaren too... Well, I will keep them isolated. I am afraid of spotted fever. Not common, but very bad. I will see no more patients. My apprentices will help you. Excuse me."

And the news, as with all bad news, had flown round the Town. Athirra made her appointed visit, and so did Jebend. They bade the travelers goodbye, afraid that it would cause too much stir if they came again on the following day. Zolg let it be known that the fever could only be caught if one of the spots was actually touched, so people seemed less terrified by the second day.

In any case, that was the day for Zolg's wiving. The owner of the House where Tilla was, kept his distance from Zolg. He'd heard about the fever too. He took the credits, though.

Tilla herself had heard, and was troubled to be coming to a house full of diseased people. She was a shy, slight creature, but with an intelligent eye and a generous mouth. If she was to be Zolg's wife, she had to be trusted with full knowledge. She entered into the conspiracy with such enthusiasm, that it was clear she had dreamed of escape herself. But she seemed delighted to be with Zolg, and he with her. She promised to make the readying of the upper house her first priority. Taza took to her easily enough. The little girl had already had so many caregivers, that she accepted yet another with equanimity.

Galt concerned himself with having Athirra bring round what he would need for the journey as inconspicuously as possible, and with making bundles for Zolg to burn on the heights which would resemble people: the supposed bodies of Ibaren and Jussy. He wrapped two large logs in old blankets, and added a generous amount of meat scraps, so that the smell of burning would cause no suspi-

cion. Ibaren thought the whole thing immeasurably grisly, but Teq helped ener-
getically.

Ibaren's shopping had produced the shirts for the boys and a dress for Ocham,
as well as a handsome wrap for her, all woven, not knitted. Galt said he would
think about how they might get a loom, or at least the plans for a loom, to Teq as
time progressed.

And then it was the second night and time for departure. Jussy remained passive to all their suggestions, becoming agitated only if she thought her father
would come for her. The infectious fever idea settled her mind. She allowed them
to bind her on to a stretcher without complaint, and even the dampening trip
behind the falls did not cause her to do more than whimper. It was a very dark
night, which was just as well, because Teq had to make three trips. On the first
he took the bundles of gifts and personal belongings of the two women. He
loaded those on to the carry and returned. On the second trip he eased through
the low place in the cave first, and then Galt pushed Jussy's stretcher through to
him. Galt had a difficult time getting through. He had put on weight in the past
year. The third trip was for Ibaren, and she could not get through at all. Her knees
would not allow her to bend and crawl so far. In the end, she lay on a blanket and
they pushed her through as they had pushed Jussy. And that was before they started out.

Galt led the way, with Teq shouting directions as needed. One end of the
stretcher was on Galt's shoulders, and the other on Teq's. But Teq was also leading the carry and trying to help Ibaren. They made very little progress and
camped early. They intended to start out again at first light, but whether it was
the excitement, or the discomfort, nobody got to sleep until just before dawn, and
then they woke up late. It was decided to stick to journey food. Everything was
hard enough without hunting as well. And then it rained a little. Just showers but
wetting. Jussy suffered the worst because she had to just lie there and get rained
on. She did not complain, but Ibaren did. Her feet hurt and she was soaking wet
and couldn't they please stop and dry out? By the third day, they got along better. Ibaren was getting her walking legs back, and Teq had devised a way to
attach the binders from the carry's harness to his belt. They made excellent
progress and covered a lot of ground. But not enough. They were heartily sick of
journey food, and fairly depressed when they set out on the last day. They waited for nothing, so that it was still mid-morning when they crested the rise of the
home valley, and Teq let out his hail.

Now everybody seemed just delighted with each other, but nobody seemed
particularly glad to see him, Teq thought. Ocham had never even looked him in
the face, since he got there. And her miserable calm about everything! You would
have thought she could have shown a little excitement. A little pleasure. He had
been away more than a week, and it was the first time they had been separated
since they met. He had felt it. He had missed her. Why hadn't she missed him?

Ocham and Ibaren finished their rounds first. "We have decided that this is the
occasion for a feast," Ibaren said. "Galt will only stay tonight, and then he must
hurry back. We've been gone far too long already. One thing, he will definitely

look thinner after his 'illness'," she laughed. "He hasn't walked so far in years either."

"What can I do to help?" Teq asked Ocham.

"Nothing, really. Put those things away," she told him with unruffled serenity, pointing to the bundles he had unloaded from the carry. "The women's house will be this one, where Jussy is, so you will want to stow your things in the other. A couple of days will finish it. We have been eating in there, so you could bring out the table and the stools, to sit on."

"You might want to wash first," Ibaren suggested. "I know I must."

"I'll go for a swim," he said sullenly. "Those jobs can wait until closer to evening."

"Swim?" Royar had heard him. "Can I come, Teq?"

Well, somebody wanted his company. "Come on, then," he answered.

"Let's all go," Doban suggested. "Sir?" to Galt.

"The lake will be freezing. Do us good," Galt agreed. "Where do we go in?"

"Beyond the trees over there," Teq told him, brightening up. "Race you," he said to the boys.

"Well, that will keep the men happy," Ibaren said. "What about that water you have warming?" she asked Ocham. "Let's all three of us have a wash by the fire in comfort."

Ibaren added a few touches to the feast. Jussy came outside for it. The moon rose clear and lovely, rippling a bright path of mystery across the surface of the lake. Compliments flew. Galt was genuinely impressed with everything they had done. He particularly liked the huge barn made of stone, which was a new idea to him. The carries seemed most docile and useful, and the insulation of the houses which Doban had invented was a real marvel. He slept that night beside the wall they had completed, and had never slept so draught-free.

But the evening promised well. After they had eaten the entire gumbuck between them, telling tales and laughing together, Teq brought out the shirts he had brought for the young men and the dress for Ocham. She had known nothing of his intention to obtain one for her, and she was speechless with delight. She caressed the cloth and the pleasure brought tears to her eyes.

"Oh, such a gift. I have never in my life... Oh, Teq it is..."she murmured, happily to him.

"Oh, yes. It is great. I always liked your shirts. This is the best." Royar butted in.

"Perfect," Doban grinned. "Thank you. You did not forget us."

"Forget you! You were never from my mind," he protested. He looked over at Ocham to see if she understood that it was her he meant, but her face was buried in the cloth and she did not look at him.

"Time for music," Doban announced. "Who plays the drum?"

"Oh, I will. Do you have a drum?" Ibaren offered. "I haven't seen a drum since... since the Honor."

"It's pretty crude, I'm afraid," Teq answered her. "Perhaps you know more about them and can help us make a better one."

"Perhaps, indeed," she said.

Doban brought out the instruments and began to play, a plaintive little tune at first. Ocham quietly sang along with him, and Royar joined in. "It is a song of the Sea," she explained. "A summer song. A happy song."

Doban looked at her, and broke into a lively melody, which he did not need to explain was happy. And another. And then one of his wild songs, with Royar pumping in his hollow-noted accompaniment, and Ibaren keeping up on the drums. Then fiercer, with the drum rhythm more emphatic, and Ocham sprang up, dancing. Teq moved to join her, but she spun away to the opposite side of the fire. He subsided again beside Galt, not knowing whether or not to follow his instinct to leap up and whirl after her. He did not. He ought to have.

The evening ended quietly. Galt sang a song of the Wilder camps which Teq had never heard before. Jussy clapped her hands at Ocham's dancing and Doban's playing, which pleased them both. Ibaren caressed the drum, and Royar bounded about full of energy. Only Teq was not infused with a spirit of well being. He went to bed almost disgruntled.

The next morning early, Galt got ready to leave.

"I'll go with you. It will be much quicker if we use a more difficult route," Teq offered.

"I do need to hurry. Can you spare him?" Galt asked Ocham.

"Your needs must be served today," she answered. "Teq will be here to help Doban another day."

"Then let us be on our way," Galt smiled. "I will have such wonderful tales to tell of you all. Teq?"

They walked in companionable silence. "She is a fine woman. She reminds me of Tarabeth, your true mother," Galt remarked towards evening. "You will be lucky to have her to wife."

"Lucky, yes," Teq answered shortly, but would say no more to Galt's quizzical questioning look.

On the second day, they noted a bare knob of a hill. "Put a flag on top of that, if you need me. I'll come and check at least two times a month, barring deep snow, or flood, or something," Teq promised.

"I will. And I'll bring Athirra to see you in the spring. We'll think of some excuse to be out of sight for a few days."

"Not spotted fever," Teq laughed.

"Not spotted fever," Galt agreed. "Though it has served us well. Leave me now, and get on back. I can see my way easily enough from here. It has been good to see you. I shall miss you all over again." Galt hugged him. "Cheer up. It will work out, you know. I shall expect to hear from you as soon as you can."

"I shall miss you, too," Teq answered, hugging him back. "It was a great thing to see you all again. Tell them all that, won't you?"

"I will."

Teq watched him swing away, climbing more easily than he had a few days ago.

I was so eager to get back to Ocham, he thought, and now I barely feel welcome. What can I have done wrong? Perhaps I should give up and go back with Galt. Perhaps that's what she expects me to do. Well, I won't do that. The Mountains are my home too. Thank the Sky and the Mountain there is plenty of work to do. At least she will have Ibaren and Jussy to talk to. I did that much for her, even if she hates me. But why? Why? And what will I do without her?

He sighed and turned away to go back. He trod the path with a heavier step than he had only two days before.

Chapter 48

They were ready for the winter. The second house was lined. There was a larder cut into the soft edge of the mountain behind the connecting covered walk between the houses. The smoke house was filled with fish and game. There were furs enough for each bed, as well as blankets. Reeds covered the floors. And there dawned one of those rare days in autumn which seem to deny that winter is on its way. They were called Summer Memory days. The sky was high and dazzling blue. Wisps of hair-blown clouds flew across it, heralding rain to come. The wind was playful, blowing first from this quarter and then from that, lifting old leaves to gambol with. Such leaves as were left on the deciduous trees were of brilliant reds, yellows and oranges, and the grass was the old, rich green of summer. The coniferous trees sang their whispering songs and sent forth such a smell as must tickle the nose awake.

What could Ibaren do but declare a holiday. "Go, all of you, and play," she announced. "I am going to cook. I want no help, except , perhaps, if Royar would dig me some wild onions and hunt for green herbs by the lake."

"Come swimming," Doban offered Jussy. "It will be cold, but afterwards we can run to the top of the Mountain and look for miles. You can see how we got here. I've been promising to show you that for weeks."

"All right," she answered doubtfully. "I did say I would." She was still more subdued than the others, but by now, nearly two months since her arrival, she trusted them. Was certain that nobody ever hit anybody, and they all worked just as hard as ever, because they wanted to. She adored Ibaren, and played easily with Royar, but he was too boisterous to be comfortable on expeditions. Doban was quieter. More secure.

Teq picked up his spears and said he was going exploring. He glanced over at Ocham, but she was not looking at him, so he just went.

"I'll help with the cooking," Ocham offered. "There is too much for one person."

"In a whole day?" Ibaren answered. "Go on with you. You'll just be in my way. Royar is more use because he just does what I ask of him, and doesn't keep doing things for me. That child is going to be a great cook, one day. You'll see."

"But surely I can do something," Ocham protested.

"Yes, you can. You can go off exploring to the south. Nobody ever goes that way and I am curious to know what's down there."

"That's Teq's job. He's the mapmaker."

"Possibly, but he's already gone, and I can't ask him. Now, get on with you. I have to think what I'm going to make." Ibaren shooed her off. She had an idea that Teq had gone south for the very reason she'd mentioned, and she was tired of watching the two of them avoid one another. The winter would be very confined, and could be cheerful or miserable, depending on the harmony among the people. Those two were made for one another and it was time they did something about acknowledging it.

Ibaren sighed a little for Bessindel. She had been such a tiny thing. It seemed so unkind that she had never had the chance to grow into a sensible woman. Life in an Honor would have done that for her. Out in the wild places, and confined in the Town, she had become too dependent and too willful. Stayed a child, in fact. It was a sad thing. But she would never have done as Teq's wife. Funny how none of them had thought of that when he had wived her. But then he was only part grown up himself at the time. Now, there were subtle changes in him. He was all man. A leader, even as Galt was. Strong and thoughtful and decisive. Ocham was the same in her way: resolute, and true; calm and passionate. Yes, they needed one another. Ibaren watched Ocham set off, a basket in her hand in case she found something, no doubt. And here came Royar with something to show her. She must get started.

Teq had gone south as Ibaren surmised. He had his mapmaking tools as well as his spears. He had not taken the long way around the lake, as Ocham was doing. He had climbed the Mountain by the scree slope and was running along its crest. He did not look either down or back. He was pleased to be alone. He needed the time by himself. This day would give him the strength to survive the coming winter confinement. That Ocham despised him he did not doubt. What had caused this, he could not imagine. Everything had been comfortable between them, and then one day they were talking, and she had changed. What had they been talking about? He could not remember. Nothing of importance, surely. Well, it must have been something important to Ocham, and he could not even recall what it was. It went to show how little he understood her. Bessindel had been all surface. He said something she didn't like and she would yell at him. Ocham was quieter. If something hurt her, she said nothing. She simply took it to herself and buried it. If only she would talk to him. He loved the way she smiled when she talked. He had to watch her offer these smiles to others, these days. He loved the way she moved: so lithe and so firm. Her every task was carried out with grace and economy of action, so that it was accomplished while others were still considering how to start. She was gentle with Jussy, and respectful of Ibaren. She was cheerful and firm with her brothers. It was only Teq she never spoke to.

Never asked for any help. Never moved to join him around the fire in friendship. He must stop thinking about her and concentrate on what he was doing, and especially where he was going, he thought. He had to look around with care to discover where he was.

From then on, Teq addressed himself to the task of measuring and mapping. The way south was not wooded like the way to the west and north. It was bounded for some way by the ridge along which he had been running. There were one or two gullies leading through the rocky terrain, and another tiny lake, duplicating the valley of their home place, but in miniature. On the farther, more southerly, side, the ground rose to a plateau of rock, sparsely dotted with vegetation, and filled with pockets of caves and gulches, which made him think of the land of the rift. He paused on its northern edge, sketching what he could see, and sat down to take a drink from the water he carried, and eat the journey food he had picked up as automatically as he had picked up his weapons. He looked at the sky. The sun was past its peak, and beautiful as the day was, it was going to be as short as any other at this time of year. He had better be getting back.

He descended from the plateau, and chose to return by the western side. It looked like easy enough terrain, and it would fill out the picture of the land for his map. No time to take any measurements, but he would be able to judge roughly. There were a couple of places where he had to scramble up over high-piled rocks, and descend again to the grass. He skirted the miniature valley, and came again close to home. There was one more pile of rocks, but it looked as if there was almost a path leading around them. And on the path he saw Ocham.

He stopped, unsure whether to run to catch up with her, or let her go ahead in peace. He looked up to see whether he could climb the rocks and outflank her, reaching the home valley by a different route. But what he saw there, froze him. Quietly perched on the rocks, sunk down so that it was close to the shape and color of the rocks themselves, lay one of the huge feline predators, watching every move Ocham made. She was bent over the ground, apparently searching for something, moving slowly and even humming a little. He caught a fragrance of her song on the erratic wind.

The same wind made the predator look up. Teq stood perfectly still. It would not do for him to frighten the animal. He was sure it was stalking Ocham, not simply watching her pass. He had to get there - in spear range - without alerting it to his presence. He scanned the terrain. The wind shifted merrily again, and the animal looked back at Ocham. Teq saw a way around behind the rocks, where, with luck, he would be above the creature, and could attract its attention to himself and away from her.

At the top of his lungs he yelled, "look up, Ocham. Run."

She glanced up, leisurely, and saw the cat, huge and feral, gathering itself for a spring. She gave one scream, short and piercing, then flung herself forward. With one mighty stride she cleared the place where she had been standing, looking around frantically for a place to hide. She could never outrun this creature. She had only seen them from a distance, before. They were usually alone, stalking the herds of gumbuck which roamed the Mountains. She had seen the sudden speed with which they sprang after their quarry. Had admired their beauty of movement. She had very rarely seen a gumbuck outrun a cat.

From the corner of her eye she noticed a crack in the rocks. If she could squeeze herself in there... She had to. There was nowhere else. As the cat landed in the place where she had been, she flung herself at the crack, and scrabbled to get her whole body in. She heard the creature snarl in rage. She tried making herself smaller. A great clawed foot raked down the outer edge of the rocks, tearing at the arm and leg which were still exposed. The leather dress and trews she had chosen to wear that day gave her some protection, although those mighty claws could pierce it like water.

And during all that time, Teq had been running. He had no idea he could run so fast. He leaped recklessly over the terrain, desperate to reach the cat before it sprang. He did not. He arrived at the top of the rock as he heard Ocham shriek in pain. He took time only for a deep breath, and he jumped. He was not all that clear where he was going to light, but he must put himself and his weapons between Ocham and the cat. He landed on its back, near the tail. He did not feel the scratches he tore in his legs as he knelt astride it. His spear was in his hand. The forward movement of his jump pushed the spear into the neck of the beast, which was as far as he could reach. The animal roared in pain. And writhed. It reached back with its gaping mouth to snatch at the thing which was hurting it. Teq had his second spear. He lunged from where he still sat, and the spear went through the cat's mouth and into its brain. With a great gout of blood spewing from its mouth, it died. Teq collapsed on to its back.

He lay there heaving for breath for a moment, until he heard a whimper from Ocham.

"It's all right," Teq gasped. "It's dead."

"Oh, Teq. It's huge. I never saw it. Oh, Teq," she grabbed him by the shoulders and pulled him upright, "are you all right? Are you hurt?"

"No, I'm fine."

"Come, let me look at you. There's so much blood. Some of it may be yours."

He let himself be helped off the creature's back. To tell the truth, the strength had suddenly gone out of him. He had no idea how he could have run so far, so fast. Or how he could have jumped from such a height. He looked up. The rock towered above him. There were scrapes and tears all over his legs, somewhat bloody, but nothing worse.

"Really, I'm all right," he assured her, "but what about you?"

"It scratched me a little," she smiled at him, "but I'm still alive because of you." It was the first smile he had seen in weeks. It made him weak. He leaned on her and turned her towards him and smiled back.

"If I had lost you..." he said. "I might have lost you. What would I have done? How could I have gone on without you?"

"But you saved me," she answered wondering. "You saved me. You did it, all alone. You killed this huge creature and I am perfectly safe."

He pulled her to him, folding her tight against his chest. "Don't frighten me again," he said. "I couldn't live without you. Even if you hate me, I need to know you're there."

"Hate you?" she said. "Teq, I thought you didn't want me. I thought you couldn't like me, and I didn't want to force you. I had to stay away."

"But, I love you," he said. "You are my life."

"I have loved you for ever," she whispered. "Even when Bessindel was your wife. I was so ashamed. And then I thought... but you turned from me."

"I did? When?"

"Never mind. I was mistaken." Suddenly she laughed. "And now it's getting dark and we must go back. What shall we do with this beast?"

"Take it with us, of course," he decided. "They'd never believe us otherwise. Do you have anything to carry?" he asked.

"Just my basket. I found mushrooms. I can take your spears," she replied. "What about those cuts?"

"Today, I feel no pain. Or at least I won't once you've kissed me. Just once, or I'll never want to move." He grinned at her as he pulled her to him and kissed her. "We had better see to your cuts. They are much worse than mine. Those must hurt a lot. Look, you're bleeding badly. Let me bind them for you." He tore off his shirt and ran down to the lake to wet it. He washed the gouges the cat's claws had left on her arm and leg. If it had been able to get at her more easily, it would have slashed her to the bone. She winced while he bound them, but such was her euphoria, she only felt the pain in her nerves. Not in her heart. He kissed her again. "We'd better go. Now."

"Or we never will," she smiled back, radiant in the quieting light.

Teq picked up the beast, staggering under its great weight. He pulled it across his shoulders and they walked back with Ocham in the lead, picking the easiest route.

That night the celebration was true. Every one of the six persons round the festive fire was celebrating something. For Jussy it was a sense of freedom realized for the first time. She had seen the immensity of the Mountains, and she knew, really knew at last, that the Town had no power here. Never could have. She laid her hand in Doban's and trusted him. When it came to music, she turned out to have a spectacular singing voice and a knowledge of all the songs the Smiths used with their work. While these were not merry songs, or pretty songs, or even loving songs, they were rhythmic, and Ibaren used the drum to accompany them with mighty bangs and booms which filled the valley and terrified the animals. Why not? It was a people night tonight.

Doban felt the warmth of friendship with a woman for the first time, and found it to be different from either his worship of Bessindel or his respect for his sister. He felt protective and triumphant for bringing Jussy to her sense of home, and he took pride in it. He played his pipes with extraordinary zest because of it.

Ibaren was at peace. Whatever had happened between Teq and Ocham and the great cat, she would no doubt hear when they told their tales at the end of the evening. She really didn't care what had happened. It had brought them together at last, and she had been instrumental in it, and she was pleased with herself. And pleased to be here. She had never before had such a sense of rightness in a place: not even in the Honor. Here she was the only elder, and they had needed one. She was needed. That was it! In her old age she had not become useless, leaving things to the youngers, as she had so often witnessed in the Honor. She was useful here, and happy to be.

Even Royar was pleased with himself because at least two of the dishes they were all exclaiming over were his creation. He had made them himself, with very little help from Ibaren, and everyone said they were good. He had always lurked in Doban's shadow, and although he knew he was a pretty good carpenter, and a fair hunter, and a decent herder, he had never actually done anything original until today. He was fairly bouncing with pleasure any time anyone praised his work. Ha! He wasn't just a child any more.

Teq had walked in to the home place, just as dusk was turning into night, carrying the great cat across his shoulders, and had caused just the sensation he had hoped. This was a day for heroics. He wanted to show off before everyone. It was the day he had won his lady and he was fairly bursting with the joy and pride of it. The cat was the symbol. It lay on the opposite side of the fire, with the light glinting off its fierce eyes, and he wanted to laugh out loud every time he looked at it.

And Ocham? With the load of her misery at last lifted from her shoulders, she saw everything and everyone as if they were new. There was a glow to the world, which twinkled in the firelight and made the taste of the food as exquisite as the feel of the air. The moon had never gleamed so warm, smiling at her, personally. Her brothers had never been so dear. She had never been luckier in the company she kept. The world was a complete and beautiful place.

She felt no pain. When she danced, Teq danced. Even Jussy danced, although they didn't notice her. Royar jumped up and capered with her a little, so that she didn't feel silly, all alone with the lovers. For them, there was not just a leaping and a twirling and a gasping at the light, bright thrill of the music. There was a place around the fire with only themselves in it. They saw nothing but one another's eyes. When the music ended they smiled, and clasped hands and sat leaning together, as Ibaren began the telling of tales. Of fantasies and realities which made a fantasy of the night.

When they ended the evening at last, having placed the body of the great cat on the roof of the connecting passage, they slept more deeply than they could imagine sleep to be. It was not sleep. It was the visit of the Mystery, who came to each, to reaffirm their happiness.

Teq was the only one who heard a voice. To the others there was just the sensation of the presence. But Teq heard.

"You have done what I intended. You have done well. Just as there was a price to pay for my guidance, now there is a reward. You will do well here. You will serve my needs and in time my priest will come. There will be a Lord, a Lady and a Servant of the Mystery of the Mountains. Think well as you plan your

Home in the Mountains. Yours is the chance for something good. Or bad. Think well. I will be watching."

Chapter 49

Twenty years or so passed and the home place became known to them all as Mountainhome. Things they had planned began to work out, and things they had not planned happened anyway. Some good, some bad. For instance, the plan for attracting Wilders to the Mountains worked rather well. A very few would hear the drumming and come to investigate. When they discovered it meant crossing a Mountain pass to find the source of the drums, the majority would turn back. Only the most adventuresome would be curious enough to follow the sound. Mountainhome members would be watching from the top of the pass, and would lead the Wilders to a campfire. Once there, they would be questioned and if they were satisfactory would be told about Mountainhome. If they were not, they would be accompanied back through the pass, the others going along with them as if they were themselves Wilders out exploring, who had found the Mountains inhospitable, and who had simply been drumming for their own company. So far, possibly a dozen new members had been recruited in this way. One was joined to Taza and another to Belletha. Through the years, many young women of the Town had "succumbed" to the spotted fever, and had come through the cave to join Mountainhome. Zolg and Galt and Jebend and Athirra always consulted carefully before they determined which of them would be able to survive in the wilderness of the Mountains, better than the Pleasure Houses, before they would tell them that there was a chance for them outside the Town. They could not allow the exodus to be more than a trickle, or the suspicions of the Town would be aroused. Only the most desperate cases came through.

Gath was one of the young men who always went on the Wilder recruiting drives. When the time had come for Belletha to be sent through the cave, he had heard the story along with his twin, and had refused to be parted from her. Both Galt and Athirra sympathized with him, though they hated the thought of losing the company of both the twins, their firstborn. The move was, of course, irrevocable. There was no going back for a man who missed the privileges of the Town. But Gath fitted in well. He and Belletha succumbed to the "spotted sickness"

together, and were brought to Mountainhome by Athirra. It was her second trip
through. Her first had been that spring twenty years before, coming with Galt as
he had promised. Both Galt and Athirra were present, then, when Teq and Ocham
were joined, the day when Teq finally gave Ocham the splendid shawl he had
bought for her the autumn before. The Mountainhomers rejected the term wiving, since they found it rather one-sided. It was a joining. Galt and Athirra's second son, Garreth, was born during the winter prior, and now compensated somewhat for their loss.

On the debit side, there had been a splitting of the People of the Mountain. Not
all were willing to accept the rulings of Teq and Ocham. A small group had gone
to live in the miniature valley to the south, and had set up a rule by council. It
was Ibaren who made the peace. It was the last thing she did for them before she
died, and she was proud of it. She had Teq and Ocham agree to a council of advi-
sors, while they took the titles of Lord and Lady. The Council would be changed
each spring, although members could remain or return to their position if the
other council members asked them to. Each household, or family group would
propose one member to sit on the Council. Ultimately, Ibaren suggested, it would
be a Council of Elders, but there weren't any yet, apart from herself, and she was
too old to be bothered.

It was Athirra who arranged for the cave floor to be deepened. After her first
visit, she was determined never again to have to creep through the narrow part
on hands and knees. It was such a miserable introduction to a fine new world, she
argued. Galt and Jebend had to do the actual work, the noise deadened by the roar
of the falls. They carried it out with small eagerness, considering themselves past
the stage in life where digging could provide any amusement. Bruises and aches,
yes. They did it, however, and Athirra praised their efforts mightily, while Zolg
treated their bruised bodies and sensibilities with balms and wine. The way
through was now a gentle slope from start to finish, floored by tamped down
earth, and guarded by thin leafed bushes.

For his part, Teq had made a path down to the ledge where he had rescued
Royar, that day long ago. He liked to sit up there and look down at the home
place, and watch the people go about their daily work. It was a privilege of age
to have a little more leisure. He could look down on fields, planted as the Honor
fields had been, but with a wider variety. At Ibaren's suggestion they had planted an area with the herbs she used for her medicines.

There was a corner of Mountainhome where Doban the Smith worked. Jussy
had discovered metal ore in the bed of the river. She had been in trouble with her
father because she knew the secrets of working it. Lo! She could teach them. By
this time, she and Doban were joined, and she would teach the secrets only to
him and Royar. Royar didn't care to learn. He was an accomplished carpenter,
and the most favored cook on feast days, so he thought nothing of the information Jussy gave him. Doban, on the other hand, was immeasurably excited to
think that they could have metal tools. He had seen how well Teq's spears - the
gift from the People of the Desert - worked. He thought of skinning knives, of
axes, of chopping knives - a million things they could use.

But they had no anvil. Jussy assured them that nothing could be done without
an anvil. With an anvil they could make another anvil, but with none ... Teq could
think of only one solution: they must steal one. Jussy would not help if it meant
reentering the Town. Most especially entering the home of her father. Teq decided he must go back to the Town to seek help from Galt. On that journey he took
Ocham and Doban, so that they could see the Town for themselves.

They arrived, as always, at night. Once they emerged from behind the waterfall, there was very little they could see in the dark. Teq led them down with care,
and knocked hopefully on Zolg's door. It was answered by Tilla, a babe in her
arms, and another child clinging to her skirt.

"Teq!" she gasped. "Come in. These are my grandchildren. Let me put them
to bed. Jebend is below with Zolg drinking ale. I will send word for my son's
wife to pick these two up. She is only visiting. And who are these?" she smiled.

Teq had pulled Ocham and Doban in behind him, and they had all followed
behind Tilla as she talked the way into the main room. It was clear how much her
influence had changed the stark house Teq remembered. It was warm and bright,
with benches along the walls, padded with some material.

"Tilla, this is Ocham, my wife, and her brother, Doban. We need some help,
so I thought they might like to come and see the Town - what little you can see
at night," he grinned.

"You are all most welcome," she answered. "Please sit down. I will bring some
ale, when I put these children down. They do not understand yet, so there is no
harm done. I'll tell Zolg you are here."

In a few moments they could hear Zolg's halting approach, and firm footsteps
following.

"Teq, oh Teq," Zolg exclaimed. "It is too long between visits. If only this foot
of mine would allow it, I would come and see your splendid home. But, at least
I get to meet your wife and her brother, Tilla tells me." He hugged Teq, and shook
hands with the other two. Jebend stepped forward, grinning from ear to ear, shaking them all by the hand and naming himself.

"I sent Tilla off with the babies to give them to our son's wife. No point in
having her come here tonight. Now. Ale?" Zolg offered.

"If he will let me get in a word," Jebend smiled as he sat down, "tell me why
you are here. I will tell Galt later, but he is in a Council meeting tonight. You
know that Kambar is Dignus now, do you?"

"No, I had not heard." Teq was not really surprised. Sedemp had been old, and
Kambar had wanted to be Dignus, then. "Liddel, who was the last one you sent
us?, didn't say a word. But then most of these young women know nothing of the
larger affairs of the Town. They have been servies, or daughters of servies, and
they are told nothing but their duties. Doban, you know, is joined to Jussy, the
Smith's daughter, and she was the exception. As a matter of fact, that's why
we're here."

"Is what?" Zolg asked, returning with a huge jug of ale and setting it down on
a table. Jebend reached mugs down from a high shelf and helped him hand them
round.

"The reason we're here," Teq answered. "This is serious business to us, but Jebend just might not want to hear of our larcenous intentions."

"You've come to steal?" he asked.

"Not steal," Doban growled. "Take some compensation for my wife's wrongs. I was there when she first arrived. I saw her injuries."

"Ah. You are the people who came from the Sea," Zolg said, enlightened. "You are the beautiful Ocham about whom Teq could not stop talking and thinking, when he was last here."

Ocham smiled. "Couldn't he? I thought never to see him again."

"Nothing would have kept him from you," Zolg assured her.

"True," Jebend agreed. "Now explain your larcenous intentions."

"We, that is Jussy, has discovered metal in the rivers," Ocham explained.

"And she has told me how it can be worked," Doban continued, "but it can't be done without an anvil."

"You can't make an anvil," Teq continued, "or so she says, and we don't know. So we've come to steal one."

"Take one," Doban said.

"What's an anvil?" Zolg asked. "I mean would you know one if you saw one?"

"A reasonable question," Jebend agreed.

"Well, Jussy has described it to us. She's also said it takes at least two men to carry one," Teq told them. "Only the Smiths have such a thing, and they have two, or at least they had when Jussy lived there. They have an old one, as a spare, in their little workshop. I have no idea how to steal it."

"I'll help you," Jebend said, astonishing Teq. "But I want something in return."

"Of course," Teq agreed. "What?"

"I have a son and two daughters," he explained. "My older daughter has just entered a Pleasure House. My wife went to the Keeper she knew and trusted, and begged him to bid for her. My daughter went willingly. My son is a green shirt with the hunters, under Chief Prodarin: the Chief who replaced Kambar. My son is doing well and is happy. But Maylin is my baby, and I cannot bear to see her go to a Pleasure House. I thought I had got over these ideas, but I cannot. She is still young. Just seven years. If I help you, I want to go back with you and bring her with me. Is it agreed?"

"Would you remain with us?" Teq asked. "Of course, you can come and bring her. You and she would be most welcome."

"I'll get you a jar of the paint, now," Zolg offered, "so that you can give Maylin her spotted fever. Just put it on with a small stick. Perhaps tonight would be a good idea for Maylin. You could "catch" the fever when you bring her to me, and come to visit. You can decide later whether to get better, eh?"

"That is a wonderful idea," Ocham said. "I will look after her while we are here, so that she will not feel strange with us. Thank you for offering to help."

"I am frankly overwhelmed," Teq told him. "I am going to ask Galt if he has any ideas. With both of you, we must succeed."

"I'll tell Galt the moment I see him. It may not be tonight, though," Jebend told them. "It would look very odd if I went into the enclave too late at night without some real disaster on our hands. I had better be going, and make sure there isn't one," he added.

"I'll walk out with you and get you that paint," said Zolg. "Bring Maylin here tomorrow. The stain works really well. I have perfected it, you know. It won't wash off for a week."

"Going already?" Tilla walked back into the room, puffing a little. She had put on weight in the last twenty years, where Zolg had become thinner and nearly bald. The only change Teq could see in Jebend was the totally gray hair. Otherwise, he looked as trim as ever. But then, Teq thought, I see no changes in any of us, either. I wonder what they see.

"I'm going to make something to eat," Tilla offered. "I am very lazy, and brought food back from an inn on the way, so there's almost nothing to do. I want to sit down with you so that we can all chat together."

"May I help you?" Ocham offered. "Food from an inn sounds delightful. We have never tasted such a thing."

"Really? No help tonight, dear. I'm just so delighted to have you here, and you've already walked a long way today. Here comes Zolg. He can bring some more ale while I set up the meal. Zolg", she called, as she bustled out.

Ocham retained her beauty and figure in spite of bearing Teq four children. They had three sons and a daughter, the youngest. The sons, Toban, Chameq and Teqan were nearly grown. Indeed, Toban was beginning to look for a wife. They were as different in looks as in personality. It was Chameq who seemed like Galt over again, where Toban favored his mother, and Teqan looked a lot like Royar when Teq first met them. Their daughter was as like Tarabeth as could be, and they had named her Tarocha at Teq's insistence. It was because of this little one, that Teq could feel Jebend's need to save his Maylin. She was exactly Tarocha's age. They could grow together like flowers in the forest.

But Teq was the father of two daughters. His oldest as well as his youngest child was a daughter. He had told Ocham the story, long ago, so that when she arrived it was only Lord Teq and Lady Ocham who were prepared for her. She walked into their lives one summer morning five years earlier, robed from head to toe, with a rippling walk and an arrogant voice and two companions.

"I am Teksana," she announced to the astonished company, assembled around the cooking fire, where Royar had made a huge pot of specially spiced food for the eve of Summer Long Day. "I am seeking Teq, my father. Which is he?"

After a pause long enough to register their shock, Ocham had risen to her feet, understanding the importance of first impressions.

"I am Lady Ocham, wife to Lord Teq. You have been expected," she said, with her gentle serenity, radiating calm to those assembled.

Toban leapt to his feet. "I am Toban, oldest son of Lord Teq. I know nothing of you. Where have you come from?"

"I am come from the Desert," she answered, unfolding her veil and allowing her glowing hair to tumble free. It was the precise color of Teq's. To look at her, tall and lithe and fair skinned, there was no mistaking that she was Teq's daughter. She turned to Ocham. "I honor you, Lady. These two are mine," she added, indicating carelessly the two warriors who accompanied her. "My mother, Shamana, Princess of the People of the Desert and once Priestess of the Mystery, would not permit me to come unaccompanied. You can do with them as you will."

"Come, all of you," Ocham said. "I will take you to Lord Teq. He will be glad you have arrived safely."

The delay in identifying himself, had allowed Teq to consider how he would handle this. He had only half believed that such a daughter existed. He had barely believed that Shamana would send her to him as she had announced, so long, long ago. Now he rose to his feet, standing a little uphill from the rest of the company, which was where he had merely happened to be when the newcomers arrived. He waited for Ocham to lead them over.

"You are welcome, daughter," he said when she was introduced to him. "Have you become a Priestess as was foretold? Do you speak to the Mystery?"

By this time the whole company had come out of shock, and gathered around. They had all discussed the tales of Teq and the Mystery time and again, when the tales were told round the festival fires. Not just Ocham and Doban, but others had encountered the feeling that there was a presence, a someone or something, who had a care of them. There was also a fair share of skeptics among them. All awaited the answer of this extraordinary creature with her extraordinary escort.

"It was the Mystery of the Desert who told me when to come," she answered, still speaking in that loud, arrogant, hypnotic voice. "I am sent to his sibling, the Mystery of the Mountains. He has spoken to me since I came to the Mountains, guiding me here. How else could I have found you?"

"Then you are doubly welcome, daughter. You will be known as the Servant of the Mystery, Priestess of Mountainhome, and will rank with Lady Ocham and myself. We are the three whom the Mystery told me would reign here, for our span. We consult with Council, whom you will meet. A house will be prepared for you. We do not wander, though we explore, the Mountains. This place is Mountainhome. Your escort is free to go or stay as you wish. There will be no fight to determine their place among us. Our customs are different from those of the great People of the Desert."

"They will stay," Teksana announced. "I will be comfortable with people who know my birth place."

"It is as you wish. You will learn and accept our customs, and then you may reign with us. Acceptance is imperative. We are the great People of the Mountains, and will be honored as such."

Teq was astonished at himself for remembering how to address her in ways she would expect. "How does Shamana, your mother?" he asked.

"She is well. She is served by those who love her. Melansa, my sister, is Priestess of the Mystery now."

"It is well," said Teq, while Ocham eyed him a little quizzically, unused to the pompous language. "Now, eat with us, all of you, and we will then see to your accommodations. Come, people, greet your Priestess, Servant of the Mystery, and then let us return to our meal."

Of course, the transition to acceptance of a priestess had not gone without clashes, especially because of her arrogance, and certainty of her ability to know the will of the Mystery. Teq's sons, in particular, were offended that their father had a daughter older than themselves, about whom they had known nothing. He took all his children, Teksana included, into his house and told them the full story of his short week in the Desert, so that they would understand why he had not forewarned them of her coming. He had been almost certain that this event would never occur.

Teksana snorted. "But my mother, Shamana, told you it would be so. How could you have doubted?"

Toban challenged, "how could my father think that the word of this woman would mean anything among his people, whoever she was among yours?"

"We are all People of the Mysteries," Ocham answered her son. "Therefore, your father had told me about Teksana. To tell me was enough. To tell you was unnecessary. We hoped she would come. Who knew what the Mystery might have decided since those long ago days? There are no certainties in life. At last we can know what the Mystery intends for us, since she is here. Her role is not your role. Your role is not hers. Accept that you each have your own place in the Mystery's design, each equally important, and be at peace."

The peace was uneasy at first. The warriors found it hard to learn the ways of the People of the Mountains, since warriors had no place there. Teq asked them to teach the young people the art of combat, since it might be of use at some time, and they in turn, learned to respect the arts which their new people could practice. In time the uneasy peace came to be acceptance, and then genuine trust.

It was just as well, Teq thought, since Teksana had been left in charge with Toban as her second, while Ocham and Doban and he made this trip to the Town. It was important that they arrive back to find harmony still in control.

Chapter 50

Galt and Athirra arrived early the next morning, followed shortly by Jebend, carrying Maylin. Jebend had sent written word round to his Chief, that Teq was at Zolg's, so that he might be the obvious person to carry his little daughter there himself. Zolg had given him a draught for her to drink, which would make her seem feverish and sleepy. The little girl made no objection to being put to bed and to sleep in the strange room. Ocham went to sit by her, so that there would be a friendly face and a cool drink when she woke. She planned to tell her all about Tarocha and Mountainhome, as if it were a magic tale. A place any little girl would yearn to visit.

When Jebend left her, he joined the others. "Have you decided to come and make your home with us, Jebend?" Teq asked him.

"I cannot. I would dearly love to, one day, but my wife was close to hysteria when I showed her one or two 'spots' on my wrist. If I die, she will become a servie. It was not something I had thought of. She has been a good mother to our children. I could not do that to her falsely. As it is, she will worry herself ill while I am gone; but there is nothing I can do about that. I must see Maylin settled." Jebend sighed. "Perhaps, one day," he added. "To tell the truth, I am getting heartily sick of confinement to the Town."

Galt nodded in understanding. Teq had been a little shocked at Galt's appearance, when he first walked in. His step was as vigorous as ever, but he was thinner. Wasted. It was as if a mighty image in the clouds was being dispersed by the winds. He had no idea how much he himself looked like the Galt he had known in Marisel's Honor.

Athirra, on the other hand, looked much as she always had. When she was a young servie, she had looked mature beyond her years. Now that she was older, she looked much the same. Her hair was a little faded, her eye a little less keen, but you had to look hard to see it. "Do you know, I had not thought of that," she said. "If anything were to happen to Galt, I too would become a servie. What an appalling thought!"

"Surely, the Dignus made new rules about that by now," Teq protested.

"Not only has he not," Galt told them, "He has made it the rule that a Dignus may have three wives, and a Chief two. Both Fergin and Prodarin have availed themselves of the opportunity. We can even take wives directly from a Distribution, just like the old Dignus, and not wait for the Pleasure House routine. Things are getting harsher for women, I think, in spite of all the years of trying. No. If I die, Athirra must come directly to you. She can throw herself on my corpse, or some such," he laughed, "in a frenzy of grief and 'die' of it. Whatever. There can be no other course."

"I shall have to plan well in advance," she smiled back, "in spite of the fact that I am not too eager to think about such an exigency. Perhaps I really will fade away from grief. What do you think?"

He squeezed her hand. "Now, Jebend writes that you have some thievery in mind. I am certainly glad that letter reached me safely."

"I trusted the messenger," Jebend laughed. "It was your own son."

"Perhaps we can make use of Garreth on our felonious enterprise," Galt suggested. "It's time he was involved along with the rest of us. He has been begging me to let him visit, ever since Gath and Belleth left, which must be eight years now."

"Since the anvil is so heavy, we could use strong arms," Teq agreed. "Besides, I have never met my youngest brother."

"Tell me what it is you need," Galt said.

So Teq did, with input from Doban and Jebend, so that the story took time to tell.

"With Jebend and Garreth, there would be four of you to carry the thing back," Galt considered. "That should be enough. Ocham will be there to look after Maylin. Now all we have to do is steal it, and get it to the cave. Ah, here is Ocham now. How are you, my dear? Can we keep everyone here for another three days? What do you think, Zolg?"

"Tilla and I would be honored. But next time you come, could you bring my Taza to visit?" Zolg responded.

"I swear it. She has asked, shyly, if she might be allowed to visit you. It was just not the time. We will see to it, though."

"And I want to meet my granchildren," Galt put in. "They are men grown, by now."

"Well, Toban at least is ready for a wife. The others just think they are grown up," Ocham chuckled. "I am looking forward to Maylin being a companion to Tarocha. They are of an age."

"I have a plan," Galt told them.

"I knew it," Teq nodded. "You always have a plan."

"Doesn't he?" Athirra agreed. "Tell it, then."

"The day after tomorrow is the Founder's Day Feast..." Galt began.

Since his elevation to Dignus, Kambar had instituted a reenactment of the battle which had been the foundation of the Town. The reason, in fact, that there was a Dignus to honor, and a regime oppressing women. The original battle had taken place within the boundary walls of the Town before they were reinforced, and had been the suppression of the first women captives. They had rebelled against their capture, had seized their weapons, and almost succeeded in escaping from the disorganized rabble which was the first men inhabiting the Town. Only the prompt action of a leader in rallying the men to some sort of disciplined action, had won them the day. They had recaptured any of the women who escaped, and had instituted the oppressive system which made women into chattels and men into Confraters of the Town. The leader had become the first Dignus, and the day of the victory had been celebrated ever since. But the population who remembered the actual event was aging, and Kambar decided it would be wise to restage the battle as part of the Founder's Day celebration. Of course, the valor of the women was shown as an evil uprising against benevolent masters; and, of course, the parts of the women were played by the newest green shirt recruits, not women with weapons, but the principle pertained. The reenactment served to stir the blood of the Confraters, and assure them that their policies for females were wise and necessary.

The battle took place at sunset. It was quite a short staging, but the resultant celebratory set-tos which took place, kept it going through the night. The Watch normally had a busy time, taking men with broken heads into custody for the night. The inns and wine shops did a wonderful business and heads hurt from more than blows by the following morning. But there was general chaos in the Town, and much more nighttime action than was normal.

The Watch was more than a little surprised to find that Chief Galt came to their briefing the evening before, and not Captain Jebend.

"I am here," Galt announced, "because your Captain has shown early signs of the spotted sickness. He must be kept isolated. But tomorrow will be a busy night and he can ill be spared. I will lead you myself."

There was a stirring among the men, but it was apparently of interest, rather than distrust. Was this not the man who had been the first Captain of the Watch, and had earned them the respect of the Town?

"I have decided," he went on, "to deploy all but two corps from the Palace to the East Gate. The remaining two corps will guard the North and South Gates. Sergeant Grid will command the Palace end, keeping his corps before the Palace itself. We do not want the zeal of the participants to carry them into the Palace to involve the Dignus. The battle will range down the main avenue from there to the East Gate. You will line the avenue to ensure that the battle doesn't -er overflow."

The men laughed. There had been trouble the year before when contingents of the actors had decided to flee or chase their opponents into the side streets.

"I do not expect any trouble at the other gates, but maintain your posts there unless I personally, or one of the sergeants whom I have sent, tells you otherwise. Any questions?"

In this way Galt left the side streets empty for the party of thieves to remove the anvil. It was judged best for Jebend to stay close in Zolg's house. It would never do for him to be recognized as part of the enterprise. Garreth, however, would go with them. In twenty years, the Town had changed somewhat, and it would not be helpful for Teq to get lost. The worst part of the matter, was that the Smith's house was as remote from Zolg's as the Town would permit. They would have to traverse the whole distance, carrying the heavy object. Carrying articles was not a normal thing to do in the middle of a celebration. They decided they would simply have to play it as they found it.

So, after two clear days of peaceful catching up and rest, the party was ready to set out at sunset. Ocham insisted on coming. It would be her only opportunity to see the Town. Since any sane woman stayed within doors during this event, she dressed in some of Doban's clothes. Garreth led the way, taking streets which were empty of people. This was easy enough at this stage. From the roars and shouts, it was clear that the entire male population was gathered to watch the battle. They reached the house of the Master Smith without incident. So far, so good. Jussy had described the house in detail, so that had no problem locating the hut where the old anvil was kept. They shoved the door open. What they saw stopped them in their tracks.

The Master Smith had been drinking all day in anticipation of the evening's entertainment. Was it not a feast day? He slept heavily in the afternoon, and woke to find his two sons playing with his latest wife. It didn't bother him. Even her screams didn't bother him. He was already getting tired of her. He had been through four wives already. Fortunately, now that Kambar was Dignus, how anyone treated their wife or servie or any woman they owned, was their own business. They could replace them as often as they liked, so long as they had the credits. Captain Jebend and his Watch could not interfere. He had been and protested when they took Jussy. The matter of his wife did, however, rouse him to excitement. He went into the back shed where the old woman and young child servies slept. He thought about doing the old woman, but decided he'd keep her till later if he still wanted her. He took the child up, and the woman started to yell at him. He thrust a cloth in her mouth, and tied her to the leg of the bed they shared. He wondered why he hadn't thought of this before. He threw the child on to the ground, ripped off her clothes and raped her. He was so intent that he neither heard the opening of the door, nor the woman's scream of fury which followed. He concentrated on his business.

Teq and Doban fell on the Smith together, to pull him off. The child slumped unconscious in a bloody heap. Ocham gathered her up. Between them Teq and Doban set about trying to subdue the Smith, to keep him quiet, still and senseless. They were motivated as much by rage, as by the need to silence him if they were to complete their mission. He was a huge man, with muscles harder than rock. He was old and strong and solid. He heaved the pair of them off, like shrugging out of a coat. Had it not been that they were used to felling trees together, working together as a team at a heavy task, they would have been stamped into the ground like insects.

Garreth had stood for a second in the doorway, summing up the situation. It would not do if the smith were to recognize him and remember who he was, if he reported the incident later. He would surely report the theft of his anvil, at least. Garreth noted a metal pole, used to bar the door, no doubt, though fortunately, not this evening. He picked it up and slammed it down on the Smith's head from behind, dropping him like felled timber. "Sorry, I could not help before," Garreth apologized, "but he might have recognized me. It would not do for it to be known I was a part of this."

"You came at just the right moment," Teq assured him. "Now, let's get away before the curious start arriving."

"We are not leaving this child here," Ocham said firmly.

"Or the old woman," Garreth added, cutting her free. "She has seen us. I would not be able to keep quiet about it if the Smith's sons questioned me. I know she wouldn't. Can you stand, old woman? Will you come with us freely?"

"As fast as I am able, sir," she whispered.

"Faster than that," Teq said. "Now where is that anvil."

"Over here," the old woman said. "Is this what you want, sir?"

"I expect it must be," Doban answered. "It looks right. And look at this. It is a hammer made of metal. I want that too."

"All right. Take whatever you want. We may as well be blamed for the flood as for the leak," Teq told him. "But let us go. Garreth, can you help me with this anvil? I can't even lift the thing."

"Here's a leather sling," Garreth said. "Carry it in this. Come on, before the Smith wakes up. We must be streets away before that happens. Believe me, he will not keep silent. He will have the Watch on us before you can blink, and this thing is not easy to conceal."

"Doban and I will take it," Teq decided. "You take the hammer and lead. Take the woman with you too. Ocham, you carry the child and stay close to him. We'll jam this door shut, somehow, and then catch up."

Half way back, they turned a corner into a party of revelers, silent as they drank from wine flasks simultaneously, in some sort of drinking contest. The group staggered past, seemingly safely until one of the revelers lowered his flask and called out, "Woman."

Ocham stopped involuntarily, the child in her arms, stirring and whimpering piteously.

"Ha!" Garreth called to them. "How could you tell? This one had the part of a woman in the battle. Good, eh? We thought the child a good touch."

"You sure?" the reveler asked drunkenly.

"Would we be here with a real woman?" Garreth chuckled. "Get on with you. We're looking for the Bloated Barrel inn. It's near, isn't it? Got friends there to fool with this lot."

"Don't know," said the reveler, losing interest. None of his fellows seemed to care. They moved on.

Meanwhile, Doban and Teq were staggering under their load, breaking their backs trying to keep from showing what they carried. They leaned on a house wall, to ease the strain, but stood up without groaning aloud, and carried on when Garreth led them out. The old woman slipped out of a shadow and joined them. Teq had forgotten about her.

"What's your name?" he whispered to her.

"Dellith," she answered, "and the child is Keela. She was new bought by the Smith to work the bellows two days ago, sir. She is but seven years old. I tried to save her from him, at least, and I don't care who knows it, but he swore I would be next when he tied me. I thank the Skies you came in. I have no need to know why, but where are we going?"

"That's an even longer story," Teq grinned, straining against the ache in his shoulders. "You will be safe, if we make it this night."

They were nearly at Zolg's house when they heard the tramp of the approaching Watch. There was no place to hide. The street was empty. The mock battle was over so long ago, that the Watch corps must have been liberated to patrol the Town. Galt could not have held them any longer. There would have been no reason.

"Stand here," Teq ordered. "Ocham, Dellith follow me."

He fled up the stairs, two at a time, beating on the door with his fists for Zolg to let him in. Jebend answered the door.

"We need you," he gasped at Jebend. "You must hold up the Watch. We are caught below."

"Good," Jebend answered, racing down the stairs ahead of Teq. The green shirt training was never more obvious. Only a green shirt would react at once. Only a man of Jebend's intelligence could think while he sprang into action. The sound of the marching Watch could be heard coming nearer.

Jebend roared at Garreth and Doban, standing helpless over the anvil and hammer. "What are you doing in this sector? Don't you know the physician declared quarantine? This is not a place for revelry. I, myself, have the spotted fever. Sergeant," he roared. "Halt those men."

"Captain Jebend?" came the sergeant's voice in query.

"Yes, sergeant. I am sending some revelers out of here. Keep your men away. The spotted fever can be caught too easily. We cannot have it loose in the barracks. March your men away. I will deal with these."

"Are you sure, sir?" came the voice.

"Of course, I'm sure," Jebend answered testily. "You think I cannot deal with two revelers?"

"No, sir. Sorry, sir. Hope you get better, sir," answered the sergeant. "Ready men? March."

Teq reappeared. "Thank you," he breathed.

"It's what Captains of the Watch are for," Jebend grinned. "Here, let me help with that thing. Straight up to the cave with it. There's wine and food inside, and everyone gathered to send us on our way. Come on, then. Let's not stand here for the next corps to arrive."

"Quite right," Teq answered the grin. "We can do without any more surprises."

Chapter 51

In the year and a half since they had brought her to Mountainhome, the child Keela had not spoken. Dellith assured them that she used to speak. It was as if the shock of her dreadful experience had bereft her of the power to talk about ordinary things. She appeared to enjoy the company of Tarocha and Maylin. She slept in the same room with them and went with them cheerfully when they played. She even joined in their lessons when Belletha held classes in the long winter to teach the children to read and write. But she made no sound.

On a morning in late spring, mists clung damply to the lake. The older children had taken the herds reluctantly from their pens in the small valley to the higher pastures. There was a chill in the air, though the day promised to warm up later on. The sun was getting stronger as the year wore towards summer. Ocham sat with Dellith and the three little girls, showing them how to use the spinning wheel, to make thread from the wool combed from the warm coats of the carries. Keela sat with her back against Ocham's knees as she tried to make the thread grow smoothly. Suddenly she arched her back, her eyes glazed and she let forth a piercing cry. It was the first sound Ocham had ever heard her make, and she was startled into dropping her spindle.

She gathered Keela on to her knee. "What is it, dear?" she soothed. "There is nothing here to hurt you."

But the child could not hear her. She was far away, somewhere in her mind. Footsteps clattered up the steps to the door of the house and Teksana burst in.

"What person heard the Mystery?" she demanded. "Someone in here heard him speak. Who was it?"

"It was Keela who cried out," Ocham answered her. "I do not think she heard the Mystery, though, come to think of it, there was nothing else to startle her. Could it be?"

Teksana knelt before Ocham and took Keela's shoulders between her hands. She gazed deeply into her eyes, concentrating on her. Focusing herself totally on the young girl. Keela gave a small moan and her eyes came back into the room with them. She looked at Teksana with the same intensity as Teksana looked at her.

Teksana spoke at last. "It is well," she said. "You can speak now. The Mystery has chosen you because of your suffering. There is always a cost. Always. For me, I can bear no child. But your price has already been paid. The Mystery has given you a message for us. He told me to seek you out to find out what it is. Speak, little one, tell us. I will take you into my house for my own. I swear it. I will train you. When I can no longer do the work, you will become the Priestess, the Servant of the Mystery of the Mountains. Now speak."

Keela's voice was faint, unsure. "Death," she said. "In the Town. A person has died. All his family must gather at the Town."

"Is that all? Is that all the message?" Ocham asked. "Do you not know who? Who has died?"

Keela's voice faltered. "You are to bring wood and game. You are to build houses. It is the father of Lord Teq who has died." And she burst into tears. Floods of tears. All the tears she had not shed for the violation and the pain and the shock. She cried and Ocham hugged her until she quieted a little.

"That is all," said Teksana. "She knows no more. You have done well, little one. Now come with me." Teksana gathered the child to her with warm arms and with care. She took her hand and held it tightly in her own. Keela gave one little sob, and then her crying was over. She accepted Teksana as her guide. Walked trustingly at her side, content.

Teksana led Keela away, while Ocham rose to her feet, stricken by the news. She knew what hurt it would bring to Teq. Tarocha and Maylin clung to her, knowing her grief, though not the reason, not really.

Teksana walked to the House of the Council. It had been built with a balcony before it. Announcements which effected all the People were made from there. She led Keela to the balcony, and let out her ululating cry. Work stopped everywhere. Everyone listened. "Bring me Teq," she called. "I speak as the Servant of the Mystery. Teq must be found."

Teq was up on his ledge, too far off to hear more than Teksana's cry. He had been watching her movements with interest. And then, suddenly, his heart misgave him. He closed his eyes and the Mystery stood before him, vague as the mist. Formed from the mist. "Be strong and honor your father," he heard in his head. And then he heard the People calling his name, and Ocham standing below, looking up at him, and he knew the news they would tell him.

In the Town Athirra sent for Jebend. She sat grim-faced by Galt's bed, dry-eyed and upright. Never more upright than now, when her heart was breaking and dragging at her breast hard enough to have bent her double; weeping great gobbets of tears, sufficient to flood the Town.

Galt lay in his bed, gasping, recruiting his strength. Zolg was on the other side of the bed, spooning a draught into a cup, and holding Galt's head so that he could sip from it. Zolg was relentless in making him drink it all down, and when he had done so, Galt's breathing was easier. But not easy. Not any more. He had risen from his bed this morning, as any morning, and a great and vicious pain had snatched at his arm. He had time only to gasp, "Athirra," when he fell, crashing like a great tree in the forest. But this tree did not fall unheard. It was a sound heard and understood by his wife and all his household.

When Zolg came, he told her what she knew. The heart in Galt's chest had lurched. More than lurched. Another lurch like it and he would die. He had trouble making the breath reach into his lungs. His limbs were heavier than he could tolerate. Galt lay as he had lain the first time Zolg saw him, gathering his strength. This time, though, it was not to march off to start another life. This time it was to gain enough of himself to say what he needed to say.

Jebend came. He came cheerfully, because the message had said nothing of Galt's fall. He was surprised to be directed the Chief's bedroom.

"Good morning, layabeds," he said. And then he saw Zolg and the stricken faces about the bed. "The hunt returned last night," he told them, seeing instantly what was important, and what must be done. "Garreth should be home within the hour. Is word of this to be allowed to circulate?"

"No, no. Not yet. I want to tell you that you must leave the Town," Galt spoke, his voice little more than a whisper. "They will want one of their own kind to replace me. What of your wife?" he asked Jebend.

"Weak. Not strong. In some pain, but not a lot. But I don't think she could make it to Mountainhome."

Zolg answered the unspoken question. "She could not. She can come to us. If Jebend is to 'die', we will take her in as our servie. In this way it will seem as if he arranged the matter. A recurrence of the spotted sickness in Jebend must be fatal. Would this do? Will your wife be content with this?"

"She has never really been wife to me as Tilla is to you, or Athirra to Galt. She is too timid. Always anxious to please me, and kind to our children, but never in charge. It might be a relief to her not to try to seem well for me. I think it would," Jebend answered.

"Take Athirra," Galt whispered. He looked over at his wife and reached for her hand. "I cannot bear to leave you, but since I must, you must go to Teq."

"I promised I would months ago. You know that," she told him. "I have even worked out how I am to die of my own knife from grief at your passing. Don't concern yourself over me. I shall have such tales of you to tell to all your children..." She turned her face away from him so that he would not see the tears in her eyes. It was not her way to pretend. He would know that. She could not tell him he would not die. They both knew as well as Zolg that he would.

"You will need a lot of wood and meat, Zolg," Galt smiled, "to make a funeral pyre for all three of us. Garreth must announce that I insist on that. We must send the boy to inform Teq. Man," murmured. "All my sons are men."

"I will send Garreth to inform Teq, once you have seen him," Athirra said. "Teq can bring the wood."

Jebend said, "I have the stain Zolg gave me, still, but I will not catch the fever until all is arranged. Galt, my friend, my Chief, you have lead us all. Always. You have shown us what we must do and how we must do it. We are diminished already that you are abed and not keeping the Town in order. It will become untenable without you."

Galt reached for his hand and squeezed it. "I trust you to see to my Athirra. I have always trusted you. Be happy in your new life."

He lay back exhausted, and Zolg beckoned Athirra from the room. "Let him rest. Stay with him if you wish. You give him peace. I will send Garreth in as soon as he comes."

"Oh, Zolg." Athirra moved into the comfort of his arms for just a moment. "What am I to do without him?"

"You will just be Athirra," he answered, "and that will be enough. More than enough."

"What will you do, with all of us gone? The Town is so terrible now, and I thought it oppressive when I first came. But under Kambar... What will you do?" she asked him.

"We will be all right, Tilla and I. I am the Master Physician, and I am needed, eh? I intend to set up a sort of secret rumor, that those who dare can escape such oppression as Kambar offers. Those who like the Town will laugh. What oppression? But the women with courage will want to know. The elderly women will have the answers. Tilla had the idea. She knows how it is for the older women. The drudgery of being a servie. She can meet one here and another there, she says, and get the word started. The spotted sickness route will have to die with me when my time comes, but there will be escapes by then, which are recognized as such, because of the rumors. You can tell all this to Galt, if you think it would ease his mind to hear it. I had intended to talk to him about it. But then this... Dear Athirra. Be brave."

She smiled at him as best she could, and wiped her face with her sleeve. "Listen. I think that is Garreth now. I must fetch him to his father. Thank you, Zolg. You have quietly helped us all for so many years." She kissed him, and turned to greet her son.

It took more than a day for Garreth, running all the way, to reach Mountainhome. In fact, he never quite got there. On the wooded rise just north of it, he met Teq, leading a large party of people, and carries loaded down with supplies. Over the rise he could hear the sound of building.

"I just caught you," he gasped to Teq. "I come bearing terrible news."

"We know of it," Teq told him. "Slow down and have something to eat and drink."

Ocham hurried forward, offering what was in her pouch. Gath and Belletha arrived with drinks from their bags. "Did he die in peace?"

Garreth gulped down the offerings and spoke more clearly. "He died in his bed. I was there and Athirra and Zolg. I had just returned from a hunt. Another hour and I would not have seen him alive. But how in the Earth and Sky did you know?"

"You forget we have a Servant of the Mystery among us," Teq smiled. "Actually two. Little Keela, whom we rescued from the Master Smith, is another such. They can speak to the Mystery, and so we were told."

"I cannot comment on that which I don't understand, but I am glad. I must return as fast as I came. Galt's death was not to be announced until today, but there will be a lying out in the Square before the Palace, so that the people can see him. It is so with the death of a Chief. I must be there."

"And then?" Teq asked.

"And then he has written his desire - which I must read, out there in the Square before many witnesses - that he wants to be burned on the place behind Zolg's house where those who die from illness are burned. His ashes will be spread on the burying place of the Chiefs behind the Palace."

"I'm sure he had a reason for that, though I can't see it," Teq pondered.

"It is so that Athirra, my mother, can plunge a knife into her breast and be burned on the same pyre. Only Zolg and I will be attending. I will return with the sad news and the ashes, to the Dignus and the other Chiefs. Zolg is always excused from ceremonies. They associate him with illness. Jebend will fall sick with the spotted sickness as soon as I return and will be burned too. Then we will all slip through the cave at dead of night to meet you. Zolg will come too. Is Taza with you?"

"We are all here. So. The Mystery told us to bring wood and game, which we did not understand. Zolg will need a lot for all those burnings. Some game for the fire and some for the feast, I suppose. We will hold a feast to honor Galt when you all come through. You are going back? Jebend is joining us along with Athirra, I take it. That was the reason the Mystery told us to build. Well, we have obeyed the instructions. You hear the building, preparing houses for Athirra and Jebend, and these carries are loaded with wood and game. We will send people with you to lead the carries. If you stop for nothing you will be back before morning. Are you able to do that?"

"Yes, of course. I will sleep and eat when I am back in the Town. And yes. I will go on living there. I am happy enough. Perhaps I will join you, one day. Or perhaps I will become Dignus, and finish what Galt started. We shall see," Garreth smiled.

"Here is journey food, and fresh water. Who will go with Garreth?" Teq asked.

Toban and Gath stepped forward at once, leading two carries which carried wood and game. Teq and Ocham and Belletha hugged Garreth, and they were off.

It was two days before the main party reached the meadow below the cave. The weather was fine, and the place dry and comfortable. Teq climbed up to the cave, and slipped through, but he did not enter the Town. The flames from the huge funeral pyre were leaping into the dark sky, illuminating the Town as it had been illuminated by the presence of Galt's great soul, Teq thought. He wept that he had not seen him at the last, and yet he felt his presence with him now. The roar of the flames contended with the roar of the waterfall in filling the night with the sounds of pain. Below, Teq could see a contingent of the Watch drawn up. They must have carried Galt's body to this place, followed by Garreth leading Athirra. Undoubtedly, they would wait and escort Garreth and the ashes back to the Square in the light of morning. Teq thought that they could expect Athirra through the cave the following night as soon as it was dark. He made his way down to Ocham, so that she could make her plans for the feast.

The whole family was gathered. Teq had seen to it that all the people of Mountainhome who were related to Galt were with him. His brother Gath and sister Belletha were there; and his niece Taza, all with those whom they had joined. Their children were there, as well as his own, excepting Teksana who had refused to come. She had known nothing of Galt, she argued. She would not belong.

The day was spent roasting meats and boiling food for the feast. People had brought their finest clothes. It was not to be a feast of mourning, but of celebration of Galt's life. At dusk, Teq went again to the cave. The Watch had long gone. The Town was eerily silent. A slight mist rose from the falls. Slipping quietly up towards him from Zolg's house he made out five figures, all carrying bundles.

Athirra entered first. He took the bundle from her, and hugged her close. They said nothing. Zolg came next, carrying a small bundle. "I have not left this Town since first I entered it. I feel as if I am on an adventure. If I can, I will come to your Mountainhome myself, one day. Here is Tilla. Which way?" He spoke in a whisper.

"Through there," Teq pointed. "Once you're through, you will see the fire. Go on down. Ocham is there, and so is your Taza, eager enough to see you that she may burst."

"Taza," he whispered, and went.

Jebend brought up the rear with Garreth. They both carried enough to break the backs of the others. "My mother would leave nothing of Galt's or her own behind," Garreth groaned. "I hope you have enough carries for all of it."

Teq hugged them both and led them through. "No problems?" he asked Jebend. "Your wife?"

"Ill, but Zolg and Tilla have taken her in. She will be there officially as their servie. She is content."

And the feast was as fine as any within the best inns of the Town. There was a huge quantity of food, and as much conversation to help it along as any gathering of family, or Honor or tribe in the world, after a long separation.

Around the middle of the night, with the moon high in the sky and the flames of the bonfire threatening to reach up and singe it, the music began. There was singing and there was dancing. Teq led the young men in a dance of the life of Galt. And then the women danced to honor his rescue of them, and the freedom he had brought into their lives. The men leapt up and danced with them with a stamping and a whirling and a leaping, because life went on, regardless of sorrow and loneliness.

They sank to the ground, and the wine was passed which had been brought especially from the Town in some of those huge bundles. In a quiet voice, Athirra began to tell tales of Galt, the Chief. Teq told about his place in the Honor as Sieur, and the manner of his leaving it. Zolg told of his first meeting with Galt, when he had been a free Wilder. Athirra went on with the tale of her rescue. And the tales continued through the night.

"When we return to Mountainhome, I shall collect all these stories, and write them down," Taza said. "it should be done."

"The stories of life in other places should be recorded, while there are people free to tell about them as they were. As they still are, probably," Athirra agreed. "I could explain about life in an Honor, where women are in command."

"And I of the role of men, and children in an Honor," Teq agreed. "Zolg knows about life as a Wilder, and so do some of the men who have come through. That must be recorded. It is so different."

"If you like," Ocham offered, we could talk about the ways of the People of the Sea."

"And Teksana about the People of the Desert," Teq put in. "It is a wonderful idea, Taza. We must use a permanent stain ink on vellum, the way I make my master copies of maps. There are no end to the tales we can tell."

"If there is no end, I had better train some of the youngs to help me," Taza laughed, "or I may never see daylight again."

"Here is the daylight," Athirra said. "We have honored Galt with an all night vigil. I am so glad you are all here to do this."

"And have a plan that tales of him will be recorded. He will never be forgotten. He was a giant among the People of the Plains." Teq lifted his glass in a final toast. "We shall all strive to be as he was, each in our own way."

Ocham smiled up at him. "Your way is good, too, Lord of the Mountains."

"Together, we are good, Lady of the Mountains. Together we are more than each of us alone. And with Teksana to talk to the Mystery, we shall do."

For the first time in his life Teq was content.